18 1/2 DISGUISES

Maizie Albright Star Detective 7

LARISSA REINHART

Past Perfect Press

Praise for Larissa Reinhart

The Finley Goodhart Crime Caper series

"This is as fun a novel as it is moving and at times heart-breaking, never the more so when the final page comes and readers are only left wanting more."

Cynthia Chow, *King's River Life Magazine*

"Con artists, murder, a cast of sinister characters, and some laughs along the way. Loved it."

Terri L. Austin, author of the *Rose Strickland Mysteries*

The Maizie Albright Star Detective Series

"The perfect combination of mystery, romance, and laughs."

Devilishly Delicious Book Reviews

"This was a fun read--a fast-paced caper that kept me entertained until the end."

Terry Ambrose, author of the Seaside Cove Mysteries

"The mystery and detective cases drive the story, but Larissa Reinhart's characters steal the show every time."

The Girl With Book Lungs

The Cherry Tucker Mystery Series

"A Composition in Murder is a rollicking good time."

Terrie Farley Moran, Agatha Award-Winning Author of *Read to Death*

"This is a winning series that continues to grow stronger and never fails to entertain with laughs, a little snark, and a ton of heart."

Kings River Life Magazine

"Cherry Tucker is a strong, sassy, Southern sleuth who keeps you on the edge of your seat."

Tonya Kappes, *USA Today* Bestselling Author

"Giggle-inducing, down-home fun."

Betty Webb, *Mystery Scene Magazine*

"The perfect blend of funny, intriguing, and sexy!"

– Ann Charles, *USA Today* Bestselling Author of the *Deadwood* and *Jackrabbit Junction Mystery Series*

"Reinhart's charming, sweet-tea flavored series keeps getting better!"

Gretchen Archer, *USA Today* Bestselling Author of the *Davis Way Crime Caper Series*

"Cherry is a lovable riot, whether drooling over the town's hunky males, defending her dysfunctional family's honor, or snooping around murder scenes."

— *Mystery Scene Magazine*

18 1/2 DISGUISES

18 1/2 DISGUISES, Maizie Albright Star Detective #7

Amazon ASIN: B08M6J7Y39

ePUB ISBN: 978-1-7345638-6-3

Paperback ISBN: 978-1-7345638-7-0

Hardcover ISBN: 978-1-7345638-8-7

Library of Congress number: 2020922780

Printed in the USA

Author photo by Scott Asano

Books by Larissa Reinhart

A Cherry Tucker Mystery Series

A CHRISTMAS QUICK SKETCH (prequel)

PORTRAIT OF A DEAD GUY (#1)

STILL LIFE IN BRUNSWICK STEW (#2)

HIJACK IN ABSTRACT (#3)

THE VIGILANTE VIGNETTE (#3.5)

DEATH IN PERSPECTIVE (#4)

THE BODY IN THE LANDSCAPE (#5)

A VIEW TO A CHILL (#6)

A COMPOSITION IN MURDER (#7)

A MOTHERLODE OF TROUBLE (in YEAR-ROUND TROUBLE)

Audio

PORTRAIT OF A DEAD GUY

STILL LIFE IN BRUNSWICK STEW

Box Set

CHERRY TUCKER MYSTERIES 1-3

Maizie Albright Star Detective Series

15 MINUTES

16 MILLIMETERS

NC-17

A VIEW TO A CHILL

17.5 CARTRIDGES IN A PEAR TREE

18 CALIBER

18 1/2 DISGUISES

19 CRIMINALS (coming soon)

Box Set

#WANNABEDETECTIVE, MAIZIE ALBRIGHT 1-3

Audio

15 MINUTES

16 MILLIMETERS

NC-17

18 CALIBER

18 1/2 DISGUISES

A Finley Goodhart Crime Caper Series

PIG'N A POKE (prequel, short story)

THE CUPID CAPER

THE PONY PREDICAMENT (coming soon)

THE HEIR AFFAIR (coming soon)

Contents

Acknowledgments

Thank you Lord for unanswered and answered prayers and for inspiring me to write this series. Anything good came from your blessing.

A huge thanks to Caitlin Burk who not only enthusiastically gave me great ideas for ways to murder a costume designer and taught me about a fascinating part of the film industry, but for being a shining example of one who took their talents and used them wisely.

Ritter Ames, you're an incredible editor, book guru, and a great friend. Thank you for all the help and support. And thank you especially for your graciousness, understanding, and lightning fast editing skills!

Terri Austin, thanks for being my beta buddy and for your friendship! I can't wait to read your next book!

The Mystery Minions, know that I'm thinking about y'all while I'm writing. You each represent the reason I burn the midnight oil. Thank you so much for your incredible support and friendship!

To my Larissa's Writing Friends on Facebook, and especially to Dru Ann Love, Lori Caswell, Lorie Lewis, and Debby Guisti, thank you for your friendship and guidance. I love the encouragement and support of the writing community. It's a wonderful thing.

To the Funks, Reinharts, and Hoffmans, thanks always for all your love, support, and Facebook shoutouts. Also to my sweet friends (too numerous to name all of you) for your encouragement, especially the Metzler-Concepcions, Schwingshakls, Witzanys (thank you for letting me borrow Maizie's name), and the Benders. Love you! And to all the folks in Andover and surrounds, thank you for your hometown support!

Gina, Bill, Hailey, Lily, Sonja, and Grandma Sally: thank you for beta reading, shipping books, receiving books, and generally putting up with me.

Peachtree City, Georgia, thanks for inviting Hollywood to town and giving me the inspiration for this series. And thanks for being such a wonderful place to live and raise my children.

And to Trey, Lu & So, you have my gratitude and my love always. xoxo

To Irma
The strongest woman I know

ONE

#PartyPrologue #NeedANash

I needed to hear Wyatt Nash's voice like I'd never needed anything before. More than chucking California and my Beverly Hills lifestyle to create a new life in Georgia. More than getting out of jail when my crazy ex-fiancé implicated me in his (secret-to-me) drug-dealing life. Even more than refusing to sign Vicki's contracts to preserve (my sanity) our mother-daughter relationship from the constraints of our manager-actress alliance.

I needed the deep growl of Nash's "what" more than I ever wanted carbs.

And that's really saying something. It could also be a very big problem. I've not had much luck relying on men in the past. I feared this set a dangerous precedent for my heart.

But then again, I'd never witnessed a murder victim before meeting Nash.

The evening had started out well. At a masquerade gala for the Clothing Kids Foundation founded by my old friend and fashion mentor, Lorena Cortez. She'd moved to Black Pine recently, like me. Whereas I moved to escape Hollywood, Lorena had retired from a long and illustrious career in costume design. Lorena and the Clothing Kids board had asked me to emcee the ceremonial speeches at the gala. Rhonda and Tiffany, my Black Pine BFFs had come as my plus twos. I'd worn my most notable costume designed by Lorena — a cheer outfit from *Julia Pinkerton, Teen Detective*.

Actually, I'd been asked by the board to wear it, bringing — IMHO — a more Comic-Con feeling to the gala. I would have chosen something a little more relevant. And with more cover-age. A woman of my size and stature should not bare her upper-upper thighs. I was no longer in high school, but unfortunately, I'd been typecast a long time ago.

Lorena had graciously adjusted the old cheer ensemble for my twenty-five-year-old body. She'd also created wood nymph costumes for Tiffany and Rhonda to go with the woodland theme she'd devised for the magazine photo spread that would highlight Clothing Kids and her career. My father's company, DeerNose, had supplied all the materials (non-scented) for the children's costumes who attended the benefit and the photoshoot.

The Clothing Kids masquerade gala was an appealing fundraiser, particularly as we entered Mardi Gras season. A local philanthropist couple, the Martins, held the party at their beau-tiful Queen Anne in the historic district. Black Pine's well-to-do had packed the rooms and garden of the Martins' home. Both old and new Black Piners longed for sophisticated events.

At least the moneyed class did. In the winter, the more down-to-earth Black Piners focused on celebrating the opening of NASCAR and mourning the end of football season.

The board had been working hard to raise funds, drive awareness, and create national chapters. Lorena's notoriety in the entertainment industry helped tremendously. The buzz had grown, and the launch looked like a success.

Until now.

Until Rhonda and I, looking for Lorena, had scurried next door and opened the door to her bungalow. Changing every-thing forever.

I couldn't reverse time, but at the moment, I desperately wished I could. Wished I'd never brought Rhonda with me. And mostly wished we hadn't found what we found.

And now, while I wished away, Rhonda was screaming. Mostly to the Lord to save her. But also at me to do something — combined with a lot of nonsensical shrieking. I clutched her hand and sucked in air through my nose and out my mouth. I couldn't blame Rhonda for screaming, but between the screaming and my own panic, I feared I'd pass out.

I needed Nash. Just his voice would do. I knew this from experience. Something about his calm, commanding presence soothed me. If he panicked, he never showed it. In the face of overwhelming situations, he quieted. And he smelled good.

But I think that's a pheromone thing.

In the face of overwhelming situations, I cried. Hyperventilated. Made bad decisions. Or ate trans-fats. I was not one you should call in an emergency.

My biggest wish — the one upon a star and to God and the universe and anyone else listening — was for me to be different. Immediately.

Currently, I hyperventilated and was really, really, really afraid of making another bad decision. I'd already made a few since entering.

My fingers slipped and fumbled on the tiny turn-lock of the Chloé mini saddlebag hanging across my body. Partly due to the shakes. Partly due to the blood that somehow got on the leather. And everywhere else.

"Maizie, we need to go," sobbed Rhonda. She yanked me backward, dripping fabric apple blossoms in her wake. I dropped the phone. It skittered across the pine floor until it hit a bookcase filled with baskets of fabric and sewing equipment.

"I can't go. I have to stay," I spoke in gasps. I couldn't even figure out how to talk and breathe. Why couldn't I be like Nash? He always managed to breathe and talk and think in emergency situations. "I'm calling the police. You go outside. Get some fresh air. I'll be there as soon as I can."

"Outside by myself. Are you crazy? What if...whoever did this is still around?" Rhonda collapsed to the floor, pulling me with her.

My knees buckled and my tailbone hit the wooden floor. Hard. But I landed next to my phone. I picked it up and called Nash.

"What?" said Nash.

I immediately calmed. Mostly. Rhonda's screaming had commenced again.

"I'm not coming to that party," he continued. "There's nothing you can say that will entice me. Except for the cheer skirt. But I would forever be indebted to you if you came over later in the cheer outfit. And by forever indebted, I mean—"

"I can't," I gasped.

"It's not really a fantasy thing, I—"

"No, no. I can't wear it ever again." My breath hitched. I pinched the skin between my thumb and forefinger to control my tears. "It's covered in blood."

During the pause that followed, I jerked in bubbly gasps, squeezed my eyes shut, and tried to block Rhonda's screaming.

"Is it your blood?" he said slowly.

"No."

"Did you call 9-1-1?"

"As soon as I arrived. I'm ignoring their return call right now."

"Where are you?"

"Lorena's."

"Your friend, the costume designer? On Scarlet Oak Drive? The old bungalow?"

I nodded. Which he couldn't hear, but he said, "Be there in five minutes. Just hang on. Stay on the line. Stay calm. Are you in danger?"

Rhonda had stopped screaming, but her face had gone an

ashy gray. "I don't think so. I don't know. Maybe? Who knows? I don't understand—"

"Is someone hurt? Someone who needs help?"

I stared across the room, but there was nothing we could do for her now. "I guess not."

"Get out of the house. Isn't the party next door? Go there."

"I can't go there. I'm all bloody," I wailed. "Everyone will freak out." Like Rhonda. Which I couldn't say out loud because it would freak Rhonda out more. "I can't leave her. It's just...just...too...too..."

"You don't have to talk. Just breathe." Nash stretched out the words and between syllables, I heard his boots pound the old wooden stairs of the Dixie Kreme Donut building. The third riser rang like a gunshot, making me flinch.

Seeing my recoil, Rhonda grasped me around the middle and pulled me against the feathery layers of her toga. We leaned against the bookcase, clutching each other, staring out at the large open room in Lorena's adorable bungalow. Previously styled in what I'd call funky artisan. Now looking more like horror splatter gore. I circled Rhonda's shoulder and patted her bare upper arm.

"It's going to be okay," I said to her. "Nash is on his way."

"Oh Lawd," she moaned. "Lawd, Lawd, Lawd."

"Who's that?" said Nash.

"Rhonda. She's in shock."

"Is it Rhonda's blood?"

"No. Rhonda is okay. Right, Rhon?"

She turned her head to bury her face in my armpit.

"Maizie, hon'," said Nash. "Now that you're calmer, could you tell me what happened?"

"I...we...you see...then—" Losing the words, I hiccuped.

"Start at the beginning."

"Which beginning? People always say that, but you never know how far back they want you to go." I gulped a mouthful of air that tasted like starch and old pennies and blew out quickly.

In my ear, something heavy banged. I knew it was only the outside door of the Dixie Kreme building, slamming as Nash left his office. But I jerked anyway. Beside me, Rhonda shook. I clutched her against me. My armpit was drenched with her tears and snot, but I felt it a good sign she was no longer screaming.

"How about starting at the party. You and Rhonda were there." Keys jangled and a metallic squeak told me Nash had opened the door of his Silverado pickup. I breathed a little easier.

"And Tiffany."

"And Tiffany," he said. "She's not with you?"

"No," I said sadly. "We left her at the gala. She's hooking up with a bartender."

"Leave that for later. Boomer was supposed to be there." Nash's voice tightened. "He's not with you now, is he?"

"No. Daddy and Remi are still at the event. Or they went home because he didn't want to be there in the first place. But I told him he had to come because DeerNose is a big sponsor for Clothing Kids and he's on the foundation's board. Lorena dressed him like a lumberjack and Remi is an armadillo. Too cute, but I couldn't tell her that—"

"The costumes don't matter, hon'. You were at this party—"

"Masquerade Gala."

"Gala. And Boomer was there, even though he didn't want to be—"

"You know it's quail season. He wanted to be up before dawn. But I said he should still come to Lorena's kickoff event…" I thought about that for a minute and shuddered another gasp. "Oh my God. Daddy—"

"But he's fine and Remi's fine, right? So you were next door—"

"At the Martins'. They're board members for Clothing Kids. They have a beautiful, turn-of-the-century Queen Anne. Which you'll see in a minute—" I opened my eyes. The pool of blood shimmered. I quickly closed them again. "Oh God, I'm in shock. I must be in shock. Why am I talking about architecture and wardrobe? Why can't I be serious? I think I'm going to be sick—"

Rhonda's face wrenched from my armpit. My eyes popped open. Her cherubic face — still ashy — hovered next to mine. Narrowing her deep brown eyes, she shoved me back against the bookcase. A basket flipped off a shelf, scattering clips and bralettes all over us. A bra petal caught on one of the twigs sticking from Rhonda's extensions.

"Don't you get sick on me, Maizie Albright. The blood is bad enough. And the whatever that is—" She waved toward the scene before us. We collectively gagged and looked away.

Nash swore. "Forget the beginning. Forget it. Jump forward. What happened? Whose blood, Maizie? Whose blood is on you?"

I clamped my eyes shut. My chest heaved. I buried my face in Rhonda's neck, inhaling her vanilla Bath & Body spray and the clay from her tree makeup along with a strong dose of her fear-produced sweat. A heady mix that reordered my brain.

"Oh my God, Nash. It's Lorena. My sweet, sweet friend. Oh, God. She's—" I hiccuped a sob.

Rhonda squeezed me, and I squeezed back.

"She's hurt?" Nash said slowly. In the background, the engine cut off and the door squeaked. His boots thudded, then pattered.

The front door of Lorena's bungalow swung open. Still clutching each other, Rhonda and I looked up. Nash's tall, brawny body filled the doorway. Stepping inside, he ran a hand over his shaved head. The little scar on his chin whitened with the tightening of his jaw. His Paul Newman-blue eyes narrowed at the blood-spattered scene.

A pool of spreading blood stained the cheery rug and wooden floor. And in the center lay Lorena's body.

"She's dead," I whispered.

TWO

#TheBeginningBeginning
#SteppedAndRepeated

*L*ater, Rhonda and I sat on the tailgate of an ambulance, draped in blankets. We told our stories to the officer on duty. Nash and I took Rhonda home, where Tiffany promised to watch her.

"Figures on the night I might have met Mr. Next-Right," said Tiffany. She'd been kidding. Mostly.

From the minute I'd called Nash to that moment had seemed like a long, long stretch of time. I felt numb and over-charged like someone had toggled my on-and-off switch too many times.

Instead of driving me to my father's cabin, Nash brought me to the old Nash Security Solutions office above the Dixie Kreme Donut Shop. Where he (temporarily) lived.

In the hall bathroom, I peeled off the bloody cheer outfit and placed it in the paper bag given to me by Black Pine Police. I burst into tears. Lorena would never again design a cheer skirt with a secret inner panel that somehow prevented muffin top. I showered, dressed in one of Nash's concert t-shirts and sweat-pants, and schlepped back to the office.

Nash waited for me on the lumpy couch in the reception area. Now his living room. I sank beside him and buried my face in his neck. One of his large hands cupped the back of my head. The other patted my leg.

He responded well in emergencies, but the aftermath made him uncomfortable.

At least my aftermath.

"Mowry's in charge of the investigation," he said.

"That's good," I sniffled. "Ian's very thorough."

"It didn't look like an accident," said Nash slowly.

I shook my head and looked up at him. "Why would someone do that to Lorena?"

He stroked my hair. "You did good tonight. You kept your head."

"I panicked. I walked through a crime scene. My bloody footprints are all over the place. I put my hands on her body when obviously she was dead. I cried and I almost threw up on Rhonda. And I made no sense on the phone. I gave the dispatcher the wrong address then hung up. It took them twenty minutes to find us."

"You checked on a victim to see if you could help. You called in the first responders. And you called me. You stayed calm. For you. That's all that can be expected."

"Exactly. As a private investigator, more should be expected. I'm not the person I would call in an emergency. In an emergency, I call you. I want to be like you. You would have handled it better."

He shrugged and patted my hand. "I'm me. You're you."

"That doesn't make me feel better." I slid forward and leaned my elbows on my knees. "And here I am, thinking about myself again when I should be thinking about Lorena."

"Let's think about Lorena. But first, tell me what you told the police. Start at the beginning-beginning," he said. "Then we'll sort out what happened with the rest."

"The beginning-beginning." I sighed. "I didn't see Lorena today. At least not until it was too late. My beginning-beginning started with the Step and Repeat."

. . .

*S*tep and Repeat — the event backdrop for taking red carpet moments — was something Rhonda had always dreamed about. And I'd made it happen for her at the Clothing Kids Masquerade Gala. Tiffany was only barely aware of entertainment news, but Rhonda was a subscriber. Rhonda and Tiffany had done a lot for me since my move home and subsequent cultural adjustment to the non-rich and not-famous lifestyle (their words not mine). Taking them to *the* Black Pine social event of the year meant a lot to Rhonda.

Free drinks and food meant a lot to Tiffany.

"I can't believe I'm here," said Rhonda through duck-face lips. We stood on the Martins' walk before a vinyl banner wallpapered with the Clothing Kids logo. "I'll never forget this night as long as I live."

"Dressed like this, I can believe it," Tiffany smirked. She'd rolled her eyes at their crepe togas adorned with foliage, but I could tell she was secretly pleased to not only be invited to the landmark event but also dressed by my famous friend. "Mardi Gras and we don't have to do anything weird for beads."

Rhonda pressed a hand to her apple-leaved bosom and tried to toss her balayage spiral extensions, forgetting several had been curled around long, forked twigs attached to a crown of apple blossoms. Trying another pose, she turned sideways, looked over her bared shoulder, and smiled coquettishly. "Just think. Me, a wood nymph."

"Better than another kind of nymph." Tiffany cocked a hip and unfolded her arms painted in cherrywood knotholes.

"Or dressed as a cheerleader over two layers of Spanx," I said then sucked in my breath. Placing my weight on my back leg, I tucked one hand on my hip and leaned forward with my other arm stretched across my cheer skirt. "I'll be lucky not to pass out by the end of the night. If I eat anything, I'll pop like a can of biscuits."

Not only was this Tiffany and Rhonda's first red carpet photoshoot, but it was also my first in over a year. Between my very (very) public fall from grace, the subsequent wrapping up of my old life (arrest), and move in with my father's family in Black Pine, Georgia (probation), I didn't get a lot of red carpet calls. Or invites to emcee philanthropic events. Or even requested to give charitable contributions. I'd been blackballed from the giving tree. Which I understood. For your cause, would you want a celebrity headliner whose fiancé had been caught using his *non-profit* to sell Oxy to senior citizens?

In my case, absolutely not. Even though I had no idea Oliver's kindness toward the elderly extended into drug dealing. Unfortunately, charity work had been my favorite part of celebrity status. Toward the end, philanthropy was the only real perk considering how badly I wanted out of the entertainment world.

But here I was, once again, smiling and blowing kisses for a professional photographer before a media backdrop. I couldn't contain my excitement.

Rhonda pulled out her selfie-stick, conveniently disguised as a twig.

"No photos," said Helmut, the photographer, and waved us on. "Don't forget I have exclusive rights to all photos and video. If you've hashtagged anything about tonight, I will find out."

And here was my first experience of getting kicked off the red carpet walk. Which says a lot about my life now. But I wouldn't change it for anything.

Except maybe wish I hadn't gotten asked to attend the masquerade in my old *Julia Pinkerton, Teen Detective* costume. I hoped Helmut cropped the photos. I'd rather keep everything below my shoulders out of the public eye. But at least my arms were toned from carrying cameras and other surveillance equipment. And from driving my dirt bike, Lucky. It's amazing how clenching handlebars for fear of dying can be an effective workout.

Although I was about to swap Lucky for a vehicle with four wheels. I would probably need a new arm regimen.

We sashayed up the brick walk to the Martins' house. The home was located in Black Pine's original downtown, the area off the town square where the old Southern and carpet-bagging families had their homes. Back when Black Pine was a Gilded Age mountain retreat for those escaping the summer heat. The lake came a bit later when those old families wanted an even better vista for golfing. And a place to put their sailboats and baby yachts. Black Pine remained a resort, and recently it also became a hub for the movie industry.

Whether it's the nineteenth or twenty-first century, some things never change: taxes, land, and labor have always been cheaper in the South. And the rich still run things.

They just have a different accent now.

"Let's hit the bar," said Tiffany. "Maizie, I know you don't drink, but if they're really expecting you to do a Julia Pinkerton cheer routine when you present the giant check, you'll need one."

I shook my head. "Sometimes it's better to face humiliation sober. Especially when it's a humiliation for charity. Which I'm all for. At least in theory."

"I want to tour the house," said Rhonda, snapping herself beneath the foyer chandelier. "I love these old houses. But only if it's a rich person's house. You head to the other side of Black Pine and houses just like this are dumps."

"Funny how that works," said Tiffany.

"Are you taking pictures for your blog?" I said, fretting per usual. "Helmut told us he has exclusive rights to the party."

"That man doesn't have exclusive rights to my face, Maizie," said Rhonda. "I'm gonna selfie my way through this house. And this party."

I found it best to nod and smile when Rhonda and Tiffany had issues with authority. It often led to raised voices and exaggerated body movements. With the crush of the party, I feared someone might lose an eye due to Rhonda's branch extensions.

"Let's selfie our way to the bar," said Tiffany. "Some dude told me it's in the back parlor, whatever that is. But judging by the folks rolling in, we need to get there before they run out of free booze."

"I thought we would hobnob," said Rhonda. "And pass out LA HAIR business cards. My goal is to eventually work exclusively with Black Pine's rich and famous. We can charge more."

Tiffany shook her head, scattering leaves. "They tip worse. Let's go. The bar calls. I also want to stock up on gift bags before they run out."

"We're at a party with gift bags and it doesn't have a bouncy house?" Rhonda turned to me, sideswiping a passing pirate's parrot and knocking it from his shoulder. "How much were these tickets, Maizie?"

"My humiliation is the price of your admission." I cocked a shoulder. "But I'll catch up with you later. I should find the Clothing Kids people and find out what time I have to present the check."

"How about talking them out of the cheer routine." Tiffany snorted.

"Daddy, Carol Lynn, and Remi should be here, too." I looked around the foyer at the clusters of costumed patrons. "And I imagine Lorena is flitting around somewhere. If you see her, tell her I'm looking for her."

Rhonda grinned. "Can you believe I know a famous Hollywood costume designer?"

"You don't know her, Rhon," said Tiffany. "We met her once. And she mostly had a mouth full of pins while we stood around in our undies wrapped in material. Not my idea of a G.N.O."

"If Lorena meets you once, you become her friend," I said. "That's why I love her. And her mouth is often full of pins, so no biggie."

"See?" Rhonda elbowed Tiffany. "I bet Lorena'll do a selfie with me. My blog will blow up after this."

"I'm gonna blow up if I don't get to the bar." Tiffany yanked on Rhonda's elbow. "Come on."

I watched them walk away, then craned my neck, trying to identify people in the room. Not spying my family or anyone from the Clothing Kids board of directors, I moved through the front rooms. I'd not grown up in Black Pine, so the only recognizable faces were the few that had hired my investigation companies — formerly Nash Security Solutions and currently Albright Security Solutions (owned by my ex-manager/still-mother who didn't care enough to get creative with names). Totally awkward doing cocktail party nods to those who hired you for cheating spouse surveillance.

Even more awkward pretending you don't recognize those you've seen with their pants down. Literally.

This was why Wyatt Nash, formerly of Nash Security Solutions and currently head of security at DeerNose, didn't do Black Pine shindigs and wasn't my plus three. Also because he doesn't like shindigs. Or people in general. But years of dealing with the underbelly of civilization does that to you.

Which, hopefully, was where I'd be after my two-year apprenticeship was done.

Okay, that sounded better in my head.

"Excuse us," said a man in a tux, opera cape, and Phantom mask.

He tried to push past me. I backed into a butler's pantry to move out of his way. His plus one, in a long gown — obviously Phantom's Christine — waved at a friend and stopped in the congested wood-paneled hall, blocking me inside. The couple leaned against the doorway of the pantry, chatting with friends. I turned and moved deeper into the pantry, in search of solitude.

Fine. In search of snacks. The Spanx were killing me, but my empty stomach was killing me more.

The pantry shelves held assorted fine china, crystal, and

silver. But the back wall had shallow shelves with vintage cookie tins. Spying a small latch (and hoping it was a sign from God), I lifted the latch and pushed a small door open. Instead of a cookie closet, I faced ornamental shrubs.

I took it as a different kind of sign from God and stepped into the cool evening air. Easing through the tall azaleas, I spied a couple dressed as Raggedy Ann and Woody from Toy Story. Not wanting to break up a secret rendezvous, I halted, poised to creep back through the secret cookie door.

"You need to calm down," said Woody.

"I'm going to kill you," snarled Raggedy Ann. "You ruined everything."

Wrong kind of secret rendezvous.

THREE

#MeanGirls #SlyDogs

*S*liding backward toward the door, I heard the sharp crack of palm on skin, followed by a crash and a thud. The bush in front of me shook, scattering leaves and twigs.

Some slap. Raggedy Ann obviously worked out.

Figuring Woody could take care of himself, I popped back through the pantry door. Finding the Phantom and Christine gone, I slipped back into the hall where Paul Bunyan stood glowering. One hand clasped an ax he'd hooked on his shoulder. A scrawny armadillo yanked his other hand.

"Maizie," said Boomer Spayberry and hauled my six-year-old half-sister, Remi, back to his side. "About time I found you. When are they doing this thing so I can git?"

"Daddy. You look perfect." I grinned. The ax was the only costume requirement for a man of his stature and dressing habits.

"I don't know why I have to be at this party. Or in the pictures. I don't mind being on the board, but I'd rather just sign the checks," he said. "Quit pulling, Remi."

"I wanna find the kids." She tipped her head up, pointing her pinkish-grey felt armadillo nose toward the coffered wood ceiling. "We're doing hide-and-seek."

I stopped myself from telling Remi she looked cute. Those were fighting words. I stroked her felt head instead. "Lorena outdid herself with this costume."

"I can't curl up in a ball, though." Remi knocked on her segmented paper-mâché shell. "And Daddy won't let me eat bugs."

"Having your picture in the magazine spread is good PR for DeerNose," I replied, insightfully moving the conversation back to Daddy and away from armadillo eating habits. "And what could be cuter than a giant lumberjack surrounded by kiddy forest dwellers?"

"It's terrible PR." A Chanel No. 5 cloud wafted toward us. "But don't let my opinion stop you."

The perfume was as recognizable as the voice. We collectively jerked and turned to face my ex-manager and still-mother, Vicki Albright. Not only spritzed but also clothed in Chanel.

"Not much of a costume," I said.

"It's vintage." Seeing my reaction, she sighed. "I'm surprised you don't recognize it. I wore it to the 2010 pre-Golden Globes party at Chateau Marmont. Hello, Boomer," Vicki said to Daddy, then patted the armadillo's head. "Remi. Lorena did an incredible job with the costume."

"Must not be that great if you knew it was me." Remi scowled, matching her lumberjack guardian.

"Vicki." Daddy nodded. Their relationship as exes had recently improved into cordiality. However, trust was still an issue. Past grievances and betrayals were tricky. Daddy made an effort to forgive, but to forget was another thing entirely. "Come on, Remi. Let's see if we can find the kids."

I waited until they moved down the hall. "Why is it bad PR?"

"Really, Maizie." Vicki rolled her eyes. "His clothing line is for hunters. And you want him photographed wielding an ax before a group of children wearing animal costumes? DeerNose's one million to Clothing Kids won't matter. Everything is about optics. I'm surprised Lorena agreed to the idea."

She had a point. "Daddy hoped it would help to show hunters' views on conservation and preservation. But I'll talk to Helmut before the shoot."

"Helmut's doing the photo spread? I thought it was just tonight's party snaps." Vicki patted her blonde coif. "I'm surprised Boomer's doing this publicly anyway. He never used to do galas. Not when I wanted to participate. All that talk about not blowing trumpets when giving alms. Everyone knows the only trumpeter at a gala is in the jazz quartet."

As a child of divorce, I'd gotten used to tiptoeing around potential landmines. I ignored the hazards hiding in that comment. "I convinced him. It's a kickoff to bring the charity to a national level. They're hoping to establish chapters in other communities."

"I also heard you promised a cheer routine."

"A reenactment from *Julia Pinkerton*." My cheeks blazed. "I find it difficult to say no."

"Interesting since you've had no issue saying it to me." Her sea glass green eyes narrowed, then widened. She jerked her chin up but softened her features. "Sorry."

"That was very good," I said encouragingly. "You're getting better."

"Kevin's having me try meditation." She lifted a shoulder. "If I concentrate hard enough, I can almost forget I'm stuck in Black Pine after you betrayed me by running away to live with your father. Which caused *All is Albright* to dive in the ratings."

"On judge's orders," I muttered. "And the dive had nothing and everything to do with the casting."

"Maizie," called a voice thickened with midwestern twang. "We've been looking for you."

We turned to peer down the hall, relieved by the interruption. A man dressed in a three-piece suit, complete with a straw boater and spats, waved.

"Who is that?" murmured Vicki.

"The homeowner, I believe. Dennis Martin. I haven't met all

the board members yet. Lorena lives next door, so their involvement is probably neighborly kindness."

"This new money in Black Pine." Vicki sighed. "Trying to pretend they are original."

"Since when do you care about Black Pine lineages? Your money isn't exactly old. It's the same age as me." I raised my brows, hoping she'd get my implication.

She slow-blinked, flashing her sea glass-green eyes. The Georgian accent she fought to hide in California suddenly appeared. In a much more refined drawl. "The Albrights have been in the area for over a hundred years. Spayberrys, too. You should learn to appreciate your family legacy, Maizie. Particularly now that you live here again."

I blinked back with matching sea glass-greens. However, I blinked in confusion, not contempt. Back in the day, the Spayberrys were considered backwoods — they literally lived in the woods, as far from town as they could get — and the Albrights were "townies."

"You couldn't wait to get out of Black Pine," I said. "You dragged me to California as soon as I got that diaper commercial."

"There was no dragging. I carried you in a Baby Bjorn." She shook her head. "Really, Maizie. Let's meet the organizers. I have an extra check for the foundation."

The suited man stood before a door to an office. As we strolled inside, a woman turned from gazing out a window. She wore a long Edwardian-style dress with long gloves and a plumed hat pinned to her updo.

"Dennis Martin," said the suited man, holding out his kid leather-gloved hand. I shook it, wincing at the firm grip. "This is my wife, Jan. We missed you at the meet and greet. Had a little emergency we needed to take care of."

Jan gave Dennis the side-eye. "Not an emergency. Just a small detail we needed to attend to."

I smiled and winced again as Jan took my hand. Another

strong grip and her gloves were damp. "This is my mother, Vicki Albright—"

"I know," said Jan, grasping Vicki's hand. "You're the *television* producer for that reality show. The movies really attract attention to Black Pine. But I told Dennis, it's not just feature films that build the economy. The small screen counts, too."

Vicki's smile flickered. "*All Is Albright* is one of the shows I produce. Among my other projects."

"And you live in the Peanut Mansion on the mountain. I know you did quite a bit of work on it. I'm president of the Historical Society." Jan arched her brows. "I'm glad to hear you passed our inspection. I was surprised considering some of the *embellishments* you made."

I took a step back, unsure of the dangers lurking in the shallow pool we trod. Some animosity of the historical variety, it seemed.

"Your in-town home is quaint, too," said Vicki. "Originally a tobacco grower's little house, I understand?"

"Like yours, this was also a summer home," Jan replied, lifting her chin. "But Mr. King of King Tobacco also had a third home on St. Simon's Island."

"Not Jekyll? Too bad," murmured Vicki. "Peanuts had so many more uses, I suppose."

I discreetly moved to elbow Vicki. She outmaneuvered my elbow and turned to study the toile wallpaper. "Reproduction, I assume?"

"Original," said Jan. "We hire a preservationist to clean it every year."

"I hope they wear a mask," said Vicki. "I understand arsenic was used to get that vibrant green. Owning a historic mansion, I've been studying architectural history, too. As my family has always lived in Black Pine, even before the Peanut Mansion was built, I feel learning local history is more than a passing hobby. It's a family legacy."

"Arsenic?" Dennis's befuddled expression turned to open

horror as he stared at their dining room wall. "Jan, did you know about that?"

"Of course, I know," said Jan tightly. "That trouble was mainly in England."

"Sorry," said Vicki. "I didn't realize your tobacco farmer wouldn't have imported his wallpaper. He bought locally? How quaint."

"Vicki," I said quickly. "Don't you have a check to give the Martins?"

Vicki opened her velvet handbag. Pausing a moment to allow the gold interlocking C's to catch the light, she pulled out a slip of paper and handed it to Dennis. "Happy to help your foundation."

Dennis glanced at the amount and chuckled. "Wow. Your reality show must do alright. Get it? Alright instead of Albright."

"*I* do alright." After a sharp glance at me, Vicki flicked a smile. "If you'll excuse me."

We turned to watch her sashay to the door. She halted at the appearance of Raggedy Ann and Woody. I studied Woody's face and noticed the slap hadn't left a mark. Must have sounded worse than it was.

"Hey, Spencer," said Dennis Martin. "Vicki Albright gave us a nice fat check."

"Really, Dennis," muttered Jan. "Don't be so gauche."

Woody quirked a grin. "Vicki?"

"Spence Newson?" Vicki placed a hand on his plaid arm. "I thought I recognized you."

"I heard you were back." He pulled her in for a hug. The leather fringe from his gloved hands dangled down her backless Chanel dress provocatively. The irony of the contrast was not lost on me. "Haven't seen you in ages, girl."

I tried to disguise my shock as she hugged him back. Hugs and Vicki didn't intermingle in the literal or figurative sense. Maybe Kevin's meditation included herbal supplements. Strong ones.

"Spencer Newson is the executive director of Clothing Kids," said Dennis. "I guess your mother knows him. Tonight you'll present the check to him and Lorena. And this is Jennifer Frederick, our CFO. She'll be receiving the check, too."

Raggedy Ann moved around Spencer and Vicki's huddled walk-down-memory-lane.

"Assistant director of finance." Even with the red triangle and circles drawn on her nose and cheeks, Jennifer's face looked flushed. She darted a look at Jan before turning to shake my hand. "I understand you're good friends with Lorena."

"Who isn't a good friend to Lorena? She makes that an easy thing to do." I smiled, wondering what Spencer had done to upset Jennifer.

Not my business, I reminded myself. But keep an eye on Vicki.

"I've known Lorena for a long time. When I was six, she and I worked on a Barbie commercial together. She even made extra clothes for the Barbies I was given that weren't part of the commercial. They became some of my favorite toys. Ten years later, Lorena was Wardrobe Supervisor on *Julie Pinkerton, Teen Detective*. She made me a tiny Julia Pinkerton outfit, too. I still have them somewhere."

"They're probably worth a fortune now that Lorena's won all those awards," said Jennifer.

"I could never sell them. Lorena helped me through some of my teenage struggles. She was never too busy to talk. And she gave great fashion advice."

"I guess you were glad to learn she moved to Black Pine," said Jan. "Once I knew who she was, I became more tolerant of the liberties she took with her bungalow. Can you believe she gutted it for a more open floor plan? Unbelievable. For someone who knows clothing history, I'd like to think she'd want to pay a little more attention to hundred-year-old architectural traits."

"Lorena's always had a unique vibe," I said. "She wanted a

large living space for all her sewing equipment. Work and play are the same to her. I think her home looks totally cute."

"Puppies are cute. The desecration of architecture brings to mind another word," said Jan with a sniff. "Lorena didn't want to be on the Historical Society preservation committee. Said she was too involved with Clothing Kids and helping at the local theater."

"She is retired," I said diplomatically. "She was supposed to retire before that indie film brought her here. Although I'm glad the indie won her another CDGA award." At Jennifer's questioning look, I added, "Costume Designers Guild Award."

"Yes, Lorena's very talented." Jan glanced over her shoulder. The ostrich feather swept across Jennifer's yarn head. "Where is she anyway? Shouldn't we do the speeches?"

Jennifer pushed back her sleeve to check her watch. "We may need to do this without Lorena."

"Why don't I go next door and get her?" Anxious to get away, I moved toward the door.

Spencer Newson caught my arm. "This is your girl, Vick? I've seen all your shows and movies, hon'. Such a pleasure."

"Always nice to meet a fan." I gave him a tight smile.

Before I could slide away, he brought me in for a hug. "I'm more than a fan. Almost like we're family, right Vick?"

"I wouldn't go that far, Spence," purred Vicki.

He bussed my cheek. Trying to dodge his overly-friendly parry, I swooped backward, bumping into Jessie the cowgirl. Looking sexier than I remembered. And angrier. Although it'd been a while since I'd seen *Toy Story 2*.

"Sorry," I said.

She grabbed Spencer's arm with her fringed glove. "Who's this, Spence?"

His hand flew off my waist. Spencer swung his gaze from me to Vicki to Jessie. His smile faltered.

Awkward.

"Maizie Albright," I offered.

A feline smile curled Vicki's lips. "Vicki Albright."

"Spencer's wife, Susie Newson," said the cowgirl, adjusting her hat to better glower at us.

"Spencer and Susie, how adorable," said Vicki. "I don't remember you from school. Spencer and I graduated together."

"You wouldn't remember me because I'm not as old as you."

"Yes, it shows."

Probably everyone got Vicki's jab except Susie, judging by her triumphant smile. She eyed me. "But you look my age."

I lifted my shoulders. "I guess? I don't know. Who can tell?"

"Now Susie, honey," said Spencer. "We were just catching up."

"Right." Susie snorted. "I've heard that before."

The Martins and Jennifer took a concerted slide backward and feigned interest in the possibly arsenic-tainted wallpaper. I crept back toward them, preferring poison over venom.

Vicki tapped Spencer on the arm. "You haven't changed a bit, Spence. Always the sly dog."

He had the decency to blush and mumble an apology.

Susie yanked on his arm. "Spencer?"

"We'll never get this show on the road," muttered Jan. "It takes Spencer forever to calm her down."

"This happens a lot?"

"More than you'd like to know," said Jennifer.

Remembering the slap she'd given him, I feared Jennifer was right. But hoped for Vicki's sake, she was wrong.

FOUR

#LoveOrMoney
#NightoftheNotLivingDead

---

*a*fter meeting the board members, I had a feeling I knew why Lorena waited until the last minute to appear for the opening ceremony. Making my excuses, I zipped out of the room and aimed toward the other end of the house where I hoped to find Tiffany and Rhonda.

Couples jammed the hall leading to the back parlor. I squeezed through and spotted Tiffany at the bar. Judging by the cock of her hip and her hand gestures, she appeared to be in a deep conversation with the bartender. Rhonda had stationed herself behind the buffet table. I circled the table, dropping appetizers on a plate as I moved toward Rhonda.

"Oh my stars, am I glad to see you," said Rhonda.

I grinned. "Having fun?"

"My branches are caught on a curtain behind me and I've been standing here for thirty minutes." She glared across the room. "I haven't been able to get Tiffany's attention. She's all into that bartender."

Leaving my plate on the table, I slipped behind Rhonda and examined her hair. "It's not the curtain. The cord for the shade is wrapped around your sticks."

"Get it off," she shrieked. "Just cut it out."

"I'm not cutting their shade pull. Jan Martin would kill me. I'm only half-kidding after meeting her. Hang on. It looks like the more you moved, the more tangled it got." I dug through her sticks, seeking the end. "Why didn't anyone help you?"

"I don't know," she wailed. "Hardly anybody came over here. The food must be terrible. One couple came over, and I said, 'You've got to help.' They clapped and tossed money on the table and left."

I glanced at the table. "You raised one hundred dollars for Clothing Kids. Nice job, Rhon."

She glared at me. "I'm a plus two guest. You're the entertainment."

"Hang on." I moved behind her again, flipped the cord over, under, and around the branches. "Freedom. Your curls are kind of frizzy now."

Rhonda jerked forward. "I'm taking the sticks out. But first I'm going to kill Tiffany."

"But look at her." We gazed at Tiffany's back. She stood on her toes, her small, wiry frame leaning toward the bar. Her scrawny shoulders were hunched near her ears and a finger pointed at the bartender's face. But with each shake of the finger, the bartender's smile grew bigger. "It could be love. Who knows."

"Huh," grunted Rhonda. "I usually don't leave her alone at a bar. After a few sips of a cocktail, she gets surly with the staff. I have to haul her off before she pops someone. But this guy looks like a glutton for punishment."

I shrugged. "It takes all kinds."

Tiffany had moved her finger from his face to form a fist. The bartender folded his arms on the bar top and leaned closer.

"That guy's going to get hurt," said Rhonda. "We should do something."

I moved in front of her. "But Rhonda, what if it's love? Who are we to get in the way of love?"

"You're a little obsessed with trying to get everyone hooked up, Maizie. Vicki and Kevin. Now Tiffany and the bartender. He'll get a black eye if he's not careful."

"I can't help it. I love being in love. And I want everyone to feel that kind of happiness." I clasped my hands together and sighed. Maybe a little too wistfully.

She squinted at me. "Trouble in paradise?"

"Oh no," I said. "Nash and I are great. He works for my father and I work for my mother."

"There's nothing in that situation that could go wrong."

"Right?" I forced a smile. "But we're working toward a greater purpose. For my two-year private investigation apprenticeship to be done and for him to pay off his debts."

"It's all about money, then."

"I don't think I'll ever make much money as a private investigator."

"Then it must be love."

"I've got to get Lorena," I said. "We need her to start the ceremony."

Rhonda riveted her attention back to Tiffany. She'd stopped shaking her fist. The bartender poured her another drink. "I'll go with you. Maybe Lorena's got another idea for my hair other than trees. These branches could be lethal."

*A*fter making our way through the crowd, we walked out of the open front doors, crossed the veranda, and traipsed the front walk to the sidewalk. A group of hired valets hung out by the gate, chatting. Rhonda took a valet selfie and we continued down the sidewalk toward Lorena's bungalow.

"These homes are beautiful," I said, gazing at the row of historic houses lit by the moon and carefully arranged landscape spotlights. "I'm glad the Historical Society works so hard to protect the original designs. Although in Vicki's case, I'm not sure why she cares. In California, she had zero interest in old homes. She wanted modern with views. Now she's brushing up on nineteenth-century wallpaper."

"I hate to say it," said Rhonda. "But I'm gonna do it anyway. When it comes to Vicki, you've got to consider the interior motives."

"I think you mean ulterior motives."

"Nope," said Rhonda. "Vicki's motives are all interior. She's the only one who understands them, and they only benefit her."

"She's doing better," I said. "Kevin's helping a lot."

"But where's Kevin?" said Rhonda. "He's a famous kung fu trainer to the stars. He belongs at a party like this, too."

That was a good question. And I didn't have an answer to it. I kept my mouth shut.

We strolled down the sidewalk toward Lorena's. As Rhonda shed apple leaves, I shed misgivings about my mother. I wanted to believe in the best in her relationship with Kevin Yuan. Just like I wanted to believe the best in my relationship with Nash.

I also wanted to believe in the best for Susie and Spencer, but they seemed like a hot mess. Instead, I hoped for the best in Spencer's interest in Clothing Kids. Mainly that their president wouldn't let his extracurricular shenanigans affect his leadership in the foundation.

"I wonder why Lorena didn't want to be president," I said aloud.

"Wasn't she born in Mexico?" said Rhonda. "I think you have to be born here or something. But I would vote for Lorena anyway."

"I meant executive director of the Clothing Kids charity. I met the president and some of the other board members. Spencer's an old high school friend of Vicki's and his wife looks to be our age. Susie almost scratched Vicki's eyes out, thinking they were up to something. I also witnessed a private scuffle between Spencer and the board's CFO. Lorena's the founder and a board member. She must have wanted other people to run the foundation, but I'm kind of wondering why she chose Spencer."

"Lorena must have had a good reason. She really wants to clothe a lot of kids."

"Very true," I said, stopping at the sidewalk juncture before her house. "I shouldn't be such a doubter. I'd trust Lorena with anything."

"You know how these CEO-types are," said Rhonda. "I learned all about it on *Billions* and *Empire*. Crazy greedy and will do what it takes to get the job done." She sliced a finger across her throat.

"I don't think Spencer Newson's that kind of CEO. He's the director of a charitable foundation, not a Wall Street titan or a hip-hop mogul," I said. "I'm more worried his marriage will cause him to lose focus on his work."

"That happened in *Mad Men*," said Rhonda. "You can only do booze and women for so long before it causes you to lose the ad agency."

"Forget the president," I said. "And please don't mention it to Lorena."

"Done and done," said Rhonda. "Selfie?"

We leaned against the picket gate to her house and smiled up at Rhonda's phone. Behind us, the bungalow appeared warm and inviting. The interior lights basked the porch in a cheery glow. Shrubs lined Lorena's walk. Pots of pansies climbed her porch steps.

"Lorena must be home," I said. "Maybe she had to fix something on her costume. She's going as *La Calavera Catrina*, the Day of the Dead fancy lady skeleton."

"Scary?" said Rhonda. "I don't do scary. I stay home on Halloween, you know."

"The Day of the Dead is not really meant to be scary. It's a family holiday."

"If she looks scary, I'm out of there. I'm just telling you now."

FIVE

#TemporaryTemptations #TigerQueen

"And Lorena did look scary," I said to Nash. "You saw how scary. Poor Rhonda. She'll probably never get over it. I'll never get over it. Poor Lorena."

I began to cry again, having held off through my story. Nash rubbed my back and patted my hand. Then found the box of tissues he bought for me and the few customers who cried. After I returned from washing my face, I found him pacing the cramped room.

He stopped and pulled me into his arms. "Do you want me to take you home?"

"No." I snuggled against him. Wrapped in his solid arms, I laid my head against his firm chest and my trembling ceased. My pulse slowed to match the steady beating of his heart and my body melded to his. I closed my eyes, saw Lorena, and opened them. Even my Nash-swaddle wouldn't stop my brain from seeing her bloodied body. "Who would want to hurt Lorena like that?"

"The police think it was a robbery," said Nash. "But seems kind of grisly for Black Pine. It looked like head trauma along with the stabbing."

I shuddered. "What did they steal?"

"They're not sure. The perp didn't take any electronics that they could tell, but her file cabinet and a safe were opened and a lot of paper was strewn about. Maybe they stole money or something like that."

"What do you think?"

"Not a typical robbery for Black Pine. Unless Lorena knew the perp. Which could be the case."

"I can't believe anyone would want to do that to Lorena. I need to understand what happened." I rubbed my temples, then moved out of his arms to sit on Lamar's La-Z-Boy. Popping the footrest, I watched Nash make tracks across the dusty floor of the front room.

"Mowry's lead detective," said Nash. "Don't worry. He'll keep us informed. And he might have a different opinion for the motive. The first responders said robbery."

While Nash paced, I thought about the state of Lorena's room. Robbery hadn't immediately come to my mind either, but I'd been distracted by Lorena's body, lying face down. Blood obscured the bright flowers and ornamentals painted on her face, making the white and black paint for the *Calavera* skull mask gruesome. Her beautiful hair had been tangled and matted in blood. A pair of scissors had been left sticking out of her back.

I hugged my arms across my chest. "Did Ian say how she was killed?"

"Nothing official. Mowry needs to wait for GBI's medical examiner's report. But we did talk about the obvious. The scissors were probably not the murder weapon."

"She had makeup on but hadn't gotten dressed. Her dress and hat were still hanging on a mannequin in the corner." I couldn't stop shaking. "Someone hit her in the back of the head, didn't they?"

"That's how it appeared to me."

"And stabbing her in the back with the scissors? Seems kind of…personal."

"That's what I would think. Symbolic." Nash stopped pacing

and returned to crouch next to me. He placed his large hands on my shoulders, slid them to my biceps, and gently unfolded my arms to take my hands. "You shouldn't be thinking about this. Not now."

How could I think about anything else? "I can't help it."

Leaning toward me, he cupped my face in my hands. "It's late. You should sleep."

Would I ever sleep again? "I don't think I can."

"I have a bed." He looked at me. Intently. "That's what I was doing when you called. Putting it together."

I glanced around the room, but it looked the same as usual. Frumpy couch. Dumpy recliner. Battered file cabinets. A coffee table with old issues of *PI Magazine* and an *InStyle*. I took great comfort in knowing the office remained like this while we took our sabbatical from Nash Security Solutions. That the file cabinets and Lamar's La-Z-boy would be here, waiting for our return. We could blow the dust off and go back to work. As partners.

"You sleep on the couch," I said. "Temporarily."

"Not anymore."

"Where is this bed?"

He jerked his chin toward the inner office door. "In there."

"That's your office."

"It was my office. Now it's my bedroom." He cocked his head. "You look upset again. I'm not trying for a booty call right after your friend was murdered. I thought you'd be happy to know I have a bed. And maybe you want to sleep on it."

"I don't know." I knew Nash wouldn't pull a murder-sympathy booty call. It wasn't his style. He was a Southern gentleman. Mainly because he was a gentleman and Southern. He believed in booty calls with a proper time and place. Like hotel rooms in Florida. Which hadn't fit in our agenda. Yet. "I should go home, I guess."

"I bought expensive sheets. I asked Carol Lynn what kind to get."

"Daddy and Carol Lynn and Remi all have camouflage-print sheets. Except Remi's is pink camo. DeerNose brand. Unscented, of course. But very camo."

"I asked what kind you had. I figured you had some kind of special designer sheets you brought back from California."

"True. I don't want to sleep in camouflage sheets. Remi wears camo jammies. It's confusing enough waking and finding her and the Jack Russells in my bed, but then to lose her in a forest of sheets is disturbing."

Nash stood and rocked back on his heels. "You don't want to see my bed?"

Biting my lip, I pushed the footrest down and slid out of the recliner. I walked to the office door and opened it. The desk and chairs had been shoved against one wall, equipment piled on top. A mattress and box springs on a simple frame took up the rest of the room. The sheets did look expensive and mostly covered by a fluffy gray duvet. The pillows looked new and plump. A plush throw picturing a Siberian tiger with blue eyes lay at the bottom of the bed. The fabric was worn and fuzzy with lint, the edges frayed.

Nash strode in, grabbed the tiger throw, and tossed it in the corner. He made a Vanna White sweeping gesture toward the bed. "What do you think?"

"What's that?" I pointed toward the crumpled tiger throw.

"Nothing." Nash leaned over and pushed on the mattress. "You can change the setting to more firm or soft, depending on how you like it. Pretty nifty."

"Nifty," I echoed. "Was that your childhood blankie?"

I'd never seen Nash blush before. "It's not a blankie. It's a blanket. But yes, I've had it for a long time."

"What's the tiger's name?"

"I take it you want to go home now?"

SIX

#31FlavorForgetIt #APersonalMurder

*T*he morning after Lorena's death, I called in a personal day to Albright Security Solutions and went to LA HAIR instead. In my previous career, calling in sick to work could sabotage production schedules. The only personal day I'd ever taken was during the filming of our reality show, *All Is Albright*, and that was to check into rehab.

A true mental health day.

Al and his crew had gotten plenty of B-roll roadside footage of the facility. The producers used lower third captioning to explain my sudden exit. Technically, my character still had screen time.

I didn't like taking a personal day. I took my new job with Albright Security Solutions seriously. And my new boss, Annie Cox, was great. So great. I had a lot more independence and responsibility than I did working for Nash. That should have made me excited to go to work every day.

But for some reason, my excitement for private investigations had dulled. Which worried me. This was a major career pivot. I'd come to a vocation crossroads and turned left. Studied Criminal Justice at Southern Cal. Worked hard to prove myself to get the job as an apprentice to Nash.

But when Nash lost the business to Vicki and Vicki hired Annie to replace him, my job had gone from rainbow swirl to vanilla. Surprisingly, since private investigations were the 31 Flavors of jobs. You never knew if a stakeout would reveal your subject prancing around a sleazy motel room in leopard print boxers or secretly reading bodice-ripping romance books in a corner of the library.

Or both. Herb Jackson turned out to be a leopard-print boxer-wearing, secret-romance reader who needed a private escape from his paranoid wife.

But for some reason, even Herb Jackson's secret rendezvous with Loretta Chase books left me feeling blasé. Each week, Annie took my digital photos and report, filed them, and gave me a "nice job." At the end of the week, I deposited my paycheck and met Nash for dinner. Then usually left before dessert to go to a local bar to watch for my next Herb Jackson to appear. I clocked hours toward my PI license, but something was missing. The proverbial bloom was off the investigative rose.

I feared my previous career had ruined me for normal work life. Not that running a honey trap was normal work life. But you get the picture.

Even though it wasn't every day an old friend had been murdered (thank goodness), I still felt guilty taking personal leave. I headed to LA HAIR early. Outside of Nash's arms and Carol Lynn's chicken pot pie, LA HAIR was chicken soup for my soul. I also wanted to check on Rhonda. I didn't think LA HAIR's manager would allow her a mental health day. The last time Tiffany called in, Faye had demanded a doctor's note. But then Tiffany had a fractious attitude toward "rules, laws, and people telling me what to do." She never felt guilty about taking personal leave.

Don't tell Tiffany, but I kind of got Faye's point about a doctor's note.

I opened the door to the salon and took a deep breath of acrylic, aerosol, and Aromatique — a diffuser oil for masking the acrylic and aerosol fragrance. Coughed but felt soothed. I moved past the shelves of nail colors and over-priced products to the reception desk. Rhonda hunkered in the desk chair, barely raising her eyes to meet mine. I broke Faye's rule and moved around the counter to hug Rhonda. Tiffany broke Faye's rule and left her nail stand to join us.

"Sit tight, Doris," called Tiffany over her shoulder. "If the light goes off in the UV dryer, hit the button again."

"Is it safe to leave me?" Doris stared at the little box hiding her fingers. "Are you sure I should be touching your equipment?"

"This isn't brain surgery, Doris," said Tiffany. "You're just getting your nails done."

"How are you doing, Rhonda?" I said. "Did you get any sleep?"

She shook her head. "I can't stop thinking about Lorena. That scared the holy bejeebus out of me. I was afraid to close my eyes."

Like Rhonda, I couldn't sleep either. Not because I was scared. My brain wanted to pick through the crime scene, but the only thing I could focus on was her body.

"She's not gonna haunt you, Rhon'," said Tiffany. "You didn't kill her."

Rhonda looked up at me. "Who killed her?"

I shrugged. "Detective Mowry's investigating the crime."

"Shouldn't you be investigating it, too?" said Rhonda. "You're also a detective."

I bit my lip. "I'm not a detective-detective. I'm a private detective."

"Look into it privately," said Tiffany. "What's holding you back?"

"Interfering in an on-going criminal investigation that just started last night."

Tiffany rolled her eyes. "Lorena is your friend."

"I'm your friend, too," said Rhonda. "And I can't sleep until I know this killer is caught. What if they saw us go inside the house? What if they think we know something? Don't you watch movies? I'm most likely to be killed next."

"I don't think it works that way in real life—"

"Maizie," said Tiffany. "Do your job."

She was right. I was friends with the detective in charge of the investigation. I could work with Ian. I'd done it before. Without him knowing. But this time, I could ask permission. I wasn't limited to search warrants and whatnot like he was. He might want my help.

Ian wanting my help in a homicide case? Probably not.

I did honey pot stings, cheater surveillance, and the like. Looked for missing persons — mainly because they owed the client money. Drew up security plans. Vetted employee backgrounds. Made asset searches. Scoured for criminal activity. Online mostly.

Solving homicide cases was not in my wheelhouse or job description. Annie would never go for it. She preferred to pull in paper-chase clients, although the cheater racket paid well.

I never handled a homicide case, particularly on my own. With Nash, we had investigations where a murder had transpired, but our inquiry never began with foul play. Although it would be an interesting challenge.

What was I thinking? Lorena was a friend, not a puzzle.

"I'll see what I can do," I ventured. "I planned on checking in with Detective Mowry today anyway, in case he'd learned anything new since last night. IMHO, the attack was personal."

Rhonda's eyes widened. Tiffany leaned forward. "Who do you think did it?"

"I don't know. Lorena was the most likable person I know. I can't imagine anyone wanting to kill her."

"Why personal, then?" stammered Rhonda. "Personal how?"

I lowered my voice. "The scissors in the back gave it away. That's pretty obvious don't you think?"

"I would never stab someone in the back with scissors," said Tiffany.

"Of course not—"

"A knife, maybe," she continued. "But something like a hatchet would do more damage. What can stabbing with scissors do? Particularly in the back. Why not the gut? It's softer. Or neck. That would do the trick."

I glanced at Rhonda. She'd gone ashy again. "I should go."

"I thought you took a sick day," said Tiffany.

"A personal day." Someone killed my old friend. You couldn't get much more personal than that. Too personal. I needed to get my head out of Lorena's murder, not into it. "I'm shopping for a car. I have enough saved to get something more than a dirt bike. I think."

"We'll meet you at Rhubarb's at three," said Tiffany. "You'll need our help."

"What? I planned on visiting a dealer—"

"Rhubarb's. Corner of Beaver Run and Chickasaw Plum. You don't need to go anywhere else. Use the time to start your investigation."

"But—"

"Trust us," said Tiffany. "And we'll trust you to figure out who killed Lorena."

SEVEN

#ShrugMuch #TheGingherGanker

*S*ince I'd promised Rhonda and Tiffany to learn what I could from Detective Mowry, I pointed my dirt bike Lucky toward downtown Black Pine. I couldn't wait to be rid of Lucky. I'd been stuck with Lucky after my Jaguar had been repo-ed and Daddy refused to cosign for an auto loan.

He didn't believe in loans. I didn't believe in adult women riding the motorized bike given to them at age 14. But with my past legal troubles and nonexistent credit history — which is what happens when your ex-manager/still-mother and her accountant "takes care of everything" — I had no choice but to learn how to endure 250 ccs rumbling beneath my thighs.

I also hadn't planned on shopping at a place named after a fruit. Or a vegetable. Not being familiar with rhubarb, I wasn't really sure what it was, except not anything that inspired my confidence in automotive quality. But friends were harder to come by than cars. I could put up with Lucky for a few more hours.

I parked on Scarlet Oak Drive, closer to the Martin house to stay out of the way of the patrol cars parked before Lorena's bungalow. I sat there for a minute, watching official-looking people with blue-bagged feet enter and exit her house. Two uniformed officers knocked on her neighbors' doors. Yellow and black tape decorated her fence and porch.

I wondered who would water her pansies.

Then wondered why that thought crossed my mind. Shouldn't I instead be wondering who killed my friend? Another reason to be more like Nash. He wouldn't make plans to go car shopping the day after his friend was murdered. He would have been here bright and early with pertinent questions to ask Mowry. Nash wouldn't care about pansies. He'd care about justice.

I hopped off my bike and waited by the fence until I saw Detective Ian Mowry exit the house. He wasn't an authoritative guy, but he had a commanding presence. Plus he was a looker — tall and lean with thick, dark wavy hair and eyes the color of milk chocolate. The neighbors watching the proceedings, including Jan Martin, couldn't keep their eyes off of him. I waved, and he waved back, then met me on the sidewalk.

"How're you doing, honey?" He leaned in for a hug, gave me a quick kiss on the cheek, and backed off. We'd gone on one lunch date before I fully committed myself to (wearing down) Nash. I loved Ian. I just didn't love-love Ian.

"I'm good." I realized I was wringing my hands and shoved them in my pockets. "Actually, not good. Is Lorena with the medical examiner?"

He nodded. "It'll take a while for the report. I know you saw the scissors. Between you and me, someone whacked her in the back of the head with something heavy. In the meantime, GBI's in there doing forensics. I hoped for some trace evidence, but there are fibers galore with all the sewing stuff, and we're not finding many useful prints."

"No prints on the scissors?"

"Wiped." He paused. "Or the suspect wore gloves. Ms. Cortez was headed to the costume party a few doors down, right?"

I nodded. "You think it was someone in a costume?"

He shrugged. "Maybe. Maybe not."

"They could have left the party and come back," I said. "There were a lot of people going in and out."

"We'll talk to everyone at the party. Right now, we're focused on the neighbors, hoping they saw something."

"Nash and I think the scissors..." I gulped, blinked away the image of Lorena lying on the floor, and refocused on Ian. "The position of the scissors made it look personal. Stabbed in the back, you know."

"Could be. Hopefully, the ME will tell us if the scissors were done before or after Ms. Cortez was assaulted with the head wound."

"You think they snuck up behind her, stabbed her with the scissors, then bashed her in the head?"

"It's possible. Maybe their original intention wasn't to kill her. They might not have realized she was in the house and grabbed something nearby to incapacitate her. Stabbing her in the back would have made her scream, I'm sure. They could have panicked and swung at her with another object."

"But why stab her in the back at all?"

"Maybe they threatened her with the scissors. If they fought, it could have been a wild swing that landed wrong. The scissors are incredibly sharp. For cutting cloth, I suppose. You heard of the brand, Gingher?"

I shook my head. "Lorena fought her attacker? Can you get DNA evidence?"

Ian studied me. His gentle expression had hardened, but he laid a hand on my shoulder and squeezed. "I'll know after the ME report. This is all guesswork right now. I'm running through different scenarios. That's one."

"Another is they killed her and left the scissors in her back because it was personal." I sighed. "What about the robbery theory?"

"Could be." Ian shrugged. "Hard to say."

He shrugged too much for my comfort. "Ian, what should I do?"

"Go home. Rest. Try not to think about this."

"I can't do that."

"We have victim's counseling. I can get you an appointment."

"Maybe I can help? I've known Lorena for a long time. We worked on projects together including *Julia Pinkerton*. Lorena helped me through some difficult teen years."

"It is useful that you knew the victim personally." Ian smiled. "Let me get things in order here. We're still taking evidence. I haven't had a chance to carefully read all the notes from last night. I just skimmed your report. We'll talk later. It'll be helpful to have some insight into Ms. Cortez."

"I didn't know Lorena that well recently, but I'm happy to tell you everything I know." I hoped that would help me to put the images of Lorena to rest. But I had a feeling it wouldn't be enough.

Strolling back to Lucky, I pulled out my phone and called LA HAIR.

"Hey Rhonda," I said. "I talked to Detective Mowry. They don't have anything to report yet, but Georgia Bureau of Investigation has sent forensics to her house to sweep for evidence and the medical examiner will do a thorough autopsy. They're doing a good job."

"It's Tiffany, not Rhonda. Do they know who did it?"

"No," I said slowly. "It's a little early for that. They're just collecting evidence and canvassing the neighbors now."

"And what are you doing to solve this case?"

"It's not my case, this is a crimin—"

"Maizie Albright," barked Tiffany. "Are you or are you not a private eye?"

"We don't usually solve murder—"

"I'll see you at three and I hope you've got something more to report," said Tiffany.

"But—"

"You know what Rhonda is doing right now? She's sitting in a stylist chair, rocking and moaning. She hasn't eaten today and she didn't sleep last night. She says every time she closes her eyes, she only sees blood. You know what kind of people talk like that, Maizie? Crazy people. My best friend is now crazy because you dragged her into that house and exposed her to a horrible crime scene. She may never sleep again. She's afraid to go home by herself, so she's just rocking and moaning until I can leave."

"Oh God, I'm sorry." A lump grew in my throat and my eyes teared. "You're right. This is my fault."

"Don't be so dramatic. You didn't kill Lorena," snapped Tiffany. "But you gotta make this right. Figure out who murdered Lorena so the police can toss them in jail and poor Rhonda can get some sleep."

EIGHT

#CorporateNash
#SeeingTheForestAndNoTrees

I needed Nash again. But this time, just his advice. Maybe a hug, too. I knew I'd find him at DeerNose, working on some kind of special project. Even though it was a Saturday, and he didn't have to work weird hours now. I supposed once you got used to weird hours, it was hard to change. I've always worked weird hours, even in the industry. I didn't really know any different.

But still. Working on a Saturday. Weird.

The DeerNose headquarters stretched through an area carved from my father's forest, miles from his cabin, but on the same land. Daddy drove an ATV to work. Another reason he had no qualms about his grown daughter driving a dirt bike around town.

I parked in the mostly empty lot, scanned my card to enter a side door (my only nepotism privilege), and walked through hallways where animals and birds peeked through trees and bushes. All painted, of course. Still a little unnerving to exit the woods and find them still in the building. And on the clothes. And in our cabin.

I guess when Daddy dedicated his life to forest motifs, he went all in.

During her negotiations for Daddy's support of Clothing Kids, Lorena had enjoyed her visits to DeerNose. I'd been surprised when she'd asked me to make the introductions. The entertainment industry wasn't exactly hunting-friendly. She'd researched textile-related local captains of industry and read Daddy's views on conservation — typical of hunters but always surprising to non-hunters — and decided it was a good match. They'd gotten along well. Both were no-nonsense, practical, and hard-working but born with a creative flair for design. Lorena had devoted her flair to clothing actors and Daddy applied his to clothing hunters.

I found it an odd alliance, but they didn't.

Hadn't.

Walking through the DeerNose office area, I realized it wasn't just Rhonda and me who needed comfort after our disturbing find. Daddy would feel the loss. Maybe Remi, too. And the other board members, come to think of it. I didn't know Lorena's family, but I supposed the police would notify them. She'd kept her private life very private as long as I'd known her. Never married. No children. Perhaps she had gotten the family life she needed from friends and from making Barbie clothes for young actors, like me.

Security was housed between the factory and administrative offices. By the time I knocked on Nash's door and entered, I'd grown weepy again, thinking about Lorena and the loss so many would feel. My tears dried upon spying Wyatt Nash sitting behind a big desk and staring at a large computer monitor. He rubbed the little scar on his chin and scowled at the monitor. A natural pose for him. But he also wore a tie. Printed camouflage and hanging loose around his collar. But still, a tie. On a Saturday.

He had such strange rules for himself when it came to work-life.

Even more disturbing, his office was clean. And bare. Clean and bare. No scattered paraphernalia. At the old office, equip-

ment littered the room, seemingly haphazardly discarded —
although he always knew where to find each piece. Unlike the
old office, there were no crumpled bits of paper jotted with a few
words — only meaningful to him — decorating his desk. No
clothing hanging in odd places or sticking out of file cabinets. No
dust or dings or not-so-gently-worn furniture.

I shook off the comparison. DeerNose might scent their
clothes with deer pee, but it was still a corporate office. With an
office manager to order furniture. And a janitor to dust and
vacuum. I wondered if Nash had a secretary. I quickly extinguished that thought before my imagination took it somewhere I
didn't want to go.

Nash glanced up.

I pasted on a smile before he saw whatever emotion registered there from seeing Corporate Nash.

"Miss Albright, I mean Maizie. What are you doing here?"

"I need...advice." If he wore a tie, logic dictated this was a no-
hug zone.

He beamed and waved me into a chair across from his desk.

"What are you doing?"

"Looking at shipping and receiving logs." He rubbed the back
of his neck and leaned back in the big office chair. It didn't creak
or sigh. And when he extended his legs, his boots didn't hit the
underside of the desk. Was he even wearing boots? I hoped he
didn't have those shoes with the little tassels.

I was afraid to look.

"I thought you were going car shopping," he continued. "Did
you want my help?"

"No, I'm good. Rhonda and Tiffany are meeting me later.
Have you heard of a place called Rhubarb's?"

"I told you, Skeeter Mason is a buddy and he'll get you a
good deal."

I'd looked up Skeeter Mason. I didn't feel any more confident
about Skeeter than Rhubarb. Skeeter specialized in 4x4's and
bass boats. I didn't know what kind of vehicle had 4x4 dimen-

sions, but I felt pretty sure it wasn't something I felt comfortable driving. And although a bass boat was a popular local purchase, it had limits in getting around Black Pine.

As a change of subject, I gave him my *Cosmo* smile, leaned forward, and placed my hands on his desk. He jerked on his already-loosened tie and ran a finger around his collar.

"I could take you to Skeeter's now." His polar blue eyes gleamed. "But let's stop at my place first…"

I turned off the *Cosmo* smile. "The advice I need is about Lorena's murder."

The smolder in his eyes extinguished and he sat up. "What's going on?"

I told him about Rhonda's agony and Tiffany's anger and my anxiety. And my conversation with Ian. Nash listened and massaged his neck. When I finished, he frowned.

"I don't know if it's such a good idea for you to 'help' Mowry."

"Because it's an active investigation?"

He shook his head. "As long as you don't interfere in the BPPD's investigation, it's not a problem. You have to wait to talk to witnesses and examine crime scenes until they're done. Report what you're doing. I've done it before. With Mowry."

"On a murder case?"

Nash leaned back, casting his eyes to the ceiling. Rubbed his scar. "I've had one homicide case. The victim's family wanted help. They thought they knew who killed the victim, but the police weren't finding evidence for a conviction. You know how that goes. They hired me to essentially prove this guy murdered their daughter."

"Were you able to do that?"

"No." His gaze flicked back to me and his shoulders slumped. "I proved the boyfriend didn't kill their daughter. The guy had an unbreakable alibi, which was why the police couldn't charge him in the first place. But I found some evidence that helped point the police in the direction of the actual killer — a drug addict who picked her up when she was walking home from a bar. Sadistic sumbitch. I won't give you the gruesome details. It turned my stomach and was hard to get over. Made me glad I'm not a cop."

I got up from my chair, circled the desk, and hugged him hard. He pulled me into his lap and buried his head in my neck.

"You never told me this before." Nash didn't share much. He was more of a "what's past is past" kind of guy.

"It was a rough point in my life." He sighed. "Mowry, too. He'd just gotten divorced and his wife wasn't letting him see their baby during the case. Jolene and I weren't doing so hot either. We separated soon after. Mowry and I were a couple of miserable jackasses. Lamar spent a lot of time kicking our cans."

I stroked his head and planted a kiss on his temple. "I'm sorry you went through that."

He gazed up at me. "Actually, this is why it's not a good idea for you to investigate Lorena's death. A murder investigation can change you. It's heartbreaking. This would be really personal for you. Not just because you knew the victim. Because you found her."

"But Nash, because I found her, my heart's already broken."

His hands tightened on my waist, and he nestled me against his chest. "I understand. Still, I don't think it's a good idea, though."

I spoke against his scratchy blue Oxford, "I think I've got to do this, if not for Lorena but for Rhonda, too."

Also for myself, but I didn't want to sound shallow. Even with my distress over Lorena's death, as soon as Nash had mentioned the feasibility of investigating her murder, I wanted to do it. I needed to learn how to handle this kind of tragedy like a cop would. Like Nash would. I wasn't serious enough for real investigation work yet. Annie had me mostly on paperwork unless we were running a honey trap. But it wasn't my brain that was useful in a honey trap, if you get my drift.

I could use Lorena's murder to get myself into the right frame of mind. To prove my worth to Annie. And Nash, Ian, and everyone else.

Ugh. I was supremely shallow. Morbid. Callous. Absolutely the worst.

I shuddered, which Nash must have mistaken. He murmured sympathetically and hugged me.

"Would Ms. Cox help you with the investigation?" Nash stroked my hair. "You can't do this alone. Does she have any experience in this kind of casework?"

I didn't want my new boss's help. If I used my friend's murder to harden myself, I didn't want a lot of witnesses. "Probably not. This is an off-duty investigation."

The stroking stopped. And was replaced by muttering.

I sat up. "What did you say?"

Nash avoided my eyes. "Nothing. I'll help you. Let me finish what I started here, and I'll meet you at Lorena's tonight. Call Mowry first and get our involvement cleared. Don't step on his toes."

"You don't need to do that. You're plenty busy. You're here on a Saturday, for goodness sakes." I played with his tie. "If I have a question or something, I can ask Ian or Lamar."

Lamar had been a cop before he took over his family's donut shop. "The perfect retirement for a cop," he'd said, but he still enjoyed giving his two cents on our cases.

Back when Nash and I had cases.

Nash hefted me to my feet and stood, shaking out his legs. "No hon', I think this investigation is a bit too personal for you to accomplish on your own. Do your car shopping with the girls and we'll meet up after."

"I don't know about that." I bit my lip. I wasn't sure if Nash should witness this cold-blooded side of me. Who used their friend's murder as a training ground? Besides, if he held my hand, I wouldn't get the chance to accomplish a case this big on my own. Like Annie, Nash took charge. They both left me with what they felt was "safe."

I'd gotten my feet wet with both Nash and Annie. I was ready to go beyond safe. To jump into the void of private investigation "no return." To develop the thick skin that made them impervious to shocks and calamities.

"You're right," said Nash. "We'll go to Skeeter's first."

Definitely not what I meant.

Nash took a step closer, closing the gap between us. His hands ran down my sides, and he gave my Stella McCartney Adidas leggings and tee a long, appraising look. His hands tightened on my hips and his fingers slipped between my tee and leggings. He leaned forward and his lips hovered near my ear.

"I hung curtains this morning," he murmured. "They match the bed."

Curtains?

This was getting too weird for me. I pecked his cheek and sidled toward the door. "I'll just meet you at Lorena's."

NINE

#SnapCrackle #Pop

*W*hen I called Mowry, he repeated a similar story about his horrific meet-cute with Nash. And similar doubts about me working on Lorena's murder case. But as long as I didn't get in the way and I reported anything I learned to him, he begrudgingly said I wouldn't be arrested for interference.

Good thing, since I was still on probation.

I checked that off my list, then headed to the office. Not Nash Security Solutions — my old office that smelled like donuts but now held a giant bed. My new office, Albright Security Solutions, was located around the corner from the old office. It smelled like Yankee Candle and Windex. Annie Cox, my new boss, regularly polished the front window.

I think she was trying to wear down the "Albright" name, but I couldn't be sure.

The front door chimed as I sauntered through. Taking my place at the front desk, I stole a look at the door to the back office which I had shared with Nash for a short time. Sighed. Told myself to get a life and focus on my friend's murder. I fired up Tracers database. Winced typing in Lorena's name. My back

My ears warmed. My shoulders tightened, and I glanced me.

"Whatcha doing?" said Annie, hovering above my head.

If I were to typecast my boss, she'd be the rookie cop trying to prove herself in a squad room of older, more experienced, mostly male cops. The type who wore a belt with a pistol holder. The kind who snapped gum, barked sharp remarks, and slicked her thick, dark hair in a ponytail every day. Worked 24/365, eager to close cases and move on.

Annie was tough, no doubt. Also severely practical, which was why she took the job. You had to be career-focused to work for Vicki.

Either that or slightly mental.

As her daughter, I was the exception to the rule. Just saying.

"I'm checking a name on Tracers." I shifted in my chair to block my screen.

Annie arched her neck to look around me and snapped her gum. "Why not IRB?"

"I'll look there, too."

"Yeah, always use two sources to check accuracy." Her jaw worked. The gum snapped, crackled, and popped. "Which case?"

"Um." I thought quickly. "A new one."

Shizzles, I was a terrible liar.

"You're in kind of late today." She walloped a stack of files on my desk. "While you're on Tracers, here are some skips I collected."

"I called in a personal day, remember?" My voice squeaked. "And it is Saturday."

"Is it?" She smirked, then strode back to her office.

I closed my eyes briefly, then looked at Lorena's information on the database. I noted her social security number and date of birth in my Hello Kitty PI notebook, then jotted down her past addresses. I glanced at the skip trace folders, pushed them aside, and dialed up Facebook instead.

When it came to clients, I learned the essential nutrients from databases. The meat was on social media.

No one had posted on Lorena's page today. The news hadn't gotten out. I buzzed through her feed, looking for anything usual, then jumped into her photos. I perused her celebrity collection, all ensembles designed by Lorena. Quickly hopped out of that rabbit hole to focus on her more recent days in Black Pine. Found Rhonda and Tiffany trying on their wood nymph togas. Various children dressed as forest dwellers. Remi in her armadillo suit, scowling at the camera. None of Daddy in costume, but there was one of him shaking hands with Lorena. And another where she selfied the two of them before a wall of camo-print fabric. Daddy blended. Lorena did not.

Sniffling, I wiped my eyes. This was harder than I thought. I pinched the nerves between my thumb and pointer finger to stop my tears and to stiffen my resolve.

Hardcore. Be like Annie.

Maybe I needed gum.

I tapped on Annie's door, and at her beckon, entered. She looked up from her computer screen. "Finished the skip tracing already?"

"No." I bit my lip, knowing I would get awkward fast. I tended to social-awkward a lot around Annie. If she was the rookie cop, I was the rookie witness easily intimidated by authority figures and couldn't help but try and please them. "I wondered if I could borrow some gum. Actually, not borrow. I plan to chew it. I won't be giving it back. But I could buy the gum from you. One stick would do. If it's alright with you."

She reached into a drawer, pulled out a pack of peppermint Extra, and tossed it on the desk. Then tipped back in the chair and appraised me. "You took today off?"

"I left a message," I said. "I need to buy a car."

"About time." She rocked and snapped, but I knew she wasn't done. I used the time to unwrap a piece of gum and began chewing.

"How's this working for you?" she continued.

"It tastes okay. I didn't grow up chewing gum because Vicki didn't want my jaw to get overdeveloped."

The rocking and snapping stopped for a moment, then resumed. "I meant working here."

"Oh." I tried snapping. The gum fell out of my mouth and landed on the desk. "Sorry." I picked up the gum, wrapped it in the silver paper, and tossed it in her trash can.

"It's a little weird, right? Your mom owns this business, but you work for me."

I shrugged. "My work life has always been a little weird. Especially when it involves Vicki. Which it always has, because you know. She's my...ex-manager." The mom-word still felt odd on my tongue.

"Yeah." Annie rocked faster and snapped louder. "So not weird for you?"

"I have to apprentice with a private investigator for two years. What else can I do?"

"Okay." The rocking slowed. "You're still seeing that guy? The other PI?"

"Nash?" Annie wasn't from Black Pine. You could tell by the gum cracking and the "yeah's". She only knew of Nash from the few minutes he took to clear his stuff from his office. Annie's new office. Nash's new old office. His PI things remained in a cardboard box in the corner of his original office. In what now, he considered his living room.

He'd probably toss a doily on top in his urge to redecorate.

"Yep, still seeing Nash," I said and hoped for the end of that topic. The good thing about Annie was she wasn't one to prolong conversations. Awkward or not.

She squinted at me. "What kind of car are you getting?"

Annie was also not one for segues.

"I'm not sure," I said. "It depends on the price."

"Yeah." She cracked her gum. "Get a Jeep. You'll thank me for it later."

Annie drove a Jeep.

"I'll see what they have," I said brightly, then spun away and fast-walked from the room. The door closed behind me, and I sagged against it.

There was nothing wrong with Annie. I wanted to like her. I wanted to girl power and superwoman with her. But she didn't seem interested. Maybe she had rules for boss-employee relationships. Nash had those rules. We were only dating because he was no longer my boss.

Well, that and other reasons.

Which made me think of the old office and my discomfort with the bed in it. And I didn't want to think about that anymore (or do skip tracing), so I left the office to meet Tiffany and poor Rhonda at a place called Rhubarb's. To buy a car.

My life couldn't get much stranger.

Oh, wait. Never mind, universe. Forget I said that.

TEN

#RhondasRegret #RhubarbClobber

*R*hubarb's did not feature a thin, barefoot man in overalls with a piece of straw hanging from his semi-toothless mouth. This is why I shouldn't typecast before meeting people. The car salesman wore shoes and a polo emblazoned with the Rhubarb's logo — "Best Deals in the Blue Ridge Area." Instead of straw, he had a tiny vape cigarette which he quickly pocketed upon spying us approach his lot.

Rhubarb's might have started as a podunk garage with a handful of vehicles bought at police auctions — or so I was told on the ride to Rhubarb's in Tiffany's Firebird — but it was now an auto superstore of vehicles. Still mostly bought at police auctions. The extensive inventory of pre-owned vehicles covered three parking lots, each the size of a football field. The single-bay garage had grown to five with a sales-building that smelled like tires and oil mixed with citrus spray and stale coffee.

Tiffany's eyes gleamed and darted. She sized up Troy, the salesman, then abruptly walked off, making him scurry after her. Rhonda and I entered the sales reception room, reached for the stale donuts offered with the stale coffee, and sank back on the vinyl chairs. We regarded each other as we chewed, and I feared what would come next.

"I'm working on Lorena's case," I said. "I have permission from Detective Mowry. I'm doing preliminary research."

Rhonda sighed and leaned her head against the wall. The extensions had been removed and her hair was a mass of tiny curls flattened against the wall. Her face was absent of makeup, which I'd never witnessed in the time I'd known her.

I took it as a bad sign.

"Lorena was my first brush with celebrity greatness," said Rhonda.

Hurt, I opened my mouth, then closed it. I really wasn't that great. But still.

"Even though regular people didn't know her, she was major league, you know? Stars knew her and not only liked her but wanted her to design stuff for them," said Rhonda. "Lorena told me how she started as a seamstress and a dresser. In Wardrobe, she worked ten to thirteen hours a day. She had to be there hours before the actors to have their costumes ready. Stayed after they left to clean their clothes and get them ready for the next day. But her pay was half that of other tech crews, like lighting or whatever."

I knew this story, but Rhonda needed to tell it. "Mostly women work in Costume," I said. "It's highly skilled work but low pay. You have to love what you do."

Rhonda nodded. "Lorena came from nothing. Her mom worked in a dry cleaner's shop. Her dad was a migrant worker. But Lorena rose to the top, working non-stop. She won awards. Knew she couldn't devote herself to a family like she should, so she waited. That's why she retired so young. She finally had a chance to enjoy life and spend time with her man. But instead, she starts a charity. And was murdered."

"I don't think she was murdered because she started a charity." I paused. I didn't know Lorena had a boyfriend. "Did she tell you all this during your fitting?"

"Lorena told me I could do the same thing." Rhonda's chest heaved. A tear squeezed out of the corner of her eye to trickle down her face. She swiped at it. "I come from nothing. I work with my hands. Lorena said I could do something great, too. Like style hair for the stars."

"Oh, Rhonda." I grabbed her hands. "Lorena was special. But you're special, too. I'm really sorry you lost her. She was right. You can do great things. You're talented. You have the drive to work hard like Lorena did."

Rhonda squeezed her eyes shut, causing a cascade of tears. "I'm so scared."

"You witnessed a really brutal crime. The victim was someone you admired and looked up to. You're doing the best you can." I pulled in a breath and let it out slowly. I knew how she felt.

"Thanks, Maizie." Rhonda yanked a tissue from her pocket and swiped her face. "Tiffany doesn't really think I'm being over-dramatic. She just says it to guilt me into feeling better."

I wasn't sure about that, but I nodded and patted her hand anyway.

"Tiffany's had a chance to scare the salesman, you should talk to him now," said Rhonda. "I'll wait here. She was priming him for y'all."

"Are you sure?" I looked around the reception room. Besides the stale donuts and coffee, a flatscreen played a twenty-four hour news channel. The only magazines were devoted to tires and fishing.

"It feels safe here." Tears plopped on her lap. "Maizie, Lorena died right before we got there, didn't she? I saw it on your face when you checked for a pulse. Whoever killed her hadn't been gone long. They could've seen us."

Her breathing became labored. I rubbed her back. "No one saw us. If the killer had just left, we would have seen them." Although, they probably slipped out the back. In that case, they could've hidden in the yard and watched us enter. "But even if they did see us, we didn't see them. We're completely safe. It's not like they're worried we can turn them in."

Rhonda's red-rimmed eyes widened. "I didn't think of that."

I rubbed faster. "Which is why you shouldn't worry about it. Because the attacker didn't think of it either."

"Oh, Lawd," moaned Rhonda.

"Um, I'm going to find Tiffany." Tiffany's threats probably worked better at healing Rhonda than my reasoning. Which seemed to make things worse. "You're totally safe here. You can see everything through these big windows."

And everyone could see Rhonda. But I wouldn't mention it.

J found Troy and Tiffany among the muscle cars. Tiffany sat in a newish red Mustang with a door inscribed with the word "Cheater." By the size of the scrawl, the writer must have used a sizable knife.

"What about the stain in the seat?" said Tiffany. "I know it's blood."

"Doubt it. Probably a juice box. That stuff's hard to get out." Troy rocked back on his heels. "Our pre-owned vehicles have been cleaned before putting them on the lot. We sell them as-is. Any extra care is, you know, extra. However, I like you. I'll talk to my manager about kicking in another scrubbing if you're interested in purchasing this gorgeous vehicle."

Tiffany popped out of the car without answering. Then leaned through the window, examining the seat. "I think it's blood."

"What about the cheater etched in the door?" I said. "Can't you buff that out or something?"

"That's cut into the metal. Some little lady was sure hot under the collar with the previous owner, right?" Troy chuckled.

Tiffany turned around, one eyebrow hovering high on her forehead and the other near her narrowed lid. She had stupendous facial muscles. "How do you know it was a woman? Could've been a guy."

"Well…" sputtered Troy.

"Anyway, I don't know how interested I am in a blood-soaked vehicle," said Tiffany. "My friend witnessed a murder, and we're not crazy about the thought of driving around in a hot rod that for all we know conveyed a dead body."

Troy's eyes rounded. I think mine did, too.

"You saw a murder?" said Troy.

"What do you have in convertibles?" I said to change the subject. "My last car was a convertible. A blue convertible. I like blue."

Troy seemed glad for a change in subject. Particularly to blue convertibles. "I have several models in stock. Is there a certain make you want? What kind of mileage?"

Tiffany shot me a look. "She's paying in cash. No loans."

Troy's grin broadened. "What's your price?"

Tiffany held up a hand before I could state what I had saved, now stashed in an envelope in my backpack. It wasn't much. But enough, Tiffany assured me, to get something better than a dirt bike. "Show us the vehicles first. We don't want to waste your time negotiating for something we don't want."

We followed Troy toward his selection of "choice pre-owned vehicles." I lowered my voice, "Rhonda's freaking out in the showroom. Maybe you should sit with her."

Tiffany cut her eyes away from the row of pickups toward the sales office. "You think you can handle this guy?"

"You've done a great job preparing him for me." I cut a look at Troy, humming under his breath and clutching his vape. "I think I can handle him from here. Besides, I need to manage this on my own. I've had people doing basic things for me my whole life."

"True," said Tiffany. "But negotiating with a car salesman is not basic. It's not even intermediate. This is an advanced level of life skills."

"Someone should sit with Rhonda," I said. "She's really scared."

Tiffany opened her mouth, then closed it. "Okay. You're right. Just one thing. Hey, Troy."

Troy glanced over his shoulder and smiled at us. "Ma'am?"

"Maizie here can't get credit. And she makes barely above minimum wage. Just an FYI before you talk her into a rolled Lamborghini or something."

Troy's smile stuttered.

Tiffany walloped me on my back, knocking me a few steps closer to Troy. "Good luck."

"Thanks," I said.

"I meant for Troy."

ELEVEN

#TurnOnSignal #JessicaFletchering

I drove to Lorena's house in my first pre-owned and completely my-owned vehicle. A Bronco convertible. I thought the name "Bronco" had a nice ring. Besides that, it had two seats, a back bench, seat belts, and an "after-market" stereo with a "mega-base." The speakers were located in the bed, which I found odd at first, but with no roof, the speakers actually offered a surround-sound-like quality. Troy said they'd deliver sound within a quarter-mile.

Not a good selling point for someone who did surveillance. However, I could afford the Bronco or a purple 1994 Oldsmobile sedan missing a steering wheel.

Bronco it was.

I wondered at which police auction Rhubarb's bought their previously owned vehicles. Somewhere with a lot of vehicular crime scenes, evidently.

When I arrived, I spotted Nash leaning against his pickup, brawny arms folded and eyes on Lorena's house. He'd lost the tie and returned to his normal uniform of a concert t-shirt and tight-ish (in a good way) jeans. As I maneuvered to get within six inches of the curb, his attention flicked to my Bronco. Then did a double-take. I think his mouth might have dropped open. He hurried from his truck to where I parked.

"I don't know if I should be worried or turned on," he said.

I wasn't sure either. "This was the only convertible I could afford. At least one that ran and didn't have bullet holes or bloodstains."

He jerked his head from studying the Bronco to study me. "Hon', just because it doesn't have a top, doesn't make it a convertible. This doesn't convert. At all. It's a topless Bronco with missing doors. Is this even street legal?"

I slid out the side of the Bronco, holding on to a homemade duct tape strap someone had handily attached to the roll bar. "Troy said, since it's from 1976, I can get one of those license plates for vintage vehicles so the police won't bother me."

"Who's Troy?

"Troy from Rhubarb's."

Nash ran a hand along the bed. "It's also not a car. This is a truck. If you wanted a 4x4, we should have seen Skeeter."

"This is a 4x4?" It looked like a rectangle to me. "It's not much bigger than a car. Certainly not as big as your truck."

Nash pulled on the roll bar. "Is the engine rebuilt? We could lift the suspension and trim the fenders to get you new wheels and some Bighorn tires."

That suspiciously sounded like making my almost-car as big as a truck. "Everything but the stereo and duct-tape is original, according to Troy. Which makes it a unique find and a Ford-owner's dream. Especially in its un-restored state. Also according to Troy."

Nash turned shining eyes toward me. A long dimple appeared, hiding his scar. "I'm officially turned on. This baby just needs some new paint and a lot of love. Also, new shocks and brakes. New exhaust. A complete overhaul. We could work on this in our spare time."

Working on my non-convertible that was really a decapitated truck was not my idea of spare time fun. But Nash's eyes had darkened from ice- to tidal pool-blue. He had the same look I got when Carol Lynn made fried chicken for dinner.

However, I wasn't sure if it was me or the Bronco making him hungry.

Before he could suggest going back to the office to try out his new bed and matching curtains (or finding a garage to swap out spark plugs), I scuttled from my new, pre-owned, vintage scrapheap toward the Martins' Queen Anne.

"The police aren't done with Lorena's house." It was still decorated in yellow and black bunting.

"We should give it a few days to be safe. After forensics, Mowry and his team will want to look through the property carefully," drawled Nash. "You want to—"

"Talk to the Martins," I said quickly. "They hosted the party and might have heard something."

Nash looked at my topless and doorless Bronco. Sighed. Then looked back at me. "Good idea. By the way, what did Boomer say about the murder?"

"Daddy?" I slipped my hand in Nash's and pulled him along the sidewalk away from the Bronco. "I haven't seen him yet. He was up and out before dawn. He'll be very upset, though. Remi, too."

"I wouldn't mention your investigation. Let him think the police are handling it."

"Why?"

"Trust me." Nash squeezed my hand.

"I'm accompanying him and Remi to the photoshoot. If they still do it. Although, I would think the foundation would want to carry on Lorena's plans. The magazine spread is a huge PR coup."

At the Martins, evidence of the party had been obliterated. We sauntered down their brick walk and up the stairs of their historic porch, hand-in-hand. All kinds of warmth, security, and peace unfurled within me.

Until I had an epiphany.

"Wait a minute," I said. "What are you doing?"

"I thought we were questioning the neighbors."

"No." I pointed at his hand in mine. "You're holding my hand. Still. And we're about to knock on their door. What's going on?"

He scowled. "I like holding your hand. Can't I hold your hand without you questioning my motives?"

"When it's you, yes. This is an investigation. I know your rules." Actually, I didn't know them all. Some, I believed, he made up as he went along. "When we're working, you don't do PDA. In fact, when we're not working, you don't do public displays of affection."

He shrugged. "I'm not working. And you're moonlighting. It's Saturday night."

"This is a serious investigation that I'm taking seriously. No PDA." I jerked my hand from his.

Nash folded his arms across his chest. "Fine."

I pressed the fancy doorbell and noted the not-fancy-yet-sleek camera above it. "We could ask to look at their security footage from last night, but I doubt we'd get much from all the people coming and going."

"Probably right," said Nash. "But another neighbor might have something."

The door swung open. I introduced Nash. Jan Martin invited us inside. She seated us in the front parlor where I hoped her wallpaper wouldn't poison us. I took small sips of air, just in case.

"It's terrible, isn't it?" said Jan.

Dennis strolled in and dropped into an antique-ish looking armchair. "Terrible. I can't believe it."

"I thought you might have heard something," I said.

"Like what?" said Dennis. "Didn't you find her? What did it look like? I heard it was a real horror scene."

"Yes," I said primly. "It was very shocking."

"A lot of blood?"

I nodded.

"Did you see the murder weapon?" said Jan.

I didn't know if the police had revealed any information about the scissors. "Who knows if I did? I was just focused on Lorena."

"But you must have noticed how she died," said Dennis.

"We love murder mysteries," said Jan. "And we're very curious."

Except we didn't live in Cabot Cove or St. Mary Mead. This was Black Pine where murder shouldn't make you curious. Murder should make you feel sad or scared.

Particularly when it happened to your next-door neighbor.

TWELVE

#TheMarryingKind #RealUgly

"*D*o you have a list of guests?" said Nash abruptly.

"Of course." Jan scurried off.

"Why do you want to see the guest list?" said Dennis.

"I thought we should check in with everyone." I didn't want to reveal my investigative purposes to the Martins. I couldn't tell if they were morbidly eager or morbidly suspicious. I was still new to snooping and the interrogation of witnesses.

"What committee's doing that? I gave Jennifer the money we collected last night. Maybe you should cross-reference with that list to see if they donated before the police came in."

"That's an idea." Perhaps the Martins were just morbidly tactless.

"How long have you known Lorena?" said Nash.

"Since she moved in — about a year or two ago. Lorena costumed a film here and said she fell in love with the area. It is a good place to retire." Dennis leaned back, then must have remembered the chair was antique-ish and sat up again. "Jan set out to meet Lorena when we learned someone had bought the bungalow. Jan likes to make sure owners of these historic treasures know what they're getting into. With the preservation laws and whatnot."

"Jan seems very passionate about preservation," I said, thinking about her passive-aggressive slight fight with Vicki.

Dennis nodded vigorously. "In fact, when Lorena started renovating her home, Jan wasn't too happy with her."

Jan walked in, waving a printed list. "Here it is. What wasn't I happy with, Dennis?"

"Lorena's house."

Jan's features briefly hardened, then she shrugged. "I didn't know who Lorena was at the time. I thought she was some kind of kooky hippy-type. This isn't Asheville. She absolutely tore apart the inside. If you want open space, buy modern. And the cottage has a gray roof. With a gray roof, a putty, dull red, or cream would be acceptable colors for a house. But not tangerine, muscadine, and apricot. I still don't understand her logic. Who had a tangerine and muscadine house in 1927?"

"In fact, we weren't interested in doing Clothing Kids until we learned who Lorena was," said Dennis. "I told Spencer Newson with all the local committees we were already on, we didn't have time for another charity. But then he told us how famous Lorena was, so we said, 'what the hell.'"

"Not that we're into all that Hollywood hoopla," said Jan quickly. "But when I told people about the movies and shows Lorena had worked on, they agreed I should work with her. Lorena simply doesn't understand historic architecture, but she was a fountain of knowledge on historic dress. I might be needed to advise for movie sets and Lorena could have recommended me."

"You only did Clothing Kids because of Lorena's fame?" I gritted my teeth.

"I wouldn't say that," said Dennis. "Spencer's a good friend. And Lorena was his *special* friend. He really made a case for the charity."

Hold up. Spencer was Lorena's boyfriend? "What do you mean by *special* friend?"

Jan and Dennis glanced at each other and looked back at me. "You know," said Jan. "*Special*."

My stomach flopped uncomfortably. "But Spencer's married to Susie. Jessie the Cowgirl."

"And he was married to someone else when he met Susie," said Jan. "It happens. Susie didn't like Lorena, but that's the pot calling the kettle black now, isn't it? A tiger doesn't change his stripes."

"That's just Spencer," said Dennis. "We don't approve, but we love him like a brother. We're golf buddies, you know."

My jaw ached from grinding my teeth.

"The party," said Nash, who was much better at staying on task and regularly ground his teeth (which might account for his stupendously well-defined jaw). "Maizie said there were a lot of people entering and exiting the house. We saw you have a camera on the front porch. Any in the back?"

"There's one on the patio door," said Dennis. "We gave the police links to the footage for both. They also checked our back gate to the alley. We don't have a camera there, though."

"Any other outside exits?"

"No," said Jan. "We also gave the police the guest list. Although there were a few party crashers."

"Really?" I said. "Did you figure out who the party crashers were?"

"No," she fumed. "I didn't know the women and they obviously couldn't afford the entry ticket. Freeloaders. They were dressed like trees or something."

A slow burn crawled up my neck. "Those were my friends, Rhonda and Tiffany. They didn't crash. They were my plus two."

Nash shifted beside me. "Anything else unusual you noticed? Maybe before the party?"

"The caterer's bartender was overly friendly," said Jan.

"Wait. Didn't something happen before you met me?" I said. "Some kind of emergency? What was that?"

"Oh, that?" Dennis cut a look to his wife. "That was—"

"Nothing important. Just related to the food." Jan's cheeks reddened and she rose from her chair. "I certainly hope you have enough for your committee report."

"Committee report?"

"Aren't you calling on all the guests to explain what happened?"

"Sure. I'll tell my committee." *My committee of one.*

I rose, noting her eagerness to be done with the interview.

Jan nodded and led the way from the parlor, ushering us out the front door with such efficiency, I barely registered the door closing behind us.

"What was that all about?" I said.

Nash took my hand again. This time I was thankful. "Black Pine is full of snobs, Maizie. But there are snobs everywhere, just like there are good folks everywhere."

"I'm used to snobs, Nash." I squeezed his hand. "I can't believe Lorena would sleep with Spencer. He's married. And the Martins were so blasé about it. Gossiping about Lorena when she was murdered? I can't even."

"You don't always know people's private life." Nash gusted a sigh. "Many times you don't want to know."

"Come on." I rushed him down the steps of the veranda, away from the camera. When we stood safely out of earshot, I looked up at him. "Here's something I do know. The Martins have another outside exit they didn't mention. I accidentally found it. Remember the cookie closet?"

"Hinky," said Nash. "They were also overly interested in what you saw at the crime scene."

I felt vindicated. But not in a good way. Mostly in a "this murder was about to get real ugly, real fast" way.

We walked to our vehicles hand-in-hand. Which felt strange but also sweet. However, Nash wasn't really known for sweet. His mind seemed to be somewhere else, and I had a feeling he'd forgotten where he'd left his hand.

"I'm talking to the other neighbors tomorrow."

"Carol Lynn and your dad expect us for Sunday dinner," said Nash.

"I can go before or after. For some reason, they eat in the middle of the afternoon on Sundays." I glanced up at him. His jaw was clenched, but his eyes were on my Bronco. Something warred within him.

Nash swung me around to face him. "Can we keep the investigation between us? Not mention it to Boomer."

"What's going on? You don't want him to know I'm looking into Lorena's murder?" I studied him. He wore the stern, emotionless look he used around most people. The Nash RBF, something a little scary to behold. Not normally used on me. "Wait a minute. You don't want Daddy to know you're helping me. It's got nothing to do with me."

He jerked a nod.

"Even when you're off duty?" I thought about Nash-motives. "What's the big project you're tackling? Does Daddy expect you to be working on a Sunday?"

Nash shifted his gaze away, then back. "No. Just don't mention the investigation. I don't want to talk shop around him."

"Fine. Whatevs. He'll want to talk about the Bronco anyway." For that reason, I wanted to escape Sunday dinner and interview neighbors.

At the mention of the Bronco, Nash's eyes gleamed. "That's a great idea. We could get under the hood."

"I'm afraid if you lift the hood, something will break or disintegrate. The Bronco is not my ideal car, but it's better than Lucky. Mainly because I can sit on it in a skirt."

Nash's gaze fell to my legs. "I forgot to notice the skirt. I should've noticed the skirt."

"You were too busy ogling my convertible."

"Maybe we could go back to the office for some more ogling." The gleam in his eyes took on a different glint. "I could look under *your* hood."

"I should get back to the cabin and see how Daddy and Remi

are doing with Lorena's murder." I didn't want to ogle in the office. I'd end up ogling the new curtains and the other disturbing non-officey features.

Grabbing the duct tape strap, I hoisted myself into the Bronco. Then leaned toward Nash. He tipped his head to kiss me, a gentle kiss that devolved into something less gentle. Cupping my face in both hands, his mouth sought to claim mine.

I clenched his shoulders, giving him permission to do all the claiming he wanted. I hung on while fissures of electricity zipped through my veins, headed to my core like heat-seeking missiles. His hands dropped from my face to slide beneath my thighs. He lifted me from the bucket seat to the floor of the Bronco and wedged himself between my legs.

I might have groaned and wiggled closer. Then remembered we were on Scarlet Oak Drive where people walked with dogs and babies this time of night. Also, I was in a skirt. I wiggled back.

"Are you sure you don't want to go back to the office." It wasn't a question. He wanted to go back to the office. The fried-chicken-dinner look had returned. Glazing his eyes and making his heart pound.

My heart also pounded and the glaze in my eyes had gone from fried chicken to chocolate cake. It took all my will power not to pull him into the bed of the Bronco. Making me realize its usefulness for the first time. "I want—"

"Yes?" He tightened his grip on my waist.

"To *not* go to the office."

He gave me a look like I had kicked his dog. "Baby. Honey. Sugar. Why?"

"It's the office."

"I'm working on it." He gave me a pained smile.

"I'm not asking you to work on it."

"I'm doing it anyway."

I wanted to say, "The more you work on it, the more I'm

aware of the changes that have happened. And I don't want to think about what those changes mean."

Instead, I said, "Don't work on it."

"Why?" he growled.

I patted his shoulders. Which didn't help. "You should enjoy your free time."

Which also didn't help.

Nash cocked his head and studied me. "I could tell you how I'd like to enjoy my free time. But I guess you're not interested. I'll see you tomorrow."

And he left.

THIRTEEN

#SinSeason #WindSwept

I parked the Bronco in the front drive of the cabin but entered through the side door into the kitchen. My mind was on Nash. I'd hurt his feelings. And probably confused him. But I did need to check on Daddy and Remi. And I did want to avoid the office. For now. I wasn't sure how to explain it to him without hurting his feelings even more.

This was a new kind of relationship for me. My previous ones were a little more traditional. Or non-traditional, depending on your viewpoint.

Dinner had finished hours ago, but I found a wrapped plate for me in the fridge. Fried pork chops and bacon-infested collard greens. Carol Lynn, my father's wife, cooks with love. As I took it, cooking with love meant the calories didn't count.

I found the family bundled up on the deck, watching the sunset on the lake. And counting ducks. Greeting them, I set my food on a long wooden table. Three Jack Russell terriers bounced onto the table. I picked up my plate and settled onto an Adirondack chair next to Daddy.

"I'm sorry about Lorena. You got to know her pretty well recently and this must be hard to take."

His beard brushed his chest with his nod. "Unbelievable. It

wouldn't have upset me as much if it'd happened out in California but in Black Pine? What is this world coming to?"

I decided not to share my initial thoughts about murders in California being as upsetting as murders anywhere. "I spoke to Detective Mowry today and they're making progress on the case. Doing forensic work and that sort of thing."

"Is Detective Mowry up to the job?" Daddy folded his arms. "Black Pine police don't usually have to deal with this sort of crime."

"I've worked with Ian Mowry before and he's a good cop. He's very thorough."

Carol Lynn murmured something I couldn't hear, then rose to find Remi.

Daddy turned toward me. "I'm sorry, baby girl. I shouldn't have such dark thoughts. Miss Lorena was a good woman. One of the best businesswomen I've ever met and an amazing seamstress. I truly respected her." His voice caught, and he paused. "I can't believe anyone would kill her, let alone murder her in such a horrible way."

I touched his arm. "I know, Daddy. I feel the same way."

"That photographer called today about the shoot. They still want to do it next week." He shook his head. "I don't know. Doesn't seem right."

"The magazine spread was a tribute to Lorena's work as well as a spotlight on Clothing Kids. Don't you think it's even more important to do now?"

"I suppose." Daddy rubbed his eyes. "There's a lot going on at DeerNose, too. I don't really have the time. The fall line is due, and I can't bring myself to draw a single pattern. I'm feeling out of sorts, I suppose. I spent the morning in my deer stand moping."

Daddy was not a moper. He was a doer. It was also not deer season. My stomach clenched. I set my plate on the armrest, unable to eat. "I'm sure Ian will solve Lorena's murder quickly. That will make you feel better, right?"

"I don't know, honey." He tipped a big shoulder. "I would like to see justice, don't get me wrong. Maybe it's my age. I thought I could protect this little corner of the world, and now I see no place is safe. Evil still encroaches upon us."

"Oh, Daddy." I wanted to rally his spirits and realized my best bet meant I couldn't keep my promise to Nash. "I'm actually helping Ian Mowry on Lorena's case with a private investigation."

"Are you now?" He straightened on his rocker. "How's that, then?"

"I spoke to the Martins this evening. Tomorrow I'll interview Lorena's other neighbors and hope they saw something. Sometimes people will tell a PI information they won't say to the police."

"Makes sense. What did the Martins have to say?"

My cheeks burned at the memory. "Have you heard anything about Lorena's love interests?"

"Her what now?"

"Do you know if she was seeing anyone?"

"Can't say we talked about our personal lives, baby girl. Miss Lorena and I kept our conversations on the work for the foundation. That and apparel design chitchat."

"What about Clothing Kids chitchat? Any juicy gossip there?"

He shot me a stern look. "I don't go in much for gossip. That's a sin, you know. If you have an issue with someone, you should confront them. Not talk behind their back."

Unfortunately, my new career was fueled by sin. But so was my old career. Just of a different nature. "I'm looking for anything troubling in Lorena's life. For the investigation. Which should ease your conscience."

He rocked while I reached for my food. My nonexistent food. My plate was still perched on the arm, but I didn't remember cleaning it off. I turned in my chair. Two wagging tails peeked behind it. Sighing, I turned back to Daddy.

"I can tell you one thing," said Daddy. "There's a lot of strife among the board members. But that's not unusual with these charitable foundations. They're filled with a lot of A-type personalities. Everyone wants to be the lead dog."

"Can you be more specific?"

"The CEO and CFO. Spencer Newson and Jennifer Frederick."

I'd witnessed that strife when she smacked Spencer at the party. It seemed hard to believe philanthropists would come to blows over leadership, though. "Do they often fight?"

"I don't know about fighting," he said pensively. "But there's some tension there. Miss Jennifer and the others don't always see eye-to-eye."

We were interrupted by squawking. Three seconds later, a pack of white and brown dogs bounded on the porch followed by their pied piper, Remi. She tooted on a duck call, making the small wooden whistle hoot, screech, caw, and yap.

"I wished I wasn't an armadillo," she said. "Ducks are more exciting."

"Don't be stirring up those Gadwalls, Remi." Daddy leaned forward in his rocker to eye her. "I want them to feel like they can winter here. Stick to calling wood ducks."

"You're not going to shoot the ducks, are you?" I said horrified.

"It's not duck season, honey. I want to see how big their brood gets."

I didn't get it. But it made me think of something else. Timing.

"Lorena was killed during or right before the party," I said. "Whoever killed her might have thought she'd be at the party. Her safe had been opened. It might have been a robbery."

"How would they know to open her safe?" said Daddy.

"Easy," said Remi. "All you need is a coat hanger. I saw it on YouTube."

"No more YouTube," said Daddy.

I studied Remi. "Have you tried opening a safe with a coat hanger?"

She gave Daddy the side-eye, then looked at me. "I'm not supposed to touch the safe."

Daddy's face had flushed and the color was deepening. Before he had an apoplexy, I beckoned my little sister. "Talk a walk with me, Remisita."

We strode off the porch. Five dogs followed. Two stayed behind to lick my plate. We walked into the cool timber. The air was scented with decaying leaves and the woodsmoke billowing from the cabin's fireplace. The shadows had deepened, but the path was easy to follow. More so for Remi in her cowboy boots. Not so much for me in my Stuart Weitzman mules.

"Did you hear about Miss Lorena?" I said gently.

"She died. Someone killed her."

I stopped our stroll. Daddy and Carol Lynn wouldn't have mentioned Lorena's murder to Remi. But Remi had a bad habit of eavesdropping. "What else did you hear?"

"Just that she was killed." Remi kicked a pinecone. "They didn't say how. I wonder if it was a hammer."

I gulped. "Why a hammer?"

"Miss Lorena had this precious little hammer. It was so teeny tiny. Miss Lorena said she used it for all sorts of things, like aging clothes. I don't know why she wants clothes to get old, but I want to use it for something else." Remi looked up at me. "I really hope nobody used that hammer to kill her."

I really hoped Remi wasn't as disturbed as she sounded. "Do you have thoughts about...hurting things with a hammer?"

"Nails, but I don't think they can feel it. I want to build a teeny tiny house for my hermit crab." She scampered down the path, leaving me to wonder how Lorena had really been killed.

I shuddered. But I didn't think a tiny hammer could produce that much blood.

· · ·

*D*espite the agitation I caused Nash, he still agreed to meet me at Lorena's before Sunday dinner. I wanted to canvas the neighbors — to find out what they had told the police and to hopefully glean more with my unofficial questioning. Having Nash with me would help me to focus. Thus far, I wasn't great at interviews. I had to learn how to harden myself against friendly chitchat and stick to my purpose.

Before heading to Lorena's, I drove to LA HAIR. I'd left Lucky there when I rode with Tiffany to Rhubarb's and needed to bring her home. I missed Lucky…wait.

Nope, I didn't miss Lucky.

But Remi might want to drive Lucky when she was old enough. At fourteen, I hadn't any interest in dirt bikes, but Remi probably would at a much earlier age. Considering she was six, any day now.

The sun warmed my back, the temperature hovered in the high fifties, and thin clouds barely marred the blue sky. Another gorgeous Sunday in winter. I enjoyed the crisp air breezing around the doorless and topless frame of Billy — my name for the Bronco. All the while I could sit on an actual seat. With a seatbelt. Which I really needed. The no door-thing kind of freaked me out. But Billy had another bonus — no more helmet head. The wind could blow through my strawberry blonde locks.

Just like Grace Kelly in *To Catch A Thief*. No scarf held her 'do in place as Grace whipped that little convertible around the curves and hills of the Riviera. I loved Grace's style but especially in that Hitchcock flick. None other than Edith Head had designed Princess Grace's wardrobe for that movie. Edith, normally very diplomatic about her feelings for actors, had said Grace was her favorite actress and *To Catch a Thief*, her favorite movie.

Cary Grant had clothed himself. But when you're Cary Grant, you could do that.

Edith Head had known Frances Stevens wouldn't bother with her hair while trying to dominate The Cat, John Robbie, by driving like a bat out of hell along that coastal highway. In fact, by not using a scarf to protect her hairstyle proved she was more than a debutante and had grit. Funny how eliminating that small wardrobe element spoke so much.

Lorena had pointed this fact out to me when we had argued over a particular wardrobe style for Julia Pinkerton. Edith had styled Frances brilliantly. Lorena strove to do the same with every character she dressed. At the time, I was no Grace Kelly, and Lorena let me know it. As a teenager, I resented her for it, but I begrudgingly respected her, too. Not everyone could put a little starlet in her place without completely damaging her fragile psyche.

As much as I loved Frances Stevens' character and style, I drove much more carefully than she did. I did not have her chutzpah or her courage. To be fair, her convertible had doors. Also, the breeze seemed fiercer than it had appeared in *To Catch a Thief*. Odd, as this was a sunny day in Black Pine, not the windswept Mediterranean coast. Possibly, Billy was less wind resistant than Frances Stevens' blue Sunbeam Alpine convertible. Come to think of it, my previous convertibles had been more wind resistant, too. But they were also blue like the Sunbeam Alpine. My previous convertibles also had doors.

My scalp started to ache.

I patted my hair and my finger caught in a tangle I couldn't push through.

Maybe Audrey Hepburn's scarf and sunglasses look from *Charade* would better suit the Bronco. Audrey Hepburn as Regina Lampert had chutzpah. *Charade* was another Cary Grant classic. And she'd been styled by Givenchy.

You could never go wrong with Givenchy. I'm sure Edith Head would agree.

At the old strip mall holding LA HAIR, I parked the Bronco, then attempted to finger-comb my locks. My fingers jammed into knots and caught. I ripped out my hands to check my rearview mirror. And gasped. For once my thin, strawberry blonde strands had body without the help of product. They also had height without the aid of gravity. My hair had not gone to the Mediterranean. It had traveled to the Caribbean and joined the Rastafarians. I had dreads. I stuck my fingers into the mass of whipped and snarled locks and pulled. Yanked. My eyes watered. I gave up.

Scarfs from now on. No more Grace Kelly as Frances Stevens.

Remembering I had parked before my salon of choice — only because my friends worked there, but don't tell them that — I walked to the door and yanked on the handle. The door didn't move. A sign announced LA HAIR's closure for the day. Unusual for a Sunday. Tiffany liked Sundays. She said the better tippers came on Sunday. She thought they felt guilty for making her work on the day of rest.

Trying to rip through my wind-woven locks, I schlepped to where Lucky had been parked. Gasped again.

Lucky looked like she'd been in a street fight. Or had been featured at Rhubarb's. Her shattered side mirrors lay on the ground. Her tires were slashed. Lights smashed. And the front fender had been battered and bent.

"Lucky," I cried. "Who did this to you? My poor baby."

I bent to wipe the ripped seat with the bottom of my coat. And saw the rips formed the word "whore."

OMG, Black Pine crime was getting ridiculous.

FOURTEEN

#LuckyBilly #CopsAndRobbers

$\mathcal{I}$t took some time to get Lucky into the back of Billy, but I managed. And cried a little while doing so. Poor Lucky. The latest victim of Black Pine violence.

When I arrived at Lorena's, Nash waited for me, pacing the sidewalk. "Where've you been?" He cocked his head. "That's an interesting look."

I yanked on a matted clump of hair. "I need a hat for Billy."

"Who's Billy?"

"The Bronco."

Nash glanced at the truck and scrubbed his face.

"Oh, Nash," I wailed. "I can't believe what happened."

"Are you worried you'll have to cut it all off or something?"

"No," I gasped. I hadn't thought about that. I hoped not. I stuck a pinky along the edge of my scalp and tried to free some hair. My eyes watered. "It'll be fine. I'll just wash it with a lot of conditioner. And maybe some Moroccan oil. Or olive oil."

"Butter?" He tried to smile.

I bit my lip.

"It's not that bad."

"It's not my hair." I sniffled. "It's Lucky."

"The dirt bike?" He paused. "I take it you're naming all your vehicles?"

"Look." I grabbed his hand and pulled him to Billy's bed. "Someone vandalized Lucky."

Nash sucked in a breath. "Looks more like an assault and battery. Where was he parked?"

"She. In front of LA HAIR."

"Did you report it?"

I shook my head. "I didn't want to take the time. I left her there overnight. I thought she'd be okay, but it was Saturday night."

"On the mean streets of Black Pine? This kind of vandalism doesn't happen here. You need to report it." He peered over the truck bed. "Does that say 'whore?'"

I nodded.

"Anything you need to tell me?" He quirked a smile and slung an arm around my shoulder. "Don't worry about it, hon'. You've got the Bronco now. We'll fix her up. She'll be as good as new in a few months."

"He. Lucky's a girl. Billy's a guy." I paused to take in his meaning. "A few months to fix her up? He just needs doors. Maybe a roof. Driving a convertible in Georgia doesn't have quite the same vibe as it did in California." In California, my hair had never looked like a home for rats, for one thing.

"We'll go to salvage yards. It'll be fun. Rebuild the Bronco into its former glory."

"Fun?"

Nash leaned to kiss the side of my head, then pulled back. He patted my hair, then wiped his hand on his pants. "Let's get canvassing. Which neighbor do you want to interview first?"

I pointed to the house next door to Lorena's. A two-story neoclassical with columns. A white picket fence edged the yard. A basketball hoop stood in the driveway and a soccer net sat on one side of the lawn. Between the two, lay an assortment of toys and bikes. I wondered if Jan had any issues with historical homes accessorized by children.

We trooped through the white picket gate and up the sidewalk. On the way, we circled a skateboard, a naked Barbie, a Nintendo Switch, and a baseball glove. At the baseball glove, Nash stopped and scooped it up.

"This is a four-hundred-dollar glove." He glared at the house. "What kind of person leaves a Wilson Super Skin lying outside?"

"A kid?"

He scoffed and jammed his thumb into the doorbell.

A woman with dark circles under her eyes and a hairstyle similar to mine answered.

My hair was trending.

Wait. She had a baby in her arms. Only trending with sleep-deprived mothers and women who drove trucks without roofs.

"Yes?" The mom moved the baby from the crook of her arm to her shoulder.

Nash thrust the baseball glove at her. She took it, thanked him, and began to close the door.

"No, wait," I said. "We wanted to speak to you about your neighbor, Lorena Cortez."

"I'm done talking to journalists. Let the woman rest in peace."

I stuck my foot in the door and hoped that worked like it did on *Julia Pinkerton*. I wore Jimmy Choo combat boots, but they had a crystal-studded strap. They might be combat boots, but they were still Jimmy Choos. "We're not journalists. We're private investigators and we're investigating Lorena's murder."

The door stopped, thankfully, before banging my Jimmy Choo. "Private investigators?" She swung the door open. "Like in the movies?"

"No," said Nash.

"Sort of," I said. "Lorena was a friend of mine, and I just so happen to be an investigator."

"In training," said Nash.

"You're a private eye, too?" She stared at Nash and stepped

backward. His resting Nash face had that effect on people. Plus his largeness. And muscle-ness. He would have made a good bouncer. I eyed him wondering if he had been a bouncer at one point. Living in the present was great and all, but in a partner, it would be nice to know a little history.

Before Nash could explain his new job title or I could ask him about any old ones, I refocused. "I assume you've spoken to the police?"

"I couldn't tell them anything. We were at the Martin's party." She rolled her eyes. "Only because Lorena made costumes for my kids."

"What were they? Maybe I saw them. I was at the party, too."

"A raccoon, fox, nightingale, and a bat." She smiled at the baby. "And she was a bunny. Lorena outdid herself. The costumes were amazing."

"You have five kids?" said Nash.

"Aww." I poked Nash. "That's wonderful. I'll see you at the photoshoot. My sister, Remi, was an armadillo."

"I know Remi," said the woman. "My son, Aiden, is in her class."

"He has Mrs. Childs? How does he like her? She's so sweet. Remi loves her." Next to me, I heard Nash clear his throat. Shizzles, I was doing it again. "Back to Lorena. What about before the party? Have you noticed anything unusual on your street?"

Aiden's mom laughed. "Honey, I barely get time to shower, let alone pay attention to unusual activity on our street."

"Thanks anyway," I said. "We'll leave you to your work. You must have your hands full."

"I can tell you that Lorena was a delightful person and a good neighbor. One of the few that were accepting of a large family." She glared past our shoulders, where I imagined the daggers hit the Martin house. "I'm going to miss Lorena. I can't believe anyone would want to hurt her."

I was, too. And I was glad to hear how wonderful Lorena had

been. I pinched my thumb. There was no crying in investigations. At least not public crying.

Aiden's mom also teared up and began bouncing the baby. "I wish I knew more. Please do whatever you can to help the police. It's scary for me and my kids. My husband installed more alarms, but I still don't feel protected. I don't want my kids going outside now, but I also don't want them trapped in the house. This was a safe neighborhood. We didn't have robberies before."

"We'll do what we can, ma'am," said Nash. "Thanks for talking with us."

She closed the door, and we threaded our way around the toys. Before we reached the gate, a young boy popped out from behind an oak tree.

I gasped, grabbing my chest. "You scared me."

"What's a private investigator?" said the boy.

"Like a detective. Are you Aiden?" I said. "I'm Remi's sister, Maizie."

He folded his arms. "Too bad."

"What was that?"

"Nothin'."

"Later, kid." Nash placed a hand at the small of my back, moving us toward the gate.

"Wait," said Aiden, walking alongside us. "Are you detectiveing Miss Lorena's killer?"

I stopped. "Yes, Aiden. Don't worry. Between us and the police, we'll catch the bad guy."

"I'll probably catch him first." His little chin jerked up. "I know stuff."

Nash squatted to face the kid. The stern look he used on Aiden made me shiver. "Don't even think about it, kid. This isn't a game. You should stay in the house and listen to your momma."

"And if you know stuff, you should tell us or the police," I said. "What do you know?"

Aiden's gaze moved to his shoes. "Never mind."

"Did you see someone go into Miss Lorena's house?"

Aiden shrugged.

"Did you see someone leave Miss Lorena's house?"

He looked up and glared at me. "Maybe I did and maybe I didn't."

"Maybe we should talk to your mom again," said Nash.

Aiden's eyes widened. "I didn't see nothing." He spun and ran toward the house.

"Do you think he saw something?"

"Kids are unreliable. I never discount them, but I don't know about this one. Sounds like he wants to play cops and robbers. I'm worried about him getting in trouble. I think I scared him off."

I wasn't so sure. I knew another six-year-old who didn't scare very easily. I just hoped Nash was right.

FIFTEEN

#FashionVictim #ClipClopSlap

*W*e spoke to six neighbors and by the seventh, I felt pretty good about my interview techniques. When I segued into non-murder topics, Nash would clear his throat. Most of the neighbors had been at the party. All had spoken to the police.

I learned many things. Like a recipe for fat-free cinnamon rolls — although I didn't believe they tasted as good as fat-filled cinnamon rolls. The local Stein Mart was closing and everything was forty percent off. The geese at the lake had been terrorizing Mr. Leonard's dogs. Mrs. Wilkin's grandchild won the local poetry contest and would appear at the county-wide competition. The city council was a bunch of crooks and thieves, out for their own self-interest. The city council was hard-working and upstanding citizens who did more for the city than anyone in years. The deer were terrorizing Mr. Leonard's dogs. This would be the worst spring in years. Or the mildest.

And no one saw anything unusual concerning Lorena Cortez the day or night or week of her murder.

At the last house, Nash glanced at his watch. "I don't want to be late for Sunday dinner. Let's vamoose."

"I'm late all the time," I said. "Carol Lynn and Daddy know my job has strange hours."

"My job doesn't have strange hours," said Nash.

"Yet, I found you working on a Saturday. I would call that strange."

"You don't need to mention that to your dad. I'd rather he think I'm sticking to the hours he gave me."

I dropped my hand before reaching the doorbell. "What's going on with you? Daddy won't care you're working extra hours. Unless he's paying you overtime, and then he might examine the bottom line and say no. He admires people for going the extra mile and all that. You know he's all about the 110-percent-whatsit."

"I don't seek extra approval for doing my job."

"That is not how to get ahead in the corporate world." But secretly I was glad. Tie-wearing, approval-seeking Nash was a turn-off.

I bit my lip. I was so shallow. Why couldn't I be turned-on by Nash's tie? It was around his neck, which I found attractive. A thick, muscular neck that fitted between his broad shoulders...

My face heated. I glanced away before Nash recognized a sign that I might want to reconnoiter in the office. Currently, the office was an even bigger turn-off than his tie.

But Nash appeared to be gritting his teeth. His scar throbbed. Which meant he hadn't recognized my blush.

"Hurry up," said Nash. "We're not getting anywhere with the neighbors anyway."

"This one is important. It's directly across from Lorena's." I reached for the doorbell again and drew my finger back. "Hang on. Lamar said you're not a Sunday dinner-kind of guy."

"You've been talking to Lamar about me?"

"All the time. Since the beginning. How do you not know that?" I planted my hands on my hips. "Why are you in such a rush to get to the cabin, really?"

His mood changed faster than my manicure colors. The chiseled jaw relaxed and the scar disappeared in place of a long dimple. His hands snuck out to slip beneath mine and hold my hips. "Why wouldn't I? I'll have you snuggled up on the couch next to me while I watch football with Boomer."

I snorted. "You don't like football. You like baseball."

"Then there's Carol Lynn's cooking."

That I could understand. But Nash didn't have my appetite. "Not buying it."

The dimple disappeared. "Why can't I just want to have a normal evening with you?"

"Oh." I slipped from his hands and into his arms. "Sorry."

"It's okay." His face lowered, then drew back to pat my hair. "Are you sure we won't need to shave this mess?"

I glared up at him and heard the door open behind me.

"What's going on out here? What are you two doing on my porch?" A short, middle-aged man stood in the doorway. He folded his arms across his chest, resting them on his belly.

"Good afternoon, sir," said Nash, shoving me to the side.

I smiled at the man while adjusting my clothing. "Sorry about that. We're private investigators looking into the death of your neighbor, Lorena Cortez. I'm sure you've already spoken to the police. We wanted to follow up with a few questions."

"I haven't spoken to the police." He tilted his head. "Lorena died? I've been out of town."

"How well did you know Lorena?" said Nash.

"She's a neighbor. We say hello at our mailboxes and that sort of thing. When I had surgery, she brought me chicken soup. I get her mail and water her flowers when she's out of town. I'm also a fan of her work. She's extremely talented if you didn't know."

"I agree. Lorena was talented." I loved Black Pine's neighborliness. "That's nice you were friendly. I'm so sorry for your loss."

"Lorena really died?" The man's face crumpled. "How? She seemed healthy."

I reached to hug him, but Nash snagged my jeans, holding me back.

"She was murdered," said Nash.

"Oh my." The man's eyes widened. "You better come inside. I'm Gary, by the way."

We followed him into the foyer. A kimono hung on the wall, the sleeves spread out to display a flowering tree and peacock.

"That's a gorgeous kimono." I tilted my head. "I wore one like it on a TV show."

"You were on *Julia Pinkerton, Teen Detective*?" said Gary.

Not wanting to sound contemptuous, I merely nodded. However, one couldn't help feeling disappointed when Gary hung *Julia Pinkerton* memorabilia on his wall but didn't recognize the titular character from the show standing before him. Another good reason to be done with celebrity life. It was a lot more disappointing than you'd think. "How did you get the kimono?"

"I bought it at auction." Gary's eyes filled with tears. "I'm a big fan. I learned about Lorena when she won the CDG award for excellence in contemporary television ten years ago."

I studied Gary anew. He wore sweatpants with a green cable knit sweater. Not someone I'd identify as a fashion geek. But there I went again, wading in shallow waters.

"Did you notice I also had the cherry blossom *kanzashi*?" He pointed to the credenza below the hanging kimono. A little stand held an eight-inch-long metal hair stick topped with dangling flowers. "I think you stabbed someone with it in that episode."

"Julia Pinkerton didn't kill the ninja, just took him out," I explained to Nash. "The ninja was actually a guy on the gymnastic team. Julia caught him pilfering the school's computer equipment."

Nash pressed his lips together and gave me a look.

"Lorena made the little cherry blossoms from kimono silk," I rambled, then looked at Gary. "I had no idea that was still around."

"Do you want to see the rest of my collection?" said Gary.

"No," said Nash. "We want to ask—"

"Yes," I said, traipsing after Gary. "Yes, yes, yes."

Gary had hung character costumes throughout his home, including a suit of armor in his kitchen. Some he'd gotten at private auctions. Several were Lorena's pieces. "I offered to buy them from her, but she asked for a donation to Clothing Kids instead."

We stood before a jade green dress that had been stained, aged, and ripped. Worn by Jennifer Able in the movie *Homecoming Court*. My eyes welled with tears. "I'll never forget the scene where Ada wore this dress. When they announced Justin and Tiffany as king and queen, it crushed her. Jennifer did a great job revealing emotion without overdoing it."

Gary's head bobbed. "I loved it when Ada pulled the knife out of her boot and threw it at Justin. Went right through his neck, just before he could rip Tiffany's heart out. It was so touching."

"Those tears in the dress were strategic," I told Nash, who clearly didn't care. "So the audience can see Ada's secret tattoo."

"Lorena used a combination of shredding, sanding, and paint to get that look of grime and blood. She showed me her technique on a jean jacket," said Gary. "I have Justin's outfit, too. It still has the blood splatter from the knife wound. But it's his falcon hood and wings I'm most proud of."

I sucked in a breath. "You have the Falcon ensemble? I thought they'd have that locked in a vault."

Gary gave me the slow nod. "Between you and me, when I go to ComicCon, I've signed autographs as Justin. I can't help it if the fans can't tell us apart. It's our eyes." He held his hand to cover the lower half of his face. "Do you want to see my albums? I wish I had the portrait done to show you."

Nash snagged my elbow before I could follow Gary back into his bedroom. "Gary, I noticed you have a doorbell camera. Do you have videos from last Friday saved? The camera might have caught something across the street."

"It's motion-activated but it can't hurt to check," said Gary, trotting off. "Let me get my iPad."

"What are you doing?" hissed Nash after Gary left. "We don't have time to look at Looney-Tunes' dress collection."

"I can't help myself," I said. "And he's so broken up about Lorena. I think it makes him feel better."

"You don't find it weird?"

"That he's a little obsessed about Lorena? Like he might have followed her to Black Pine and bought the house across the street?"

"That part's hinky. I meant weird for a grown man to collect teenage girl movie artifacts."

I scoffed. "I've known a lot of grown men who...well, it is unusual for Black Pine, yes. And Gary doesn't look like the typical fashionista. But now I've been in Gary's house and can report all this to Mowry."

Nash's eyebrows quirked. "Good idea, Miss Albright."

I smiled up at him. "Thank you." Noting the darkening of his eyes as he grinned down at me, I stepped away. "Gary will be back."

"He already caught us once." Nash moved forward. His hand snuck behind my back and he swept me against him. "Anyway, I'll hear him. Those shoes he's wearing make an annoying sound. We've got a minute."

"It is odd he's wearing penny loafers with sweatpants." I squirmed in Nash's arms. "I don't want to get caught again."

"I have to say, it's pretty sexy seeing you use the fashion stuff to nab a suspect." Nash's dimple flared. "At first, I thought you just wanted to look at his clothes."

I did want to see the costumes, and my excuse for gaining information for Mowry was an afterthought to make myself look less superficial. But I kept that to myself.

"You need to control yourself, Mr. Nash," I said coyly.

"Then you need to stop wriggling against me, Miss Albright." Nash's head ducked toward mine. The clop-slap resounded in the hall behind us. Nash let me go with a wink.

Heat crawled up my neck and smacked my cheeks. Now I

understood Nash's rules. Although I found it irritating that he didn't follow his PDA rules for my investigations, only his own.

Gary clomped into the living room. "I pulled up Friday's footage. Not much there."

Nash took the iPad, skimming through the videos. "You're right. Not much we can tell from this. Would you mind if I send it to our office anyway?"

At the words "our office," I squinted at Nash.

"Of course. Anything to help. Poor Lorena." Gary sighed. "I can't believe it's true."

"I'll be in touch, Gary." I handed him the card to my new office. "If you think of anything let me know. By the way, Detective Ian Mowry might call on you. He's talked to the other neighbors, so I'm sure he'll want to speak to you, too."

"Isn't it enough to talk to you?" said Gary.

"The police still have to conduct their own interviews." At Gary's befuddled look, I wondered if he only invited us in thinking he wouldn't have to speak to the police.

And if that was the case, why didn't Gary want to speak to the police?

SIXTEEN

#DuckDuckEdna #CrazyExDirtBikeKillers

I followed Nash to the cabin, wishing I could ride with him. Not just because I needed better protection from the wind. I wanted to discuss Gary. And the "our office" comment.

Likely a Freudian slip. However, I felt something was hinky. With Nash.

I caught Nash's arm before we walked inside the cabin. "About the office comment…"

"What office comment?" He looked at the front door, then at me. "Can this wait?"

"No. You said you were sending Gary's front door surveillance footage to our office. What does that mean?"

"Oh, right." Nash's eyes gleamed. "We got him."

"Got who?"

"Gary. He was right about the camera not picking up anything across the street. But his doorbell camera did pick up a delivery guy dropping off packages on his doormat. Then the camera showed the door opening and someone grabbing the packages."

"Gary said he wasn't home," I squealed. "That's awesome. He's a suspect for real. I have a real suspect."

"He had the opportunity to kill Lorena if that was his hand dragging in the packages. However, we need a better motive than a man who loves prom dresses."

"Gary's a stalker."

"We don't know that. Yet." Nash cracked a grin. "But it's a lead. Good job, Miss Albright."

I frowned. "But you found it. Not me. I was too caught up in his awesome wardrobe collection."

"Your interest probably caught Gary off guard, if he did want to hide the fact he wasn't home. He probably forgot about the packages."

Still, that was like giving me credit for a great meal when I only chose the restaurant.

"Anyway, I sent the video to your email address."

"Oh," I said a little too despondently. "I thought you said *our* office."

"Habit, I guess." He shrugged. "Boomer will say something about the time. I know it."

I rolled my eyes. "He's obsessed with time and temperature. And the weather. The price of gas. All things we have no control over. That's his schtick. I don't pay any attention to it."

"You're not working for him."

Inside the house, we said our hellos to Carol Lynn, who did things in the kitchen — cooking, I presumed — and found Daddy in the family room, staring up at a flat-screen above the fireplace.

"Georgia at Auburn," he said. "1996. I still have it on VHS."

I felt Nash's cringe, but he nodded and made some remarks that sounded on topic. I had no clue as to their secret language, other than football was involved. Nash lowered himself to the couch to stare up at the screen. I snuggled against him, per his earlier instructions.

Daddy glanced at us, then did a double-take. "Baby girl, what on earth?"

"You do know we're seeing each other, right?" I scooted a few inches from Nash just to be safe. Daddy owned a lot of weapons and most of them shot bullets.

"Do you think I'm blind? Why else is he here every Sunday? I'm talking about that." Daddy pointed at my head. "Is that some kind of new style?"

"This is Billy's fault." I sighed, stuck a finger in my scalp, and teared up trying to jerk free a tangle.

Daddy's eyebrow rose. "Billy's a hairdresser?"

I snorted. "Not in the least."

Color rose in Daddy's cheeks. He spoke slowly and quietly. "Wyatt Nash, do you know what she's talking about?"

Nash rolled his eyes. "Yes, sir. Unfortunately. You see—"

"And you did nothing to prevent it?"

"I wasn't there."

Daddy cut him off with a harsh look then turned his eyes on me. "Did this happen to you during a surveillance whatsit?"

"No," I said. "It sort of happened while driving."

"He was in the vehicle with you?" Daddy rose from his chair. "My Lord, you didn't hitchhike, did you? I have warned you about that."

"Hitchhike? What are you talking about?"

"Sir." Nash stood. "She named the Bronco, Billy. Her hair's just wind-tangled."

"It's more than wind-tangled." Daddy eyed me. "It looks like you've been attacked by a wild animal. You've been out in public like that?"

"You're the only person who's said anything about it." I looked at Nash. "Right?"

"Black Pine folks are too polite to make remarks to your face," said Daddy, easing back into his chair.

Nash lowered himself onto the couch. "A few people asked me if you were okay when you were out of earshot. But don't worry. They meant well."

I left to shower. An hour later I exited the shower with a pink scalp and twenty-percent less hair than when I started. Remi sat on a stool in my bedroom, holding a jar of Crisco.

"My hair is so soft," I said. "Your mom was right. Much better than olive oil."

"She does like this stuff." Remi drummed the jar lid. "You're gonna smell like fried chicken, though."

I sniffed a lock. "I think it's okay. I used up a bottle of Shu Uemera conditioner, too." I stared into my open closet, then turned back to Remi. "I met a kid named Aiden today. He's in your class."

Remi stuck out her tongue and gagged.

"What's wrong with Aiden?"

"First off, he's a boy." She rolled her eyes and wrinkled her nose. "And he's a fibber. He lies all the time. Momma says he does it to get attention. Aiden said I stole Edna's candy bar. Edna ate that dang candy bar, and she went along with him."

"You have a classmate named Edna?" Old-fashioned names were really trending.

"Naw, she's our rabbit. Edna belongs to the class, but Mrs. Childs never lets me take her home. Because of Aiden."

I had an inkling as to why Edna never visited the cabin. "Do you give Edna candy bars?"

"Can't very well give her snacks when Aiden keeps stealing them, can I? He's a liar and a thief."

"First off, candy bars aren't healthy for bunnies."

"They ain't healthy for anybody."

She had a point. "Second, if Edna ate the candy bar, then Aiden didn't steal it."

Remi glared at me. "He's still a fibber."

"Does he lie about other things?" If Aiden wasn't reliable, I wouldn't bother trying to find out what he knew about the night of Lorena's murder. Despite Nash's warnings about the unreliability of kid testimonies, I still wanted to talk to him.

However, this example likely proved his point.

Remi bobbed her head.

"Did you see Aiden at the costume party?"

Remi's eyes narrowed. "He was a bat. Bats also eat bugs. Just because they fly doesn't mean they're better than armadillos."

"You wanted to be a duck, anyway."

"Oh, right." She beamed, tossed the Crisco can on the floor, and slid off the stool. "I'm getting my duck call."

"Hold on there." I blocked the doorway. "Did Aiden say anything about seeing something at Miss Lorena's? Did you see him leave the party?"

"He didn't say nothin' and if he did, I wouldn't believe him anyways." Remi stuck her tiny fists on her spindly hips. "And he might've left. We were playing hide and seek and we couldn't find him for a while. That house was really fun to play in. All kinds of places to hide. Aiden's really good at hide and seek, but since he's a fibber, he might have left and snuck back. He's probably a cheater, too. I wouldn't put it past him."

She shot forward. A minute later a squawk sounded in the hall.

Followed by, "Remington Marie, we said no duck calls in the house."

*A*t the doorway to the family room, I hesitated. Nash's voice had caught my attention. The smooth bass had a similar quality used when he interrogated witnesses. Slyly. In such a way, they didn't realize he was interrogating them.

Except he spoke to my father, not a witness.

"No shop talk on a Sunday, Nash. Catch me at DeerNose tomorrow." Daddy looked up as I entered the room. "About time. It's getting late. Although you look a heck of a lot better now. We're holding dinner on you. Carol Lynn made cowboy beans and you know how I feel about beans."

He exited the room with Nash's eyes on him. I also recognized that thoughtful, blue-eyed gaze. Nash's "something's hinky" expression.

"What? What's that look for?"

"Hey, sugar." Nash stood, his face once more placidly stern and adorably scary. "You look gorgeous. And you smell great, too." He sniffed. "Like —"

"Don't say fried chicken. What's going on with you and Daddy?"

"I don't know what you mean." Nash took one of my hands and pulled it to his lips. "You taste great, too. Listen, after dinner, let's go back to my place."

"If by 'your place,' do you mean, going back to the *office* to discuss Gary and Aiden and the rest of our interviews?"

His brows drew together. "That wasn't exactly what I had in mind."

I knew exactly what he had in mind, but I've found a deliberate obtuseness helps with the small blows to the ego. And libido. "I called Ian after my shower and told him we canvassed the neighbors."

"You made your dad wait more than an hour for his beans and during that time you were chatting with Mowry?"

"I wanted to talk to Ian while the interviews were still fresh in my mind. No biggie, we chat all the time."

"You and Mowry call each other *all the time*?"

"Sometimes we text." I shrugged. "He likes to help with my cases."

"Isn't that your boss's job?" Nash's jaw tightened and his scar pulsed. "Is Mowry seeing anyone now?"

"I don't think so. He hasn't mentioned it. Why?"

"It might be the reason why your dirt bike's a wreck."

I sucked in my breath, remembering the name that had been sliced into Lucky's seat. Poor Lucky. A victim of domestic violence. Which made more sense than a random assault. "I've got to call Ian."

Nash folded his arms. "Seems to me 'calling Ian' is the last thing you should do."

"Shouldn't I warn him? What if he doesn't know he has a

crazy ex-girlfriend? Or a crazy current girlfriend? What if she goes after Billy? A knife and a baseball bat would kill him. Lucky had been in better shape and can be repaired. But Billy? He's one broken taillight away from the eternal junkyard in the sky."

Shizzles. I'd be back to driving Lucky. Or Remi's abandoned Big Wheel.

Nash took a deep breath and let it out. "Why Ian?"

"You're busy. You've got a corporate job. You're a nine-to-five nose-to-the-grindstoner." I hitched a shoulder. "Sometimes I call Lamar, too."

"What about Ms. Cox?"

"She's busy, too." Saying so wasn't fair to Annie. She would help me if I needed it. But I felt awkward enough around her. After helping me, she'd probably hand me a pile of subpoenas to serve. Or a stack of client vetting. I didn't want to mention it to Nash, but Annie knew how to bring in the business. Bringing in the business wasn't his strong suit.

But he'd been great at doing the business.

"I'm not so busy I can't take a call from you." Nash glanced toward the kitchen. "Maybe texting would be better though. I don't want Boomer to think you're calling me all the time."

"That's why I don't do it." I snuggled against him and sighed when his arms tightened around me.

His hands slid over my rear and he hiked me closer. "What time is Mowry coming to the office?" He nuzzled my ear and his lips slid to my jaw. "Do y'think we'll have a minute?"

"Ian's coming here. For dessert."

Nash pulled back. "You're kidding."

I shook my head. "I can ask him to meet us at the office. But since it's more bed than office these days, I figured the cabin was safer."

"More bed than office?" Nash cocked his head.

I decided to change the subject. "What's going on with you and Daddy? You've been giving him the side-eye since we got here. I heard you questioning him earlier. If I didn't know better, I'd think you were investigating him."

"I investigate *for* him." Nash began striding toward the kitchen. "Better hurry up. Beans are waiting."

I watched him disappear through the doorway and folded my arms.

Something was hinky.

SEVENTEEN

#SnapCrackleVicki #BungledBungalow

*T*he next day, I arrived early at the office — the new, non-donut-scented one — to start on my work to give myself more time for Lorena's case. Also to avoid Annie as much as possible. I halted in the doorway, letting it shut behind me. Key tapping and gum-smacking assaulted my ears. I had failed to arrive before my boss.

Possibly Annie Cox wasn't human. Obviously, she didn't have a life.

"That you, Albright?" Annie called.

"Yes, sir. Ma'am. Ms. Cox. Annie, I mean. Yes, I am here." I flopped into my chair and stared at the pile of folders on my desk. They'd been stacked higher than my monitor.

"Got some new leads yesterday. Shouldn't take you too long."

I blew a silent raspberry at the stack and tossed my Moschino backpack beneath my desk. Running background checks had never been fun, but they hadn't felt as dreary and boring at Nash Security Solutions as they did at Albright Security Solutions. I shoved the stack aside, opened a blank spreadsheet on my computer, and began typing in my notes from the previous day's interviews.

A pop behind my head caused my hand to jump. My fingers slammed the keys, typing "FS5ua;w" instead of "Gary."

"What'cha doing?" said Annie, peering over me. "What's that? Some kind of code?"

"Typo," I said. "You scared me. Just logging some interview notes."

"Sorry to scare you. I find it helpful to list all the names in column C and make check box columns to the left of C. And beneath the checkbox you can put the date and time you spoke to the witness." With her gum grinding between her teeth, she leaned across and tapped keys. New boxes appeared. "There you go. Much more efficient."

"Thanks." I stared at the screen, willing her to leave.

"Interviews for what?"

"The new case I told you about on Saturday," I hedged. I grabbed a folder off the top of the pile. "I'll start on these now instead."

"Always try to finish your paperwork before starting something new. It's more efficient. But obviously, triage the other stuff first."

"Obviously."

"D'you hear about the murder of Lorena Cortez?"

I spun around in my chair and leaned back so it didn't feel like Annie hovered over me. Which she was. "Yes. I was at the Clothing Kids gala."

"Police are keeping the details pretty quiet." Annie smacked her gum, staring down at me. "You and Lorena were tight, weren't you?"

I wondered if this was Annie's way of getting me to spill. It was pretty effective. I snuck a pen and my notepad in my lap to take notes on her technique. "I've known Lorena a long time but mostly from working with her when I was a kid. She was the costume designer for *Julia Pinkerton*."

"Lorena Cortez made you the clothes for the show?"

"She designed the style and wardrobe. The director and actors work with the designer some, but Lorena did all the research. The costumes reflect the character, mood, and style of the show. The wardrobe department bought, sewed or altered, and dressed me. Then Lorena would check all the principal actors before a scene."

"You couldn't get dressed on your own?"

"The dressers are there to make sure everything fit and looked right. Small details make the picture. And continuity is important. They have to log every detail for each scene to make sure we look the same in each shot." Reminiscing, I tipped my head to the side and smiled. "Sometimes we had disagreements about what Julia should wear for certain scenes. But Lorena was always right."

"Anyway, Vicki knew Lorena Cortez, too."

"Of course. Vicki was my manager. She had a lot to say about my wardrobe, too."

Annie snorted. "I bet."

I tilted my head to study Annie. That had been a derisive snort, considering Vicki owned Albright Security and had hired Annie to manage it. Kind of a cheeky snort before the owner's daughter. But then Annie didn't hide her feelings. Much. For a robot.

Perhaps Annie struggled with Vicki. She wouldn't be the first or the last.

"Has Vicki been hands-on with the business here?" I'd thought after Nash had left, Vicki had given Annie the reins and turned a blind eye to the PI office to focus on her celebrity management career. "Is she micro-managing or anything like that?"

"Not particularly," said Annie. "I just turn in the numbers. Let her know if anything major crops up."

The snort had also been a bit scathing for someone who let Annie do her thing.

What was going on with Vicki and Annie? Nash and Daddy

were already giving me heartburn. My hands twisted in my lap. "Why did you want to know if Vicki knew Lorena?"

Annie shrugged and snapped her gum. "Just wondering."

Vicki had known Lorena. She also knew Spencer. The Martins had insinuated an affair between Spencer and Lorena. I hadn't talked to Spencer yet. Jennifer Frederick had slapped him at the party.

"I gotta go," I said. "I forgot to check on something."

Annie leaned back and crossed her arms, eyeballing me. "What about the background checks?"

Shizzles. "I'll be in later to do them. Technically, I'm early and not on the clock."

"Technically." Annie snorted. Happily, just a common-variety snort. "By the way, what kind of vehicle did you get?"

"Huh?"

"You know. You left work on Saturday to buy a car..."

"Right. A Bronco." I waved vaguely toward the window. "It's the blue one."

Annie pivoted and walked to the window. "You got a 4x4. Kind of looks like a Jeep."

"It's not a—"

She spun around, smiling. "Cool."

I shrugged. "It's missing doors and it looks like the roof was cut off with a hacksaw. But it runs and I can sit in it. Unfortunately, I have to wear a hat, so I'm still dealing with flat hair."

Annie waved away my complaints. "You need to jack that baby up and get bigger tires. I know a guy."

I didn't want to climb into Billy. I could effortlessly slide into my previous convertibles. Now I had to step up, using a duct-tape handle. Thankfully Billy wasn't as high as Nash's truck which involved some core strength to climb inside. Particularly if I wore a skirt or heels.

"I'll see you later." Annie trotted to the back office, snapping and popping in time with her steps. She glanced over her shoulder. "I'm ordering in for lunch. You want me to get'cha something?"

I gaped, then closed my mouth, and nodded. I guess we were bonding over Jeeps. Whatever. I needed to speak to Jennifer Frederick and Spencer Newson, to learn what I could about Lorena's alleged secret romance.

Hopefully before lunch.

⠀

*T*he Clothing Kids Assistant Director of Finance, Jennifer Frederick, lived in old Black Pine, a few blocks from the Martins and Lorena's home. She also had a bungalow, probably built in the twenties. Unlike Lorena's colorful cottage, Jennifer's retained the original look of the era in moss green with cream trim. The natural color and large magnolias almost hid the house from passers-by, awarding the cottage a mysterious, enchanting feel.

Adorbs.

I traipsed up the brick walk and climbed the wooden steps to the porch. A "no soliciting" sign hung near the video doorbell.

"I'm not expecting any packages," said a woman's voice through the doorbell's speaker.

Perhaps the camouflaged cottage was less inspired by whimsy and more strategic. "Jennifer, it's Maizie Albright. We met at the party. I'm Lorena's friend."

"I work from home. Will this take long?"

"I wanted to ask you some questions about Clothing Kids. And the party," I waffled, then realized Nash would be more direct. I pulled my shoulders back and lifted my chin. "I'm investigating Lorena's murder. It's important we talk now."

"I thought you were an actress."

"I was, but now I'm a private investigator." I said, then muttered, "In training."

The door cracked and a pretty, dark-haired woman peered out. Jennifer's smooth complexion, trim figure, and bright brown eyes reminded me of Lorena. However, her personality seemed forty degrees cooler. "You're better off asking Spencer Newson. He's the president."

"I didn't recognize you without your Raggedy Ann costume." I smiled. "Spencer's next on my list. But I want to hear all the board members' opinions."

The door widened. "Opinions?"

"About what happened that night. And anything else you can tell me about Lorena and her...relationships with the other board members."

"Come in," she huffed. "I don't have long, though. I'm in the middle of an audit."

"You're being audited? Man, I'm sorry to hear that. That really sucks. I hope they're not raking you over the coals or anything."

"I'm the CPA conducting the audit," she said starchily. "My company provides external audits for companies like your father's."

"DeerNose is being audited?" I squeaked.

"No, *like* DeerNose. I can't reveal whom I'm auditing."

"Right." I followed her into the cozy living room and sank onto the edge of her couch. "Sorry about that."

"What do you want to know about Lorena?" She remained standing, her arms crossed over her long hoodie.

"Anything that might shed a light on what might have happened."

"I have no idea. It's a horrific tragedy. I told the police the same thing."

"Uh-huh." I floundered, wondering if I should match her stand. I wasn't sure what Nash would do. Probably not sit down in the first place. "With the big gala, you must have been working closely with her."

"There was a lot of logistics and planning involved. My work's mostly budgetary. Keeping track of the expenses and reining in her more elaborate ideas. That sort of thing."

"I'm sure Lorena had a ton of elaborate ideas. She always told me, 'Go big or go home.'" I caught myself before I took a turn down memory lane. It still hurt to reminisce. "I understand Spencer Newson worked closely with her, too."

Jennifer stiffened. "I suppose so."

I studied her, wondering if her reaction to the mention of Spencer and Lorena meant the rumors were true. Possibly the tension between Jennifer and Spencer was a result of those rumors. Jennifer seemed pretty strait-laced. She wouldn't approve of an affair, particularly one that could jeopardize the success of the Clothing Kids foundation. "I suppose Lorena and Spencer had a lot to coordinate for the gala and the magazine spread."

"Of course, they did. I can't comment on the particulars since it's not my area."

"Did you notice anything unusual in the last few days?"

"No. We were all busy preparing for the opening."

I wasn't getting anywhere with Jennifer. I couldn't tell if her coolness was due to her nature or from protecting the board's reputation. Clearly, she wasn't prone to gossip like the Martins. "What about the robbery?"

She shifted and tightened her arms. "What about it?"

"The police said it looked like Lorena had been robbed. Her safe was open and there were financial papers scattered about."

Her intensity sharpened. "Her safe? I didn't know that. What kind of financial papers? Anything to do with Clothing Kids? I should have been told."

I gulped. Had I just revealed something the police wanted to be kept quiet? I hoped I hadn't screwed up Ian's investigation. "I'm not sure if the papers had anything to do with Clothing Kids."

"I certainly hope not." She averted her gaze. "I'll take care of it. I'll look through our accounts and see if anything's amiss."

"Let me know if you find anything." I rose and moved to the door. "You should tell the police, too."

Her gaze snapped back to me. "I know how and what to report, believe me."

"Of course, you do. If you think of anything else, please let me know." I handed her an Albright Security Solutions business card. One perk I'd gained after working for Nash.

Too bad I hadn't gained the art of interviewing.

"One last thing." I watched her. "Why did you slap Spencer Newson?"

Her eyes widened and her face contorted, trying to control her expression. "He did something inappropriate."

Somehow that didn't surprise me. A better question would be, why would Lorena want this kind of man as director of her charity? But if they were having an affair, I didn't need to ask.

*O*wing to handle the questioning of the Clothing Kids CEO better than I had the CFO, I drove along the lake toward the mountain. The Newsons didn't live in the historic district like the other board members but in a new, gated community on Black Pine Mountain. I felt relieved to not be subjected to poisonous wallpaper or lead pipes. But when Susie Newson answered the door in a bikini, I figured I'd rather take my chances with toxicity.

"Susie, I met you at the Clothing Kids' gala. I'm Maizie Albright."

"I know. I thought you were here about the filter." Susie crossed her arms over her bandeau top. "I've been waiting to do laps all morning. It's freezing."

Considering she wore a ruffled strapless with a thong bottom, I didn't figure her to be particularly serious about her strokes.

"Um," I said, hating to state the obvious but feeling it necessary. "It is winter."

"We have an indoor pool." Susie cocked a hip and studied me. "What did you want?"

"I'd like to speak to Spencer."

Her eyes narrowed. "About what?"

"Clothing Kids. The Martins gave me a guest list and they thought I should…" Why was I trying to come up with an excuse to talk to her husband? Nash wouldn't use an excuse to make Susie more comfortable. "I want to speak to Spencer about Lorena Cortez."

"Why?"

"Maybe you didn't hear. She was murdered."

"Oh, I heard. I've heard all about it." She studied her nails. "That's all anyone talks about right now."

"It's pretty shocking."

"Why are you interested?" Susie looked up and arched a brow.

"I'm a private investigator. I'm investigating Lorena's death."

"No way." Susie dropped her arms and her hip to lean against the doorway. With her claws retracted, she appeared younger and prettier. And less irritating. Slightly. "I thought you were an actress turned beautician."

"I was an actress." I wondered why she thought I was a beautician. My hand darted to my hair, seeking tangles. "Now I'm a PI in training. Can I come in?"

"Sure." She backed out of the doorway and grabbed a coverup lying on an entryway table.

Their dramatic marble foyer rose past the second story. An elegant chandelier hung across from a picture window, filtering sunlight and gilding the room with prisms and rainbows. I followed Susie into a formal living room. She flopped onto a velvet loveseat and motioned for me to take the wingback across from her. Pictures of Susie and Spencer in cute frames decorated a carved marble fireplace, a grand piano, and custom built-ins. The walls were decorated with inspirational sayings about love, families, and life.

It was like *Town & Country* had shopped at Kirkland's. I had a feeling the house and furniture had been chosen during

Spencer's previous marital period, then redecorated by a twenty-year-old.

"What's it like being a detective?" Susie grabbed a pillow covered in sequins and hugged it against her flat belly. "Is it pretty cool? Like in the movies?"

"Not really. I starred in a PI show, and I've found little to no similarities." I straightened in my chair, happy to share my insights from a professional point-of-view. Rarely did I get asked questions linking my former and new career. Usually, it was one or the other. And in both cases, most questions were about my love life. "There's a lot more paperwork in real life, for one thing. And rarely any murders."

"You've got one now."

EIGHTEEN

#SusieAndTheBanshee #MashupMania

Susie leaned forward, speaking excitedly. "They're saying some women found Lorena."

"That was me and my friend, Rhonda. Remember when we thought Lorena was late to the party? I went to her house and found her. Unfortunately." I shuddered at the memory and focused on Susie's "Live, Life, Love" signboard to give my brain a refresh.

"Yeah, right. Your hairstylist friend. I heard about that, too." Susie bobbed her head. "I also heard Lorena was really bloody."

I nodded, not wanting to think about that again. *Be like Nash. Or Annie. An Annie-Nash mashup character. Focused. Perceptive. Bulldogging for the truth. Hard-bitten, yet not washed-up.*

I'd already done washed-up in my real life and would not enjoy bringing that insight to a new persona.

Getting into character, I adjusted my posture by slouching. Tilted my head. Tightened my jaw. Eased back in the chair, spreading my arms over the rests and pushing my knees to touch each side of the chair. A power position.

Then I remembered my skirt and closed my legs. Probably why corporate women wore pantsuits.

Susie leaned forward, squishing the pillow. "Why do you want to talk to Spencer? He didn't see anything that night."

"He worked with Lorena on Clothing Kids. I thought he'd give me some insight into the victim's final days."

"You sound just like a detective."

"Thank you." I grinned, then checked myself. My Annie-Nash character wouldn't smile at a compliment. I gave Susie a cool nod. "Did you know Lorena?"

"Not really. I mean, she's been over here to talk with Spencer about Clothing Kids. I sat through some boring dinners." Susie rolled her eyes. "Spencer usually went to Lorena's house. And lately, all the time. You know, because of the kick-off fundraiser. It was a lot of work."

"I bet."

I couldn't tell if Susie knew Spencer and Lorena might have been having an affair. Her earlier antagonism seemed like jealousy but with Spencer's past who could blame her? Susie had been the "other woman" when he married her. And still seemed focused on seducing him by wearing bikinis in the house.

Unless that was for the pool guy.

Confused, I forgot about my mashup character and leaned forward. "What do you do, Susie?"

She looked surprised. "I'm a student. I just got married, so I'm decorating and stuff, too." She pointed at an "Our Happy Place" plaque. "I worked at Home Decor and More part-time. Not as much now. I'm super busy."

"How did you meet Spencer?"

She gazed into the distance, a dreamy smile on her face. "It was truly romantic. He was at Home Decor and More buying a gift when he saw me. He waited like forty-five minutes to check out until I wasn't busy. Then asked me if I wanted to get a drink after work. We started going out after that."

"Very romantic." Not creepy at all. "It must have been a whirlwind romance."

"Sort of." Susie pouted. "It took a while to get married, though. Because of his divorce."

Not having an appropriate comment, I nodded.

"The divorce took forever."

My head bobbed.

"I broke up with him a few times, too." Her voice rose, then mellowed. "And when he finally proposed, I made sure he was serious. Marriage is serious, you know."

"Oh, I know. Super serious. That's why I called off my past engagements." Love also tended to blind me until it was almost too late to realize the kind of person I'd really be marrying. Probably because I fell in love too easily.

Wait. Was I doing that again?

I straightened my slouch and slid my thumbnail between my teeth.

But we were taking things slow. Nash worked for Daddy while he fixed his financial issues. I worked for Annie to finish my two-year apprenticeship toward my private investigator license. Two years was a long time to wait. We weren't even engaged. Just committed.

All good. I slipped back into my slouch.

Susie prattled on about her long engagement to Spencer. I continued to nod, and my mind wandered. If I was blind to Nash, it wasn't because I was love-struck. He was a tough nut to crack. Like his weird behavior toward my father.

If we weren't engaged, I hadn't made the same mistake again. Right?

Wait. What was I doing? This conversational thread about Spencer and Susie needed to end. My Annie-Nash detective wouldn't have felt sorry for Susie and her obvious loneliness. My new character would have sought out Spencer, leaving Susie to rant and deform pillows alone. She definitely wouldn't have let Susie segue into her entire dating history, pre-Spencer. The girl sounded like a character from a Carrie Underwood song.

Being hot and young had its drawbacks when it came to the kind of men you attracted. I felt sorry for Susie.

But not too sorry. She was still a suspect. Just like the Martins and Gary. And Spencer, too, if he was sleeping with Lorena.

I reclined in the wingback, disentangled my hands from their wringing, and draped them over the armrests. Good for me. I already had a list of suspects.

Like I knew what I was doing.

"Look at the time." I glanced at my wrist. No watch. I looked up. "I know you're super busy. Is Spencer here?"

Susie tossed the mangled pillow and got up. "He's in his office. I don't know what he's doing. Let's see."

I trotted after Susie, then fixed my gait to something less eager and bouncy. Nash and Annie never bounced.

Susie stopped at a hall door and opened it without knocking. In his desk chair, Spencer gazed out a window. Startled, he looked over his shoulder. He turned back toward the window, cleared his throat, then rose. When he moved around his chair, the beaming, easy-going countenance had returned.

"Maizie Albright, good to see you, girl. What brings you here?" He shot a glance at Susie. "Thanks, hon. Maybe we could all have some tea or something?"

"Sure," she chirped at Spencer. "Whatever you like, honey."

"You feel like coffee or a glass of tea, Maizie?"

Coffee sounded good. But Annie and Nash never took offers of sustenance — something I didn't quite understand. Maybe a personal rule — so I refused, too.

"Maizie's here to ask you about Lorena, honey," said Susie. "She's a detective. Did you know that?"

"Private investigator," I said.

"Maizie's still training. She said she has two years to go," said Susie. "But I bet she's pretty good. After all, they're letting her out to ask questions."

Letting me out? "Well, this isn't exactly an official case," I said. "I knew Lorena, so it's more personal."

Spencer stood slack-jawed for a minute. Probably from the overload of unnecessary information. "Of course, she's pretty good," he drawled, catching up. "Have a seat over here, Maizie. How's your momma?"

"My what? Oh, you mean Vicki?" I perched on the edge of a club chair. "I haven't seen her since the party, but I assume she's fine. You know Vicki. She keeps pretty busy."

Spencer laughed and slapped his thigh. "She sure does. I could tell you some stories about her in high school." He glanced at Susie. "But maybe another time. You wanted to ask me about Lorena?"

Spencer was making a brave face. A wide smile that didn't reach his eyes. Before we came in, it looked like he'd been crying. My heart squeezed, knowing how he must feel with the loss of Lorena. Especially if he'd been having a relationship with her.

But now wasn't the time for me to be empathetic. I had a role to play.

I mean, duties to perform.

"Did Lorena make your Woody and Jesse costumes for the party?" I started with a softball question and planned to lob hardballs later. I'd learned that from Annie. Except for the ball game analogy, which was all Nash.

He chuckled. "They're from Costume City. Susie's idea. Thought the kids would like it. Lorena had her hands full with the woodland costumes. Those were really for the photoshoot, but she wanted the kids to get a chance to wear them at the party. That photographer was supposed to have a few shots of the party in the spread, too."

"Did you see Lorena the day of the gala?"

"Let me think." Spencer's eyes wandered the room. "I might have stopped by to check on a few things. I can't remember now. Getting old. I could check my calendar."

Or they had met for a secret rendezvous and he wasn't sure if anyone had seen him or not.

I smiled, pleased with my deduction. "Did you notice anything unusual about Lorena lately?"

"Not really, no." He smiled tightly.

I took that as a yes. "I'm sure continuing Clothing Kids without Lorena will be hard."

"Lorena's vision made Clothing Kids happen," said Spencer. "We'll muddle through somehow. As executive director, I must continue with her plans. The foundation is important to me. Sadly, I've never had children myself."

My heart clenched. "I'm sure you still have time. Susie's young."

He blinked. "I don't think we'll go that route."

"Oh, right." To each his own, I supposed. Just the same, I filed that nugget into my "odd things to tell a detective" box.

"How long have you and Susie been married?"

"Five years."

"Sorry, I thought you were newlyweds. Susie said she was a student."

"She's been taking classes on and off for a few years. I met her when she was still in college."

Ew. But whatever. I was a detective, dangit. It didn't matter if Susie was my age and Spencer had gone to high school with my parents and...Ew. I blew out a breath. Better to get back on the subject of my murdered friend. Much easier to take.

"Any guesses as to why Lorena was murdered?"

He shook his head. "No clue. I heard someone say she was robbed. Can't believe something like that would ever happen in Black Pine."

"I don't think she was robbed," I said. "Or at least, I don't think it was a home invasion intent on robbery. I think the perpetrator intended on killing her."

Spencer's eyes grew wide. "On purpose?"

"It's a theory we're working on." And by we, I meant me, but whatever. I was supposed to meet Ian later to go over my theories and evidence. He'd missed dessert — called away and couldn't meet us. I couldn't tell if Nash had been relieved or annoyed. Instead, we'd spent dessert talking about the new camouflage design Daddy had recently painted. If you weren't a camo aficionado, it was really hard to see the difference. But then I'd been told the same thing about Birkin bags.

But come on, just by color alone, Hermès had camo beat.

"Don't worry, Mr. Newson. I'll figure out who killed Lorena," I said in my best reassuring but professional private investigator tone. "I won't stop until I know what happened. Lorena was my friend. I want to see justice delivered."

I also wanted to see if I could actually solve a case on my own, but those were the petty thoughts I kept to myself.

Most of the time.

NINETEEN

#DeadMeet #BrotherBrigade

I'd planned on meeting Mowry for lunch, but since Annie had offered to pick up something, it looked like I was forced to lunch twice. First world problems.

But not for me. I loved lunch.

I also wanted to ask Vicki about Spencer. It'd been a long time since they were acquainted, but his past might offer some insight. As Lorena's secret lover, he was a big suspect. Maybe Vicki could tell me if he'd done something like date the prom queen, who was later found murdered. It happens. I was pretty sure I'd seen that on a *Cold Case Files*. That's why investigators had to look into those past connections.

Wait. Had I learned that from Annie, Nash, or TV?

In any case, I had two lunches and Vicki on my agenda. But it wasn't lunchtime yet and there was always the possibility that Vicki would put me off my lunch. I swung by LA HAIR instead. I also needed to check on Rhonda and to report to Tiffany.

I parked Billy before the strip mall and walked into LA HAIR. Rhonda wasn't at the desk. I peeked around the corner to the row of stylist chairs. Tiffany wasn't at her nail stand. Ashley trimmed a wriggling toddler's hair while the toddler's mom took pictures with her phone.

"Are they out back?" I called to Ashley.

Ashley looked up. The kid jerked forward, narrowly missing the pointed end of the scissors hanging before her face. The mom shrieked. Ashley dropped the scissors.

My heart pounded in my ears and my vision spotted. I grabbed the edge of the reception desk.

Great, I had scissors PTSD.

"Oops. Sorry." Ashley picked up her scissors, then looked at me. "Tiff and Rhonda didn't show. And they didn't come in yesterday either. Faye's pissed."

The mother glared at Ashley and held a cookie before the girl's face. The little girl stopped moving. "Hurry it up," said the mom.

I hollered my apologies and scooted out of the shop. After climbing in Billy, I called Tiffany.

"Where've you been?" she snapped.

"Why aren't you working? I'm at the shop. Ashley says you haven't been in for two days."

"We've got a problem here. A big problem. You better get over here."

I parked down the street from Tiffany's small ranch. Cars and trucks filled her driveway and curb. Hurrying to her house, I could only assume one thing. Okay, two things. Either a family member had died, or she was having a party. With Tiffany, kind of a fifty-fifty hunch. She had a big extended family in Black Pine. She also liked to party.

Wishing I had stopped to buy flowers or food, I waited on her front stoop after pounding on her door. Locks turned, a chain rattled, and the door cracked open. "Who is it?" said a deep voice.

Clearly not Tiffany.

"Maizie?" I said, hating the shaky quality of my voice. My

new character would've sounded a lot fiercer. Something I needed to work on. Maybe before a mirror.

Inside the house, I heard Tiffany holler at Deep Voice. The door closed, a chain rattled, and the door swung open. A man, taller than a refrigerator and just as wide, stood in the doorway. He wore an Atlanta Falcons jersey and an Atlanta Hawks hat. His eyes were narrowed and hostile, and he barred my entrance with one powerful arm.

"What'd you want?"

My heart skipped a few beats. I needed intensive mirror practice. "Tiffany asked me to come over."

"You're the detective? Rhonda's friend?"

"Yes," I squeaked.

The eyes warmed, his shoulders relaxed, and the arm dropped. "Praise the Lord. Come in, come in."

I entered the tiny living area and spotted Rhonda on the couch, staring at the ceiling. Her hair hadn't been brushed, nor had her makeup been applied. She wore sweats and a stained t-shirt. Big, brawny men surrounded her. They had the same round cheeks and dark brown eyes as Rhonda and were trying to get her to eat.

Her brothers, I deduced.

I rushed to her side. "Rhonda, what happened? What's going on?"

"Rhon won't eat," said a brother holding a dinner plate dwarfed by his giant hand. "And she won't talk."

"She also won't shower," said the man on the other side of her. The couch sagged under his weight. "Or sleep. This is serious."

"Oh God," I said. "This is all my fault."

Four sets of angry brown eyes glowered at me.

Rhonda held a hand up. "Not her fault."

"It sort of is," said Tiffany, walking into the room. "Maizie subjected you to that hell house and now look what happened."

"What happened?" I said. "Is she still in shock?"

"She's in shock all over again." Tiffany held up a piece of paper. "This was on the door of LA HAIR yesterday when we arrived at work. She's been sitting on my couch ever since. She hasn't moved."

"Rhonda needs to eat," said a brother.

"And shower," said another.

"She really needs to shower," said a third.

"Shut it, Chad," mumbled Rhonda.

"What are you going to do about it?" Tiffany shoved the note at me.

"Dead meat," I read. I looked up. "That's it?"

"Isn't that enough?" said a brother. "That's from the murderer."

"Are you sure?" Personally, I found it a bit vague. Besides Tiffany and Rhonda, four other women worked at LA HAIR. And Tiffany was a bit notorious for feuding with other hair-dressers in town. And her ex-husband. And unsatisfied customers.

However, they did have a point. Rhonda had been the only one of the six to walk in on the scene of a murder.

"He wants to kill me." Rhonda trembled. "The killer thinks I witnessed the murder."

"Why didn't you tell me this before?" I said to Tiffany. "Why didn't you call the police?"

"Like the police can protect Rhonda." Tiffany scoffed. "I called in the big dogs. She's much safer this way."

"Her brothers can still watch Rhonda, but we need to tell the police about this. It's an important piece of evidence in the investigation."

"That's your job," said Tiffany. "And now you know. What were you doing yesterday? I figured we'd hear from you."

"Investigating," I said. And eating Sunday dinner while passively aggressively arguing with Nash, but I kept that to myself. "Oh, shizzles. Someone beat up Lucky. I had left her at

LA HAIR overnight and when I returned on Sunday, she'd been beaten and knifed."

"That's when we found the note," barked Tiffany.

"Lawd," Rhonda moaned. The brothers threw their hands in the air and moaned with her.

"Just what in the hell have you been doing, Maizie?" yelled Tiffany. "What if that had been Rhonda?"

The brothers looked at me. The temperature of the room dropped sixty degrees.

"I've been interviewing potential witnesses. I spent all day yesterday and this morning doing that," I said quickly. "I have a few suspects. And I have a meeting set up with Detective Mowry."

"That's it?" said Tiffany. "You've had the whole weekend."

"This isn't an episode of *CSI*," I said. "It takes a lot of time to interview people."

"Then do something else," shouted Tiffany. "Rhonda's gonna wither away and die if the killer doesn't murder her first."

Rhonda moaned, causing sympathetic growls from her brothers.

I wasn't sure what else to do besides interview possible witnesses. But I didn't want to say that in front of this group. Tiffany had an itchy trigger-fist and Rhonda's brothers looked like they lifted small cars as a workout.

"Hang in there, Rhonda," I said. "And please eat something. At least to make everyone feel better."

"And shower," said Chad. "That would be helpful, too."

If Lorena's killer was threatening me and Rhonda, that meant they thought we knew or were capable of discovering who they were. Ironically, I had no idea who they were. Therefore I had to solve the case due to a misunderstanding between the killer and me.

Miscommunication was supposed to be the hallmark of comedies, not tragedies. Figured I'd get a case of mixed-up dramas.

TWENTY

#CatTails #CrazyExBoyfriend

I decided to forget about lunch and drive straight to Black Pine police station. The dispatcher at the front desk recognized me. After a few minutes, she buzzed me through the fireproof door and Ian Mowry walked me to his desk. I liked visiting his cubicle. His daughter was six, like Remi, and he kept her fresh drawings pinned on the walls.

"Maddie's getting better at drawing people," I said.

He squinted at the drawings. "You think? They still look like blobs to me."

"But they're blobs with hair and eyelashes," I pointed out. "The blob with long eyelashes, hair, and a gun must be you."

"Really?"

"You have great hair and long eyelashes. Plus there's a gun."

"Gee, thanks." He winked and ran his fingers through his wavy, dark hair. "Except that's supposed to be a cat. The muzzle is really a tail. That's why it's orange. Maddie's got an orange cat named Pumpkin."

"Maddie is quite the artist," I said diplomatically.

Ian smirked then turned sorrowful brown eyes on me. "Why do we have to talk now? I really looked forward to lunch."

Poor Ian. He loved lunch as much as I did. "I needed to see you right away. I have to ask you a personal question."

"Shoot."

"Are you dating anyone?"

He quirked a smile and leaned an arm on his desk. "No. Why?"

"Do you have a jealous ex? Or maybe just a garden-variety crazy ex?"

His smile flickered and his brows pulled together. "My ex-wife and I have a pretty good relationship now. Cordial, you know. She's getting married again, so I don't believe she'd get jealous of...Just what are you asking?"

I explained the state of Lucky, focusing on the slanderous name cut into her seat. And Nash's theory about what might have happened to Lucky. Then showed Ian the note stuck on the door of LA HAIR. And Tiffany's theory as to who "dead meat" was and why.

"First off," said Ian. "That note's a little vague. And knowing your friend Tiffany's reputation..."

"Say no more. Those were my first thoughts, too. However, it doesn't change the fact that Rhonda is truly freaked out."

"Understandably. I can send someone over for victim's counseling if you think that would help."

"I have a feeling the only thing that'll help is figuring out what happened to Lorena Cortez."

"We'll talk about that in a minute." Ian gazed at me steadily. "As for your bike, did it occur to you to ask Wyatt Nash the same questions you asked me?"

"About a crazy ex? I don't think beating up my bike is Jolene's style. And why do it now? If she wanted to scare me off, she should've started that months ago." Which she had. But she preferred the legal route, like threatening my probation and to sue me. She had a reputation to uphold.

"I was thinking about other crazy exes."

My heart stuttered. "What are you saying?" I whispered.

Then wondered why I was whispering. "Nash has more exes than Jolene?"

"He's thirty-two, not nineteen, Maizie. Haven't y'all talked about his dating history?"

"No. That's in the past. Why would he talk about that?" I said, but in my head, it sounded more like, "NO!" and "WHAT DATING HISTORY?" and "DON'T CRY IN A POLICE STATION." and "OH MY GOD."

"Does he know about your past?"

"Everyone knows about my past. It's been in the headlines." I steadied my eyes on Maddie's orange cat-gun so I wouldn't have to look at Ian. "Let's return to the murder. And let's say, hypothetically, the murderer killed Lucky."

Ian grabbed a pen and his notebook. "There's been another victim?"

"My dirt bike, Lucky."

"Right." Ian sighed. "Here's the thing, Maizie. If the suspect in the Cortez case wrecked your bike and wrote that note, it means they're taunting you. Why would they do that?"

"I took it more as a threat."

"Still, what would be the purpose? If you or Rhonda could reveal the suspect, you'd have done it that night."

Ian had a good point. I slumped in my chair, telling myself to be relieved.

"Don't worry." He patted my hand. "I really doubt it has anything to do with Ms. Cortez's murder. It's probably a crazy ex like Nash said."

I chewed my lip. That didn't make me feel any better. Particularly since it wasn't Ian's crazy ex. "But you'll analyze the note? I can give you Lucky as evidence now that I have Billy."

"Sure, sure." He patted my hand again. "Who's Billy?"

"My new old Bronco."

His eyes sparked. "You got a Bronco?"

I wasn't having this conversation again. "I interviewed most of Lorena's neighbors, the Martins, Jennifer Frederick, and

Spencer and Susie Newson. Did the Martins tell you about their secret door?"

He cocked his head. "Secret door?"

"A side door located in their wet closet. Mrs. Martin would call it a butler's pantry. When we asked about exits from the party, they didn't mention it. But I used it that night. Opens behind some bushes into a side yard."

"I know the door in question. I can't remember if the Martins reported it or we found it." Ian tapped his pen, reached for the pad, and jotted a word. "I'll have to check my notes. We've taken a lot of witness testimony in the last few days."

"Have you heard gossip about Spencer having an affair with Lorena? That's the scuttle from the Martins."

Ian leaned back and tossed his pen on the desk. "I think it's just a rumor. We didn't find any evidence at Ms. Cortez's house and Spencer point-blank denied it."

"He seemed pretty upset when I saw him. I caught him crying."

"Crying?" Ian massaged his chin. "They did work together on the nonprofit a lot, but that's to be expected."

"What about Susie? What did you think of her?"

"I think she's young and obsessed with keeping Spencer." Ian leaned forward. "I think Spencer realized too late he made a mistake marrying her."

I thought so, too, but that didn't prevent me from feeling indignant. "Then he should've stayed out of her pants from the beginning. She was barely legal when he met her. Of course, Susie's obsessed with trying to make the marriage work. She was a child and in love. It was wrong and he knew it."

Okay, that was Marion Ravenwood's line from *Raiders of the Lost Ark*. But still a great line.

Ian held up his hands. "Hey, I'm just calling it like I see it. Anyway, they're both persons of interest, but I'm focused on some other leads right now."

"Like Gary?"

"Who's Gary? Wait a minute. Why is that name familiar?" Ian grabbed a folder from a basket on his desk. He skimmed a finger down a list. "The neighbor from across the street? I haven't talked to him yet. He was out of town."

"So he says." I reported Gary's fashion obsession and the sneaky package pick up. "I'll forward you the video."

"I'm impressed, Maizie." Ian smiled. "Good work. I'm moving Gary up my to-do list."

"That was Nash's catch." I scowled. All I had were rumors, a vague note, and a busted bike that might have been the result of a Nash stalker. "What are the leads you're working on?"

Ian rocked in his chair, grinning. "Recently, someone down-loaded files from the victim's computer and tried to get into her bank accounts. Probably why her safe was opened."

I gasped. "That's big stuff. Better than Gary."

"Gary's still good." Ian patted my hand. "I can't wait to see his costume collection. It'll be an interesting visit."

I gave him a Julia Pinkerton stink eye. "Are you thinking robbery now?"

"Well..." Ian drew out the word, and I could tell he was choosing his words. Which probably meant he wouldn't tell me everything he really thought. Or he'd tell me something I didn't want to hear. "We learned Ms. Cortez had an old boyfriend — before moving to Black Pine, mind you. She filed a restraining order in California when this guy threatened her after she broke up with him. Her friends in California said that's why she moved here."

"I thought she fell in love with Black Pine after doing wardrobe for that indie film." My chest tightened. "Lorena never said anything about an old boyfriend to me. She must have been really scared if she wouldn't tell me...I mean, tell everyone she decided to retire here."

"The ex-boyfriend claimed Ms. Cortez stole money when she left. They'd shared an online business. Selling custom-designed something or other. Anyway, her friends said his claims weren't true. However, Ms. Cortez did quit the partnership after winning some award. Her side of the business skyrocketed after that. His did not. I imagine the guy felt pretty bitter."

"Oh my God." I felt an onrush of tears and pinched my thumb hard. "I had no idea. I didn't even know about her side business. How could I not know about that? I thought the outfits I saw on her social media accounts were costumes from the shows she worked on."

"Hey, it's okay. She probably didn't want to relive the issues with her boyfriend. Or burden you with them. It isn't unusual for people to keep secrets like this."

"Maybe I could have helped her."

"Hon', you don't know that. We don't even know if the ex-boyfriend has anything to do with the case. He's just a suspect right now." Ian leaned forward, placed his hands over mine, and squeezed. Belatedly, I realized I'd been pinching my thumb. "Maizie, it's really hard to work on a case when you know the victim personally. You often learn new things about them. Often stuff you don't want to know. Unfortunately, in a case like this, the violence usually isn't random, even if it wasn't premeditated."

"I know." I pulled my hands from under his in an effort to steel my nerves. Nash and Annie wouldn't need a cop to hold hands with them after learning tragic news about a victim. "I'm okay. It was just a shock. I can do this. It wasn't like Lorena was my best friend. She knew me professionally. When I was young. Of course, she had a life I wasn't privy to."

Ian nodded sympathetically. "The boyfriend's name is Kyler Blick."

"The mask maker?" I really didn't know anything about my supposed friend, Lorena, if she'd been dating Kyler Blick. "Kyler's a lot younger than Lorena."

Ian lifted a shoulder.

"Right." I sighed. Didn't matter.

"More to the point," said Ian. "Blick would know his way around sewing tools, right?"

"You mean, he'd know which would make a good murder weapon."

Ian nodded.

"What's Kyler's motive other than jealousy or revenge? Did Lorena have the kind of money worth murdering over?"

"Hard to tell," said Ian. "That money wasn't in her US bank account. She had a foreign account. In Mexico. We're trying to access that one, but we have to sort through some red tape."

"Foreign..." I squinted at Ian. "Are you trying to tell me Lorena could have been stealing Kyler's money?"

Ian shrugged. "That'd be a good motive for murder, wouldn't it?"

TWENTY-ONE

#LunchLowdown #HippoHypothesis

*J*returned to the office for lunch. And learned, for Annie, lunch meant eating at our separate desks in separate rooms. While running background checks. I punched in a background check on Kyler Blick instead of one from my giant stack of folders. I ate the burrito Annie had brought me and let myself wallow in even more shallow waters than before. This pool didn't even include the possibility of Nash having a crazy-ex-dirt-bike-killer-girlfriend. There wasn't room for relationship doubts in this pond. This mud-hole was only big enough for Maizie insecurities.

My new spirit animal was a hippo.

Kyler was almost twenty-five years younger than Lorena. I didn't know how to feel about that, so I set that aside. The emotion I felt toward Lorena was similar to betrayal. I'd thought Lorena and I had been close. But not close enough for her to tell me she'd really escaped to Georgia, not retired here. Who was this person who might have stolen money from an ex-business partner and lover? The one who had an affair with the married director of her philanthropy?

I couldn't fathom this other side of Lorena.

Betrayal was not what I should be feeling about a murder

victim. So what if Lorena had made me feel like I was a good friend? She did that with everyone. That was her gift as much as her talent for costume design.

However, this conclusion didn't make me feel any better either.

Facts were facts. I hadn't really known her. At all. To Lorena, I must have been Maizie Albright, washed-up teen actress, trying on a different role. Same as everyone thought.

My hippo roared in agreement.

This was why Nash didn't want me taking this case. He knew I'd take a personal case too personally. I wasn't like him. I was soft and emotional, and I would overlook things I didn't want to know. Instead of unburying the truth, I had to learn the uncomfortable details from the police like everyone else.

A snap sounded behind me. I laid down the burrito and turned in my chair.

"Whatcha doing?" said Annie.

"Thinking," I said, truthfully. "I'm wondering if I'm really cut out for this PI business. Or if I'm just trying to show everyone I'm more than a has-been actress. That I can actually do something other than pretending to be someone else."

As soon as the words left my mouth, I regretted saying them. Why would I spill my most vulnerable thoughts to Annie? What in the Hades was wrong with me? A good PI would not be an open book. Sam Spade never got gooey and boo-hooey.

I girded myself for a snide remark from Annie. Instead, Annie said, "Isn't that why you're doing the two-year apprenticeship? To prove you can become a PI?"

If I were being honest, I was doing the apprenticeship to get my license. Checking a box. I'd been focused on a goalpost. I wanted the job title. At first, my goal was to be a private investigator and not a washed-up actress. Mainly because I had played a private investigator and enjoyed the role. Then I decided I wanted my own office so Nash and I could work together again. Almost like *Charlie's Angels*. Except he would be Kelly Garrett and not Bosley. I wanted to be Sabrina, but I'd probably get type-cast as Jill or Kris because of my boobs.

All in all, those were really dumb reasons to become a private investigator.

"I learned some things about my friend, Lorena — the murder victim — that surprised me," I said instead.

"You're investigating her death, aren't you?" Annie chomped on her gum.

"Mostly in my free time," I admitted.

"You could've asked me for help. That's what I'm supposed to be doing. Training you. But you haven't really seemed like you're into this. When you said that stuff about not being cut out—" She snapped her gum. "—didn't really surprise me."

As much as I wanted to do this on my own, I couldn't refuse some assistance. "You'd help me with investigating Lorena's death? Even though it's not on the books?"

Annie shrugged. "Beats serving papers and background checks."

"*W*hat next?" I said to Annie after telling her what I learned from my interviews and Ian Mowry. "Should I ask Vicki about Spencer? Do surveillance on Gary? Dig into Lorena's background in California?"

Annie wrinkled her nose. "What about this ex-boyfriend, Kyle whatsit?"

"Kyler Blick. The mask maker."

She wrinkled her nose again and snapped her gum. "What'd you find out about him?"

"Ian said Kyler's working in Wardrobe on a monster movie."

"Here?"

"No, in New Orleans. A vampire piece."

Annie curled her lip. "I suppose the cops are looking at his alibi."

"Probably." I rocked in my chair, facing Annie, who sat on my desk. She'd set my giant pile of files on a file cabinet. And my unfinished burrito. "What about the money trail? Aren't we always supposed to follow the money trail?"

Annie blew a bubble and cracked it. "Yeah, but if it's in Mexico, not a lot we can see. The police will poke into that account if they can. Did'ya look up her business online?"

I pulled up Lorena's website and flipped the screen towards Annie.

She squinted, then tapped the mouse. "Huh."

"What? What do you see?"

Annie lifted a shoulder. "I thought it'd be, you know, costumes. These are just clothes. Fancy clothes but clothes."

"Anything an actor wears is a costume. A lot of times we wear outfits repurposed from thrift shops or other stores. Although stars might get couture for their important pieces. Monsters get the fun stuff."

"People are willing to pay a lot more for custom designs than I thought. I figured if someone was gonna pay a lot of money, you'd want a brand people would recognize."

"If you can easily afford a name brand, someone like Lorena — who has exclusively dressed movie stars — would be considered chicer. Therefore, you'd want to wear one of her designs."

"Even if other people didn't know her name."

I nodded. "It betrays their ignorance and makes you look more important."

"I don't understand rich people." She shook her head.

Annie reminded me of Nash. A female Nash. I was their complete opposite.

I sighed. "Anyway, you can see why Lorena's boyfriend would have a beef if he helped her design these pieces."

"I thought he did masks."

"Seamstresses in Wardrobe have specialties, but they all know how to sew and design a lot of different things. There's more money in apparel like these suits and gowns. Wardrobe members are one of the most underpaid crews in the industry. And they work longer hours than most of the other unions."

"There's a motive there for Kyler," said Annie. "Would he have gone to the gala? Maybe not tell anyone who he was?"

"The Martins gave me the guest list. I already checked, though, and didn't see his name on it."

"Why would he use his real name?" said Annie. "Ask the whosits and the whatsits if there was a man on the guest list they didn't know."

I shot up in my chair. "The photographer. Helmut. He took pictures of everyone at the party. I'll ask to look at the photos and see if I can spot someone who looks like Kyler. I'll see Helmut at the photoshoot anyway. I promised Daddy I'd go with him and Remi tomorrow."

Annie squinted at me. "You're clocking out for this photoshoot, right? I'm not paying you for a photoshoot. And don't forget the background checks today. But tonight we'll do surveillance at Cortez's house. That'll be fun. I'll bring dinner."

TWENTY-TWO

#StakeoutSnacking #BarelyBear

*I*f Annie was willing to take time to teach me things, I figured I wasn't a total lost cause. I decided to take the high road. I spent the afternoon doing background checks. I didn't even call Nash to ask him about his dating history. When I finished the background checks, I researched Kyler, Gary, and Spencer Newson. I also bought a salad. Then ate the cold burrito anyway.

There was only so much self-improvement one could do in a single afternoon.

At four-thirty, Tiffany called. "I haven't heard from you all day. What's going on? Did you catch the killer yet?"

"No. But I've done research and had meetings."

"How will meetings help Rhonda?"

"The meetings were with Detective Mowry and my boss, Annie Cox. About the case."

"In the meantime, someone called LA HAIR and asked for Rhonda."

I took a beat to ponder the significance of that statement. I couldn't come up with anything. "So…"

"Why would anyone do that, Maizie? No one comes to LA

HAIR for Rhonda." In the background, I heard a "Hey" from Rhonda. "She's not a stylist yet. She's a receptionist."

"What you're saying is…"

"Come on, Sherlock. Obviously, the killer is looking for Rhonda."

I wasn't sure that was obvious. If the suspect really called for Rhonda, why would they make a hair appointment? But I'd give Tiffany the benefit of the doubt. She was watching out for Rhonda, after all.

"I'm doing a stakeout tonight. I'll let you know if anything turns up."

*E*ven though Annie wanted to take my Bronco for a spin, we decided her Jeep would be a better stakeout vehicle. Mainly because it had doors, windows, and a roof.

"Surveillance on a dirt bike," said Annie, handing me a chili dog. "How'd that work?"

"It didn't," I admitted and slurped on my Icee. "Usually I'd park it somewhere, then act like I was taking a walk."

"Did the neighbors get suspicious?"

"To be honest, I haven't had a lot of stakeouts on my own, Annie." I took a bite of chili dog. Annie knew how to choose a tasty dinner. "With Nash, we'd take his truck. That was…romantic."

Annie cocked a brow. "How'd you watch your subject with the windows all steamed up?"

"Not romantic like that." My face heated. "We just had a lot of time to talk. And listen to music. Sometimes we'd listen to a baseball game." And hold hands, but I wasn't revealing that. "Nash is very proper when it comes to his professional life. He'd never do anything to jeopardize a case, particularly PDA. He's not big on PDA in general."

"I like audiobooks," said Annie. I looked at her, and she

jerked her chin toward her radio. "I mean, during surveillance. It's a lot of time to kill, so I listen to audiobooks."

"Good idea." I smiled, and she smiled back. "The one thing Billy has is a good sound system. He might not have doors, but he does have a giant speaker."

"Are you talking about your truck?"

"Yes." My face reddened again. "My Bronco."

Annie slapped her dash. "This is Dixie."

"You get it," I said excitedly.

"Sure. I mean, this is a Wrangler, but it's pretty close to the one Daisy Duke drove."

"I wouldn't take you for a *Dukes of Hazzard* girl."

"Not many do." She quirked an eyebrow. "It's because of my brothers. And my dad. He was a fan and had all the shows on VHS."

We chewed our chili dogs and gazed out at Scarlet Oak Drive. Most homes blazed with lights. However, Gary's and Lorena's houses were dark.

"How bad was it?" said Annie. "The crime scene."

"Pretty bad. A lot of blood. Not like on TV."

"Did you puke?"

"No. Of course not," I exclaimed. But I'd wanted to hurl. I almost had. All over Rhonda. I kept that information to myself. One vulnerable confession a day was all the humility I could handle.

"I would've puked," said Annie. "I can't stand blood."

"That is the nicest thing you've ever said to me."

"You're really weird, you know?" Annie peered through her windshield, then picked up her binoculars. Like Nash, she had a pair of Celestron SkyMaster for long-range viewing. I made a mental note. "The whosits have company."

I squinted down the street. "The Martins."

Annie handed me the binoculars. "Are they suspects?"

"I guess." I sighed. "Ian's more focused on Kyler and the money angle. I thought the Martins acted overeager in their interview, plus they didn't mention their secret door. But that probably means nothing."

"Ian Mowry? The cop?"

"He's a detective for Black Pine PD." I confirmed the Newsons' arrival in my logbook and handed the binoculars back to Annie. "We dated for a minute."

"Jeesh. You get around."

I turned in my seat to face her. "Not really. I've always been hung up...I mean, interested in Nash. Ian asked me to lunch a few times and I went. No biggie."

"What's wrong with Ian?"

"Nothing. He's very sweet. And good looking. We have some similar interests, like food and crime. But he's not Nash."

Annie rolled her eyes. "I don't get it. But then there's a lot I don't get."

Ready to list Nash's wonderful traits, I leaned forward. Then adjusted my angle. Movement through Annie's window had caught my attention. I picked up the binoculars and focused on the yard across the street.

Someone scurried between trees, bent low.

"Be back in a minute," I whispered.

Opening the door, I slid out quietly. Like the night stalker, I kept low and hurried to cross the street. Ducking behind some bushes, I observed the shadowy figure as they snuck up to Lorena's house. I waited for them to round the back of the house, before approaching on the side.

Slipping through the shadows, I heard a door rattle. I rounded a corner and with the flashlight I'd grabbed from the Jeep, beamed it on the stoop. A six-year-old boy squinted at me. Aiden held a hand before his face, warding off the glare.

"What are you doing?" I said. "You shouldn't be over here."

"Neither should you," said Aiden. "It's called tra...tris...tredessing?

"Trespassing," I hissed. "And you can get in a lot of trouble for it. What are you doing over here? Does your mom know you're out? I bet she doesn't."

He poked out his chin and folded his arms over his chest. I recognized the belligerent glare. Remi used it all the time.

"I'll walk you back home. Before your mom finds out."

"I'm not scared. I don't need you to walk me home. I live next door. It's not scary."

"Is this like Ghost in the Graveyard or something? If you touch Miss Lorena's house, it proves you're not scared?"

"Maybe," he drawled.

"Seriously, what are you doing here?"

His lips pinched while he thought about my question. "I got to check on some stuff."

"Like what?"

"I water Miss Lorena's flowers for her."

"At night? In the winter?"

He considered that point. "I forgot to get something. I'm just coming back to get it."

I shined my light on the door. "You see that yellow tape? That's police tape. It means no one should go into the house. The police are still working in there. If you go through the tape, you'll ruin their chance for catching who hurt Lorena."

"I wasn't going through the door."

"Where were you going?" I watched him scan the house and yard, searching for an alternative answer to my question. "Look, you know you're not supposed to be over here. And if you go home now, I won't tell your mom."

His little shoulders slumped. "Fine." He jumped from the stoop, narrowly missing a pot of rosemary. He ran around the corner of the house, gave a shrill shriek, and ran back.

I shined the light on him. "What happened?"

"I saw something moving in the bushes." He stared at his feet. "It was big. Maybe a coyote. Or a bear."

"A bear?" I moved the flashlight over the camellia bushes in

Lorena's backyard. I hadn't heard of a bear in downtown Black Pine, but there were plenty in the mountains. Georgia Wildlife Management had worked hard to restore their numbers in recent years.

Sweat broke on my neck and my palms felt clammy. What was the proper bear procedure? Nash was always harping on safety. Of course, he'd meant with the lowlifes and criminals sometimes associated with this job, but one shouldn't wait to learn if a bear was an upstanding citizen before they attacked.

"Okay don't panic. My father taught me a rhyme. 'Red touching black, safe for Jack. Red touching yellow, kill a fellow.'"

"That's snakes," said Aiden.

"Right. Hang on…" I squeezed my eyes shut, trying to remember the other rhymes about deadly wildlife. "'Black fight back. Brown lay down.' What color bear?"

"I don't know. It's in the bushes."

"Are you sure?" I took out my phone. "I'll call…" The police? Animal control? Annie?

"Maybe it was a panther."

"A panther?" I squeaked. "Like a mountain lion? Or more like a bobcat?"

Aiden rooted in the rosemary pot and held up a key. "We should go in the house. Until it leaves."

I shined a light on the key. "Wait a minute." A six-year-old was trying to outsmart me. Not for the first time. But I wasn't related to this first grader. Taking the key, I dropped it back into the pot. "We're not going into Lorena's house. It's a crime scene."

"I want to see it."

"Come on." I shone the light on the path around the other side of the house. "Let's go."

"But there really was something over there. Something big. I heard it."

I placed a hand on his shoulder and steered him down the path on the other side of the house. "I'll give you something big to worry about. His name is Wyatt Nash and he told you to leave Miss Lorena's death alone."

TWENTY-THREE

#KeyControl #AlleyFinale

"What were you doing?" said Annie after I had taken Aiden home. "Chasing after a kid?"

"He was going to contaminate the crime scene. I met him earlier when Nash and I were canvassing the neighbors. Aiden's a troublemaker. He tried to tell me a bear hid in the bushes."

Annie smirked. "Did you believe him?"

"Of course not," I said, hiding my crossed fingers in my lap. "I'm wise to stories of six-year-olds. They'll say anything for attention. Or in Aiden's case, to hide the fact he planned on breaking and entering Lorena's house."

"Kids'll say anything. I've got nieces and nephews. They're crazy." Annie stretched. "How long d'you want to do surveillance? Seems pretty quiet."

I tapped my chin. "Maybe Aiden did see something in the bushes."

"Really don't think bears are hiding in the bushes in this part of town—"

"Not a bear. What if it was a person? Like the killer?"

Annie cracked her gum. "You think Lorena's killer is sitting in her bushes, doing what?"

"Watching the scene of the crime. Maybe they're worried they left some clue behind."

"Wouldn't the police have found all the evidence by now?"

"What if the police didn't recognize whatever they left as evidence?" Goosebumps broke out on my skin. My voice dropped to a hoarse whisper, "What if they're watching the house like it's a game to them? To see if the police can catch them?"

Annie blew a small bubble. "Yeah, I dunno. That sounds like a movie, not real life."

"Then why are we doing a stakeout?"

"I told you, beats background checks. Consider this a team bonding experience."

Feeling disappointed, I scrutinized the bushes on the far side of the house. However, I couldn't shake the feeling something had been there. "What if they saw Aiden take the key? Holy Hellsbah, I should call Ian."

"Ian, huh?" Annie smirked, then snapped the gum. "Not Wyatt Nash?"

I cut her a look. "What're you talking about, Annie?"

"Just seems you're quick to pick *Ian* as the one to call."

"He's the lead detective on the case."

She gave me a half-shrug. "Just sayin'. After all, you did date for a minute."

"Don't be ridiculous," I hissed and shoved my phone in my pocket. "I'm checking it out."

"Somebody's defensive."

I sucked in my lips to keep from responding.

"I'll watch from here." Annie picked up her binoculars. "Maybe you should go around back. Look over the fence in the alley. Just in case *the bear* is still hiding in the bushes."

"Fine. Good idea. Great." I only had to walk around the block to get to the alley. In the dark. Where Lorena's killer might be lurking. Or a bear. No biggie. Grabbing my backpack, I slipped from the Jeep and wished I could go home and eat a salad. The chili dog wasn't feeling so hot in my stomach.

"Hey, Maizie. Come here." Annie handed me a Canon through her unzipped window. "If you see anything, don't forget to take pictures."

"I'll call or text if anything," my voice cracked, "happens."

"Sure thing." Annie chuckled. "I'll keep my eyes peeled for the bear."

The laugh didn't build my confidence. But to be fair, not much did.

*A*lleys ran behind the homes in downtown Black Pine, something I once found quaint. Accommodations had been made for modern use, but many of the stately homes still had their garages and drives opening to the back streets, making the front streets an even more pleasant place to walk. Stables and garages were located at the back of the properties in bygone days. Likely, the alleys were also meant to keep the riffraff off the front streets, but I didn't want to think about that.

I was too busy thinking about how alleys were a good place to murder someone. In films, the dangers of the alley had become a trope. I couldn't tell you how many *Julia Pinkerton* climax scenes were filmed in backlot alleys. *Kung Fu Kate*, too. Particularly city alleyways with fire escapes, Dumpsters, chain link fences, and locked doorways ready to help or hinder the protagonist.

You didn't see a lot of turn-of-the-century resort town alleyways in films. But they still had all the obstacles. Garbage cans. Tall fences. Hidden gates. Lots of shadows. Dark and gloomy. Probably raccoons, too. The country version of the city alley rat, but three times as big. If an angry raccoon surprises you, it'll make you tinkle. One night at Daddy's cabin, I met one as I took out the garbage.

Lorena had a fence painted to match her house, therefore

easy to spot. Her gate sported a Craftsman-style arbor. Super cute. I tried the latch and found it unlocked. But I stopped myself from opening the gate.

If Lorena's killer (or a bear) lurked in the bushes in her side yard, should I be waltzing through the gate? My mashup detective character said no. Check the perimeter. Move quietly. Carefully.

As Maizie, I decided to pull out my selfie-stick. I left the Canon hanging around my neck and grabbed the retractable wand from my backpack. I hadn't found a lot of articles in *PI Magazine* on the use of selfie-sticks, but I'd personally found them handy for taking candid photos. If you posed while taking the picture, most people didn't realize you had your phone aimed at someone else.

After getting several over-the-fence shots at different angles, I lowered my phone. Thumbed through my pictures and breathed easier. Nobody there. But the planters of herbs on the back stoop reminded me Aiden had taken the key out of the middle pot. He'd return if I didn't grab it. Why hadn't the police found that key?

The gate creaked at my push. I waited, listening for movement, and peeked through. Coast was still clear. I scampered past Lorena's shed, down the path through the shrubs ringing her backyard. Reaching into the rosemary, my fingers combed through dirt and dead sprigs. I squatted to root through the other pots, then looked around and beneath them. Using the flashlight function on my phone, I searched the area, then followed the path Aiden and I had taken back to Annie's Jeep.

"See anyone?" said Annie.

"No. But Lorena's hidden key is missing. Aiden must have taken it. Now I'll have to talk to his mom." I handed her my phone. "I took a bunch of pictures of the back of the house. Worthless, right?"

She thumbed through the photos. "Did you see the kid put the key back?"

"I put the key back. He must have snatched it when I wasn't looking."

"I don't know." She tapped on a photo. "Look at this."

I leaned over the seat console. "What am I looking at?"

"Look at the ground." Her finger traced a shadow blocking the pool of light from the exterior floodlight. "Is this one of those motion-sensitive lights?"

"Not sure. The light was on both times when I was in the backyard." I enlarged the photo. "I can't see anything. What's making the shadow?"

Annie grabbed the phone and magnified the picture until it became pixelated. "Why didn't you use the Canon? It has a tele-photo lens."

I shivered. "What do you think that is?"

"Not a bear."

$\mathcal{A}$nnie dropped me off at the office, but instead of driving back to the cabin, I drove one block and parked in front of the Dixie Kreme Donut building. The second floor was dark. I stared at the old Nash Security Systems office and inhaled the donut-scented air. Tasting invisible donuts soothed me. Their invisibility also frustrated me, but my stomach was still getting over the chili dog-possible bear disaster.

After a few minutes of wondering if my subconscious had me on another kind of stakeout, I heard the rumble of a truck engine. Nash's Silverado pulled up beside me. I kept my eyes glued on the office until he climbed into the passenger seat next to me.

"If you'd have called, I would have come sooner," Nash's deep voice rumbled, breaking the stillness.

"I know." I sighed. "I was on a stakeout."

"Lorena's?"

"Yeah. Might of saw a person in her bushes. Or a bear. They

might have stolen the key to her house. Or the little kid across the street did." I shrugged. "Who knows? Certainly, I don't."

Nash squeezed my shoulder. "What's going on?"

I hooked my right leg under my butt to face him. "Nothing. Everything." I gave him a hard look. "Where were you?"

"Getting something to eat." He cocked his head.

"What's going on at DeerNose? Why were you interrogating Daddy yesterday?"

His look slid from passive to wary. "What do you mean interrogation? That was office chitchat."

I glared at him. "I know you. That was not shop-talk. You wore your 'something's hinky' look."

"Look, it's just work." Nash bared his teeth, trying to smile. "Let's not talk about your dad. I get enough of Boomer at the office."

"What's that supposed to mean?"

"It means, I don't want to talk about it." The smile hardened, and his scar flexed with his jaw. "How was your day, dear?"

"Fine." I tilted my chin up. "My murdered friend Lorena had a secret life and might have been embezzling money from the business she had with her ex-boyfriend. Allegedly. Or something like that."

Nash eased back in his seat. "Wow."

I scooted forward and used my Julia Pinkerton stink-eye on him. "And Ian said he doesn't have any crazy ex-girlfriends, but you might."

"He said what?" The cool blue eyes narrowed into two icy slits. He drew himself closer. "Anything else Mowry said about me? Or you?"

"We were talking about the case, not relationship stuff."

"Uh-huh." Nash turned, climbed out of the Bronco, and walked around to my side. He looked at me, his composure seemingly calm. However, the rigidity of his body made him look like one solid block of muscle. "Listen, Maizie, I don't want you talking to Mowry about us."

"We don't really—"

Nash firmed his lips and cut his head to the side. "I mean it."

"He's your friend. You think he broke the bro-code or something?"

"Something." He let out a long breath, placed a hand on the back of my seat, and tilted toward me. "You want to come in?"

I looked up at the office that wasn't an office. "You want to come back to the cabin?"

"No." His fingers walked up my shoulder to the nape of my neck. One long finger stretched to rub against the base of my skull. "Why don't you want to come upstairs, Maizie?"

I turned to face him, allowing his fingers more accessibility. My hand skimmed up his arm. I squeezed his tricep. "I want to be with you."

"I want to be with you, too." Nash placed his other hand on my thigh and slid it to my waist. He nudged my legs apart, placed a knee on the Bronco's running board, and nuzzled my neck. Placing a kiss near my ear, he whispered, "I really, really want to be with you."

I caught my breath and tipped my head back to give his lips greater access to my neck. My hands moved over his arms and broad shoulders to slide down his back. His hands roamed from my waist and neck to other parts. I moaned. Panted a little. Nash might have growled. But with every inhalation of donut air, I reminded myself we were necking on a public street. Half-falling out and completely exposed in Billy's topless, doorless frame.

"Come on, baby," drawled Nash, his breath hot and sweet against my collarbone. "I'm trying to make things nice for you upstairs. It's not so bad."

"I don't want to go inside the office," I moaned. "It's no longer a suitable environment for work."

"The only work I'm planning on—" Nash pulled back. "Wait. What?"

It was worse than I thought. We had not only switched roles, but we'd also swapped dialogue.

"It's the office. We don't fool around in the office."

"We have too fooled around in the office," he grumbled.

"When it was an office."

"You're not making sense." He pinched the bridge of his nose. "What's the problem with the office?"

"It's not an office anymore."

He gazed at me, unable to mask his pain and confusion. "Sugar, it hasn't been my office since I went to work for your parents. Plural. Both of them. First one and then the other. Are you telling me, I lost my business and now I've lost you?"

"You haven't lost me." I grabbed his hand and placed it on the spot that had made him growl. "I am right here."

He yanked his hand back. "But you won't go upstairs."

"I will when it's an office."

"I don't think I can do this 'Who's On First' office-thing." He sighed. "What do you want from me, Maizie?"

"You're wearing camo ties and filling out forms." My lip trembled. "You're worried about impressing my father. And buying a house. I don't want a house. I want you to get your office back."

"That takes money I don't have right now." He slanted me a hard look. "And in the meantime?"

"We could go to my office?"

He shook his head. "I don't think so. This whole office thing is too much work."

TWENTY-FOUR

#ScoobyDon't #TarnishedSilver

*T*he next day I woke confident in my immaturity and ability to destroy relationships. Also in my inability to communicate my true motives and intentions. All the things I had been working on with my ex-therapist, Renata.

All the things I couldn't work on with my new therapist. He was still in jail.

Before sleeping, I'd texted Ian about the key and the possible bear/intruder at Lorena's. I had a good chance of seeing Aiden and his mom at the photoshoot since his family encompassed the majority of Lorena's woodland creature designs. I also planned to ask Helmut the photographer about the party snaps so we could scan them for Kyler. Ian had responded with "good work, Daphne." Resulting in thirty minutes of *Scooby-Doo* banter.

Making me wonder why Nash and I never had thirty-minute conversations about *Scooby-Doo*. Lately, our relationship seemed to have a one-way track leading to Nash's non-office office. Shouldn't there be more than snogging and Sunday dinners? Did I want the office back because I only wanted Nash as a business partner, not a partner-partner?

At the breakfast table, I tripled my caffeine and contemplated all these things. *Frigtastic*. What was I doing?

I knew what I was doing. Ruining the best relationship I ever had over *Scooby-Doo*.

Across from me, Remi fed her sausage and egg scramble to an assortment of Jack Russells under the table. Next to me, paper hid Daddy's face. He still read newspapers on actual newsprint.

"Remi," said Daddy. "A girl's got to eat if she wants to grow."

"Maizie says that's the problem."

Daddy turned a hard eye on me, and I chose to segue to a new topic. "Do you think women and men can be friends? For example, can a woman who's in a serious relationship be friends with a single guy? Hypothetically, let's say they work together, but they also like to joke around and eat lunch. And text late at night. Does that mean she's subconsciously sabotaging her real relationship with her boyfriend?"

Daddy laid his paper to the side, took a long breath, and let it out.

Remi set down her glass of milk and leaned her elbows on the table. "This is gonna be good."

"No, it's not," said Daddy to Remi. He turned to me. "What's all this?"

"I have a bad history with men. I make poor choices. I need help."

He glanced at Remi. "We need to set up some parameters for this conversation. I don't want details."

"I want details," said Remi. "What do you do with these men?"

"She does nothing," said Daddy. "You are excused."

"Are they bad men?" said Remi, ignoring her father. "Did you let them go instead of arresting them?"

"No. Not that kind of bad. I'm not the police. Bad like unhealthy for you."

"Like candy?" said Remi.

"They can be like candy," I said in reflection, my voice turning soft and gooey as a marshmallow.

"Not like candy," said Daddy. "Boys are not like candy. Remi, you may go."

I caught his meaning. "Yes. More like poison."

"I don't know if I am the right person to have this conversation with you," said Daddy. "Where's Carol Lynn?"

"But Carol Lynn never made bad choices with men."

"You're damn right she didn't." He looked at Remi. "Go find your mother."

"But some might say you made a bad choice in Vicki. Although if you hadn't made that choice, I wouldn't be here."

"Remi, if you go to your mother, you can have a Pop-Tart," he said, desperation ringing in his voice.

She scooted from the room, the dogs yapping and following her.

Daddy looked at me. "I am not comfortable with this conversation."

"I can tell. Just tell me what to do. I fall in love quickly. For the wrong reasons and the guys turn out to be bad news. But this time, I think I'm the bad news."

"What have you done to Wyatt Nash." It was not a question.

The hair on the back of my neck stood up. "Nothing? Yet?"

"I knew it." He slammed a hand on the table. "I knew I shouldn't have hired him."

"No, no. Hiring Nash has been great. He's very good at what he does. I mean, if we weren't dating, you still would have hired him. Wouldn't you?"

"Yes." He pressed his lips together. "But the very fact you're dating made me not want to hire him."

"Just forget I said anything."

"I'm fixing to do just that." He glowered at me. "Baby girl, when are you going to screw that head on straight?"

"I don't know, Daddy," I said miserably. "I keep trying and it keeps getting more crooked."

"Tell Wyatt Nash you're sorry. Immediately. Stop talking to the single guy. Immediately."

"Okay."

"And ask the good Lord to forgive me for allowing your mother to take you to California. I blame Vicki." He eyeballed me. "Don't you dare bring this up with her, though. She's the last person you should get relationship advice from. You need to give her some. I like the new guy, Kevin, but Vicki's been seen around town with Spencer Newson. Black Pine is a small town in a lot of ways. People talk. She's doing the same thing to Kevin Yuan you're doing to Wyatt Nash."

I felt my eyes grow wide with shock. Not because Daddy accused me of acting like Vicki. Although I would have to unpack that horrible thought at another time. When I felt more mentally and emotionally prepared. Perhaps never. "Vicki and Spencer Newson? What have you heard?"

"They've been seen at the club, playing tennis or some such nonsense. Lunching. I don't know. I don't usually abide such gossip." Daddy shook out his paper. "Clothing Kids is already suffering from the loss of Miss Lorena. That idiot Newson should be working on rebuilding, not providing more dirt for the grapevine."

"Were Spencer and Vicki a thing in high school?"

He laid the paper on the table. "Your mother and I were a *thing* in high school. Has someone told you different?"

My face felt hot. This had become a subject in which I didn't want to participate. "You went to high school with Spencer Newson, too. What was he like back then?"

"Evidently like he is now." Daddy picked up the paper and opened it, disappearing. "I don't want to discuss high school."

Neither did I.

"That was a long time ago," he continued. "And if it wasn't for Miss Lorena, I wouldn't have anything to do with Newson now."

"I'll speak to Vicki this morning."

The newspaper slid down a few inches to expose the top of

Daddy's white-flecked auburn brows and his deep blue eyes. "I thought you were going to the photoshoot with us?"

"I am. I'll meet you there." I rose.

"Call Wyatt Nash first. He's been uncannily grumpy lately. Now that I know the cause, I want the problem fixed. And if this single man is anything like Spencer Newson, you best drop that friendship."

The paper rattled, hiding Daddy's face.

*N*ash didn't answer his phone when I called. He also wasn't at the office. I left apology messages in both places. And decided visiting my mother would be a good punishment.

I found her breakfasting in her dining room. The Peanut Mansion was a Gilded Age monstrosity with a stone edifice, two wings, and a phenomenal view of Black Pine Lake. It had been modernized and updated over the century, most recently by Vicki. And now seemed to be under construction again.

I dropped into a chair across from her. "What's going on?"

"I'm having a few things done." Vicki waved vaguely at the walls. "Don't worry. The contractor is licensed in historical restoration."

"I wasn't worried." Although I wondered if the restoration had begun before or after her verbal tussle with Jan Martin, the vanguard of Black Pine historic homes.

"Coffee?" Vicki indicated the antique-looking silver service on the table. "There's also tea. Kevin likes tea."

"Speaking of Kevin, is he in town?" I poured coffee into a dainty china cup and sipped. It didn't taste like historic coffee like I feared. "Tasty."

"Kevin's working on set on the West Coast." Vicki smiled. "It's the silver. It's non-reactive. Everyone should drink from silver."

"Isn't silver expensive and hard to clean?"

"Isn't a little money and elbow-grease worth it? All these plastics and cheap metals today." She sighed. A little too dramatically for my taste. Not only did Vicki have money, but she also had a maid.

"I need to talk to you about Spencer Newson."

Her smile reappeared, although the return trip looked smugger. "Spence?"

"There's been talk in town."

Her green eyes glittered. "Really?" she purred.

"Talk in town is not good." I stopped. "But you look like you enjoy the notoriety."

"Really, Maizie. Have you learned nothing from your years in the industry?"

I had learned many things. Most importantly, I learned one shouldn't let your mother manage your career. Particularly if your mother was Vicki. "Remind me why you want the town to gossip about you and Spencer Newson."

"Bad publicity is still publicity. Don't you care about Clothing Kids? Do you want people to forget about all the work Lorena's done to build her foundation? If people are talking about two board members, then they have the non-profit in the back of their minds."

"I don't think it works that way. Patrons are less likely to contribute if there's a negative association with the charity." I studied her. "Wait. What do you mean two board members?"

"Spence wants me to join the board of Clothing Kids."

I massaged my temples. "You need to stop doing whatever it is you're doing with Spencer. There's a murder investigation and it's getting ugly. Spencer might have been having an affair with Lorena. He's a suspect."

"I don't believe it." Vicki shook her head, then tapped her chin. "Well, I'll admit, Spence is not the most faithful person in the world. But he'd never murder anyone."

"High praise, indeed." I rolled my eyes. "Also, you need to think about Kevin's reputation. You might not care what people say about you, but this affects Kevin, too. And he might not like you gadding about with Spencer Newson."

"Gadding about?"

"It's all the antiques and historic whatnots, they're affecting my vocabulary." I gave her a stern look. "Do you love Kevin?"

"Of course." Her chin rose.

"Then have some respect for him. It's difficult enough working on a closed set away from your loved one. But hearing they could be cheating?" I glared at her. "Don't put Kevin through that."

"Speaking from experience?"

I jerked a nod. I'd been in high school, shooting a TV movie while *Julia Pinkerton* was on hiatus. He'd been a producer's son. We hadn't gone on a real date, just made out in my trailer, but it still hurt. "What does Spencer say about Lorena's death?"

Vicki examined her nails. "We've mainly talked about the foundation. And of course, we've chatted about all that's happened over the years. The murder's not come up."

"Not come up? How does a murder that happened less than a week ago not come up? A murder involving someone you both know." I set my cup on the table. "You didn't mention it?"

Her shoulder lifted. "I asked if he'd heard anything. He said he told the police everything he knew, which wasn't much. Spence looked upset. We moved on to another topic."

"Do you think he was having an affair with Lorena?"

"If he was, it's not my business. And it's not yours either."

"Actually it is. I'm investigating Lorena's murder."

"Digging up dirt on a friend will solve her murder?"

"Unfortunately, it seems that way, yes." I gave her my best stern schoolmarm look. "And I would like to avoid digging up dirt on you at the same time. So, cool it with Spencer Newson."

"If I join the board of Clothing Kids, we have to meet." She rolled her eyes. "But for the sake of propriety, we'll meet at my office. Perhaps you'd like to chaperone?"

Not really. "Fine."

TWENTY-FIVE

#PhotoFollies #SuspectCentral

*C*lothing Kids had rented a cargo room in an empty warehouse for the photoshoot. DeerNose had supplied the backdrop and props from their marketing department. Lorena's friends in the glam squad — hair and makeup — had volunteered their time and talent. The photographer, Helmut, had proffered his time minus his production costs. Local children were the models. And, of course, Lorena had provided the handmade costumes. In all, a good example of community giving with cooperation and compromise. The mutual feeling of all involved was to continue with the photo spread for Lorena and the sake of the Clothing Kids foundation.

I had a feeling the magazines interested in covering the philanthropy were likely eager to write the article from a new angle. What would have been a feature on an award-winning designer's lifetime achievement in the entertainment industry and her new career as a philanthropist, would now be an exposé on a murder.

When I arrived at the warehouse, children ran amok, half-dressed. Their parents struggled to quell their excitement while dealing with the intricacies of dressing them in costume. Hair and Makeup astutely set up a monitor with Disney videos while they worked their magic on the children. Helmut and an assistant fiddled with lighting checks and scenery placement. I watched the proceedings before finding my family.

Daddy sat in a folding chair with a laptop, ignoring the scene. He looked up when I joined him. "Hey there, baby girl." He squinted at me. "Maybe those gals over in Hair and Makeup can help you with your hair. Looks like you tussled with a wildcat again."

"Tying a scarf didn't work. Luckily, I brought a ball cap for the ride home." I leaned over to peck him on the cheek. "Where's Remi?"

He pointed to an area where racks of hanging clothes created a dressing room. "Carol Lynn's over there, too, helping Remi get her stuff on. The child's all riled up."

Remi was always riled up. "It looks like all the kids are excited."

"Remington got in a tussle with a boy. I had to pull them apart." He chuckled. "That little thing packs a mighty wallop for her size. I don't know what that boy did to set her off, but she was having none of it."

I had a feeling I knew the boy and set out to find a bat. And his mother.

Near the wardrobe area, I found Aiden sitting cross-legged on the floor by himself, his wings drooping around his slim shoulders. "Where's your mom?"

"Changing a diaper." He squinted at me. "What are you doing here?"

"My sister is Remi, remember? Why were you fighting with her?"

He rolled his eyes. "She started it."

That could be true. I had more pressing issues to discuss. "Did you take the key from Miss Lorena's house last night?"

Shaking his head, he stared at his lap, his lip quivering.

"What's wrong?"

He looked up. "Nothing."

"What did you want in Miss Lorena's house?"

He shrugged and bit his lip to abate the tears threatening to fall.

"Aiden, I've got to talk to your mom about you going over to Lorena's. I don't think I can trust you not to do it again."

His trembling lips firmed in a line. Popping up from his seat, he leaped past me and ran off.

Aiden left me with no choice. I moved toward the teeming group of kids and their mothers. Aiden's mom wasn't among them. While I waited for her, I asked Carol Lynn to introduce me to the moms. I explained my new career — with starts and stops from all the interruptions by the kids — and asked them about Lorena.

"Did you see anything unusual the day of the gala?"

"Not at all," said one mother, fixing her child's antlers. "I can't believe it. One minute Miss Lorena's here, and the next she's gone."

"You know what they're saying?" said a mother holding a baby ladybug. She glanced down at the fox staring up at her, listening. "Never mind what they're saying. But it's what they're saying."

The others nodded.

"What are they saying?" I asked for clarity's sake.

The moms collectively widened their eyes and dropped their gazes to the children. The fox stared back at me, then slowly inserted his finger into his nose. The mom batted the finger.

"So, you heard something…" I suggested.

Fox Mom sighed and leaned in. "I didn't see anything 'suspicious,'" she marked the word with finger quotes. "But Mr. Newson and Miss Lorena were arguing when I arrived."

The moms collectively grimaced, then glanced at their woodland animals.

"You're saying Spencer Newson was at Lorena's house the day of…" I cut my eyes toward the kids. "…the event in question."

Fox Mom bobbed her head, and the other moms shook theirs.

"The thing 'they're saying'," I added my own finger quotes. "Is the *thing* between Newson and Lorena. And seeing the argument confirmed the *thing* for you."

Smiling, the moms bobbed their heads, proud I'd finally worked out what was obvious to them.

I grinned, too, then spotted Susie Newson leaning against the wall near us. Feeling not so proud and more embarrassed, I thanked the moms and handed out business cards. "If you think of anything more specific, call me."

Nodding, the moms herded their flocks, packs, and kits toward hair and makeup.

"Hey Susie," I called, moving toward her. She wore a cute wrap dress and four-inch heels that showed off her long muscular legs. Maybe she was confused as to the kind of photoshoot she visited. "How's it going? What are you doing here?"

"Spencer said he needed to supervise the shoot so I came to watch. Why are you here?"

"My father and sister are in it. His company is a sponsor. Remi's an armadillo."

"I saw an armadillo get in a fight with the bat-kid."

I sighed. "That would be her. She's what they call a 'pistol.'"

"You're still asking questions about Lorena's murder? I saw you talking to those moms."

"Yeah." I felt my cheeks heat. I hoped she'd only seen and not heard.

"What are they saying?"

I also wanted to protect Susie from Spencer's and Lorena's argument. But Nash and Annie wouldn't have such qualms. Susie's husband was causing the gossip and Spencer was a prime suspect. Although maybe not as much as Lorena's other boyfriend, Kyler, whom she'd allegedly ripped off.

My stomach turned over. Just thinking about these men in Lorena's secret life made me regret all the coffee I'd had earlier. I wondered if PI's had issues with reflux. I needed to ask Annie if she regularly took an antacid.

"One of the moms witnessed a dispute between Spencer and Lorena on the day of the gala," I said hesitantly.

"Spencer said he wasn't at Lorena's the day of the gala."

"I know." I waited for a beat, but Susie didn't offer an explanation. "Has Spencer mentioned a disagreement between himself and Lorena?"

"We don't talk about Lorena anymore."

"Because it's too upsetting for Spencer?"

"Because I'm sick of the subject." Susie scowled. "If you'll excuse me."

I watched her clomp away, looking a little like a young girl playing dress-up. Knowing I should find Spencer, I chose instead to speak to Helmut. My stomach would feel less queasy asking him about photos than interrogating Spencer about his alleged argument with Lorena.

I wasn't making progress in the field of investigation.

Also, I couldn't find Helmut. But an assistant pointed me toward the woodland backdrop. "He's back there. Fixing a tear."

Faux trees and bushes had been erected before the vinyl background. I threaded my way through the mini forest. Hearing voices, I stopped before moving around the backdrop.

"For that?" Helmut's strong voice carried naturally. He scoffed. "Do you know who I am?"

"Come on. Name your price," said another voice, sly and wheedling. "I'll take whatever you don't use."

"Get out," Helmut's voice rose. "Out."

A slender man wearing droopy jeans and classic checkerboard Vans hurried out from behind the backdrop. Spying me, he zig-zagged through the trees, speeding toward the open door. Helmut walked from behind the drop, shaking his head.

"Who was that?" I said.

"Paparazzo." He pretended to spit. "He wanted any footage I don't use."

"Why would he want pictures of kids dressed as animals?"

"Not of today. From the party. They've been hounding me since Lorena's murder." He grimaced. "Disgusting. The media loves murder. Especially the tabloids."

I nodded in agreement. "Actually, I wanted to talk to you about the party shots, too. For a different reason. I'm assisting the police in investigating Lorena's death."

Helmut unsuccessfully tried to contain his snort. "You?"

"I'm working as a private investigator now."

"But you performed—" His eyebrows lowered, and he smiled. "I heard about this. I thought it was a joke."

"Not a joke. I wanted to check your party pics. I'm looking for someone in the photos. He was probably disguised, though."

"It was a masquerade. Who do you look for? If it's the local people, I don't know them. But perhaps one of Lorena's friends, I might know and could show you. It would go faster."

"That would be great. Do you know Kyler Blick? He's also in costume design. Specializes in masks."

"He's also Lorena's ex." Helmut nodded. "He's a suspect, right? The boyfriend and husband are always a suspect."

"Yes," I agreed reluctantly. "I can sort through the pictures. I know you're busy."

"Nonsense. Maybe tomorrow. I have my hands full with this today."

Happy to have him so agreeable, I nodded. By far, the easiest ask in Lorena's investigation.

I skirted past the scenery, headed toward Daddy's chair where an armadillo bounced at his feet. Glancing back with a smile for Helmut, I spotted him watching me. The amiable countenance he'd worn for me had been replaced by a glower. I still felt his scrutiny when I turned to continue my scurry to the other side of the room.

. . .

"*M*aizie." Remi pounded toward me. She tried to throw her arms around my legs, but the shell stopped her. She looked up. "Armadillos are better at catching bugs than bats, right?"

"I have no idea." I cocked my head. "Is that why you were fighting with Aiden?"

"Gotta go." She ran toward the group of kids herded by Hair and Makeup to their chairs.

Daddy looked at Carol Lynn. "Honest to Pete, that child…"

"I've gotta go, too," I said, spying Aiden's mom near Hair and Makeup.

Seeing me, Mrs. Jessup waved, then left her nightingale with Makeup. She approached, bouncing a baby bunny in her arms. "The other moms said you were looking for me. I'm so sorry."

"You don't need to apologize."

"I don't know why Aiden doesn't get along with Remi. They seem to antagonize each other."

"That's not why I want to talk to you. It's actually about Aiden and Lorena Cortez."

"Ms. Cortez and Aiden? I don't understand."

"I think Aiden saw something the night of the murder, but he won't tell me." I lowered my voice. "And I found him at Lorena's house last night. He was going to use her extra key to get in the house."

"What?" shrieked his mom. She spun around, searching the group of kids. "Aiden, get over here. Now."

"I just need to know—"

She shoved the baby bunny into my arms, grabbed Aiden by the shoulder, and marched him toward the bathroom.

The baby bunny looked at me and began to howl. I bounced her, searching the room for help. "Um…it's okay. Your mom will be back soon."

The other moms didn't seem to notice the bunny's distress. I stood rooted to the spot, afraid to move. The little bundle of faux fur and cotton turned rabid with rage. I bounced and jiggled, speaking in the most soothing tones I could muster. The screaming prevented me from thinking clearly. And she had a grip on my hair that made my eyes water.

In all my roles, I'd never played a mother. I was always the kid. This was the hardest one yet.

"Help?" I called while spinning in a slow circle. No one seemed to hear me over the baby's ear-splitting cries. How did mothers not lose their minds? How could something so small be so loud?

"With this kind of projection, you could easily do theater, kid. They wouldn't even need to mike you." I halted my pivot, spotting Spencer Newson enter through a side door. He held the door and Jennifer Frederick, the board member who had slapped him, moved through.

"Come on, baby. This can't wait. I'm sure your mom will be done with Aiden soon."

I strode toward the two of them, then paused. Jennifer's arms were folded over her chest, her shoulders hunched, and her expression pinched. He had half-leaned into her, speaking, while his gaze moved around the room.

I flipped the baby to my opposite shoulder, trying to raise my voice over the bunny's bellow. "I need to talk to you."

Neither looked as though they noticed me. Spencer jerked the door open and disappeared through it. Jennifer stalked toward the set. I hurried toward the door with the baby gnawing my shoulder.

"Miss Albright?"

I looked behind me, saw Mrs. Jessup, and stopped. She had a hand clamped on Aiden's shoulder, nudging him forward. "Aiden has something to say to you."

"I'm sorry. I will not go to Miss Lorena's house anymore. And I won't fight with Remi no more." Judging by Aiden's expression, these were not words he wanted to say.

"I don't want you to get hurt, Aiden," I said. "Miss Lorena's house is a crime scene. The police won't want you to go in there. They're still looking for clues and you might accidentally harm their investigation."

His mother's mouth was a thin, grim line of exasperation. "I don't understand why Aiden would think he could go into Miss Lorena's house."

"I went there all the time," said Aiden. "She told me I could. I helped her."

"But she's not there anymore," said his mom. "You don't go into someone's house when they're not home. And you can't go into someone's house after they've passed."

I studied Aiden while his sister drooled on my shoulder and jerked on my hair. "Did you go to her house on the night of the party? While you were playing hide and seek?"

"Oh my stars," bellowed his mom. "You left the party? You went to her house when…Your father is going to…Oh my…I can't even…"

Aiden looked at his mom, then narrowed his eyes at me. "We were just playing hide and seek. I didn't go nowhere."

Alternating shades of white and crimson besieged his mother's face. I dropped the subject before she had an apoplexy. "It's okay, Mrs. Jessup. I'm sure Aiden's sorry for scaring us. I know he won't go into her house again. I need the key to her house so I can give it to the police."

"I don't got the key."

"Aiden Anthony Jessup," Mrs. Jessup's voice sounded strangled. "You give her that key this minute."

"I don't got—"

"Then when we get home, you will give me the key." She looked behind her.

A nightingale pulled on her jeans. "Momma?"

Her attention swerved to the nightingale. "Don't you look pretty?" cooed Mrs. Jessup. She cut her eyes back to Aiden, her voice switching back to grim. "You will give back that key."

"She put the key back in the pot." Aiden pointed to me. "I gave it to her, and she put it back."

"The key's not there anymore—" The baby thrust her little feet into my stomach. I swapped her to the other shoulder and crouched to face Aiden. "Are you sure I put the key back?"

He nodded.

"And you didn't see anything that night?"

He kept his gaze across the room and shook his head. Slower this time.

Clutching the baby, I rose carefully to keep my balance. "I don't think he has the key, Mrs. Jessup."

"Thank God." She lifted the nightingale. "I need to get your brother. He's still watching *The Lion King*. Come on."

Gripping Aiden's shoulder, she began to trudge toward Hair and Makeup.

"Mrs. Jessup," I called.

She looked back, and I pointed to the baby bunny.

"Oh, my stars." She pulled the baby off my shoulder, deftly disentangling her fists from my hair. "You're good with her. She's normally scared of strangers. You're a regular Mary Poppins."

"Thanks." But Mary Poppins would have gotten the truth out of Aiden.

I believed he didn't have Lorena's key. The person hiding in the bushes had seen us and taken it. However, my gut told me Aiden had lied about not leaving the party the night Lorena was murdered.

I just hoped Aiden hadn't been seen by Lorena's killer.

TWENTY-SIX

#InstaFacement #SouthernFriedGuilt

*A*s Helmut began to assemble the motley crew of animals into his scene, my phone buzzed. Noting the number, I exited the noisy warehouse for the parking lot.

"Hey Tiffany, how's Rhonda?" I climbed into Billy and relaxed into the seat, squinting at the sky. Although today was typical with sunny and clear skies, I needed to find Billy a roof before the weather changed.

"Not good. That's why I'm calling."

My attention sharpened on Tiffany. Hearing her quick intake and exhale, I imagined her on a smoke break behind LA HAIR. "You're both back to work? That's good."

"I am. She isn't."

I chewed my lip while guilt gnawed on my gut. "Her brothers are still with her?"

"At my house. And she still hasn't showered. It's getting worse, Maizie. Have you seen Rhonda's blog thingy?"

"No." My skin prickled. "Why?"

"Someone hacked her blog and posted a bunch of porn. It was reported and the website shut her down."

"Oh, no. Poor Rhonda."

"Her brother Chad thinks it's the Russians or something, but I know it's the killer."

"Okay," I stretched the word out, giving me time to think. "To Chad's credit, that sort of thing happens a lot. I don't think it's necessarily Russians, probably just some trolls who get a kick out of hacking—"

"Maizie. Rhonda's been outed by a killer. The Russians don't care about her stupid fake-celebrity blog." She jettisoned an angry stream of air. "It's the killer. Toying with her."

"If the killer wanted to toy with Rhonda, why attack her website?"

"I've got a better question," barked Tiffany. "Why are you questioning the motives of a homicidal maniac?"

"Right. I'll report this to Ian. He'll need Rhonda's login and password, probably. Do you know it?"

"It doesn't take an IT genius to hack into Rhonda's blog. Her login is Rhonda and her password is Rhonda123. I can tell you that without even asking Rhonda."

"You should tell her she needs better passwords."

"You think that didn't cross my mind?" she growled. "What have you done to help Rhonda?"

"Last night, I did a stakeout." And inadvertently helped a possible intruder find Lorena's extra key. "I questioned some people at the photoshoot today." Mostly moms. And a six-year-old.

I brightened. "And the photographer is letting me go through his pictures so I can see if Kyler Blick was at the gala. He's Lorena's ex-boyfriend and has a real grudge. Kyler is the number one suspect."

"Then why's he not arrested?"

"To arrest him, the police need evidence—"

"Rhonda's blog. There you go." Tiffany blew out another noisy gust. "Maizie, you get on this. Rhonda's losing her mind. Stop stalling."

"I'm not stalling." I sighed. "I'm just not very efficient. Yet. I've been working on this new character, who's kind of a PI mashup between Nash and Annie. But I need help understanding their motivations so I can get inside their heads a little better. I have no clue about their real backstories. Not even Nash's. I feel like I have the physical characteristics down, but I need the emotional—"

"What in the hell are you talking about? If you need help, ask Nash and Annie. What's there to understand?"

"They're not always available. To fully develop this PI role, I thought I'd—"

"Stop thinking and find this Blick guy."

"Okay. Right. But the police are on—"

"Why are you relying on the cops? You don't need them. You're a detective, aren't you?"

*I*f Kyler had shown up in Black Pine and murdered Lorena, why would he hang around, terrorizing Rhonda? There had to be a point. However, internet mayhem could be done anywhere in the world. Tiffany had not thought of that. If that were the case, Rhonda was relatively safe.

Unless Kyler was the person who had stolen Lorena's key. Then he was still in Black Pine and Rhonda was still in danger.

Frigtastic.

I called Ian.

"Hey, Daphne," said Ian. "Got any Scooby snacks?"

I grimaced. Maybe *Scooby-Doo* references weren't necessary for a relationship. "I have new information." I told him about Helmut's pictures, Aiden, and my beliefs about the key. Then reported the distressing news about Rhonda's blog.

"I'll have our cybercrime gal look into it. Thing is, it doesn't really fit the crime we're investigating. Although I guess it could match up with the threatening note on the door."

"Those were my thoughts, too. But what about the person hiding near Lorena's house? If Kyler's in New Orleans, who took the key?"

"I don't know, hon'. But I'll send someone over to check the house again. Don't worry."

"Why didn't the police find the key when you did your initial search of the house?"

Ian blew out a long breath. "Honey, I know you're not questioning my unit or GBI's ability to secure a crime scene. You're upset. I get it. If there had been a key in a flowerpot, I'm sure we would have seen it. Isn't it possible the little boy had it all that time?"

"I guess so. But what will I tell Tiffany?"

"You reported the information you learned. How about we talk all this over tonight? Do you want to meet me at Ms. Cortez's house? We can do a walk-through and explore this key issue. I want you to show me where you thought someone was hiding." Ian paused and gentled his voice, "If you can handle going back to the victim's house, that is."

"For real?" I felt a rush of adrenaline, then reminded myself of Daddy's advice. Told myself to play it cool and tried Annie's tone and swagger. "Yeah, I can handle it."

"Did you have dinner plans? If you don't, I'll get takeout. I'll be starving by then."

"Awesome," I said, then checked myself. "I mean, I'm sure I could eat."

"Great, it's a date. See you at the Cortez residence." He hung up.

My excitement fizzled and panic took its place. What did I just do? Maybe something Freudian was afoot. My ex-therapist, Renata, and I hadn't spent time on fear of commitment. She thought I committed too easily and without a lot of thought.

Evidently, Renata was wrong.

Although probably not wrong about the too easily and without a lot of thought part.

I dialed Nash's number.

"What?" He growled. But more distracted than irritated. I took heart that he answered and wasn't ghosting me.

"I'm meeting Ian Mowry at Lorena's tonight to look at the crime scene. And to show him where someone might have been watching the house."

"Okay."

"He's bringing takeout."

"That's nice."

"Why is that nice?"

"I've noticed you tend to get hungry. Especially at crime scenes. Maybe it's how you cope." He paused, but this time he sounded more focused. "Have you seen Boomer today?"

"He's here at the photoshoot." My face heated, thinking about my breakfast conversation with Daddy about Nash. "You know, Daddy's supportive of our relationship. A lot more than you'd think."

"Right. I forgot about the photoshoot. I'm kind of busy. Is there anything else?"

"Are you upset with me?"

"I got your messages. I appreciate the apology, but every-thing's good." He paused. "I might be out tonight, too. We'll catch each other later."

I hung up, feeling more worried than before. Nash was busy a lot lately. And distracted. He seemed to take more interest in my father than me.

Maybe it wasn't an ex-girlfriend who'd trashed Lucky. Maybe it was a current girlfriend.

"No," I told myself. "That's ridiculous. Nash wouldn't put up with Sunday dinners if he was getting a side helping of some-thing else. He's focused on his work and that's an admirable trait. Plus it distracts him from trying to get me to stay at the non-office."

But I really feared it also distracted him from returning to the old office. What if he found corporate life more fun than private investigations? He already found it more lucrative. We could become two ships passing each other on his king-sized, ergonomic bed. If he continued the corporate thing during the day and I worked honey pot stings at night, what would happen to us?

"This is why you should stick to thinking like your mashup character," I muttered. "She doesn't worry about future failures. She stays focused on present ones."

I started Billy, turned to look behind me, and spotted a man loitering near the empty loading dock where the photoshoot took place. The man looked familiar. My gut clenched.

A positive clench. Not an "I might not realize I'm cheating on my boyfriend" clench. A "something's hinky" clench.

I cut the engine, hopped out, and used the parked minivans and SUVs as cover to stalk closer. Crouching behind a Honda Pilot, I took a picture of the lurker. Enlarged it on my phone. I recognized him. The man Helmut indicated as a paparazzo, wanting to buy pictures from the party. But why was the tabloid-story dealer still hanging around?

My Annie-Nash mashup insisted I confront him. But I hung behind the Pilot and watched. I had a lot of experience with paparazzi. Mostly negative. My instincts told me not to bait the bear.

A few minutes later, Helmut opened a side door on the dock. He leaned down to speak to the photographer. The paparazzo handed him something, and Helmut returned through the door. The paparazzo strode to the parked cars and climbed into a blue Kia hatchback.

Staying behind the row of vehicles, I ran back to Billy, grabbed the strap, and swung into my seat. I waited until the small Kia had turned out of the parking area before backing out and following him.

My gut was right. There was something hinky going on. Helmut had said paparazzi buzzards had been circling him, wanting pictures from the night of Lorena's murder, but he'd rejected them.

Had he lied to me, too?

TWENTY-SEVEN

#HotPursuit #ChildTherapy

*T*he Kia driven by the tabloid hawker headed toward downtown Black Pine. I kept a few vehicles between us like Nash had instructed. Strictly followed the rules of the road, like Annie had warned. As Maizie Albright, I donned my incognito attire. Ball cap, sunglasses, and a blaring Kenny Chesney cd left by the Bronco's previous owner.

By age ten, I'd learned best practices for dealing with the paparazzi. Avoid them as much as possible. Today, the hunters were now the hunted. And it felt marvelous.

I could be wrong but felt sure Helmut had lied about the paparazzo. He'd been clear about not selling pictures of Lorena. I'd deal with Helmut later. After I scoped out the potential ruse.

As we sped through town, a gust of wind pushed my cap up. I slapped my arm over my head to hold it down and drove one-handed. The blue hatchback took a left onto the business highway. We drove past an older warehouse district. Once used by the railroad, scaffolding now enclosed the brick buildings. Men and trucks surrounded the area. A construction worker holding an orange cone and a stop sign forced the Kia to stop. I pulled over to keep my distance while Kenny Chesney sang about his love of island life.

I kept one eye on the Kia and another on a billboard advertising the upcoming lofts. As part of Black Pine's gentrification, a land developer was retrofitting the old warehouses into apartments. Maybe Nash and I could compromise. Instead of going all-in on the house and traditional stuff, we could live in urban (for Black Pine) accommodations. I loved lofts. Vicki had bought one for me in Tribeca when I got a part with a New York set. She'd sold it before I had a chance to live in it. The pilot hadn't been picked up. I'd looked forward to that apartment more than doing the show. Super disappointed when it didn't work out. All's well that ends well, though.

Except in my case, staying in California had ended in probation.

I scanned the sign, promising upscale amenities in historic accommodations. Totally me. If I could afford it. Of course, I'd have to wait until my probation ended and the judge let me move out of the Spayberry cabin.

However, I couldn't picture Nash in a trendy loft. I had trouble picturing him outside of the office, which wasn't a home at all. And definitely not trendy.

"Although, the office is brick and old, like these buildings," I muttered, craning my neck to see the apartments. "Maybe I just miss the office. I definitely miss Lamar."

While I waited for the Kia to proceed through the construction site, a cement mixer backed out of the drive next to me. The beep-beep-beep of the cement truck drowned out Kenney Chesney. But the construction worker flagging the truck grinned, pointed at Billy, and gave me the thumbs up. Smiling, I waved, then noticed the road crew had moved their cone. The Kia shot forward, drove over a set of railroad tracks, and disappeared behind the buildings. I chewed on my thumbnail. The cement truck stopped its reverse to change direction. Kenny Chesney blasted his love of swing shifts. The friendly builder shot me a one-minute sign, then waved at the truck again.

I blew out a long breath and adjusted my sunglasses.

The cement truck reversed. I counted beeps until it crossed the street and maneuvered into the correct lane. Kenny sang his love of margaritas. My friendly orange-helmeted worker gave me another thumbs up. I yanked out my thumbnail and pulled away from the curb. At the tracks, Billy hit the first rail and jumped the second. We bounced onto the road. I stomped on the accelerator, taking a tight corner around the building. The wind rushed through my hair and my hat sailed off. My hair flew. I flapped a hand before my face.

Pulling over, I looked around. I'd lost my hat and the Kia.

I followed the road, searching for the Kia, and spotted a flash of blue turning into a residential neighborhood. In various stages of decline, these houses likely didn't make the Historical Society's list. The area looked like the *Julia Pinkerton, Teen Detective* B-roll shots for seedy neighborhoods — home to nefarious characters, literally across the tracks. In Black Pine, this neighborhood housed young families and older residents who had likely lived in the same house all their lives.

Older neighborhoods got such a bad rap on TV.

Driving past a small house with asphalt shingle siding, I spotted the blue hatchback in the drive. I parked three houses down. Across the street, a trio of kids left their yard and approached me. I figured an open vehicle made me approachable. And noticeable. But not quite as noticeable as a twenty-five-year-old woman on a dirt bike.

"What'cha doing?" said the oldest kid, who looked about Aiden and Remi's age.

"Thinking," I said. "I've parked here for a bit to think."

Truthfully, I was working up the courage to confront the skeezy journalist. My Annie-Nash mashup tried to hurry the process, but plain ol' Maizie needed a script before accosting him.

Another boy, a bit smaller than the first, ran a hand over Billy's rust-spotted exterior. "What'cha thinking about?"

"Um, life, I guess. How to handle a problem."

"What's wrong with your life?" said a girl younger than the two boys. She wore overalls over her coat. A pink, glittery bow clipped in her hair had slid from its starting point and hung off the ends.

I swung my gaze from the house to the girl. "Actually, I'm not sure."

"Do you have a boyfriend?"

"I do." I paused. "I love him. And yet, I seem intent on destroying my relationship."

"Girls are weird," said the boy, examining the rust on his hands. He patted them on his shirt, looking pleased with the orange handprints.

"So are boys," said the little girl, watching the boy. "What are you gonna do?"

"I think we need to talk." I sighed. "We're not good at communicating. There are expectations but nothing clearly stated. And I'm not sure what I want."

"I don't get it," said the oldest boy.

"Don't you want to get married?" said the girl, clasping her hands together. "I want to get married. I want a pink dress and a crown and then we'll dance and sing with our friends."

"That's stupid," said the boy. "You don't dance and sing at weddings. You just dance."

"I'm going to dance and sing," she said. "And eat cake."

"You can eat cake. There's always cake," said the boy. "But I'm not coming to your dumb wedding if you're gonna sing."

Her lip trembled.

"It's your wedding. Do whatever you want. If you want to sing, get a karaoke machine," I said quickly. "Listen, do you know the guy in the blue car who arrived before me? He parked at the gray house."

"We're not supposed to talk to strangers," said the girl. Making me wonder how they viewed me.

"That guy lives there," said the oldest boy. "That's Mrs. Sexton's house. She keeps candy in a bowl. But it's old people's candy." He stuck out his tongue.

"Maybe the man's Mrs. Sexton's son?" I also wondered what constituted old people's candy. And if it was really as bad as he made it sound. "Does he visit much?"

"Yep," said the boy. "He's probably her son. Or her grandson. She's kind of old."

"So is she," said the smaller boy, jerking his thumb at me.

"Who me? I'm not old. I'm young."

"You're old enough to get married," said the little girl. "I'm not."

"I don't feel old enough to get married. Maybe that's the problem." I paused. "Or maybe because my parents married young and didn't work out. I'm just starting out on my own, finally independent from my ex-manager. My ex-therapist might say I need to explore the roads around me before choosing a path of permanency."

"I don't get it," said the boy.

"Before I settle down, I need to know I can take care of myself. Accomplish something on my own. My whole life people have taken care of me. Done everything for me."

"Me, too," said the little girl sadly.

"Maybe that is the problem," I wondered aloud. "I'm just not mature enough to get married. Yet."

"That's what momma says," piped the little girl.

I hoped she was talking about herself. I wasn't looking for confirmation on that opinion.

"Can we play in the back of your truck?" said the younger boy. "This marriage stuff is boring."

"No, that's dangerous," I said. "I need to figure out how to handle Mrs. Sexton's son. Or grandson, whatever the case may be."

"What did he do?" The oldest kid yanked on the duct tape strap, testing it.

"I'm not sure. He wanted pictures, but he was told no. I think he might have gotten pictures anyway."

"He robbed them?" gasped the girl.

"Not exactly. He was going to buy them."

"What were they pictures of?" The girl hopped on one foot. "If they were pictures of kittens, I would buy them."

"No, you wouldn't," said the boy. "You don't have any money."

Her lip trembled again.

"I'm not sure about the pictures, but I doubt there are kittens in them." How could boys be so blind as to what made girls cry? "I guess I'm worried the pictures may have something to do with a murder."

"Murder?" said the boy. "Are you a cop?"

"No. I'm a private investigator. That's like a detective."

"Cool," said the boy. He shoved the girl toward the yard. "Let's go."

"Why?"

"We're going to play detective."

I needed to play detective, too. For real. No more games.

TWENTY-EIGHT

#GrandmaGridlock #SpyKids

_I_nstead of hiding in Billy, wondering if I should confront the paparazzo or let the police deal with the vulture, I strode to the little house and rang the bell. An older woman, looking much like a grandmother, answered the door. "Mrs. Sexton?"

"Yes?" She peered at me through oversized glasses. "Who are you, honey?"

"I'm Maizie Spayberry." The buzzard would figure out who I was soon enough, but I wanted a small element of surprise. Also, I couldn't lie to a grandma, no matter what my mashup investigator thought. "Is your grandson here? Can I talk to him?"

"Oh, sweetie, I'm sorry, but Johnny's not here."

I blinked, not sure how to handle a lying grandmother. Annie and Nash might argue with her, but I had a thing about grandmothers, not having one myself.

"I thought I saw him pull into the drive a short time ago." I gave her my _Tiger Beat_ smile. Winsome, wholesome, and grandmother-approved.

She pursed her lips. "I think you're mistaken, honey."

I dropped my smile. "I would really love to talk to Johnny. It'll only take a minute. Please?"

Mrs. Sexton cocked her head. "You seemed to have done something different with your hair, but I know you're Maizie Albright. Your father is Boomer Spayberry, though. Didn't your mother, Vicki Albright, change your Spayberry family name to her maiden name?"

"Um, yes. It was my stage name. And then we kept it."

"Why did you tell me you were Maizie Spayberry?"

"So Johnny wouldn't know who I was right away?" I whispered, casting my gaze on my shoes.

"I think you should go home now, honey. If you have to lie to get Johnny to see you, then I don't think he should come to the door. And that hair-do is a terrible disguise. Unless that's some sort of fashion statement?"

I patted my hair, trying to finger-comb through the new knots. "I'm sorry, ma'am."

"That's better. Go on, now." She nodded, shooing me out the door.

Not only did I not get past the grandma, but I also didn't get offered grandma candy.

I trudged back to Billy and found the three children sitting in his bed. "You shouldn't climb into stranger's vehicles. That's dangerous. Haven't your parents told you that?"

"Of course," said the oldest boy.

"And don't take candy from strangers," said the girl. "Momma says that, too. Also, don't take kittens. But I really want one."

"We're playing detectives," explained the smaller boy.

"We're playing spy, not detective," said the older boy.

"Whatever you're playing, you need to hop out. I've got to go."

The boys jumped out. I took the little girl's hand to assist her. "Remember, don't climb into stranger's vehicles. Even if your brothers do."

"We didn't climb in the other one," said the girl. "Just yours."

I caught myself mid-nod. "What other one?"

"The car we were spying on." The oldest made a finger gun and aimed it down the street. "They parked across from Mrs. Sexton's house. Didn't you see them drive off when you walked over there? They were watching you."

"No." I glanced at the Sexton house over my shoulder. Goosebumps broke over my skin. "I wasn't paying attention."

"You're not a very good detective, are you?" The little girl patted my arm. "That's okay. Everybody makes mistakes."

It didn't feel okay. "Are you sure they weren't just sitting in their car, thinking? Like a neighbor. Having a think."

The three nodded. Then shook their heads.

"What did the car look like? Who was in it?"

"It was a black car," stated the oldest boy. "And there was a man inside."

"No, a woman," said the smaller boy.

"Which was it?" I looked at the girl, hoping her observation skills would outshine the boys.

She shrugged her tiny shoulders. "I was too scared to look."

I knew how she felt. "How long were they there?"

"At first, they stopped back there. While you were thinking." He pointed past Billy to the entrance of their street. "Then they parked across from Mrs. Sexton's house while you were talking to her."

I gave myself a mental face-palm. They could have been following me all day and I hadn't even noticed. "Did you know detectives and spies write down license plate numbers? I'll come back. If you see them again, write down the license plate number. But don't—"

"Get in their car," moaned the oldest. "We know."

"I was going to say, don't talk to them. But that, too." I waved them off and climbed into Billy. I wasn't sure if I should take their spy comments seriously. But someone had hidden in the bushes at Lorena's during my stakeout. Were they watching her house or me?

I'd keep my eyes peeled for a black car. Of course, in Black Pine, one-third of the vehicular population was black. You couldn't get more inconspicuous.

Probably something to think about for my next vehicle.

*G*iving up on the paparazzo for the moment, I drove back to the warehouse where the photoshoot had been held. The shoot was finished, but I hoped Helmut would still be there. Two DeerNose employees packed up the scenery and loaded supplies into a van. They didn't know where Helmut was or where he stayed. Figuring Daddy might know the photographer's whereabouts, I tried calling him. When I couldn't get him on his cell phone, I tried his administrative assistant, Mrs. Peters.

I'd always known Mrs. Peters. Besides Carol Lynn, no one knew my father better. She'd been with Daddy since DeerNose opened in his garage. Mrs. Peters knew everything related to DeerNose. She also kept her mouth shut about everything she knew, which I'm sure had a lot to do with her longevity at DeerNose.

"Your father isn't in right now," said Mrs. Peters. "After the photoshoot, he was called into a meeting. I've been scrambling to reschedule his other conference calls."

"Do you have any idea where the photographer, Helmut, is staying? I need to talk to him."

"I believe your father said they were putting him up at the resort. Boomer felt a week's stay at the resort an unnecessary expense, but Ms. Cortez wanted Helmut for the magazine shoot and for the gala. I'd hear her trying to convince Boomer about the 'PR optics,' but you know your father. Give me a minute and I'll get Helmut's room number."

From what Jennifer Frederick and the others had said, I gathered Lorena had been willing to spend a lot of money on the launch of Clothing Kids to make it a success.

Or she just liked to spend money.

Kyler Blick had accused her of stealing. I really wanted to meet the man who'd scared Lorena into moving to Black Pine. But my probation officer wouldn't let me fly to New Orleans. Not for a personal case.

The line beeped. "Maizie? Room 356. He's supposed to fly back to Miami tomorrow. Good luck catching him."

"Mrs. Peters, keep this under your cap for now, but I might have caught him dealing with the paparazzi. I'm going over there to see what's going on. I worry it has something to do with Lorena's death and I want to shield her the best I can."

"Such a terrible shame, what's happened to that lovely Ms. Cortez. I really liked her. I never would have thought she and your father would get along so well. They seem different, you know, but they complemented each other. Boomer's really shaken up about her death."

I was a horrible daughter, running around after a killer when I should be home hugging the bereaved. I promised myself after I figured out who killed Lorena, I'd start hugging again. Hugs all around.

Except for Ian. Didn't want to press my luck.

"We finally got news about a funeral service for Ms. Cortez," Mrs. Peters continued. "It's in California, where some of her extended family live. They're waiting on the body to be released from the medical examiner's office. I'm getting your father and Carol Lynn on a flight. Should I add you to a ticket, honey?"

"Unfortunately, I can't go to California." I bit my lip, hating that I couldn't properly pay Lorena my last respects.

"I'm sure your boss will give you time off for a funeral. I can get you a red-eye home."

"I'd have to get a judge to allow it," I muttered, feeling my face heat. "But I'll check with my probation officer."

"Oh my stars, I forgot about your probation. I'm sorry, Maizie. I didn't mean to embarrass you."

"It's okay, Mrs. Peters. I'm the one who gets myself into these messes. I'm sorry my dumb mistakes keep me from something like a funeral."

"I'm sure the family will appreciate anything you can do to protect her image from the press."

"That's what I aim to do right now."

I felt better already. I was going after Helmut.

TWENTY-NINE

#TeslaTussle #Photobombed

*B*lack Pine Golf and Yacht Club Resort — colloquially known as The Club or The Resort since everyone silently acknowledges the founders should have worked a little harder on the name — took up much of the valuable real estate along Black Pine Lake (as did Daddy's personal acreage). Besides the four-and-three-quarters-star hotel and cottages, the resort featured The Cove — a fine-dining restaurant mainly used for its bar — two golf courses, a gym, tennis, and a marina.

The resort and club personnel knew me by my Spayberry and Albright heritage and as Maizie Albright, the former celebrity. Unfortunately, they also knew me as the wannabe-detective. I'd embarrassed some of their guests, working on cases with Nash and now Annie. You'd be surprised how many of the well-to-do were under investigation for all sorts of interesting things — and I'm not just talking about your average white-collar crimes. Cheating spouses didn't stay within a socio-economic bracket. Neither did alimony and child support deadbeats. Or subpoena receivers. The Cove was extremely handy for honey traps.

A hotbed for bed-hopping, in other words.

Needless to say, not all of the staff were happy to see Maizie Albright saunter through their doors. Therefore, I was particularly nice to the staff who didn't care about busting guests. And by nice, I mean, Annie and I bribed them. Annie had a petty cash system just for payoffs.

This was something I never brought up with Nash. By the time I started working with him, he was using petty cash to pay off bill collectors. To be fair, Annie didn't own our PI business, nor did she have an ex-wife who tried to run it into the ground (successfully).

I parked Billy at the far end of the lot, near the road, and hoofed it to the hotel's timber, stone, and glass edifice. Under the portico, I found Carlos at the valet stand and tipped him a twenty.

"Who're you after this time, Maizie?" said Carlos, pocketing the money.

"Just visiting a guest, actually. A photographer who flew up from Miami to take pictures for the Clothing Kids Foundation launch."

"Oh, yeah. I know who you're talking about. Very famous dude, right?" Carlos leaned forward on the valet stand and motioned me closer. "I think he was taking pictures in his room, too."

"What do you mean?"

"This other dude came two or three times to see Helmut. Most times, he carried a garment bag. Real bulky one. A little travel case, too. But he wasn't staying at the hotel. He had me ring Helmut's room before I'd park his car."

My heart thudded. "What did this guy look like?"

"Kind of short and pudgy. Real white. Kind of an ugly dude. Maybe it's why he wanted his picture taken privately. I don't know if he was getting his picture taken, but you know, I put two and two together with Helmut being the photographer and the suitcase and all."

Holy smizzles. Gary. Had to be Gary. A bulky garment bag had Gary written all over it. But how did Gary know Helmut?

"I'm getting pretty good at deduction, don't you think," said

Carlos, interrupting my wild flurry of thoughts. "You think your boss could use another detective?"

My attention snapped back to Carlos. "I could ask Annie. I didn't know you were interested in becoming a PI."

"Valet parking isn't my life's ambition. It pays the bills. How much d'you make?"

I told him.

He grimaced. "Maybe I'll just keep working with y'all on the sly. Like we've been doing."

"Okay," I said. "If you change your mind let me know. By the way, what kind of vehicle was the guy driving?"

"The guy must have some cash. Tesla, Model S." My eyebrows curved inward and Carlos added, "The sedan. He had all the upgrades, including long-range—"

"What color?" I interrupted before he started his vehicle soliloquy. Something Carlos enjoyed a little too much, IMHO. But then, I didn't care about cars. As evident in Billy.

"Black." He grinned, probably noting my excitement. "You want the license plate number?"

"You betcha." I bounced on my toes to prevent myself from snatching Carlos's valet binder out of his hands.

He looked up from writing down the plate id and eyed me. "Did we make a break in a case? What did this photographer do? Porn or something worse?"

I didn't know what was worse than porn. I didn't want to know either.

"I'm not sure if it's a break. I need to know why Gar—Helmut's guest was here. But if you happen to see that car, can you text me? Or if you see another black car, could you text me then, too?"

"Um, sure, Maizie." Carlos's grin dimmed. "Any black car?"

I nodded.

He pointed to the parking lot, row after row of black, white, and silver vehicles. One lone yellow truck had been parked in the monochromatic sea, like a beacon in a storm. "You want to do a walk through before going in?"

I sighed. "No, that's okay. Just holler if you see the Tesla."

*B*efore knocking on Room 356, I stood in the hall, preparing for my mashup role. I needed someone harder-edged and focused to get Helmut to spill the beans.

Also, my persona should avoid phrases like "spill the beans."

I shook out my arms and rolled my neck. Imagined myself not growing up in my Beverly Hills home but something simpler. The office popped in my brain. Two rooms and one big bed.

Putting that image away, I focused on vocal tones. Drawing back my chin, I lowered my voice. "Helmut."

Tried again with a quieter intensity, "Helmut."

Louder with a growl, "Helmut."

The door swung open. "What?"

Helmut wore a robe. Perhaps nothing else. Personally, I was a little tired of visiting people undressed or unshowered. But maybe that's just me.

"Oh, Maizie," said Helmut in a smarmy voice he used on celebrities. "What can I do for you? Oh right, you wanted to see the snaps I took at the party. I didn't expect you so soon."

"I heard you were leaving tomorrow. I thought I'd come right away. You didn't tell me you were flying out, but I expect it slipped your mind." Mentally, I high-fived myself for getting to the point. So unlike me.

I loved this role.

He beckoned me inside his room. The furniture had been shoved to one corner. Clothes were draped over the chairs and the TV. The bed hadn't been made and an open laptop laid on it. He motioned toward the bed. "Have a seat and we'll look at them together."

"I prefer to stand, thanks."

Helmut lowered himself on the end of the bed, placing his hands behind him. The V in his robe opened, exposing a lot of chest hair. I silently prayed he had on Jockeys. Although I grew up around semi-nude men (actors), I had my limits.

"There's something else that might have slipped your mind, Helmut." I fisted my hands on my hips. "In the warehouse parking lot, I saw you take something from the paparazzo, Johnny Sexton. You want to explain?"

"What? You're mistaken," said Helmut, crossing his legs. Making me wish he hadn't.

I averted my eyes and focused on the laptop. Sidling closer to the bed, I continued, "I'm open to an explanation. It looked like you were selling pictures to Johnny Sexton. In the picture I took with my phone, that's how it appears, too. How awkward. Kind of like how the paparazzi takes snaps of celebrities that in a certain context, makes them look guilty."

Helmut turned, following my movement toward the side of the bed. "What are you saying? Are you threatening me?"

"When word gets out that a photographer like you will sell photos, it'll be difficult to get celebrities to trust you. And isn't the relationship between a photographer and his clients built on trust?"

"Of course. But Maizie, you know there's a difference between the private sitting and the public shots. The party was a public arena. Completely different than what I took today. And today was especially…" He grimaced. "*Corporate.*"

I sucked in a breath, resenting our shared distaste for the same word. But I set that thought aside for later and focused on my ire. "I don't know Johnny Sexton. Maybe he's not a vulture. His grandmother seemed nice." I paused. "Actually, his grandma was kind of judgy. But perhaps he's not interested in some kind of exposé. It shouldn't be hard for me to figure out. After all, I'm a private investigator now."

He forced a chuckle and patted the bed next to him. "So you

say. Shall we get back to looking for Lorena's ex in the party photos?"

I wanted those pictures. But I also didn't want Helmut to think he could get away with selling Lorena's image to the tabloids. I leaned toward the laptop, keeping my eyes on Helmut. "Just what did you sell to Johnny? I'll find out anyway. Better me than the police, Helmut."

"Nothing untoward," he huffed. "Just the glitz and glamour red carpet shots. People preening before the camera. Everyone loves those."

"What about pictures of Lorena? You must have met with her earlier in the day to talk strategy."

He shrugged. "I had a few shots. Nothing candid."

"You slimeball." I threw up my hands. "You told me the tabloids have been hounding you since her murder and you found it disgusting. You sold shots of Lorena in her final hours, didn't you? That's what they'll call it."

He swiped the laptop from the bed and tucked it under his arm. "Get out. And if you think your little threat scares me, it doesn't."

"I want to see those pictures."

"Get them from Johnny then, if you think you can." Helmut grabbed my arm and pulled me toward the door. I twisted and jerked in his grip. He thrust me forward and my cheek slammed into the door. His body pushed against my back, taut and hard, unforgiving. His hand gripped my neck and his breath tickled my ear.

"You're a joke," he snarled. "Nobody takes you seriously. They never have. Not as an actress, not as a detective. Never threaten someone like me, Maizie Albright. You'll regret it."

Releasing me, he shoved me out the door. "And your new hairstyle? That's a joke, too."

THIRTY

#ShakenNotStirred #LinkintheChain

I didn't want Helmut's threats to shake me. I hurried through the hotel, acknowledging friendly staff with a smile and ignoring everyone else. I thanked Carlos, fast-walked through the parking lot, and climbed into Billy. But my trembling hands wouldn't allow me to stick the key into the ignition.

Helmut had shaken me.

But, I must have shaken him, too. I wasn't sure if he feared my outing him to my celebrity friends or if I had touched on a greater risk to Helmut than gossip. Something to do with Lorena's murder.

Despite my success in learning Helmut's true nature, I felt terrible, not triumphant. I didn't like threatening people. Even oily Helmut with his suggestive robe and too-furry chest.

This might be a problem for my career. I still wasn't tough enough. Growing up with Vicki should've hardened me. For Vicki, idle (and non-idle) threats were part of her daily banter. She didn't even realize the waiter scrambling to get her pomegranate rosé martini chilled to 14 degrees Fahrenheit feared losing his job if he returned with vodka only cooled to 18 degrees.

Back in LA, I'd carried a temperature gun in my Chylak belt

bag for just such emergencies.

While I waited for my trembling to subside, I covertly glanced about for the black car that might or might not be following me. Then remembered Gary's Tesla and the very important lead I'd missed. I hadn't asked Helmut about Gary's visit.

Sucktastic.

A new flurry of career-crisis panic enveloped my chest. I should call Nash. A few words from him would do…

Hang on, I couldn't tell Nash about Helmut. He'd use his lunch break to threaten Helmut in a very different way that might get him fired from DeerNose. And he'd seemed distracted last time we talked. I couldn't call him every time I had a panic attack.

Besides that, I'd rather wait until I had a real success to report, not a mini-success that ended in me getting kicked out of a hotel room and my certain failure at forgetting an important piece of information.

I took deep breaths and focused on positive affirmations.

What about calling Ian?

No, Ian might try to stop my investigation by moving our date from Lorena's house and into an actual restaurant.

Instead, I called Tiffany. If anyone could straighten my spine with a few words it was Tiffany. Seeking a reason for my call, I told her to be on the lookout for "a black car."

"You're kidding, right?" snarled Tiffany. "That's all you've got? A black car driven by a man or a woman? That narrows it down."

"I know, I know. It could be Gary, but then again, who doesn't drive a black car in this town? Besides you, of course."

"At least if you're being followed, now you might believe Rhonda is in danger."

"I don't *not* believe you." I just found it hard to believe. Sort of. "But what's the point in terrorizing Rhonda? It's obvious she already talked to the police. What's the motive?"

"I don't make up the rules for criminals, Maizie. Do psychopaths even follow rules?"

"If the culprit is Kyler, I don't think he's that kind of psychopath. The motive is revenge for Lorena stealing from him and probably robbery, although if it is his money, does stealing it back count as —"

"Why are you defending a man who murdered your friend, Maizie?" shrieked Tiffany. "According to Rhonda, it was a blood-bath. Sounds like a psychopath to me."

"Head wounds bleed pretty bad...Okay, you're right, you're right. It doesn't matter. I'm not even sure if it's Kyler who did this anyway. And in that case, it might be a psychopath."

"That makes me feel so much better. Why can't it be Kyler?"

"He's in New Orleans on a movie shoot."

"He doesn't get time off?"

"Wardrobe is really long hours. Longer than most anyone else. They have to be there before the actors, stay until the actors are done, then prepare for the next day. We're talking thirteen to fifteen-hour days. That's not a lot of time to fly or drive to North Georgia and commit murder, not to mention stick around to follow me and haunt Rhonda."

Tiffany exhaled, long and angry. "In other words, you have no idea who did this and the maniac is still out there."

"I'll report back soon. Gary's still on my list. And now, possibly, Helmut."

"The photographer? He was at the party taking pictures during the murder. He's got the best alibi by far."

"There's something fishy going on between him and this paparazzo."

"Who cares?"

I had to protect Lorena from the tabloids as best I could. Shielding her dignity was the least I could do for her, no matter what she might have done to Kyler. "I need to see the pictures he sold to Johnny Sexton."

"Stop wasting time on these photographers—"

"But they might have evidence and—"

"Isn't that *your* Detective Mowry's job? What's he doing other than flirting with you?"

She had a point. "I'm meeting Ian at Lorena's tonight. I'll make him give me more details on the police investigation. Or else."

"Or else what?" She snorted.

I couldn't say "refuse to eat his dinner" out loud. Instead, I said, "I'll think of something."

*A*t the Albright Security Solutions office, I sat at my desk with a deck of notecards and a pen, noting every person related to Lorena in Black Pine. Possibly Kyler Blick had flown in for a quick murder visit, but I had other suspects to examine. Suspects I had gotten on my own before Ian's Kyler Blick lead sidetracked me…

Hold up. I wasn't being fair to Ian. Kyler had the best motive. My suspects were all based on location and opportunity. Why couldn't I be more focused and organized like Ian?

I considered adding Ian to my mashup character. But if he somehow learned I was imitating him, he might get the wrong idea.

The front door banged open and the bell tinkled. I looked up from the notecard I held.

"What are you doing to the window?" shouted Annie.

"Making a link chart of people and evidence related to Lorena's murder. We don't have a bulletin board and the sticky notes wouldn't adhere to the brick, so I'm sticking them to the window. Instead of using yarn to trace the connections, I bought window paint markers. I also printed everyone's Facebook profile for their link chart photo. Handy, huh?"

"Haven't you ever heard of a spreadsheet?" growled Annie. "We don't have the wall space to put up link charts. We don't do the kind of cases that need link charts."

"That's why I used the window. And we do now."

"Is someone paying you to investigate Lorena Cortez's murder?"

"Um, no."

"Then it's not an Albright case," she fumed, chomping on her gum. "Take it down."

Technically, it was an Albright case but also technically, a personal one. "I thought you enjoyed working on this case. You know, a change of pace from background checks."

"It's not a case. It's you trying to figure out who killed your friend." She stared at the window, folding her arms over her chest.

Annie liked the front window a little too much. But we all had our idiosyncrasies.

"Who's this guy?" She pointed at the window. "Spencer Newson?"

"The CEO of Clothing Kids. He allegedly had an affair with Lorena. And he lied about being at her house the day of her murder."

"I just saw him at Vicki's." Annie turned around. "I had to run by some expense reports. She likes me to bring them in person and wait there while she looks them over. She doesn't even read them. It's all about me waiting on her like I'm some kind of servant and she's the queen."

"Yep, sounds like Vicki," I said absently.

Craptastic. I was supposed to chaperone that meeting. Vicki had conveniently forgotten to contact me with the details. That kind of forgetfulness didn't bode well. Her memory was as sharp as my Louboutin So Kate stilettos.

"Did you overhear anything Vicki and Spencer were discussing? Or not discussing?" I bit my lip. "I mean, did they look guilty? Like maybe they were doing something they shouldn't be?"

"What d'ya mean?" Annie narrowed her eyes, but her lips

curled. She smacked her gum with relish. "Like I caught them doing the horizontal mambo or something?"

"No," I squeaked. "Gross. No. But did you get that kind of vibe?"

She shook her head, grinning. "I'll pay closer attention next time. Thanks."

What did I just do? I sighed. "Do you know why Spencer was at Vicki's?"

"Some kind of meeting for that fundraiser."

"Oh, right. I think Spencer wants Vicki to fill in for Lorena's absence. This seems kind of soon after Lorena's death, IMHO. Her family is still waiting for the medical examiner to send the body back to California. I mean, shouldn't he hold off until the funeral out of respect for Lorena?"

"Business is business, I guess." Annie blew a small bubble and popped it. "Anyway, if you're done making a mess, why don't you get on that pile of folders."

I internally winced. If I'd known most of private investigating took place at a desk, I might have chosen a different second career. The only desk Julia sat behind was a school desk. But not often. She cut class a lot. To catch criminals, but still. Normal high schoolers would have been expelled by the end of the first season. And how does a valedictorian get those kinds of grades when they're never at school?

Writers cut a lot of corners.

"I have a quick errand to run first," I said. "But I promise to take down my link chart tomorrow."

"Where are you going now?"

"I'm meeting Mowry at Lorena Cortez's house. We're going to talk about the case, but this time I'll make him give me details instead of the other way around."

"You're going to force a cop to talk about details on an active investigation?" Annie snorted. "Good luck with that. What time should I post bail?"

THIRTY-ONE

#PoGirl #DazzleMe

---

*I*nstead of driving to Lorena's house, I walked the six blocks. A breeze punctuated the air, more cool than cold. A half-moon peeped above the treetops. As I moved into the historic district, the scent of donuts changed to woodsmoke. I shoved my hands in my coat pockets, appreciating the exercise after sitting at my desk.

To be honest, by not riding in Billy, my scalp also enjoyed the relaxation. I'd spent a good forty-five minutes in the office bathroom dampening my hair in the sink, combing it through, and French braiding the result.

I'd also gotten over my earlier jitters. With the help of the office's security camera, I'd watched for a black car, but the street had been quiet all afternoon. Even Helmut's threats seemed more reflexive and defensive than serious. His career had been built on discretion as much as creativity. I'd made him vulnerable. I shouldn't have been surprised that he'd lash out.

However, I would remain vigilant. Just in case. Not that I was as paranoid as Rhonda.

On Lorena's street, I checked all the driveways for black vehicles. Most homes had garages by the alley, which didn't help. But I did spy Gary's Tesla and noted a black Mercedes in the Martins' drive. Mrs. Jessup drove a black minivan. But if Aiden had somehow convinced his mom to follow me, I'm sure the kids would have noticed and climbed inside hoping for juice boxes and kid candy.

Reaching Lorena's home, I spied Ian in his truck. With his eyes on his phone, he hadn't yet noticed my arrival. Open investigation or not, I needed to convince Ian to share more. All his Daphne comments indicated he didn't take me seriously.

But why should he take me seriously? I could be rash and seem silly. When excited, I had trouble pulling my thoughts together. The very reason for my new mashup PI character. This walk-through could be my chance to show Ian I was more than eye candy.

Quickening my step, I kept my gaze fixed on Ian, determined to prove myself. Ian glanced up, grinned, and slid out of his truck.

Speaking of eye candy... When Ian smiled, his face lit up. If the beam shone on you, you felt like the only girl on the planet. He wasn't stingy with the smiles either, not like Nash...

Hang on. I stopped on the sidewalk. *What the Hades, Maizie?*

Shiztastic. Was I still trying to sabotage my relationship with Nash? Good grief, when would my subconscious give me a break? Relationships had highs and lows. We were in some kind of early rut, so what? Too busy with our own lives to work on us. For example, like right now. I had to focus on this murder for Lorena and Rhonda's sake.

Although, Nash didn't act like he minded my diversions. He seemed pretty focused on his workaholic corporate life and obsession with my father.

That was weird, wasn't it? His obsession with Daddy?

Focus Maizie. Working on this case would give me much needed maturity and experience. I needed to concentrate on my career.

My stomach knotted. Thinking of Lorena's murder in those terms still made me queasy.

"You're walking?" called Ian, interrupting my thought-train. Thankfully. It headed in a direction I didn't like. Across the very wrong side of the tracks.

"Is something wrong with the Bronco?" said Ian. "I could've picked you up."

"No. Nice night," I replied in my mashup voice. Deep, direct, and dedicated. "Just felt like it."

"Great idea. Although sounds like you might be catching a cold. I might have a throat lozenge in the truck."

I shook my head. Darn it, I still needed to work on my intonation.

"We have a lot to discuss," said Ian. "I want to pick your brain about a few things."

Satisfaction fluttered in my chest. Not many people wanted to pick my brains. Unless it had to do with fashion trends. Since moving to Black Pine, I didn't get a lot of those questions either.

"Do you mind if we eat first?" Ian opened his truck door, reaching for two Styrofoam boxes. He glanced over his shoulder. "I thought we could tailgate. But we can sit it in the cab if you want."

I sniffed, trying to snatch a whiff of whatever was in the boxes. Then caught myself. What was more appropriate for a crime scene non-date? The bed or cab of a truck? This wasn't covered in my etiquette classes.

"I don't mind standing," I said. "I mean, if we don't need a knife and fork or anything."

"That's what I like about you, Maizie. You're not too cool for school."

"What do you mean?"

"Guys like Nash get on me about my love of food. I can't help it if investigations make me hungry. I'm not pretending other-wise to make myself look tough." He winked. "I got us some po' boys. Roast beef debris is good warm or cold. Although hush puppies are better hot."

My stomach rumbled. *Stay strong, Maizie. Stay in character.*

"That sounds..." I tried to formulate my mashup PI's response and weakened. I couldn't stay in character with po' boys and hush puppies before me. Some temptations were too powerful. "...totally awesome."

"Tea?" He handed me a large, lidded cup then reached for a paper bag spattered with grease spots. "Hushpuppy?"

I took the tea and a hushpuppy, chewing fast. Then slowed to savor the hot crunchy bites. Sweet and savory. Like a donut meant for dinner. "I haven't had a po' boy since my last trip to New Orleans."

"To be honest, looking into this Kyler Blick got me thinking about Cajun food." He laughed. "Don't tell the guys, they'll think I'm demented."

"What's going on with Kyler Blick?" I said, taking another hush puppy from the open bag Ian held. "Did the New Orleans police check out his alibi?"

"Well, hon', that's something I wanted to talk to you about." Ian took a long sip of tea. "Seems that Mr. Blick's alibi wasn't all that airtight."

"I thought he was working on a closed set in New Orleans? Working in Wardrobe?"

"Blick is working on a TV shoot there. When we called the studio, they confirmed this. But my man in NO has had some trouble locating him on set the day in question. Blick's wardrobe assistants are the ones putting in all the hours. There are days when Blick is 'researching,'" Ian air-quoted, "and he doesn't come to the set at all."

"Is he the costume designer for the show?"

"What's the difference?"

"Everything. Wardrobe hours are crazy long during filming. Unless you're the designer. It's a little confusing, but the costume designer's position is in the wardrobe department, but they're not literally working in Wardrobe. Wardrobe works in Wardrobe. Also called Costumes."

Ian studied me. "You're right, this is confusing. Why isn't he at work?"

"If Kyler's the costume designer for a big show, he would have done a lot of his work preproduction. The costume supervisor oversees the daily work. Blick should be checking with the supervisor to make sure the actors are happy with the look and fittings, his costumers are keeping the continuity books correctly, and the wardrobe trailers are staying orga- nized. The designer might double-check the actors' costumers on set, depending on the size of the show." I sipped tea, thinking. "If it's a TV show, as the designer, it wouldn't be unreasonable for Blick to be off set, doing research. He'd also work directly with the director, producers, and principal actors. They might be meeting somewhere other than the studio."

Ian frowned. "That's a lot of time unaccounted for. I don't like it. Blick says he was in his hotel room the night of the gala. Alone."

"Ian, this is terrible. I told Tiffany and Rhonda that Kyler had an alibi."

"Maybe I should go down there myself. I want more evidence than his word he was working the day of the gala. The studio could be protecting Blick." Ian set down his tea and the bag of hush puppies. "It's an eight-hour drive from New Orleans to Black Pine. But there are multiple daily flights through Atlanta. Homeland Security red tape is taking some time to cut through to get flight log details."

A chill ran up my spine. "A lot of rental cars are black, aren't they?"

"I suppose so. What are you getting at?"

"It's a bit of a long story." I sighed. "Today I followed a paparazzo named Johnny Sexton from the photoshoot. There's something hinky going on between Johnny and Helmut, the offi- cial photographer."

"What?" Ian pulled out a notepad. "A papa—"

"Paparazzi singular. His grandma wouldn't let me talk to him, but I think Helmut sold Johnny pictures of Lorena."

"Hang on. Helmut's grandma wouldn't let you talk to him?"

"No, the paparazzo's grandma. Mrs. Sexton. I should've stayed in character, I might have gotten around her." I sighed. "Anyway, while I was there, I learned someone in a black vehicle might be following me."

"What makes you think that?"

"Some neighborhood kids saw a black car approach and park after I went into Johnny Sexton's grandma's house. They left when I did."

"It doesn't necessarily mean someone's following you." Ian's brows furrowed.

"That's what I'm hoping. After all, a black car's not following Rhonda, she's just harassed on the internet. But then again, she can't be followed since she never leaves Tiffany's house. However, Gary has a black Tesla and he's been going to Helmut's on the sly. And now Helmut's scared of me—"

"Helmut's scared of you?" Ian looked up from his notebook. "Hon', you're confusing the heck out of me."

"Welcome to my world."

*W*e finished our po' boys while I gave Ian more details about Helmut, Grandma Sexton, and Gary's visits to the resort.

"Carlos is probably right about Helmut taking photos of Gary." I wiped my mouth on a napkin, tossed it in the empty Styrofoam box, and sighed with contentment. The po' boy was as delectable as Ian had hinted. "Gary's such a huge fan of Lorena's work. If he could afford Helmut, he'd want Lorena's chosen photographer to take his portrait. His costume collection is really amazing. And I have a feeling Gary doesn't leave them unworn."

"The more time I spend in this career, the less I want to know about people." Ian rolled his eyes. "Sounds harmless."

"Still, he did lie about being home the night of the gala. And for a groupie, it's kind of weird he didn't buy a ticket. Maybe his adoration wasn't reciprocated. If I were Lorena, I'd be uncomfortable with a super fan across the street."

"I had the same thought, Daphne. We got a hit on Gary. He's got a record."

"What?" I lowered my voice, remembering he lived across the street. "What's Gary done?"

"He's been caught trespassing multiple times at the studio in town. They didn't press charges the first time. He's got a good lawyer and gotten off with fines for the other two occasions."

"Was he trying to get into the indie movie set Lorena was working on?"

"Yep." Ian pointed at me. "I should see about getting you a reward if we arrest him."

I smiled back weakly. I didn't want a reward. Okay, I did want a reward. But I really wanted the tip-off to have been mine and not Nash's.

"Ready for the walk-through?"

I swiveled my gaze from Ian to Lorena's house. A shudder ran through me, but I tried to repress it.

"Are you sure you're alright with seeing the house, hon'? It's okay if you aren't."

"I'm fine," I said stiffly. "The worst is over, isn't it? Maybe it'll be good for me to see the living room without Lorena's body in it."

"Just be prepared, the place is not cleaned up. We've left the scene preserved." Ian patted my shoulder. "If you feel sick or anything, walk on out. I'll be right behind you. I'd like a fresh set of eyes on the place. Tell me anything that stands out."

We walked the path together. I waited for Ian to remove the crisscross of police tape and unlock the door. He stepped inside and I followed, stopping inside the door next to him.

The living room looked like a hazmat zone. Debris from the ambulance crew littered the ground. The baskets from the bookshelf had been left where Rhonda and I had knocked them over. My gaze flitted away from the large bloodstain still visible on the rug. Another stain darkened the wood near the stand where Lorena's Day of the Dead costume still hung.

"What's that?" I pointed to the other stain.

"Water," said Ian. "See the big, stainless steel box lying on its side? It's a boiler for an iron. Holds about a gallon."

"It tipped? That's a heavy-duty steam iron. Those things don't just tip over. They're solid."

Ian nodded. "Weighs about sixteen-and-a-half pounds without the iron."

"They also don't leak. That's a professional-grade steamer. I saw the costumers using them in Wardrobe all the time."

"The iron's hose was disconnected from the unit." Ian looked at me. "Seems like the water ran out after the hose unplugged."

"Is the iron the murder weapon?" I'd directed a lot of energy on not revisiting the scene of Lorena's murder to keep my emotions in check. Now I let my memory return and wander the room. That night, I'd been so focused on Lorena's body and calming Rhonda, I hadn't paid much attention to other details. I didn't remember an iron lying near her body. Just the scissors jammed into her back.

"The iron is missing," said Ian.

I shook off the image of Lorena and the scissors, forcing my brain to recreate the crime instead. "The culprit must have stabbed Lorena near the steamer. That's where most of her sewing equipment is located. Lorena was probably making last-minute adjustments to her costume." I stared at the stainless-steel box. "Steaming her dress, I guess."

"My guess, too. Good job, Daphne. What happened next?"

"The culprit wouldn't have taken time to unplug the hose, obviously. Those hoses are long. Like six or seven feet."

Ian nodded.

With my eyes, I traced the path from the upset steamer to the bloodstain on the other side of the room. More than six or seven feet. I sucked in a breath. "When they yanked the iron off its stand, would the momentum tip the machine?" Before Ian could speak, I held up a hand and continued, "No, they must have grabbed the iron, followed her across the room, and jerked the iron from the machine when the hose length ended."

"Wrenched it hard enough to tip a stainless-steel box filled with hot water."

"Oh my God." I twisted my hands. "They bolted toward her, didn't they? Picked up the iron and ran across the room. Ripped it free. Swung the iron at her head."

Ian nodded. "Confirms what the ME believes. The blow to her head matches the shape of the iron. The burns confirm it as the likely murder weapon, too."

My stomach lurched. I turned away from the steamer and kept my eyes on Ian. "Lorena tried to get away. With those scissors lodged in her back."

"Ms. Cortez ran maybe ten to fifteen feet," said Ian. "Looked like she was headed to the front door."

"That's some rage, isn't it?" I shuddered and didn't mind when Ian placed an arm around my shoulders. "This was personal. Not some random robbing."

"Probably. That's why the boyfriend Kyler Blick worries me."

"And Gary?"

"We brought Gary in for questioning." Ian squeezed my shoulder and dropped his arm. "Let's move on. Your statement said you didn't go into other rooms that night. But had you seen the rest of the house before?"

"Lorena gave me a tour the first time I visited. She was proud of her renovations." I thought about the neighbors next door. "Although not everyone else likes what she did to the house."

"What do you mean?"

"The neighbors, the Martins. The wife's the president of the local Historical Society. Several times she brought up her dislike of Lorena's remodel. Mrs. Martin seems a little obsessive about sticking to historic details. She even got into it with Vicki."

"That happens in towns like Black Pine. Part of a small town's charm is the folks who mind everyone else's business because they think they know what's best."

"Sure," I said slowly. "That's why I didn't mention it before. But they lied about the secret door. And now that I'm thinking about it, when I met them at the party, she seemed anxious about some emergency."

"Be careful. If you allow it, your mind will see all kinds of mundane actions as suspicious. Jan Martin hosted a huge fundraiser with local celebrities at her home. I'm sure there were a million emergencies that night." Ian stepped in front of me. "Let's move on. Don't veer from the path I take and don't touch anything."

"Of course." I followed him through the large open room to a back hallway. Her master bedroom looked undisturbed, thankfully. Same with her bathroom. "Nothing strange to me here."

"Good," he said.

"Can I poke around?"

"No. We already poked." Ian tugged my hand and we walked down the hall and into an office. "We took all the files and the computer."

Behind a wooden desk, the large floor safe stood open and covered in print dust. "Did you get any prints?"

"Ms. Cortez's, of course. And partials from two others." Ian glanced at me. "One isn't identifiable yet."

"The other?"

"Sorry, Daphne. Keeping that one close to my vest." Ian winked, then grew somber. "Do you know if Ms. Cortez had jewelry or other kinds of valuables she might have kept in the safe?"

"Not that I know of. Lorena wasn't ostentatious. She might have worn some special jewelry for award ceremonies, that sort of thing. I can't remember anything specific, though."

"According to her insurance papers, she had some kind of crown."

"Oh right, but that's not jeweled. It's made from fur and feathers and probably some other kind of material, like paper."

"Why would it be insured for 100K?"

"It's the evil queen's crown from *Dazzle*."

Ian blinked at me. "Come again?"

"*Dazzle* made over one hundred billion at the box office worldwide. Lorena won her first CDGA as the costume designer for *Dazzle*. She probably kept the crown as a keepsake but had it insured. That's not unusual and neither is insuring it for one hundred thousand. The role of the evil queen made Jemima Sinclair a huge star."

"The movie about elves and fairies and whatnot, right?"

"Yes."

"Just checking." Ian sighed. "The crown wasn't in the safe. Did Kyler Blick work on *Dazzle*?"

"I'm not sure. Possibly he made the crown. With a specialty in masks..."

"Damn it. If he made that crown, I want him picked up." Ian placed his hand on the small of my back. "To the kitchen, Daphne. You've been a big help."

THIRTY-TWO

#NosyNeighbors #FreudianSlips

*F*eeling pleased, I didn't mind when we rushed through the kitchen. Not allowed to touch anything, I wasn't getting much visually from the walk-through. But I felt I learned plenty from talking through the crime scene evidence with Ian.

"While I lock up, I'll make a couple calls," said Ian. "I really want Kyler Blick picked up. I might arrange to go down to New Orleans to talk to him myself."

"That reminds me, did the missing key turn up? I really don't think Aiden has it."

"Tell you what, Nancy Drew. While I'm securing the front door, why don't you walk around back. See if the key fell somewhere around those pots. I'll give you a ride back to your office when you're done."

"Sounds like a plan." Stepping off the porch, I stepped between pots of herbs and spied a six-year-old in the yard next door. I zipped through Lorena's garden to the adjoining lot and stopped at their fence. "Aiden, what are you doing? Does your mother know you're out here?"

He squeezed his lips to the side and stood on his toes to look around me. "Who's that?"

"Detective Ian Mowry. He's a policeman."

Aiden looked at me. "What are y'all doing?"

"Checking Miss Lorena's house. We're trying to catch the person who hurt her." I eyed him. "What are you doing?"

"Not leaving my yard."

"That's good. But what else are you doing?"

He rose on his toes and peeked around me again. "I've seen him before."

"He's in charge of the investigation. Detective Mowry's probably been here a lot."

He squinted. "There's been some others at Miss Lorena's house, too. Are they policemen? Nobody wears uniforms. I thought police wore uniforms."

A chill ran up my spine, but I squashed it, remembering the unreliability of kids as witnesses. The alleged black car was a great example. "What did the people look like? I'll find out if they're police."

"A man and a woman. I dunno what they look like. Old."

"Like grandma and grandpa old? Mom and dad old?"

"Yeah, like you."

Children didn't do much for my self-esteem. "I'm not old enough to be a grandma."

"You're old enough to be a mom."

"Technically, yes, but I'm not..." Why did all these children want me married with kids? I forced my thoughts to move on. "What else did this man and woman look like?"

"Dunno. Normal."

Super helpful. "Did they come together?"

Aiden shook his head.

"Did they go into the house?"

Aiden shrugged. "They scared me."

I glanced behind me. Ian had replaced the crime scene tape and walked back to his truck. He sat inside the Tahoe, speaking on the phone. "How did they scare you?"

Turning back, I found Aiden sprinting across his yard. "Where are you going?"

"Bedtime."

"What if I bring the policeman to your house so your mom and dad can meet him?" I shouted after him.

"No. It's bedtime."

*S*till immersed in his phone call, Ian barely acknowledged my point toward Aiden's escape. The back porch flowerpots waited for my search for the key. Before reaching the backyard, I peered around the edge of the house. Took a picture, then fell back against the house.

I scanned the picture, paying attention to the shadows this time. Nothing looked odd. I slunk around the corner. And felt silly. After all, a cop sat in his truck in front of the house. I walked around the backyard, examining the camellias. Looked for tell-tale signs of bears and lurkers. Footprints. Wrappers. Murder weapons. Finding nothing interesting, I turned my attention to the flowerpots.

Found nothing interesting there either. Most importantly, I couldn't find the key.

Giving up, I dusted my dirty hands and moseyed toward the front yard. Ian appeared to still be on his phone. And behind a tree in her yard, Jan Martin appeared to be watching him.

I waved at Jan, but she slipped behind the tree, then walked toward her backyard. Like she hadn't seen me. Or, like she didn't want to acknowledge that I'd seen her.

Ian wasn't *not* correct about small-town busybodies, but the Martins were right next door. Even if a warped sense of civic pride made for a weak motive, the Martins had proximity and accessibility. Lorena's remodel wasn't something Jan could ignore. She saw Lorena's house every time she went outside. Jan would also be dealing with Lorena's rejection of joining the

Historical Society. And Lorena was sleeping with their pal, Spencer.

Just like in the *Julia Pinkerton, Teen Detective,* Season 4 Episode 13, "The Loser's Loss." When a cheerleader died at Julia's high school, everyone believed she'd committed suicide. Except for Julia, naturally. At first, Julia thought an extremely bitter gamer girl had orchestrated the murder. The girl not-so-secretly despised the cheerleader and had filled a notebook with lurid scenes depicting various ways to fix an accidental death.

Total red herring. The murder notes were just notes. A major video game company had sponsored a contest for high school coders, and Gamer Girl had entered with a game called "The Cleaner." Turned out the killer was a rival cheerleader who suffered from mat-rage when she didn't make captain. Every time she had to use the victim's cheer choreography, her anger deepened until it became deadly.

In the epilogue, although their high school had expelled Gamer Girl for bringing murder-filled notebooks to school, after seeing her video game, several tech universities offered her early admission. Despite the audaciously violent game, Gamer Girl also won the contest and a scholarship.

Win some, lose some.

However, I couldn't help but wonder if Jan Martin was Gamer Girl or Rival Cheerleader in this episode.

I mean, case.

The more I fretted over Jan's possible murderous intentions, the more I worried about Vicki. Vicki was no real threat to the Historical Society or to Spencer's marriage (I hoped), but Vicki had the incredible ability to sense a person's nerve and press it until the nerve snapped or withered. And like Lorena, Vicki was impervious to small-town snideness and would do whatever the Hades she wanted. And more.

Plus, Lorena and Vicki had star quality. Fame easily ruffled small town feathers.

Spying me standing on the sidewalk, lost in not-so-deep

thoughts, Ian waved me toward the truck and rolled down a window. "Get in. I need to get back to the station."

As soon as I climbed in the Tahoe and buckled, Ian took off. "What's going on?"

"Kyler Blick hasn't responded to our calls and looks like he hasn't been in his hotel room for a few days. New Orleans police reported the hotel said his room hadn't needed cleaning. Blick also hasn't checked in at the TV set."

Thoughts of Jan Martin's murderous intentions dissipated. Ian was right, petty behavior didn't equal a homicidal rampage. My imagination made for poor detecting skills.

Or maybe I knew too many TV scripts. Writers were notorious for making something out of nothing.

"Are you going to New Orleans now?"

"I'm not sure it's necessary. The police have an APB on Blick and someone assigned to the case. If they find him, I'm going." He glanced at me, worry creasing his brow. "But I think I better stay here for now."

"You think Kyler might be in Black Pine."

"Possibly." He stopped the Tahoe, and I realized we'd already arrived at the new office.

"Thanks for the ride." I turned toward my door and felt Ian's hand on my arm. I looked over my shoulder and saw the concern marking his face. "Is there more?"

"It's just..." Ian's hand slid down my arm to my hand and squeezed. "Be careful, Maizie. I know you're anxious to learn who did this to Ms. Cortez. But if Kyler Blick is hanging around, there has to be a reason for it."

"You haven't found the iron. Do you think he's worried about where he left it?"

"Or worried y'all might have seen where he left it. Or something else." Ian sighed. "Although the threatening note and cyberbullying done to your friend don't make a lot of sense to me in terms of this case, we're treating it seriously. Tell Rhonda to continue to stay home. I've had patrol cars routed to that house several times a day. But with this new information, we can pull someone from another assignment to sit outside the house."

"I'll tell her. Thank you, Ian."

"The thing is Maizie, I'm not as worried about Rhonda as I am about you." He patted my hand. "I'd prefer if you left this to me."

I couldn't do that. If Kyler Blick was at large, I really needed to step up my game.

Not that this was a game. Or a career move. Or a friend in need. I could poke around where Ian couldn't. Suss out the ...

Oh, who was I kidding? All I had on my suspect list was a cheating womanizer, a nosy neighbor, and a cosplay super fan.

"Don't worry, I'll watch my back. And Rhonda's." I slipped my hand from under his and gave him my *Marie Claire* smile — less wholesome than *Girl's Life*, but more wholesome than *InStyle*.

He frowned. "Don't take this lightly."

"I won't, Ian. I promise."

Opening the door, I slid from the truck and onto the sidewalk. The Tahoe roared down the street. I grabbed the duct-tape strap and hopped inside Billy. Pulled on a ski cap to save my hair and drove one block to park in front of the Dixie Kreme Donut building. The neon "hot and fresh" sign was off as were the lights upstairs. The parking slots empty. If Nash had a gal on the side, they weren't meeting in the office. But then again, Nash had spied on so many cheaters in his previous investigative career, he'd know how to hide a rendezvous.

Not a thought I wanted to have.

Instead, I reminded myself what a dedicated workaholic he was. More than likely, Nash had holed up at DeerNose, looking at spreadsheets or security logs or whatever it was that he did. He probably still wore his tie.

I climbed out of Billy and walked to the stairwell door. Used my old key. I entered, climbed the stairs — skipping the step that sounded like a gunshot — and unlocked the office door.

Relocked it, moved through the front room, and into the back office. Stared at the bed and matching curtains. Grabbed the frayed snow tiger throw, wrapped myself in it, and laid down.

The bed was comfortable, I'd give him that.

I played with the buttons until I achieved the right amount of softness. Texted Tiffany the news about Kyler Blick and the extra detail on Rhonda. Then closed my eyes and went over my day. A long, exhausting day. One where I forgot to tell Ian about Aiden spotting the man and woman at Lorena's house.

Reaching for my phone, I struck something solid on the bed. Opened my eyes to a darkened room. Rolled over. Spied a large body next to me.

And screamed.

THIRTY-THREE

#FreudianShtick #AnOfferTooGood

A light flicked on. Nash peered at me through half-opened eyes. "Is this screaming a habit? Something I have to get used to?"

I held my chest, panting. "When did you get here? I didn't hear you."

"About three or four hours ago. You were asleep." He slipped his arm beneath his head and gave me a long look. A smile curled between his scar and a dimple. "I'm glad you changed your mind about the office."

I sucked in a breath. Had I succumbed to some Freudian call for booty? "About that…"

"Uh-huh." Nash stroked my hip. His eyelids remained at half-mast, but flames licked his ice-chip blues as they studied me. "Can't tell you how I felt, finding you here when I got back. But I can show you—"

"And where were you exactly?"

"DeerNose." The light in his eyes dimmed. Momentarily. Undeterred, his hand skimmed over my hip to my waist and back. "Just working on something."

"What are you working on to keep you out— What time is it anyway?"

A long sigh gusted from his nose, ruffling my hair on the pillow. He cast a look at his watch on the overturned box next to the bed. "Around three."

"Three in the morning?" I sat up. "Oh my God, Daddy's going to kill me."

Nash rolled onto his back and stared at the ceiling. "You're an adult, Maizie."

"But I live there. And Daddy's big on propriety."

"You don't have to live at the cabin."

"Yes, I do. I'm still on probation. Besides, I can't live here."

"Why the hell not?"

Before I could think of a delicately-phrased answer, Nash sat up and mopped his face. "Right. It's a converted office and storage room for a donut shop. What am I thinking? You can't live here."

My heart squeezed at the sound of his despair. I scooted toward him, wrapped my arms around his waist, and laid my head on his bare shoulder. "It's okay. Really it is. We'll get the business back. You won't work at DeerNose forever. We'll make this a PI office again. As soon as possible."

"That's not what I meant, but thanks." He sighed and turned to kiss the top of my head. "It'll be okay, sugar. You're here anyway. That means a lot to me."

He rested his cheek on my hair, and we relaxed against each other for a long moment. Beneath his skin, a slow, steady thrum began to quicken. My pulse accelerated and my toes curled. Slipping an arm around my waist, his other hand rose to cradle my face. Lifting my chin, he planted a soft kiss on my lips. Then another. And another.

When I realized he'd lowered us to the bed, I opened my eyes.

"You're not paying attention," mumbled Nash against my lips. "What am I doing wrong?"

"I forgot to check if there's a black car outside. I need to be more detail-oriented, like you. But it's hard to think like you when you're doing this with me. It's a little weird, to be honest. And I can't switch to Annie when we're like this either. That feels even more strange."

"Sometimes I swear you're speaking a foreign language that only sounds like English." Nash raised himself onto his elbow to look at me. "Maizie, why did you come here tonight if it wasn't to stay with me?"

"I wanted to talk about the case."

He thunked his head on the mattress, then looked up. "I don't know how it was in your past relationships—"

"Do you want to talk about my past relationships?"

"Not really."

"Your past relationships?"

"Definitely not." I opened my mouth and he pressed a thumb to my lips. "Here's how I should've begun that sentence, relationships are give and take, right?"

I nodded.

"Even though it's three a.m. and we've both had a long day, we're going to talk about your case. And in exchange…" He gave me a look. "Okay, we don't have to do everything I want. I'm not that kind of guy. But I'm begging you. Please, sugar. Give me twenty minutes of your undivided attention. Hell, I'll take ten minutes. Make me a happy man. Five minutes with no mention of murder, please?"

How could I resist such a good deal?

*L*ater, wrapped in a frayed snow tiger plushie, I sat on the admittedly soft and now rumpled bed. A box of assorted donuts lay open before me. My skin smelled like Nash's juniper and sage body wash. I chewed a chocolate glazed and wallowed in happiness. My joy skipped and danced beneath and over my skin. Crackling and fizzing like the static electricity that had zinged me earlier from Nash's childhood blanket.

Before you get any ideas, my excitement mostly hinged —

Maybe not mostly. I'd given Nash his turn first. — on watching Nash pace the wooden floor. The creak and groan of wood under his feet meant the silent whirring of cogs and gears in his brain. After I finished telling him about my day, his eyes had lit with another kind of fire. The fire I recognized from our investigation days. His brain buzzed with details, reordering of information, and questions. A lot of questions.

He moved into the front room. I followed him to the window, where he peered between the blind's slats. "No vehicles outside. We can't confirm anyone's watching you until someone other than kids witness it, too. But with Kyler Blick at large, we'll assume they are."

I nodded and slipped my hands around his waist to lay my cheek on his bare back. He turned from the window, gave me a half-hug, and returned to pacing. I eased onto the couch to watch him. This was the Nash I knew and loved. Focused like a Pointer, he was on the hunt, undistracted by temptation.

Of course, we'd already given in to temptation, but he really did seem back on track.

"I have to agree with Mowry about the Martins. Unless you can find more evidence." He held up a hand. "And I don't want to hear your cheerleader argument again. That seemed a little far-fetched to me."

"What about Spencer Newson?"

"Again, you don't have any evidence. And I think you're more worried about Vicki and Newson than him murdering his lover with no motive other than you don't like him."

"Spencer argued with Lorena the day of her murder and lied about it."

"Not cool, but not surprising if they're having an affair."

I scowled. "I still don't like him."

"But this missing crown...didn't Mowry originally think the murder related to a burglary?"

"The police didn't know about the crown until they had gone through her insurance papers. Because the safe was open, they assumed robbery. And when they checked her computer, they found someone had tried to get into her financial information and bank account. At first, they thought Lorena's Mexican bank account might hold Kyler's share of their business. But I don't think they've been able to prove that yet."

"The crown could point to Gary or Kyler." Nash gazed at the ceiling. "Kyler has a personal motive and Lorena had previously placed a restraining order on him. Gary has a history of trespassing and odd behavior. He could be Looney Tunes."

"Cosplay doesn't mean he's Looney Tunes."

"What's cosplay?"

"People who like to dress as fictional characters and go to conventions."

"I didn't know he dressed in those costumes. I thought he just collected them. I was referring to Gary lying about being at home the night of the murder. And secretly meeting with Lorena's chosen photographer."

"I assumed Gary wore costumes if he went to see the photographer." I tapped my chin. "Gary might steal costume pieces, but I don't think he would try to hack into her bank account. They feel like different crimes to me."

"Speaking of the photographer, I want a word with Helmut." Nash had stopped pacing to flex his fists.

I catapulted from the couch, slung my arms around his waist, and looked up at him. "I didn't tell you or Ian at the time for this very reason. Helmut tried to scare me, but he didn't hurt me. I can handle Helmut."

"You didn't tell Mowry?"

"I told Ian about Johnny Sexton, of course. He could have evidence from the night of the murder. But I didn't want Ian to get the wrong idea about Helmut..."

Nash's eyebrow arched. "Why's that?"

"I was afraid he'd make me drop the case. Tonight, when we were in his truck, Ian said as much. He'd prefer I'd leave the investigating to him. He's afraid Kyler might be in Black Pine.

But I can't stop now. What kind of investigator drops a case based on a report of alleged stalking by a black car?"

"Ian told you to drop the case." Nash eyed me for a long moment. "In his truck. Last night?"

I nodded, but my thoughts had returned to Helmut. "I really need to see Johnny Sexton right away. I'm staking out his house in the morning to wait for him or his grandma to leave. I don't want to face Mrs. Sexton again. But I can't let him sell pictures of Lorena. It might already be too late."

THIRTY-FOUR

#TMI (#TooMuchIck)

*I*n the Spayberry cabin kitchen, Remi danced in a circle, holding two donuts above her head. Chocolate with sprinkles and strawberry frosted. With sprinkles. A pack of Jack Russells bounced at her feet, each doing their best to grab a donut. While she shrieked and hooted, the dogs yipped and whined.

My father shook out his newspaper and glowered at Remi. "I didn't know the Dixie Kreme shop was open at four a.m. We thank you for thinking of us, but you don't need to run to town for donuts, Maizie. Carol Lynn makes a good breakfast."

I shot him my *Young Miss* smile and crossed my fingers behind my back. "I was already up. No problem at all."

He eyed me. "Remi sure appreciates it, I give you that."

"How are you dealing with Miss Lorena's death, Daddy? I've been worried about you."

He sighed and dropped his newspaper. "I'm alright. A little shook up, I'll admit. She was such a wonderful gal. You can't believe what they're saying about her."

"I've probably heard it." I sipped my coffee, wondering if he meant her relationship with Spencer Newson. I didn't believe the police had divulged any information about Kyler Blick yet. But word traveled fast in Black Pine. "But what are they saying?"

"Jennifer Frederick reported missing funds in the Clothing Kids account. When Newson went to pay some of the bills from the party, he came up short. Miss Lorena made the withdrawal." Daddy shook his head. "I can't believe it."

I stared at him for a long moment. I couldn't believe it either. "You mean Jennifer thinks Lorena embezzled Clothing Kids funds? It was Lorena's foundation. Why would she do that?"

"I don't understand it either, baby girl. Miss Jennifer said it's easily traced. Miss Lorena made the withdrawal online. From her own computer."

"When did you learn of this?"

"Last night. We have an emergency meeting about it today." He pulled on his beard. "I hate to complain, but I barely have time for this mess. I've got a pickle at DeerNose, but I'll have to fit this meeting in somehow. You'll never guess who's been nominated to take over Miss Lorena's seat. We're supposed to vote on that, too."

I could guess. "Vicki. How do you feel about working with... the new board member?"

He rolled his eyes. "Maizie, my biggest and only regret in life is allowing your mother to take you to California. Even with you becoming a big star. Of course, becoming a big star landed you in the hoosegow and brought you back here, so it turned out alright. God works in mysterious ways."

I knew this. I'd heard this many times throughout my life. I nodded, waiting for "The Point."

"There was a time when I refused to go to the Tru-Buy because I didn't want to see your mother's face on the cover of some paper or magazine. For that matter, your pictures, too. But only if you weren't dressed decently. Or were involved in some jackass behavior. I love seeing your picture, otherwise, honey. When you're fully dressed and acting like a reasonable human being. That's why I've saved every magazine and movie you've been in that didn't cause me discomposure."

I sipped my coffee. More old news.

"As I was saying, your mother is a different story for me. Bitterness is an ugly pill to swallow, Maizie. It casts everything in a negative light and turns your stomach sour. Makes you distrust their every action. Loathe their every decision. We are supposed to forgive and forget for ourselves, you know. When we become resentful, Maizie, we are not at peace. And when we are not at peace, it affects every aspect of our life. Especially our relationships with other people. Carol Lynn, for instance."

This was new. I'd never heard my father dish on Carol Lynn. He sang her praises noon and night. Deservedly. But still, sometimes you'd like to know the woman your father married was human.

"What happened to Carol Lynn?"

"I don't like to speak of this. Particularly with you." He folded his arms across his massive chest. "But I suppose it's a good life lesson."

Daddy loved nothing better than a good life lesson. Normally, at this point, I would tune out. But I leaned forward. "What happened?"

He shifted on his chair. "I am not a young father to Remi, as you may have noticed. Neither is Carol Lynn particularly young."

I slunk back in my seat and bit my lip. These were the times I wished my father was a man of a few words. A quality I found attractive in Nash. Usually.

"We could not get with child, Maizie. Not until Carol Lynn sat me down and spoke the frank and utter truth. My seed would not spawn until I had rid myself of that hatred and ugliness."

Burying my head in my hands, I slipped lower in my seat until my tailbone hit the bottom edge of the chair.

"When I forgave your mother, we conceived Remi. Remi is a

constant reminder that I cannot live my life in a state of resentment. I was the one who let Vicki take you to California. Any idiot could foresee she would stay out there. But I lacked faith. I feared she would ruin you or ruin my relationship with you. I didn't want to trust her, because it was easier to hate her. She almost ruined you, but it turned out all right. My prayers were answered when—"

A long howl set off a succession of barks and a peal of giggles. Daddy turned in his chair. "Remington Marie, eat those dang donuts or give them to the dogs. Y'all are driving me half out of my mind with all the hooting and hollering. Can't you see I'm trying to have a conversation with your sister? I swear if you don't stop teasing those dogs, I'm never letting you have another donut again."

Remi quickly licked the frosting off the donuts and tossed them on the floor. The dogs pounced on the fallen donuts like a pack of hyenas on a downed wildebeest.

"Remi," he growled.

"You said I could feed the dogs." She fluttered her lashes. "'Sides, I'm your forgiveness reminder."

She skipped out of the room, and Daddy turned back in his chair to face me. Mopping his face, he cleared his throat. "As I was saying, my prayers were answered when you were arrested."

"Thank you for telling me. That was very...enlightening."

"You see, if Vicki's on that board, I may not like it. For the sake of our relationship, I may quit if she gets too irritating. But I can deal with it."

"I understand completely." I slid out of the chair and hopped to my feet. "I need to do a stakeout. But can you tell me — just yes or no — do the police know about the embezzlement?"

"I believe—"

"Taking that as a yes." I leaned over to peck his cheek and hightailed it from the room before he enlightened me on anything else.

. . .

I couldn't believe Lorena would embezzle funds from her own foundation. Not for a minute. But then I couldn't believe she'd have an affair with Spencer Newson. Or had stolen money from her ex-boyfriend. My feelings about Lorena were discombobulated at best. Nevertheless, I still felt I had an obligation to protect her from the tabloids as well as I could. Criminal or not, she didn't deserve to die the way she did.

Before doing my stakeout, I stopped at the new office. My link chart remained in the window. I noticed two new hand-drawn sticky notes had been added — a bear and a key. Taking a cue from Annie's cards, I sketched an iron, a crown, and a dollar sign and stuck them next to the key. Then wrote "Missing Evidence" on a note and placed it above the illustrations. I added notes to Gary's card, listing his prior arrests, and drew a line from Gary to the crown. Drew another line from Kyler Blick to the crown. Then drew a black car and a stick-figure woman and man, each with question marks above their heads.

"Don't think they use stick figures on real link charts."

I jumped and twisted around.

Annie stood behind me with a cup of coffee and a Dixie Kreme donut in her hands. "Like my bear?"

"Very funny."

Annie moved forward and squinted at my new pictures. She tapped on a sticky note. "What's that? A boat?"

"An iron. Most likely the murder weapon. It's missing. So are funds from the Clothing Kids Foundation. They think Lorena embezzled."

"The plot thickens." She dipped her donut into her coffee. "Where're you off to today?"

"Sorry. I'm going on another stakeout. Just until Johnny Sexton's grandma leaves the house. He might have evidence of the murder."

"I guess that means you're not going to do those background checks?" She cocked her head toward my desk.

I glanced at the pile of folders. "I promise some overtime. Just as soon as I get back..." Who was I kidding? "As soon as I sort out Lorena's murder."

Annie snorted. "You're so lucky I can't fire you without your mother's permission."

*R*eturning to Grandma Sexton's neighborhood, I did a reconnaissance drive-by. Johnny's little blue hatchback sat in the drive. Not spying Grandma's vehicle, I parked in front. Then remembered the black car and checked the street. No car. Also, no kids.

Thumbs up.

I pulled off my ski cap, climbed out of Billy, and darted up the walk to ring the doorbell. Taking some deep breaths, I centered myself and focused on my mashup detective character. When Johnny Sexton opened the door, I stuck my foot in the door — I wore my Stuart Weitzman lug-sole ankle boots for this purpose — then wedged myself inside.

"Hi, Johnny. I'm Maizie Albright."

"I know who you are." Tall and lanky, Johnny's smirk did not become him. Friendly smiles flattered his body type. That being said, smirks didn't flatter anyone. "I think I know why you're here. Come in."

I followed him past a living room crammed with furniture and knicknacks. Framed photos of Sinatra and the Rat Pack hung on the walls. Along with Doris Day. James Dean. Ricky Nelson. Elizabeth Taylor. Gene Tierney. Marilyn Monroe. The room was like a New York deli decorated in floral fabric and heavy drapes. Smelling of kitty litter and Lysol, rather than rye and corned beef.

Now I knew where Johnny gained his interest in following celebrities.

We tromped into a kitchen and the scent of day-old fish assailed my nostrils. Johnny stopped at the counter where a gutted fish lay on a cutting board. He picked up a knife and waved it at me. "You want to buy the pictures, right?"

"Helmut's pictures?" I gasped, trying to breathe out of my mouth.

"Helmut didn't take them. I did."

I pinched my nose, not caring that I sounded like one of Alvin's chipmunks. "I saw you buying Helmut's pictures. He said you sell stories to the tabloids."

"Helmut." Johnny rolled his eyes and scoffed. "I thought you wanted to buy the pictures I have of you and your friend."

"What pictures of me and what friend?" My mind ran through a zillion photo ops I hoped would never see the light of day. Between the stinky fish and the threat of more public humiliation, I found it difficult to focus on Lorena. "Can we talk somewhere else? I can't breathe."

"My Gran wants these fish filleted. She's frying them for our lunch." He held up the knife. "She'll be back any minute. Talk money or get out."

"I want to talk. But your gran won't want me losing my cookies on her floor either. By the way, I didn't have cookies for breakfast. Leftover grits and sausage. And four donuts."

Huffing, he tossed the knife on the cutting board and strode to the kitchen door. "Come on. To be honest, she won't want you in her house at all. She's not a fan."

"I could tell." I hurried after him. Stepping onto their driveway, I drew in a lungful of fresh air before I continued. "I want to know what pictures you bought from Helmut. Were there any of Lorena Cortez?"

"Possibly," he drew out the word.

If Johnny was a cartoon figure, dollar signs would flash in his eyes.

No longer able to harness Annie-Nash, I tuned into my Julia

Pinkerton "I seriously want to kick your butt" teenager voice. "The photos could be evidence of a serious crime."

"You mean Lorena Cortez's murder?" He leaned against his car, unconcerned. "I heard you were working as a private eye. Taking your new role seriously, are you?"

"Yes, I am." I tilted my chin. "Super serious. I want to see those pictures."

"No worries." Johnny smiled with his teeth. "But it's pay to play. We can add the pictures I took at Lorena's house that night to your bill."

"Pictures *you* took at Lorena's? You were at Lorena's house? The night she was murdered?"

"Not inside the house, unfortunately. Across the street with my Canon."

My heart thudded in my chest. "Did you tell the police you were there that night?"

"No. Are you crazy? I don't want to get tied up in a murder investigation."

"What were you doing at Lorena's?"

"There was a small buzz about the party. With Cortez's connections, I hoped it would attract some celebs." He frowned. "You were the biggest. Disappointing."

My Annie-Nash mashup wouldn't allow me to feel hurt. I could explore that feeling later. I was (hopefully) on the brink of breaking the case and felt too delighted for the pangs of humiliation. "Did you see anyone go inside Lorena's house?"

"I definitely saw you and your friend," Johnny smirked. "Got some good snaps of the two of you sitting in the back of an ambulance after. I had the scoop on the murder. Got a great shot of them wheeling out Lorena Cortez's body. Totally awesome."

I shuddered. Dante needed a new ring of hell specifically for tabloid hawkers.

"And Maizie Albright covered in blood in her *Julia Pinkerton* cheer uniform?" He whistled. "That kind of speculation's worth a hella of a lot of green, too. I held on to those snaps, knowing as the case progressed, they would be worth more. Anyway, I didn't want to tip off the police that I was there."

"You slimeball," I shouted. "How could you?"

"That's how I get paid. If people want the story, it's considered news. The more clicks, the more ad dollars pour into the story. Doesn't matter if it's true or not. By the time a retraction is written, or the story is pulled, the photo's already paid off." He slid me another toothy shark smile. "That's how it works, baby."

I fought off the impulse to argue and focused on breaking the case. "Did you see anyone else at the house? Before Rhonda and I arrived at Lorena's?"

"I thought I saw someone. Grabbed a couple shots, hoping it was a celeb sneaking in to get their costume."

"Who was it?" I held my breath.

"Dunno. And I don't want to know. Like I said, I don't want to get mixed in with a murder investigation."

"What are you saying? You didn't examine the photos?"

"It wasn't anybody I recognized. I'm hanging on to them to see if they'll be worth more, too. I have a few 'news outlets' interested," he said, making air quotes. "They're always interested, even if the pictures don't really show anything. They can use them with 'suggestions' as to who's in the pic."

Frigalicious.

I massaged my temples. "You can't do this. You're talking about withholding evidence needed in a murder investigation. That's illegal."

"We're also talking about a hella of a lot of dough. And I'm not withholding anything. How many crimes are recorded on people's phones today? Are they withholding evidence?"

"But you know it was a crime. A homicide."

"The police don't know I know." He leaned forward. "How about we make a deal? You buy the pictures and keep your mouth shut, then I won't spill the pictures of bloody Julia Pinkerton? That seems fair. 'Cause I know I can sell them, even if your career is kaput. Hell, your mother would probably pay good money for them."

My lips tightened along with the air in my lungs. "The police need to see those photos. All of them."

"I wonder how much shots of you in the cheer skirt would go for? I should ask around."

"I want to see the photos you took at Lorena's that night." I narrowed my eyes and lowered my voice. "Now."

"Not without payment."

I gritted my teeth. "How much for all of them?"

"Hmm. I need to see what they're worth on the market first." Johnny smirked. "How 'bout I text you a figure. It'll give you time to round up the dough. No checks from you, though. I've heard you're broke. But if Vicki Albright is paying...does she Venmo?"

I had no idea if Vicki Venmo'd, but she'd want the money retrievable, if necessary. "She'll only pay by check."

"I'd rather have cash."

"Cash would take longer," I lied. "Her accountant would have to make the withdrawal and he's still in California. Vicki doesn't touch paper money because of the germs. Check or credit card."

"Fine, a check." He held up his phone. "Your digits?"

Shiztastic. I didn't want my phone number in the hands of a skeezy slimeball. But now I needed to protect Rhonda as well as Lorena. I gave him my number. "Do not sell those pictures to anyone else. If you leak them to anyone other than the police, I'm not paying anything."

"Yeah, yeah. Heard it before." Johnny rocked back in his checked Van's and shoved his hands in the pockets of his baggy Levi's. "But remember if you're buying, the deal's off. I want Vicki Albright money."

THIRTY-FIVE

#Talegating #VenusDeVicki

*D*iscouraged, I schlepped onto the sidewalk. Hearing the roar of a car's engine, I pivoted. A black sedan turned the corner at the end of the block. Across the street, the kids hopped and pointed.

"That's it!" screamed the oldest boy. "They were parked right by your truck."

"Did you get a license plate?" I shouted. "Or the make and model? Who was driving?"

"It was black," shouted the girl, jumping. "Black, black, black."

"Can you come back so we can play in your truck?" said the younger boy.

Giving up on my spies, I leaped into Billy and yanked on my ski cap. Too hard. Rolled the brim and shoved on my sunglasses. I accelerated toward the end of the street where the car had turned. Rounding the corner, I entered another neighborhood street. The black car had disappeared. Side streets spoked off the main road. I glanced down each one as I approached. The older neighborhood was a maze of branching arteries. Staying on the main street, I followed it until it looped back to the entrance.

I drove around for another ten minutes. Black vehicles proliferated. Parked in driveways. On streets. Sitting in traffic on the business highway. A black minivan passed me as I meandered through the neighborhood. A teenage girl drove. The rear window sported stickers of a Mickey Mouse-eared family of five. I figured the kids would remember Mickey Mouse people. I also didn't think my stalker was a teenage girl.

Giving up, I drove back to the office. I needed Vicki Albright-money to rescue crime scene photos. I also wanted to know how much money had been embezzled from Clothing Kids. I hoped for a better explanation than embezzlement. Possibly Jennifer Frederick had jumped to a hasty conclusion. She had seemed touchy about the subject of Spencer and Lorena anyway. I also felt I should see Rhonda.

I called Ian first.

"I can't talk," he said. "We have a warrant to search Gary's house. How about lunch after?"

Before I could answer, he hung up.

I called Rhonda.

"She can't talk," said Chad. "She's too busy watching the street for a black car."

"Why don't you watch the street for her?"

"Why does anyone need to watch for a black car? Do you know how many black cars drive down the street? Besides, there's a cop who drives by every thirty minutes. I told her that would keep any black car from stalking her. This is getting ridiculous. I'm starting to think nobody wants Rhonda dead. And if she doesn't take a shower, I'm going to kill her." He hung up.

I called Jennifer Frederick.

"I have to prepare for a meeting, I can't talk," she said.

"If it's about the missing Clothing Kids funds, that's why I called. Just give me a minute of your time."

"How do you know about that?" She paused, likely remembering I was a private investigator. Or more likely that both of my parents were now on the board. "What do you want?"

"Do you believe Lorena would really steal funds from the foundation she created? What evidence do you have?"

"It's easy to see money in the Clothing Kids account was transferred to her bank account. Lorena stole the money."

"What if she took out money to pay for something and —"

"I'm a professional auditor. And I don't have time for this." She hung up.

Zero for three.

My phone chimed and I glanced at the number. Johnny Sexton. Wanting an outrageous payout.

I needed faith in humanity restored. Making me even more reluctant to call my mother. If I had to deal with one more bad conversation, I might as well text.

Fortunately for me — or maybe not, depending on your point of view — this wasn't the first paparazzo Vicki and I had to bribe. Not trusting our phones, we used emojis as coded messages.

I texted, "angry face, pile of poo, vampire, camera, bag of money."

A moment later, I received Vicki's reply, "angry face, money with wings, and finger pointed down."

Vicki had returned my text with one requirement: I had to pick up the money now and in person.

"I'm leaving again," I called to Annie.

"Not surprised," she hollered back.

*K*eeping my eye out for black cars — I saw six — I drove through town to Black Pine Mountain. I turned onto a drive lined with topiaries, leading to the stone monstrosity known as the Peanut Mansion. When I pulled before the stately porch, I found Vicki waiting for me. I pulled off my helmet and slid out of Billy. Vicki's Manolo Blahniks made quick work across the fieldstone walk and stopped before reaching my door.

Since I last visited, the porch had gained gas lights and new topiaries — pineapples — in verdigris-encrusted urns. A Neoclassical-styled statue stood nearby — a woman in a flimsy toga bearing a basket of grapes. A Roman-Greco-ish woman resembling a definitely non-Greek-nor-Roman Vicki. I grimaced, preferring Vicki's likeness in a heavier drape with full coverage. Greco-Roman Vicki could also use a sports bra.

"What did you do?" I said. "Buy out Restoration Hardware?"

"I only use real reproductions." She pointed at the Bronco, curling her lip. "What is that?"

"My new car."

"I'm not sure what it is but certainly not a car. And definitely not new. Why are you driving it?"

"Because it's more comfortable than a dirt bike."

"Then why are you wearing a helmet?"

"I left my ski cap at the office. My other hats blow off. And I'd rather have helmet-head than ratted hair."

"You've never heard of a scarf?" She waved the check and a piece of paper. "He signs the affidavit first. We're suing him if the photos are released. Don't give him the check until you see the pictures to confirm he has them. And make sure you get his memory card."

"I want you to cancel the check after I have the pictures," I said in my firm mashup voice.

She raised a perfectly drawn eyebrow. "Parasites don't take kindly to bait and switch, Maizie."

"We're not dealing with your usual parasite. The photos could be evidence—"

She held up a hand. "I don't want to know evidence of what. I just hope it's something from your past and not a present bad judgment call."

"Speaking of bad judgment calls, I heard you had a conference with Spencer Newson yesterday."

She arched a brow. "Checking up on me?"

"I'm doing it for your own good." I crossed my arms. "I thought I was chaperoning that meeting."

"That was a joke." She sniffed. "Besides, you were busy with the photoshoot."

"So was Spencer. I saw him there. With his *wife*."

"Really, Maizie." She rolled her eyes. "We were going over financial information for a charity. A charity that needs me. Now. As in, I need to leave immediately. Clothing Kids has an emergency meeting."

"I know all about it. I'm going with you. I want to know more about what Jennifer Frederick discovered. It might be connected to Lorena's murder."

"No, you're not. This isn't a Miss Marple moment. It's a board meeting. The public isn't invited." She strode up the stone stairs to her porch. The front door closed behind her.

I stamped my foot and gritted my teeth. I sounded like Annie-Nash. I just couldn't get Annie-Nash results. So frustrating.

Jumping back into Billy, I grabbed my helmet, but before I could pull it on, my phone rang again.

"We got him," said Ian. "I'm buying lunch. I know this great place you'll love. I'll text you the address. Fried chicken and pimento cheese sandwiches."

"Wait. Got who?"

"Gary. I'll tell you all about it at lunch. Meet me there in an hour."

I should've been happy. It sounded like Ian had arrested Gary. There was no black car stalking me. No one stalking Rhonda. Lorena could be laid to rest. I was going to have an incredible lunch. I don't know if a better lunch could be created than by combining fried chicken and pimento cheese.

To be honest, the words "fried chicken and pimento" had thrilled me more than "we got him."

"I suck," I said to Billy since no one else was with me. "Why am I not excited the police caught Lorena's killer? I'll tell you why. Because I suck. I wanted to catch the culprit. I wanted to prove who did it. I wanted Tiffany and Rhonda to call me Sherlock. Which, I know they already do. But Sherlock in a non-sarcastic tone would be nice."

I shook my head. "And Ian. He's just as bad. Is it because I'm a ginger he calls me Daphne? Or is it because everyone knows Velma is the brains behind Mystery, Inc.? For once in my life, I want everyone to think I'm Velma, not Daphne. I don't even like purple."

Vicki's black Escalade pulled around from the side of the mansion. The driver waved, but Vicki was on her phone and didn't notice me. They sped down the drive.

"This is why I can never live up to Annie-Nash. I'm shallow and selfish, Billy. I could have gotten a 1986 Chevy Impala with doors and windows, but because it wasn't a convertible I wouldn't consider it. Also because it was purple. And had questionable stains on the back seat. But I was so stuck on having a convertible, I ended up with you. What kind of mountain dweller buys a convertible? As a main mode of transportation, that's a really immature choice."

I patted the dash. "But you still have seats, seatbelts, and an awesome stereo, which is a major upgrade from Lucky. Don't feel bad."

Pulling on my helmet, I accelerated down the drive, almost catching up to the Escalade. I followed them into town. Nearing the old downtown and the historic district, we passed the Dixie Kreme Donut building and the new office where a pile of background checks waited for me. However, I didn't stop. I took a secondary street, then an alley, and parked behind Jennifer Frederick's house.

Gary may have killed Lorena physically, but I still couldn't believe Lorena would have ripped off her own foundation. Was I selfish and shallow? Yes, I was. Was I Annie-Nash or even

Velma? No, I wasn't. But I was a friend. One who would fight to protect Lorena's memory.

Johnny Sexton wanted me to meet him later in the afternoon, but I could do something for Lorena now.

Give this board a piece of my mind.

THIRTY-SIX

#RighteousRebellion
#BreakingAndEnding

*J*ennifer had a back gate to her secluded cottage. More importantly, a gate that wasn't locked. I stalked toward the house, keeping my mind focused on the Lorena I knew and loved growing up. One who made me Barbie clothes. Who insisted Julia Pinkerton wouldn't wear orange bedazzled low-rise jeans. Or Ed Hardy anything. Who listened to my sad teenage stories — about loneliness and lack of boyfriends and work exhaustion and homework and my manager/mother — with real empathy and understanding. And hugs. And cookies. Who would also bawl me out for my teenage stupidity. Like drooling over a gaffer who was too old for me. Or for taking diet pills and starving myself because my cheer skirt needed a less restrictive fit.

The woman I knew was not the Lorena described since her murder. A cheater, a thief, and good gravy, an embezzler? Not the Lorena I knew.

By the time I reached Jennifer Frederick's back porch, I had filled myself with good memories of Lorena and righteous anger for the Black Pine elite. Lorena had asked for their help in clothing children. They had repaid her by stripping her bare and destroying her name.

Jennifer's back door opened into her kitchen. I hesitated, knowing I was about to criminally trespass. I could possibly be arrested. While on probation. But I also knew I'd be ignored at the front door.

No doubt, my bravado had something to do with the knowledge that both of my parents were inside Jennifer's house. But I would save that thought for a later therapy session.

Creeping through the kitchen door, I heard voices coming to my left. A swinging door connected the kitchen to what I guessed was the dining room. I stood before the door, building my courage, searching for the right words to use for my tirade, and trying different voice styles. Annie-Nash seemed the appropriate choice, but so often affronted, Julia Pinkerton gave a great rebuke.

A rumble sounding like my father stopped my whispered recitation. "How do you know Miss Lorena wasn't using those funds to pay for materials or the caterer or some such?"

"We always discussed transactions before they were made." The crisp tones told me Jennifer Frederick had answered him.

"And the police said she had a bank in Mexico," drawled a man's voice. Spencer Newson. "She could have moved the funds into that account."

"Let's not make those speculations, Spencer," said Jennifer. "We'll just stick to the facts. The money in the account is missing and it was withdrawn by Lorena. There are no receipts or orders to show for it."

"Doesn't it seem strange to any of you, that on the day Lorena purportedly stole this money, she was also murdered?" Vicki's intonation was as clear to me as the scent of her Chanel No 5. "Maybe she was forced to withdraw that money, then killed."

Holy frigalicious.

I sucked in my breath, unable to believe my mother had articulated the very thought that had nagged my brain. The police had originally believed the murder was related to the robbery. The scissors in the back had been personal. That's why Kyler

Blick had seemed the most obvious suspect. And why Gary didn't make as much sense as the murderer. Gary had enough money to purchase a mini-mansion across the street from Lorena and fill it with expensive costumes. As a stalker, he did everything top rate. He probably paid full-price for Helmut's photo session. Helmut was not cheap.

Then why would Gary steal the Clothing Kids funds? To pay for his stalking? It seemed more sensible for Gary to rob a bank if he wanted to park an upgraded Tesla across the street from Lorena. Not that murdering the woman he most admired was sensible.

This wasn't just about being selfish and shallow. I didn't want Ian to arrest Gary because I didn't believe Gary had killed Lorena.

Maybe I didn't suck as bad as I thought I did.

The door swung open. Jennifer Frederick shrieked.

Okay, I did suck. Certainly, I made a terrible spy. But I had also regained my righteous anger and Julia Pinkerton's indignant spirit.

As if I hadn't been caught eavesdropping in her kitchen, I pushed past Jennifer to stride into the dining room. "It is strange that Lorena Cortez embezzled and was murdered on the same night. I don't believe she stole that money and you shouldn't either. I will continue to investigate these crimes until the whole truth comes to light. I. Will. Not. Stop."

The Martins, Spencer Newson, and Daddy gaped at me from their seats around a dining room table littered with notebooks, electronic devices, muffins, and coffee cups. Vicki also sat at the table across from Jan Martin and next to Spencer Newson — likely a strategic move on her part — but she did not gape.

She rolled her eyes and gusted a long, bored sigh. "I told you this wasn't a public meeting. And certainly not a Jessica Fletcher moment. Or whatever that was. But thank you for backing up my very obvious conclusion that certainly didn't need a dramatic response."

"Vicki, did you invite Maizie?" said Daddy.

"This is your problem, Boomer, you don't listen. Couldn't you infer that from my response?"

"Hold on now," said Spencer. "Your daughter is a delight, Vicki, but we can't have her coming in and interrupting a board meeting."

"She's my daughter, too, Spencer," said Daddy. "Sit down, Maizie."

"I don't want to sit down. After I told everyone off, I planned to leave."

"This never happens at Historical Society meetings," said Jan Martin. "Does it, Dennis?"

"No, never," said Dennis. "But I will say most people on that board are too old to have young children."

"I'm not that young," I said, then regretted it. "I'm here to defend Lorena Cortez's honor. Spencer Newson, you of all people, should be speaking up on behalf of Lorena instead of trying to prove she embezzled. Shame on you."

"Really, Maizie," said Vicki.

"She's right," said Daddy. "Don't defend Newson. Let Maizie speak."

"Not when she's stealing lines from old TV scripts." Vicki leaned back in her chair and crossed her arms. "Would you take your Julia Pinkerton-isms and go do some real work? I know you've left Annie Cox stranded."

Dangit. But I wouldn't be deterred by Vicki. I was on a right-eous roll.

"Whatever Lorena did..." I gave Spencer the stink-eye. "... you people need to support Lorena for the sake of the charity. I can't believe the Clothing Kids board could even consider Lorena stealing from her own foundation. She deserves a lot better from her board. It makes me question why any of you are here."

I noted among the gasps, Daddy's stormy face. I quickly added, "Except Daddy. I know he loved Lorena."

When Vicki narrowed her eyes, and I added, "In a purely platonic sense. They understood each other creatively."

"I've seen you snooping," said Jan Martin. "You told me you were working for the board."

"No, I didn't. You assumed I was when you gave me the guest lists."

"Are you working for the police?" said Spencer.

"Investigating Lorena's death is a personal mission."

"This is ridiculous," said Jennifer. "I don't know who's paying you for this so-called investigation, but it doesn't give you the right to break into my house. I ought to call the police."

"Don't bother," I said, recognizing my cue to leave. "I'm late for lunch with Detective Ian Mowry. And you better believe I'm going to tell him I was at this meeting."

*A*s I stalked out of the living room and through the front door, I decided not to tell Ian I had broken into Jennifer Frederick's house, eavesdropped on the Clothing Kids Foundation board, then made a bunch of dumb accusations and ultimatums. I'd embarrassed my parents, ticked off the Martins, and infuriated Jennifer Frederick.

Really more of a Shaggy than a Daphne move.

Approaching the sidewalk, I realized I'd also exited out the wrong door. I mentally facepalmed. Black cars, including Vicki's Escalade, lined the road before Jennifer's house. Every board member drove a black car. Even Daddy's King Ranch pickup was black. I spotted Susie Newson sitting in the driver's seat of a Mercedes (black) and filing her nails. Deciding to leave my humiliation for a later analysis, I approached her.

"Are you waiting for Spencer?" I asked her after she rolled down the window.

"I'm always waiting for Spencer. He's forever in some meeting or another. I'm never invited. He calls them networking, but I know better, right? He has some nerve telling me I need to work more. It's his ex-wife that took everything, not me."

Her pout hid other feelings. Likely the heartache of being replaced as the other woman. Then finding out her sugar daddy wasn't as rich as she thought. No wonder she was irritated with Spencer. What had Lorena seen in him?

Or Vicki for that matter. Which made me worried for a whole different reason.

"I was told the meeting was private," I said gently. "That's probably why you weren't invited."

"Private meetings are so stupid. If I sit in there and listen, what's going to happen? Do they think I'll leak the flavor of Jennifer's non-fat muffins to the press? Believe me, nobody cares about her tasteless blueberry muffins."

Ouch. "I don't think you missed much. I got kicked out."

"Wow. That's harsh." She examined her nails. "What will you do now?"

"I'm meeting Detective Ian Mowry for lunch."

"You're dating the cop?"

"No, to talk about the case," I exclaimed. Not defensively. At all. "We've been working the investigation together. Sort of. I've also got another meeting. Sort of. And some work at the office. Busy, busy."

"Where's your truck?"

"It's not a truck, it's a—" I sighed. "My truck is parked in the alley behind Jennifer's house. I went in through the back door."

"Come on. I'll give you a ride."

Slipping inside the Mercedes, I drew in the scent of cupcakes or cookies. "Smells like you've been baking muffins in here."

Susie tapped on an air freshener. "It's extra strong because my workouts can make me a little rank."

At a loss for words, I nodded. TMI. Susie was what my father would call "plainspoken."

As I clipped my belt, Susie pulled away from the curb and sped around the corner. She jerked to a stop behind Billy.

"Thanks a lot," I said. "That would have been awkward cutting back through the house, and I'm kind of tired of walking around these yards."

"No problem. I need to do something anyway."

I got out of the car and waved her off. The Mercedes zoomed out of the alley. I wondered how Spencer would get home. Then wondered if Susie had been spying on Spencer. Then figured a man like Spencer probably deserved a little spying on. The PI office cases were filled with men like Spencer. Probably another reason why I didn't like him. I'd spied on a lot of Spencers in the last few months.

That thought brought me to my lunch with Ian. Which wasn't a date. But I fretted over Susie telling Spencer I was dating Ian. Those kinds of rumors spread like small-town wildfire in Black Pine. It would get to Vicki…

I called Nash. "Are you busy for lunch?"

"Doubt I'll take lunch. I'm busy in general." Corporate Nash had returned.

"The restaurant's called Sophie Lu's and it's in an old house. They have fried chicken and pimento cheese sandwiches." I didn't know why I bothered to try to seduce Nash with food. That only worked on me. And Ian.

"Gotta go, hon'."

Oh right, not the food. Ian. "Ian invited me. It's a working lunch. Just an F.Y.I."

Nash had already hung up. I spoke to a dial tone.

I huffed out a frustrated breath. I had bigger fish to fry anyway. Gary and Johnny Sexton.

With fried chicken and pimento cheese in between.

THIRTY-SEVEN

#LunchBunch #SouthernFriedSlam

I entered the shabby-chic restaurant, a converted cottage. The homey scents of frying chicken, baking biscuits, and a blend of spices surrounded me. I had entered a place of peace and comfort where I could set aside my mounting self-doubt and insecurities and recenter myself.

Fried chicken worked better than yoga that way, IMHO.

Ian sat at a small table near a window. Spotting me, he waved me over, then handed me a menu. "I know you're gonna love this place, Maizie."

"I already do." I smiled at him, then remembered to swap to my mashup character. To keep myself on track and keep Ian squarely in the friend-zone. "What evidence did you find on Gary? Did he force Lorena to empty the Clothing Kids' coffers? It doesn't seem like a Gary move to me, but I also don't believe Lorena would—"

"Cool your jets, Daphne." Ian grinned. "Let's order first. I've only got an hour before I need to get back to the department. They're processing Gary as we speak."

He waved over the waitress. The thirty-something woman cooed over his choices, then gave me a once-over when I ordered the same thing.

Not everyone was a fan. As clearly evident this week.

"Tell me about Gary," I said.

"The crown-thing was in his safe. That goofball even had the same kind of safe as Ms. Cortez."

"Gary stole the crown?"

"He claims he bought it from her. But he had no receipt and the details were sketchy." Ian leaned forward. "And guess what else we found?"

I put my folded arms on the table and leaned forward. "What?"

"The iron was in his garbage."

"What? Why would he leave the murder weapon in his garbage?"

"Outside can. According to the routes I checked, the pickup would have happened tomorrow. Can you believe it? We barely made it. All thanks to your tip, Daphne."

"That seems kind of convenient. And dumb on Gary's part."

Ian shrugged. "Takes all kinds. Most criminals aren't very intelligent. Look how many times he broke into the studio after getting arrested."

"Did Gary confess?"

"Of course not. But I'm questioning him today. The physical evidence is fairly condemning."

"What about prints? Were his prints on the iron?"

Ian chuckled. "Listen to you, Miss CSI. Nobody's prints were on the iron in our initial test. But I sent it to GBI to have them look at it microscopically."

"What about the money?"

He shifted in his chair. "I know you don't want to hear this, but it looks like Gary just stole the crown. The missing funds seem to be a different crime that's unrelated but complicated the homicide investigation. That happens sometimes."

"This doesn't sit right with me, though. I don't understand Gary's motive for killing Lorena."

"Tell me about it. My guess is he wanted the crown, got her to open the safe, and killed her. I'm sure his lawyer will go for an NGRI, an insanity plea. If the defense can prove Gary's crazy, he'll only get voluntary manslaughter." Ian grimaced, then looked over my shoulder. His scowl turned to glee and he practically bounced in his chair. "Here it comes. You'll love this."

The waitress returned, bearing a large tray overflowing with manna in the form of fried chicken and pimento cheese sandwiches. My eyes grew round, my mouth watered, and my stomach clenched ecstatically. She set the plates in front of us, gave Ian a more-than-friendly wink and smile, and sashayed into the kitchen.

"I think the waitress likes you."

"I'm just here a lot." He shrugged, oblivious, then turned his beaming smile from his plate to me. "You want to try my broccoli salad?"

I did want to try his broccoli salad. I also wanted him to take me seriously.

"I know you're doing your job, Ian. But I'm not satisfied. Maybe Gary went berserk and killed Lorena. But I still can't believe she embezzled funds. I'm continuing my investigation."

"That kind of news is always hard to hear." Ian took a bite of the sandwich and moaned. "Can you believe how good this is?"

"Remember the paparazzo who bought Helmut's photos?" I continued. "He has photos of the crime scene." I recounted my conversation with Johnny.

"No kidding," said Ian. "Good work, Daphne. I'll put Johnny Sexton on my to-do list. Have him picked up in a jiff."

"Before you send an officer over there, you should let me talk to him first. He made me an offer to buy the photos. I'll give them to you. He has some sensational pictures of me and Rhonda after we left the house, and he thinks that's why I really want them."

"Evidence, hon'. I'll pick him up. Save your money. That's sweet of you to offer, though."

I wasn't trying to be sweet. I lowered my voice, trying for a better Annie-Nash resonation. "If you send an officer over there, Johnny will trash the photos. He doesn't want to get mixed up in a murder investigation."

"We'll get those pictures anyway. Don't you worry."

But I was worried. I knew guys like Johnny Sexton.

"You're gonna love this. Very tangy." Ian pushed his bowl toward me.

I dipped my fork into his broccoli salad and felt eyes on me. A giant in khaki's, a blue button-down, and a camo tie stood at our table, silently watching us.

Nash.

Ian's eyes followed mine. "Hey there, buddy. Have a seat. Let me get the waitress back here with a menu."

Nash kept his icy blue gaze on me. "Looks like you're sharing, Mowry. Maybe I'll eat off your plate, too."

A flush crawled up my neck and slapped my cheeks. I scooted my chair closer to the window, making room for him. "Glad you could make it."

"Me, too." His gaze was heavy but inscrutable. He grabbed a chair at an empty table but centered it on the far side of the table, between us. "Are you discussing the Cortez homicide?"

"Yep," said Ian. "We nabbed our perp very early this morning."

"Who'd you arrest?"

Ian finished chewing and swallowed. "The neighbor, Gary. Maizie gave me that lead and now she has another one on a photographer who might have evidence of the crime."

Nash arched an eyebrow. "Who's the photographer?"

"Some creepster trying to get photos of celebrities at Cortez's house the night of the homicide. He might have shots of our perp. And he's got pictures of Maizie from the night in question. Wearing that cute, little cheerleader outfit that got all bloody."

Nash's scar pulsed with the tightening of his jaw. "That so? Her *cute, little* outfit?"

"Can you believe this jackass wants to sell pictures of Maizie?

He doesn't care if the photos compromise her. Really too bad that outfit was ruined, though."

"I'm worried Johnny will dump the pictures," I gabbled, trying to move their attention away from the cheer skirt. "He doesn't want to deal with the police."

"I told you, I'd get a warrant, hon'. We can get those photos even if he deletes them. Don't you worry." He nodded and picked up his sandwich. "Nash, this is amazing. You need to order one."

"But I want to see those pictures, too," I blurted. "It's my break and I want to know if Johnny took a picture of the killer. Maybe Gary didn't do it. Who throws the murder weapon in their own garbage?"

"Now, Maizie." Ian laid down his sandwich.

"Don't 'now Maizie' me, Ian. You're being really patronizing." I pushed his salad bowl to the other side of the table. "You're treating me like...I don't know...a..."

"A civilian?"

Nash reached for my tea glass and sipped.

"I'm more than a civilian, Ian. And I can continue to investigate if I want."

"Now, don't get upset, hon'. I'm saving you a lot of wasted effort and time." Ian forked a piece of broccoli. "You sure you don't want more of this salad?"

"I'm sure," I fumed. "It's not wasted time and effort. How can I rest when everyone thinks Lorena stole from her own charity? It's horrible. She was my friend."

"Hon', I told you this might be too personal for you." Ian swung his gaze from me to Nash, who watched us through hooded eyes. "Nash, tell her how it is when I have an active investigation."

"I don't need Nash to tell me how it is. I understand the rules." I realized other diners had turned toward our table and lowered my voice. "I also understand that if I'm not breaking the law, I can do what I want. Like talking to Johnny."

Nash picked up my sandwich and took a bite. "Very tasty. I'm so glad you recommended this place, Mowry. It's been enlightening. Think I'll order this to go."

I placed a hand on his arm. "To go? You're not staying?"

"Got to get back to work." He smiled. "Besides, I think you can handle Detective Mowry without me."

"I didn't ask you to lunch to help me with Ian." I jumped up, knocking my chair into the table behind us. But my eyes were on Ian. "And I didn't come to lunch so you could call me Daphne."

"Call you Daphne?" said Nash.

"Help you with Ian?" said Ian.

"I don't need anyone's help. I'm not even going to use my mashup. I'm taking this Sinatra."

"Do you know what she's talking about?" said Ian.

"Not a clue," muttered Nash. "But I have a feeling I'm sleeping alone again."

"Doing it my way. This is me, dropping the mike." I unclenched the fist I shook, flicked out my fingers, and strode out of the restaurant.

I accelerated through town. I had an appointment with Johnny, but he refused to see me any earlier because his grandma was still at home. Knowing it would take Ian more than a minute to gain a warrant to take Johnny's computer, I breathed a little easier. I decided to visit Rhonda and tell her the police had arrested Gary. Make someone's day, since mine had gone downhill.

I really hoped Johnny's pictures would show Gary sneaking into the house the night of the murder. To abate Rhonda's fears, so she could go back to work and on with her life.

At Tiffany's house, I knocked on the door and called out my name, hoping her brothers would remember me. Rhonda opened the door. Her color looked better. She definitely smelled better. But she still wore sweats, no makeup, and her hair hadn't been styled.

"Where are your brothers?" I said after grabbing her into a tight hug.

"They went back to work," she said. "They got bored of babysitting me. Nothing's happened. Once I started eating and showering, they left."

"Good news. You're not being stalked anymore. The police arrested Gary this morning. I just met with Ian and got the deets. He had the murder weapon and a stolen crown."

"Thank you." Her eyes shone with unshed tears. "I thought I was going crazy, Maizie. Maybe I am paranoid and delusional like Chad said. Maybe the killer really wasn't out to get me. Other than nasty notes and stupid blog attacks, nothing happened."

"I think you had a major shock. Who wouldn't after seeing the scene of a crime like that? It takes time to recover. Don't feel bad."

"I never want to see something like that again."

"I don't blame you." I paused. "I hate to leave you now, but I really need to meet with a sleazy paparazzo named Johnny. A real slimeball. He took pictures of Lorena's house, maybe even when the murder happened, and he's planning to sell them. I want to stop that from happening before he deletes them."

"Why would he trash the pictures?"

"I outed him to the police. Ian's working on a warrant to take his camera and computer. But this guy will know how to erase the hard drive. I've got to get over there before he does."

"If he knows you told the police, he's not going to let you have the pictures now."

"He doesn't know I told Ian. I convinced Vicki to write a check to make Johnny think I'm buying the pictures." I pulled the check from my pocket and waved it.

Rhonda looked at the check and sucked in her breath. A tinge of rose leaked into her cheeks and her eyes widened. "Vicki was willing to pay that much for pictures? I've not seen that many zeros on a check before."

"At one time, she would have. She's canceling this check. It's all a ruse." I felt flushed with excitement and tampered it down. "Johnny has pictures of you and me coming out of Lorena's house and sitting in the ambulance."

Her eyes narrowed. "This jackass took pictures of us after we saw Lorena's body? Why would he do that?"

"That's what they do. Pictures of victims tell a good story. And pictures that compromise actresses, even ex-actresses, sell a lot."

"My picture could be in a newspaper?"

"Possibly. With Johnny, more likely on a tabloid or entertainment news site. Particularly the sleazier ones. He thinks showing my bloody cheer uniform at the crime scene will make him a lot of money." I shook my head. "Even worse, he has photos of Lorena's body. I don't want those getting out. And he possibly snapped the perp. I have to get those pictures."

"I'm coming with you," said Rhonda. "He can't publish pictures of me at the scene of Lorena's murder. That's wrong in so many ways."

Rhonda's ire was a welcome joy. "Let's bust this slimeball."

"I'm ready to get out of here."

I hugged her. "I'm so happy to hear that."

THIRTY-EIGHT

#RhondaRoused #OopsIDidItAgain

*B*ecause Rhonda wanted to ride in something less "ridiculous," we took her car to Johnny's. While she drove, I filled her in on everything I knew.

"You said nothing's happened. I take it you and your brothers didn't spot any vehicles watching the house?"

Rhonda shook her head. "Naw. Before they left, I almost wanted something to happen. They were getting annoyed with me."

I let out the breath I held. At least the black vehicle hadn't been watching Rhonda.

"Chad said you don't have to be hunted by a killer to get stalked on social media." Rhonda grimaced.

"He has a point, but it's still not a good feeling."

She shot me a guilty look. "Chad thinks you and Tiffany riled me up."

We turned onto the street where the Sextons lived. Spotting the kids playing in front of their house, I asked Rhonda to pull over. The children tossed aside the shovels they'd been using to dig a hole and ran to hide behind a bush.

"Why d'you want to talk to the babies?" Rhonda gave me a

skeptical look. "Their mom won't want them talking to strangers. They look scared of you."

"They probably don't recognize your car. I'm not a stranger. We met earlier." I snapped my fingers. "I forgot to bring candy. I was going to pay them in candy."

She looked at the ceiling. "Girl, you are one odd bird."

I rolled down the window and waved at them. "Hey, kids. You see anything?"

Creeping out behind the bush, they studied the car, then ran to my passenger door. The oldest boy saluted me. "Aye-aye captain. We've got your booty."

"You switched to pirates?"

"Argh," said the little girl.

"Here." The boy shoved a piece of torn paper through the window. "We wrote some stuff down."

"Awesome, you three are the greatest." I smiled at the little girl. "And you're the cutest."

She hopped on one foot and clapped her hands.

"Pirates don't hop," said the smaller boy.

"Peg-leg pirates hop," I corrected. "She can hop if she wants."

"How old are y'all?" said Rhonda. "For the record?"

The little girl held up her hand. The boy pushed down two of her fingers.

"Uh-huh," said Rhonda. "What about you two? Y'all four or five?"

They nodded.

"Let me see that paper," said Rhonda.

I smoothed the piece of green construction paper. A vehicle had been drawn on it in black crayon. Actually, more like a rectangle with wheels. A stick person drove the car and appeared to be shooting a red gun out the window. Or firing a cat.

Rhonda shook her head.

"What about the license plate?" I said.

"It's there." The boy pointed at a lopsided square hanging off the end of the rectangle. They'd written a backward C and a number — possibly a five, but maybe a two — in red. "We ran out of room."

"What were the other letters and numbers?" I said.

The boys argued for a minute. "Maybe a six," said the oldest. "Or the letter D."

The little girl shrugged. "I was too 'fraid to look."

I sighed. "Thanks. I'll be back another time with candy."

"No Grandma candy," warned the boy.

I rolled up the window.

"Why'd you have them draw you a picture of a car?"

"It's kind of a game we're playing."

"Girl, you better be glad Tiffany isn't here." Rhonda shook her head. "Wasting time, playing games with children."

She was right. Tiffany would have scarred my self-confidence for life. I didn't realize the kids weren't literate. Remi could read.

Or she'd memorized all the books she made me read to her.

"To be honest, I thought they could watch Johnny's house for me."

Rhonda patted my hand. "You tried."

"That's all I'm doing. Trying. I thought I could handle this case. I wanted to prove to everyone I could do this. And I wanted to help you, Rhonda."

"You got me out of the house. That's something."

"To help me defraud a shyster." I smiled, but her comforting words only reminded me that I'd failed again.

"Now let me at this guy," she growled. "He's the one who's lucky Tiffany isn't here. She'd kill him."

J knocked on Mrs. Sexton's front door, but no one answered. "Can you check the drive on the side of the house? Johnny drives a hatchback. His grandma has a Chrysler. A black sedan."

"Like the one the kids drew?"

"Yes but no."

Rhonda trotted down the sidewalk and returned. "Grandma must be out. Only a Kia is here. You think he's hiding from us?"

"Or he's with his grandma." I looked at Rhonda. "You know what I'm thinking?"

"If you already planned to commit fraud, what's a little breaking and entering?"

I bit my lip. "I could jeopardize my probation. But I can't let him get away with deleting those pictures. If I could see what he has, I'd feel better."

"I'm trashing pictures, with or without you," said Rhonda. "I'm fixing to delete any picture of me."

"It's evidence, Rhon. We can't touch the photos." I wrung my hands. "But I want to see them. If he has a picture of Lorena's murderer, I need to know. I guess we'll wait until someone shows."

"Who, like the cops? Then you're never seeing those pictures."

"If Ian comes, I might be able to talk him into it." I puffed out my cheeks. "Although, he's keeping a lot from me. More than I realized."

"Tell him you won't share anymore unless he does."

"I can't do that. He may be my friend, but he is the police. I have to play by his rules. And I don't want to hurt our friendship."

"No wonder you can't solve this case. You're too worried about things, like getting arrested and hurting people's feelings."

"And breaking chains of evidence, obstruction of justice, and anything else that could screw up an arrest."

Rhonda scowled. "You got me all het up, Maizie. I'm finally out of Tiffany's house and feeling like I want to get even for scaring me so bad. I'm going in and getting my pictures. I don't care."

She left me on the porch and stalked around to the side of the house toward the kitchen entrance. The pride and joy of freeing

Rhonda from her paranoid-induced prison shifted toward feelings of regret and fear. I took a few *ujjayi* breaths to clear my mind and evaluate the situation.

I was on probation. Breaking and entering was a big no. If Ian found out, he could report me. And Rhonda could jeopardize the warrant Ian was now securing. He'd be super ticked.

Shizzles.

I ran to the kitchen entrance and found her staring at the open door. "You can't do this, Rhon. There's too much at stake."

"It's too late."

"How are you that fast? You were here maybe thirty seconds." I chewed my thumbnail. "Okay, we're not going to panic. Did he junk the photos? What did you see? Did you leave fingerprints?"

"What's wrong with you? I haven't gone inside yet." Rhonda pointed. "Look."

I moved next to her and followed her point to the floor. A trail of blood led from the open door into the kitchen. "Oh my—"

"Lawd." Rhonda teetered and collapsed on the ground. "Lawd. Lawd. Lawd."

Rusty prints dirtied the inside of the open kitchen door. The blood must have originated in the kitchen. My gaze followed the drips and splatters to the stoop, onto the cement, and toward the Kia. The driver's door appeared ajar. I gulped air and blew it out slowly.

I really, really didn't want to look inside the hatchback. But I'd done it again. Exposed Rhonda to another bloody body. Two in a week. That had to be some kind of record.

Why couldn't I just find the culprit instead of the victims?

Willing the shudders to stop coursing through my body, I turned to Rhonda. She huddled at my feet, staring at the bright splashes on the cement stoop. I bent over, placed my hands on her shoulders, and looked her in the eyes. "Go to your car. Get inside. Lock the doors. Do not get out of the car."

Her eyes squeezed shut and her lips trembled.

"I can walk you to your car. Do you need me to walk you to your car?"

"No." Rhonda blew out a breath and opened her eyes. "But you need to tell me the coast is clear."

"I can do that." I steadied my gaze on her. "If you see a black car, duck. Get out of sight."

Her brown eyes narrowed. "What?"

"Gary couldn't have done this. He's in jail." A quivering spasm ran through me. "The person in the black vehicle might have heard me talking to Johnny. We were standing in the driveway when he told me he had pictures of the crime scene."

She slapped at my hands and shoved them off her shoulders. "Why didn't you tell me that before? The killer friggin' heard you make a deal to buy pictures of them coming out of Lorena's house? Nice job, Sherlock."

"I wasn't totally sure they were following me. I never saw them. The kids reported it. Who listens to kids? And I thought they were like six or seven, not preschoolers."

"You are unbelievable," she hissed.

"I really thought we were just going to defraud a photographer, not find a body," I pleaded.

"You made me leave the house for this. Oh, Lawd, someone *is* stalking us." She whimpered. "What if they're still here? What if they're in the house right now?"

"They're not in the house because…" I thought for a moment. "They would have already attacked us. And they didn't. Yes, that's logical. We're perfectly safe. But you should run to your car and stay low. Just in case. I'll be there in a minute."

"This is like *Halloween*. Or *Friday the 13th*. Or *Scream*. What have I done to deserve this? I'm not a sex-craved teenager on a drinking binge. I'm just a hairstylist to the stars. Oh, Lawd, how did you get me into this mess?"

"You're the one who wanted to break and enter—" I stopped myself. "Just go to the car. Now. Go."

"Maizie Albright, you know Tiffany and my brothers will kill you for this. Twice in a week I'm witnessing murder."

"Maybe we'll get lucky and they won't be dead?"

She shook a finger in my face. "For your sake, you better hope so."

For Johnny's sake, I hoped so. Or for his grandma. I really hoped it wasn't Mrs. Sexton. I would never forgive myself for accidentally getting a grandma killed.

I waited until Rhonda had safely locked herself in her Nissan, then I turned toward the Kia. I dialed Ian's number, then added in Nash's.

"Maizie?" said Ian. "What was all that about Nash helping you with me? What did you mean by that?"

"Why are we on a conference call?" growled Nash. "And Ian, why exactly are you calling Miss Albright 'Daphne?'"

"Ian, I'm at Johnny Sexton's grandma's house. I need an ambulance," I said. "And some squad cars. Probably a homicide unit. Nash, I just needed to hear your voice. I feel better. If you need to get back to work—"

"Ambulance—"

"Homicide—"

Their voices clamored while I studied the hatchback. A checkered Vans sneaker hung over the driver's running board. What should have been white checks were now splattered red. I slapped a hand over my mouth and fought to quell the roiling in my stomach.

"Miss Albright," Nash's voice broke through. "Who needs an ambulance?"

"Johnny. I just need to catch my breath before I look."

"Don't touch anything," said Ian.

"Of course not," I shouted. "I know that much."

"Why are you even there? I haven't gotten the warrant yet. I got called into another meeting." Ian scoffed in frustration. "I told you I'd handle it."

"Mowry," growled Nash. "Shut up. She's already upset."

"Watch it, Nash," Ian's voice deepened. "Maizie told you to hang up. Now you're infringing in a law enforcement matter."

"You have the details you need, get the rest when you get there. I need to talk to Maizie. She said she needed to hear my voice."

"She also called me. It's a homicide, Nash."

"Hopefully not," I whispered.

"I'll be there in a minute, Maizie," said Ian. "Dispatch is sending the closest patrol car."

"Ian, get off the line," said Nash. "Maizie, talk to me."

"I'm in the driveway. He's in his little Kia. There's a trail of blood from the house to the car." I gulped air. "Okay, I'm going to look now. There's just a lot of blood, and I don't want to get sick."

"You don't have to look," said Nash. "Go wait in Billy."

"Billy's not here. I came with Rhonda."

"You brought Rhonda with you again?" exclaimed Ian. "What is she? A corpse divining rod?"

"That's not funny, Ian."

"Where's Rhonda?" said Nash.

"In her car. I made her leave the scene."

"You did good there," said Nash.

"Yes, that's good," said Ian. "Go sit with her. You did your job. First responders will be there in a minute."

"He might still be alive." I felt queasy, but I forced myself to walk up to the car. Using my elbow, I pushed the door open. The car keys lay on the floor mat. Johnny Sexton lay across the driver's seat. His head had tipped into the passenger seat, dripping blood onto the tan cloth. I held my hand over my mouth, trying not to gag.

"You still there, hon'?" said Ian.

"Mowry, hang up now," growled Nash. "Get your ass over there and do your job, but she needs to talk to me."

"Do I have to remind you of our roles in this situation?" said Ian gruffly. "Don't make me threaten you with obstruction."

"Bite me, Mowry."

I tuned out their argument. Something struck me as odd at the way Johnny lay sideways across the seat. It appeared he'd tried to escape but succumbed to his injury before he could leave. His position was strange, though, like he'd slid in and fell sideways. I maneuvered around his dangling foot and leaned into the car. Something stuck out of his back.

"Johnny's been stabbed," I said. "But also hit on the side of the head. He might be alive, but I'm afraid to touch him. He's lying at a weird angle."

"The ambulance is on its way, hon'," said Ian. "Don't touch him."

"Nash?" I said. "Hello?"

"I ordered him to get off the line," said Ian. "Don't worry, I'm almost there."

"How long?"

"Maybe five minutes."

That meant I had five minutes to sneak into the house and look for the pictures. I'd gotten over my fear of breaking and entering.

It was overridden by my fear of a cold-blooded killer on the loose.

THIRTY-NINE

#NoHugsForYou #JustAnotherBody

"*A*nother stabbing followed by a blow to the head," said Ian, handing me a cup of coffee. "This time with a fish knife. I'm guessing the perp stabbed him in the house but walloped Johnny as he attempted to enter the vehicle to escape."

"They were having catfish for lunch," I said. "Poor Mrs. Sexton. How is she?"

"Her friend took her to their house. Obviously, she's distraught." He shook his head. "If only the judge would have worked quicker on that warrant. The camera and laptop are gone. Damn."

This I already knew. I also knew I had a little blood on the toe of my sneaker that I'd hoped came from the driveway and not the kitchen. My stomach lurched.

"Do you think your friend will be okay?"

"Rhonda?" I glanced at the ambulance bay where she sat with a blanket wrapped around her shoulders watching her brothers and Tiffany arguing. "She's actually doing a lot better than the last time. I think it helped she didn't actually see the body. And she was angry with Johnny. Rage helps to lessen the blow."

But this time, Rhonda was also mad at me. She refused to speak to me. Tiffany and Rhonda's brothers felt the same.

I didn't blame them.

"I brought the killer to Johnny's door," I said. "Whoever was in that black car listened to our argument and learned Johnny might have pictures of the killer. They were covering their tracks with this murder."

"You're probably right about that. But don't take this to heart. It's not your fault, hon'."

"Tell that to Rhonda and Tiffany," I muttered.

"I had the photographer, Helmut, brought in for questioning," said Ian.

"Helmut? You don't think he had anything to do with this?"

"I'm not ruling anything out. He knew the victim and made a deal with him."

"Helmut's odious, making money off Lorena's death by selling the party pictures. But it doesn't make sense he'd kill Johnny. Helmut was taking pictures at the party," I said, echoing Tiffany's words. "He has an alibi."

"There are a lot of angles we have to rule out, Maizie. Cortez's house was next door to the gala. It would be easy to slip out and back in. The ME said, possibly she was murdered before the party began, but he can't narrow down the time enough to tell how long before."

"It doesn't feel right," I said, but my tone didn't convince either of us. "What will we do about Rhonda? The earlier threats don't seem serious, but she's scared. Shouldn't we treat them like it's the killer, particularly now there's a second body?"

"I advised her to get out of town for a bit. She said she can't afford it. With the hunt for Blick, we don't have the manpower to sit with her, but I do have patrol cars doing regular loops by her friend's house." Ian shifted his glance from Rhonda to me. The concern in his brown eyes made me squirm. "I'm worried about you. Rhonda didn't see anything, but you're directly involved. It's time you give this up."

"I can't do that. Rhonda's depending on me and I need to clear Lorena's name."

"Come on, Maizie. We're doing what we can for Rhonda. Kyler Blick is still at large. You need to be more careful."

"I didn't think bringing Rhonda here would be dangerous. You had Gary. Even when I didn't believe Gary didn't do it." I bit my lip. I didn't mean to say the last part out loud.

Ian folded his arms over his chest. "Obviously Gary didn't kill Johnny. But there was physical evidence that worked against him in the Cortez case. The prints on the safe were his. He had the crown. He could still get charged with theft. And I'm not ruling him out as a suspect. Not yet anyway."

"You don't still believe he threw the iron in his own garbage, do you?"

"I'm not discussing my opinion on the murder weapon."

"You know, you're really irritating sometimes, Ian."

His smile was grim. "I'm an officer of the law, Maizie. I protect and serve. You need to let me do my job."

"I've got a job, too." Except I wasn't getting paid for this case. "And I owe it to Rhonda. And Lorena."

"It's an unfortunate situation. Listen, chances are Rhonda will be fine, especially if she's vigilant and careful. Like you said the threats haven't been serious." He kept his gaze steady on me. "So, you agree? Drop this and go back to your other work? You need to be vigilant and careful, too. Keep me apprised if you see or hear anything unusual. Particularly this black car."

Staying "vigilant and careful" wasn't good enough for me. Not when it came to Rhonda's life. She couldn't stay at Tiffany's house forever. She was missing work. How long before she lost her job? I wasn't dropping the case. I could tell Ian knew this, but if I didn't speak what I felt, we could both pretend I agreed.

"You alright, Maizie?"

I nodded, but I wasn't anywhere near all right. I was a lot closer to all wrong. In more ways than one.

Ian cocked his head. "You look like you could use a hug."

"I don't want a hug, Ian," I said stiffly. "I want justice."

· · ·

My y friends weren't speaking to me. I no longer wanted to speak to Ian. I assumed Corporate Nash was corporate-ing. I thought he might come to the crime scene, to see how I was doing. There was a good chance Ian had ordered him not to come. Not that Nash would have paid attention to that threat if he thought I needed him. Maybe Nash thought I could handle witnessing this murder victim. It wasn't my first body, after all. Maybe he thought I could get a hug from Ian.

Who, by the way, seemed more than willing to hand them out.

But I didn't want Ian hugs. I wanted Nash hugs. At this point, I'd even take another hug in the old office. Except now the old office really reminded me of Corporate Nash, and if Corporate Nash couldn't even leave work for a minute to give me a hug at the scene of a brutal murder, I didn't want a hug from him either.

However, I also knew untimely deaths clouded my thinking. I was fairly certain murder wasn't good for the soul. Maybe Nash had been right about me handling a homicide case on my own. For my first independent case, I probably should have started with a simple cheating spouse. Fraud, even.

Kidnapping might have been nice.

I bummed a ride from a patrolman to Tiffany's house and retrieved Billy. Then I drove to the new office to look at my link chart window. I needed a suspect refresher. Gary needed to move from homicide to a burglary suspect.

But when had Gary obtained the crown? Before or after the murder? I should've asked Ian.

I parked in front of the office, my thoughts consumed with Gary. If he had snuck into Lorena's house, he might have seen her killer. But why wouldn't he tell the police? Because he was scared? Or maybe he hadn't seen anything and was too worried about how compromised he looked with the crown. I wanted to believe Gary had bought the crown with no receipt.

Except, a piece like that would need the receipt for the insurance.

I gave myself a mental pat on the back for thinking more like Ian. And stopped because I was annoyed with Ian. I was supposed to be doing a Frank Sinatra. My way.

Oh, wow. I totally forgot Sinatra had played a noir private eye in *Tony Rome* and in the reprisal, *Lady in Cement*.

While trying to recall the plot for *Lady in Cement* — all I could remember was Raquel Welch. Probably all anyone could remember and not for her performance. — I trotted through the office door and halted. A man stood in front of the window, studying my link chart. A big man in a blue button-down with his hands clasped behind his back. Probably wearing a camo tie, but I couldn't tell because his back was to me.

"Where's Annie?" I asked.

"She left to get a chicken sandwich." Nash cast me a look over his broad shoulders and nodded at the sticky notes. "Investigation board on a window, Miss Albright? You do know this is visible from the outside? I traced your links from the sidewalk before coming inside."

"Tape doesn't stick to brick." I folded my arms. "Where were you? Isn't there some kind of relationship clause that says if one of us finds a murder victim, the other shows up to pat their hand and offer words of comfort?"

Nash swiveled to face me. "Last I heard, you didn't want pats, just my voice, *Daphne*."

"Who are you mad at? Me or Ian?" I straightened my shoulders. "I'm irritated at Ian and you. When it comes to finding dead bodies, you know how I feel about hugs."

His jaw tightened, then relaxed. "I'm mad at Mowry. But not really angry. Just annoyed. Are you okay?"

"You know what they say, the first victim is the hardest and it's all downhill after that."

"Cops don't say that. Nobody says that. Every victim is hard. Come here." He opened his arms and I fell into them. A large hand cupped the back of my head. He held me against his shoulder and massaged my nape with his thumb. "I was told I'd be arrested if I showed up at the crime scene."

"Never stopped you before." I looked up at him. "But you are forgiven. You knew I would come here next. And you knew I would need a hug."

"Lucky guess." He stepped to the side, planting us before the link chart. "Gary's on the wall next to the boyfriend."

"Now that Gary's moved down on the list of murder suspects, do you think they'll still hold him?"

"Probably not. They've already questioned him and searched his house. Even if they charge him with burglary, he'll make bail." He pursed his mouth, then looked at me. "Why? Are you planning on seeing him?"

"I want to hear Gary's side of the story." I looked up at Nash. "Are you going to tell me to stop investigating because it's too dangerous? Johnny Sexton was killed because of me. I believe whoever drives the black car heard us talking. But it wasn't Gary's Tesla."

"Johnny Sexton was killed to stop him from leaking evidence." His gruff voice deepened. "They'll want to do the same to you."

I noticed he didn't answer my question. "I don't want the police watching me."

"Then I'll watch you."

I shivered. I wasn't entirely sure if my body responded to anticipation or fear.

Nash moved his gaze back to the window. "Who else besides Johnny Sexton and you would know about the murder?"

"Possibly Gary. Rhonda. Except she doesn't know anything, although they might think she does." I sighed, thinking about what I had done to Rhonda. I sucked in a breath. "Oh my God. Aiden. I couldn't stop him from watching Lorena's house. He saw a man and a woman there recently. He said they scared him. I don't remember if I told Ian or not."

"Call Mowry."

While I talked to Ian, Nash lowered himself into a chair and watched me. "What'd he say?"

"He already sent an officer to the Jessups. Someone who works with juveniles. They also detained Helmut from flying out and have a warrant for the photographs he took of Gary. I think to see if he had a portrait taken with the alleged stolen crown. I also know they're still looking for Kyler Blick."

Nash nodded. "What's the deal with Kyler Blick?"

"As the costume designer for a TV show, he doesn't need to be on set all the time. Apparently, he's not been on set at all lately. The New Orleans police are looking for him and there's a manhunt locally here, too."

"This is what mainly concerns Mowry."

I nodded reluctantly.

"You should take that concern more seriously."

"I know," I said slowly. "But I have a—"

"Don't say hunch," warned Nash. "The first homicide might not have been premeditated. The second was. If Blick is the perp, he's dangerous. Work with facts, not feelings."

"I was about to say *theory*." I glared at him. "Whoever left that threatening note and hacked Rhonda's blog had to know who she was and where she worked. Possibly Kyler looked her up, but it seems like a lot of research for threats. He's not from Black Pine. That's a waste of time for a visitor. It must be someone local."

"It's a good premise if the killer is the same person threatening Rhonda. The threats toward her could be coincidental. You said the note wasn't even addressed to her." At my pout, he added, "But let's go with your theory that the culprit is local. What about the people who scared the kid? One was a woman. The board shows your main suspects are men."

"The women don't really have a motive. Other than my homicidal cheerleader theory." I strode to the window. "Is this a crime of passion or money? That confuses me. If Kyler Blick thinks Lorena stole his money, it's both. That's what didn't fit for Gary unless he's totally mental. But if Lorena stole from Clothing Kids and was caught..."

"The culprit could have gone to her house to confront Lorena. Maybe an argument got out of hand." Nash stood up and began pacing. "Couldn't be blackmail because that's killing the golden goose."

"What if they were so incensed, they flipped out?" I moved Jennifer Frederick's photo into my suspect lineup. "Except I got the feeling that the embezzlement was a new revelation. I wonder when the money exactly disappeared from the Clothing Kids' account? Maybe Lorena didn't embezzle. Just because she has a Mexican bank account, doesn't mean she was skimming. Maybe Lorena created that account to keep her boyfriend from stealing from her."

"Someone stole that money, if not Lorena. Who are the other women connected to Clothing Kids and Lorena?"

"There's Jan Martin. But that's my rival cheerleader motive. But I can't make myself believe Jan would kill Lorena over a renovation project. Then again, I've seen crazier on *Snapped*." I tapped on Susie Newson's photo. "She's my original suspect. Susie as the wronged other woman. She does stalk her husband quite a bit. And she's angry that Spencer's broke and having an affair."

"That sounds more legit. Why hasn't Mowry picked her up?"

"He questioned both of them, but Ian said Lorena's affair with Spencer is just a rumor. He doesn't believe it. Even though Lorena's neighbors and Spencer's good buddies, the Martins, think otherwise. Spencer was overheard arguing with Lorena at her home the day of the crime. And he lied to me about being there."

"That's odd that Mowry would ignore something like that. Unless..." He stopped pacing to face me.

"Unless what?"

"There's some kind of physical evidence to prove otherwise. They could have an unbreakable alibi."

I sucked in my breath. "Or Mowry knows Spencer is sleeping with someone else. Craptastic. I need to see Vicki."

FORTY

#CarpetBagged
#MyTractor'sNoLongerSexy

s far as I knew, I had two tails. One was the phantom black vehicle. The other was a Silverado pickup. No more Sinatra for me. I couldn't even pretend to handle this investigation on my own with Nash following me. I had to field a call from Daddy asking why Nash called in a vacation day. I explained his employees were allowed vacation days, particularly when Nash was basically leaving work early. It was late afternoon, for goodness sake. And the CEO shouldn't interrogate the employee's girlfriend anyway.

Daddy blamed Nash's absence on me. Guilty as charged. Corrupting his work ethic with dead bodies.

Reaching Vicki's, I checked my rearview mirror. Nash had pulled into a scenic overlook near her drive. A strategic spot where he could observe vehicles and remain undetected by Vicki. I drove past the topiaries and parked in the circle before the Peanut Mansion. I yanked off my helmet, dashed up the stone stairs, and rang the bell. A moment later her assistant, Charlene, opened the door.

"Is Vicki with anyone?" I asked.

Charlene pointed toward a massive fish tank in the foyer.

Vicki stood to the side, pretending to study a school of clownfish when she really studied the front door.

"Were you expecting me to be with someone?" said Vicki drolly.

"You know who." I crossed the parquet to face her. "Spencer Newson is a murder suspect."

"Really?"

No. At least not according to Black Pine police. But I crossed my fingers behind my back and said, "Yes. And so is his *wife*."

"Why do you attempt that intonation whenever you say the word 'wife?' Didn't they teach you nuance in that improv class you insisted on taking?" She pivoted away from the fish tank and crossed the floor.

I followed her into the living room. Now papered in arsenic. "Stop being such a pain in the tuchus. I'm worried about you. Not just morally, but physically. Your life could be in danger."

She lifted a teacup from what used to be a bar and sat primly on a couch that used to be leather and now appeared to be horse-hair. "My life is not in danger. Unless I die from boredom. I'm not having an affair with Spence. And I turned down the offer to be on the board of Clothing Kids."

"What? Why? When?" I pressed pause on my mouth. "Start over."

She sipped her tea and sighed. "After the board voted in favor of me joining Clothing Kids, I thought about it and declined their offer. I can only handle the Martins on one committee."

I pinched the bridge of my nose. "You're on the historic whatsis thingy now?"

"Of course. We can't have the history of our town and culture run by these carpetbaggers."

"Our town was created by carpetbaggers. The literal kind. Black Pine is a turn-of-the-century resort town."

Vicki shook her head. "It's such a shame you don't appreciate your heritage."

I stared at the ceiling. Counted to ten. Took a deep breath. Counted to ten again. "Why did you want everyone to believe you were having an affair with Spencer Newson? It's appalling and disgusting and morally reprehensible. Particularly during a murder investigation."

"Can I help it if you and the rest of the town have a dirty mind?" She raised a shoulder. "We're old friends from high school. That's it. Besides, Spence wanted me to connect the Clothing Kids account to my personal banking and that's a hard no from me."

"He wanted you to—"

She slammed her teacup onto the antique coffee table. Earl Gray sloshed. The cup cracked. More tea pooled onto the lacquered veneer. "I'm bored, Maizie. Black Pine is too slow for me. I'm flying out to be with Kevin on his movie set. Quentin Tarantino can bite me. I'm spending time with my husband."

"Husband?"

"Fiancé, whatever."

"You're engaged?"

"I said, *whatever*." She stormed out of the room, calling for Charlene to bring her bags. "Vuitton, not carpet."

I stared at the pool of tea, glad it wasn't blood. It wasn't my week for liquids. Then I pulled out my phone and called Nash. "Something hinky's going on with Spencer Newson and the Clothing Kids money. He wanted Vicki to link that account to her personal banking."

"Did you tell Mowry?"

"Not yet. I called you first."

"Good." He cleared his throat. "I mean, call Mowry."

*A*fter leaving Ian a message, I decided to pay Jennifer Frederick a visit. As the financial guru, Jennifer would know if connecting the accounts was fishy. She could connect the dots and show Ian Mowry that Spencer Newson was not only a seducer of women and a terrible husband but also an absconder of charitable funds. And a framer of my friend Lorena as an embezzler.

Righteous anger pinged around my helmet. Like I'd stuck my head in a pinball machine.

Too much. My heavy breathing fogged my visor.

I waved to Nash as I speeded past him in Billy. Kept my eye out for Batman's car. And drove back to the historic district, this time parking in front of Jennifer's house. Nash parked behind me and followed me up her cloistered path.

"What are you doing?" I said. "I thought you were hanging back, watching for stalkers?"

"If I'm taking a vacation day, Miss Albright, I might as well get in on the action." He winked. "And I didn't want to talk to Vicki."

That I could understand. I ding-donged Jennifer's door and waited. "Jennifer might not be thrilled to see me. I already trespassed and eavesdropped on her once today."

"Really?" A smile unfurled from Nash's lips, but the door rattled, and the smile disappeared like a honey badger slipping back into its burrow. He folded his arms and planted his feet in a wide-legged stance behind me. l felt like Whitney Houston in *The Bodyguard*. Or Dakota Fanning in *Man on Fire*.

Which might not be such a good example. Denzel Washington went a little too dark in that role.

Jennifer pulled the door wide but blocked our entrance with her body. "What now?"

"When was the money stolen from the Clothing Kids' account?" I could feel Nash silently applauding my directness. I wanted to bounce on my toes but felt my mashup wouldn't approve.

That improv class did pay off.

"I don't need to share that information with you," said Jennifer.

"It's my belief, the transfer of funds happened after her

murder. You didn't seem to be aware of it until recently. But I know the funds don't appear in Lorena's US bank account."

"She also had a foreign account the police can't access," said Jennifer tightly. "Think what you want. Here's what I believe: Lorena and her boyfriend planned to abscond with the money. They got into some squabble and he killed her. They're a pair of criminals and now our nonprofit is sullied and broke."

The door began to close, and I slipped a foot into the frame to stop it. "Do you know why Vicki Albright quit the board?"

"Because she and Jan Martin are besting each other for Queen of Black Pine." Jennifer rolled her eyes.

"Also because Spencer Newson wanted Vicki to connect her personal account with the Clothing Kids banking. That. Is. Hinky." I stamped my foot, then remembered professional private investigators don't throw tantrums.

Jennifer blanched, then composed herself. "All the board members with access to Clothing Kids funds have connected our personal account to the foundation's. It's an efficient way to transfer funds without fees. It doesn't matter anyway. At the next meeting, we're voting to disband the foundation."

I moved to lunge toward her and felt Nash's hand on my elbow. "What? How can you do that? The foundation was Lorena's dream."

"Dream or not, the name is dead. Who wants to give to a charity connected to this kind of crime?" The door swung shut. I slipped my foot out just in time. The heavy wood banged against the jam.

I looked up at Nash. "Do find this suspicious?"

"I find it unfriendly and unhelpful," he said. "She has a point about the crime blackening the charity, unfortunately."

"What about Spencer? Isn't the connected accounts thingy hinky?"

"Sounds like all the board members did it. I can't see the point, but they all agreed to it. It must make sense. Vicki was probably being difficult."

"It's like Lorena died for nothing." I sulked as we walked down the steps of her porch and through the secret garden. "The foundation meant so much to her. Lorena's not a criminal. She's a victim."

Nash took my hand, then moved around to face me. "Hey, don't let the negativity get to you. You need to stay focused. How can you help Lorena?"

"By clearing her name?"

He nodded and pulled me closer. "You did really well with Ms. Frederick. You didn't come close to tears. Or talk too fast. Or go off on a tangent. You've improved a lot since working with me."

"I have?"

"You have. Makes me think Annie's a much better mentor than me."

"Don't say that." A chill passed through me. "I love working with you. I learn so much. You had me at my roughest. I was a hot mess. Annie got me after I had some real-world experience with you."

"You were mine first." He smiled and skimmed his fingers over my hair, then under my chin. "My hot mess."

I tipped my face toward him as his phone rang. His hands dropped. He checked his phone, then stepped away to answer it.

There were a lot of things I wanted to say — like, "What's with all the past tense?" and "Aren't I still your hot mess?" and "Won't we work together again?" — but something had happened over the week. Something stood between us. My friendship with Ian? Maybe working for my father had created our rut. Especially so soon after working for Vicki. And losing his business.

Oh my God, my parents broke Nash.

No, that wasn't it. Well, maybe. But I had a feeling something else was going on.

He had moved onto the sidewalk and stood next to his truck, his face set to grim and his eyes darting between me and some spot in the distance. Nash ended the call but continued to stare into space. Or stare at the telephone pole halfway down the street.

"Nash? What's wrong?"

He shook off his musings and shoved his phone in his pocket. "Gary, right? Let's talk to Gary. He's right around the corner. I'll follow you."

I cut him a look but climbed into Billy. Something was wrong. I could sense it.

But I didn't want to face it.

Instead, I turned on Kenny Chesney and blasted the historic district with a love song about tractors.

FORTY-ONE

#IfTheCrownFits #WackADoodleDoo

I parked in front of Gary's home and glanced across the street. Lorena's house still had crime tape draped over the porch rails and door. Next door, the Martins' Queen Anne looked the same. But on the other side of Lorena's, a police car was parked in front of Aiden's house.

The poor Jessups. They must be totally freaked out. I hoped Aiden behaved himself.

Nash parked behind me and walked up to Billy.

I yanked off my helmet and hopped out. "I wonder if Aiden gave the police anything useful."

"I wish that kid had listened to me." He glanced at their house, then switched his gaze to Gary's. "Let's get this done. Getting late."

"Okay." I gave him a quizzical glance. The sun had set, but I didn't keep normal business hours. Corporate Nash must want to go home. I sighed and hurried up the walk to Gary's.

At my ring, Gary answered in a Georgia Bulldogs sweatshirt and sweatpants. Disappointing. I hoped we'd catch him secretly dressed as the evil queen from *Dazzle*. Or as Justin the prom king. Even Batman would have been interesting.

"Did you turn me in to the police?" said Gary. "I'm thinking about suing you."

"You'll lose," said Nash. "But go ahead and try it."

"Gary, I'm sorry you were arrested," I said quickly and sweetly. Win or lose, I didn't want to get sued. People in Black Pine loved to threaten litigation. It was almost a sport. "If you'd been honest with us and the police, things might have turned out differently."

"They accused me of murdering my friend," he gasped. "The police are confiscating my portraits. Unbelievable."

"The portraits of you with the *Dazzle* crown?"

"No," he exclaimed. "Why would I wear that? What do you think I am?"

"I'm an actress. I'm from California." I shrugged and raised my hands. "It's no big deal. It's a costume."

"I'll have you know I wore a suit," he huffed. "I'm in real estate. I needed new photos for advertising."

"You had Helmut, a celebrity photographer, take photos for real estate ads?"

"I only collect costumes." Gary crossed his arms over his chest. "I love movies."

"We'll find out either way," said Nash. "No shame in telling us. The police have confiscated Helmut's camera and laptop."

"Do you know how much I paid for those portraits?"

"What did you do with the crown?" I moved toward him. "Did you make a display for it?"

Gary's eyes widened and he licked his lips before adjusting his features back to the maligned man. "Good night and goodbye."

"Why would you steal that crown, Gary? You know how it looks." I stepped closer and gently put my hand on his arm. "Gary, I want to help you. Let's sort this out so I can clear your name. Just like I'm trying to clear Lorena's name."

He looked at me, his eyes watery and his nose reddening. "She let me borrow it. I tried to explain. But it got all confused.

And with her murder, it felt too hard to clarify. They were accusing me of murder."

I placed my hand on his shoulder. "I know you didn't murder Lorena. You loved Lorena, didn't you? I know you admired her very much."

He nodded his head. "It looked bad. I could see that. I had the crown and my prints were on the safe. Probably in other parts of the house, too."

"And you'd been in trouble before. For trying to see her on the movie sets."

"That wasn't my fault. I knew she wanted to see me. But she was working so they would never let me in. She had terrible hours. She was really busy. I just wanted to bring her dinner or coffee to make her feel better."

"So you tried to sneak in? Past the guards to bring her dinner?" Behind me, I could hear Nash's restless movements. Tension bounced off his large body. I gently guided Gary further into his foyer to keep him from getting alarmed and to continue talking. "But you were caught."

"The police didn't understand. I don't even think they told her I was being helpful."

"Lorena never found out why you were trying to see her. Just that you were arrested." I patted his arm. "I guess when you went to see Lorena at her house, she didn't take it well."

"Right. She didn't understand. If I could've explained." Fat tears dribbled off his cheek. "She didn't like me living this close, I could tell. I left her alone. I didn't get her mail or water her flowers like I told you before. She never brought me chicken soup," he wailed.

"It's okay," I continued in soothing tones, keeping my attention on Gary while listening for Nash. He readied to pounce. "That must have been hard. Living so close to her, yet not being able to see her. Or the costumes she made. Like the crown."

Gary swiped at his eyes. "I heard about the crown on a

Reddit thread. It's an amazing piece. I never liked *Dazzle*, but her craftsmanship was superb."

"Did Lorena make it or Kyler Blick? They worked together on *Dazzle*."

He blasted a curse. "That man is a liar and dangerous. I can't believe she would go out with such a hideous beast. He accused her of deliberately stealing clients. Everyone knows Kyler was sponging off Lorena. She put in the work and he would take the credit. I'm glad she left him. She got a restraining order on him, too, you know. He stalked her. People reported seeing him follow her in his car. He bullied her on social media, too."

"How awful for Lorena." I chewed my lip. If I didn't get a confession from Gary, Kyler had jumped to the top of my suspect list over my cheerleader theories. "Is that why you took the crown? To get back at Kyler?"

Gary's head bobbed. "I worried he would do something. Like steal it from her." Gary frowned. "No, I didn't plan to take it. I just saw it in her safe. I didn't open the safe, you know. I didn't even mean to go into that room. The door was open. Papers everywhere. Almost like the crown meant for me to rescue it."

"Papers everywhere? You're talking about the night Lorena died."

"What?" Gary had gone somewhere else. The tears had stopped, but now his eyes had a glazed expression. He backed further into the foyer, bumping into the credenza below the hanging kimono. He reached behind him to steady himself on the display table. "You know, I think it occurred to me that Kyler might take the crown. After he killed Lorena. I thought the crown would be safer with me. I wanted to rescue Lorena's *La Calavera Catrina* costume, too, but I couldn't…There was blood everywhere."

I hitched in a breath. Tapping broke the silence. Nash texting. "Gary, did you see Kyler kill Lorena?"

"Who else would have done it? All that blood… But then

you." Gary's eyes fluttered shut and he shook his head. "You and that other woman. Just walked in the front door."

"You were there?" I gasped.

A menacing sneer crossed his face. Gary sidled forward. "I saw you. You've been there many times. You wanted that crown, too. Didn't you?"

"No. I'm Lorena's friend. I played Julia Pinkerton, remember?"

His eyes narrowed, then widened. "Right. Julia Pinkerton. I remember."

"That's my kimono from the show, hanging on your wall."

Gary glanced over his shoulder at the kimono, then back to me. "*Your* kimono? Do you know how much I paid for that kimono?" He lunged. His right hand swung up, arcing above me, and his left shot toward the door.

"Gary? What are you doing?" I backed up, then stumbled. "What about Kyler Blick?"

A hand grabbed me, yanking me onto the porch. Nash pushed around me. "Get in your Bronco, Miss Albright. Now."

"Wait, Nash." I tried to grab him, but Nash had already moved, blocking the door. "Gary," I shouted behind Nash. "Did you see Kyler kill Lorena?"

Behind me, the lights on the police car across the street had flipped on. An officer ran up the sidewalk, his head cocked to his shoulder, speaking in his walkie. "Move aside, ma'am."

"Gary, did you see Kyler that night?" I yelled. "Gary, it's Maizie Albright. I played Julia Pinkerton. I was Lorena's friend, remember?"

The wail of another siren tore through the evening's peace. The officer pushed past me through the doorway. A moment later, Nash walked out of the house, grabbed my arm, and hustled me down the sidewalk.

"That guy has more than one screw loose." He shook his head. "What a nutjob. Why in the hell didn't Lorena get a restraining order on that guy? She should've moved. And why in the hell didn't Mowry get psych to take him? I've got more than a few words to say to your friendly detective."

"I almost got his witness testimony," I fumed. "Gary might have seen Kyler. He didn't tell the police any of this. He told me."

Three police cruisers squealed onto the street. The sirens cut off and the officers piled out of their cars, running up the sidewalk. Across the street, Jan Martin strolled from her porch to the sidewalk to watch.

I turned my attention to Nash, too angry to pay attention to the commotion behind me. "We lost Johnny's pictures of the killer. Now you ruined my chance of getting Gary's testimony that Kyler killed Lorena."

The scar on Nash's chin pulsed. "I didn't ruin your chance of anything. You can't trust anything Gary says. Even if you could have gotten him to say Blick killed Cortez, it'll be inadmissible. The prosecution will prove he's certifiable."

"But Gary was there that night."

"Maybe. It doesn't mean he saw the murder. And if he did, it made him more wacko. He's probably the one leaving nasty notes for Rhonda."

"But—"

"That man thought *you* killed Lorena for a minute. And he looked like he wanted to kill you. I am not waiting behind you, hoping a lunatic says what *you* want to hear, when I can see that wackadoodle turning on you."

"What *I* wanted to hear?"

"You were feeding him. Couldn't you see it in his eyes?"

"Gary was troubled, yes. He was crying."

Nash clenched his teeth. "He was acting. I have more experience dealing with these sociopaths. I could tell he was leading you where he wanted to go, just like he did the last time we talked to him. It's my fault. I should've handled questioning Gary."

"You? This is *my* case."

"It's not your case. It's not a case at all. I warned you about taking this too personally."

"Just because Lorena was my friend doesn't mean—"

Nash grabbed me by the shoulders, forcing me to look him in the eyes. "You need to step back and see the bigger picture, Miss Albright. It's not all about you."

I gasped.

"I'm sorry." He dropped his hands. "It's just— You're trying too hard to prove something. I don't know what's going on with you. If this is more than clearing Lorena's name, you need to drop the investigation. For your own sake. You're not being careful, Maizie. Your life is in danger."

"I'm being careful. Nothing's happened—"

"Nothing's happened?" Nash barked a rough laugh. "Miss Albright, you almost got stabbed. Gary had grabbed that metal hair stick. And you didn't even notice."

FORTY-TWO

#TwoCanPlay #LifeWithBoys

*N*ash followed me home. During my drive, I couldn't hear Kenny Chesney over my teeth chattering inside my helmet. The thought of Gary stabbing me with Julia Pinkerton's hair stick unnerved me. How could I miss something like that? I thought I'd been doing a great job as my mashup PI. Like Helen Mirren in *Prime Suspect*. I wanted to make Gary confess to stealing the crown and to reveal Lorena's killer, but Gary had played me like a violin.

No. He played me like a kazoo.

When Mowry arrested Gary, I'd felt sorry for Gary, couldn't see him murdering Lorena. Couldn't believe he'd be dumb enough to leave the murder weapon in his garbage. I was right about that but so wrong at the same time. I'd thought I was a good judge of character. It looked like I wasn't. I shouldn't be surprised. How many times had I been engaged (four) and learned my soul mate had no soul (four)? Why did I think I could do better with potential suspects?

But Nash's point about me trying to prove myself upset me the most. I'd been struggling with my decision to investigate Lorena's homicide since the beginning. Had pride clouded my judgment? Vanity and I had issues. Not as deep-set as some of my other problems but growing up in front of a camera did make humility difficult to achieve.

I didn't blame my friends for being angry with me. And I'd done little to protect Lorena or find her killer.

At the DeerNose cabin drive, I pressed the button for the gates to open and drove through. In my rearview mirror, I watched for Nash's truck. But instead of pulling through the gates, he used the drive to make a U-turn.

I parked in front of the cabin, yanked off my helmet, and grabbed my phone.

"Where are you going?" I said. "Are you so angry you can't even say good night to me?"

"I'm not angry. I'm in a hurry. Good night."

"Hurry to do what?"

His silence reminded me that Nash never lied. He preferred to keep the truth to himself.

"Are you going back to work? You're allowed to take time off, you know. You don't have to make it up later. Don't let my father bully you—"

"Boomer's not bullying me," growled Nash. "Nobody bullies me. It's a special project and I need to work on it."

"At night?"

"What I need to check on happens at night."

"Uh-huh," I said. "You know what else happens at night? Things that get my dirt bike attacked."

"I don't have a crazy ex-girlfriend. Gary probably attacked your dirt bike, just like he's probably stalking Rhonda." His voice lightened. "There's an idea. Call Rhonda and tell her about crazy Gary. It might make her feel better."

"Rhonda's not talking to me. I have to go through Tiffany and she's not talking to me either. They're also blocking my texts." I stared up at the moon's ascent above the trees and wondered if Rhonda would ever trust me to never show her a dead body again. I missed my homies. "Anyway, you're changing the subject. I know what kind of project happens at night at an apparel company. No project. DeerNose isn't even open."

"The factory is open. There's a swing shift. I told you, it's a special project. Don't go questioning Boomer, either. He's too far up the chain to know about this." In the background, I could hear his turn signal dinging and a frustrated grunt. "Look, you didn't notice before because you work a lot of nights, too."

Speaking of work, I hadn't done a lick of real work in days. Likely, Annie was on the list of people mad at me, too.

"Actually," continued Nash, his voice growing gentle and smooth. "Because you work a lot of nights, I found this project to keep me busy. Because I missed you."

I narrowed my eyes at the phone. I wanted to believe him, but there was something in his tone. It was the kind of thing my (four) ex-fiancés used to tell me. When they didn't want me to know what they were really doing.

"What are you saying, Nash?" I tried to keep my voice from sounding prissy, which resulted in me sounding pissy. "You involved yourself in an extra-credit project to keep yourself busy when I'm working at night?"

"That's…" He paused. "A good way to think about it."

*A*t the breakfast table, while Remi pretended to eat, I made a to-do list. If I was working on this case for the wrong reasons, I could make it right with more effort. And being more observant. And not trying to act like Helen Mirren.

I was determined to reinvent myself. Again. I just hadn't decided on the right character.

My phone rang. Ian. I gave myself a quick pep talk about light, love, and lying to police detectives and chirped a hello.

"I've been on a manhunt all night," said Ian. "I learned what went down with Gary. Dammit, Maizie, I thought I told you to leave this alone. Now I've got Nash all over me for not admitting Gary to a psych ward."

"Nash was pretty upset. But he was with me and there was a police officer across the street." I crossed my fingers. "I was being careful. I just didn't see Gary grab the hair stick before he tried to stab me."

Remi looked up from her bowl of biscuits and gravy. I rose from the table and moved down the hall, out of earshot of Remi.

"What did you say to him?" said Ian. "Gary didn't show signs of being a danger to himself or others when we questioned him."

"Gary was at Lorena's the night of the gala, Ian. He saw something. And that's when he stole the crown."

"That's unconfirmed. Nash thinks Gary got off on feeding you lines. He's in a state psychiatric center now for an assessment. When that's done, I'll try questioning him again." Ian paused. "Hon', don't make me ask you to drop this a second time."

"Ian, you can't unless I break the law," I said. "We talked about this in the beginning. I can investigate as long as I don't step on your toes."

"Honey, it's not my toes I'm worried about."

"Maybe don't worry so much?"

He paused for a beat. "Listen, we found evidence of someone trying to break into Gary's house. Since we arrested him the first time. The locks are scratched up and one of his window alarms had been set off while he was in jail."

I sucked in a breath. "They think Gary does know something about the murder. What if it's like Johnny Sexton all over again?"

"Gary's plenty safe now. The psych hospital doesn't serve fillet o' fish."

"That's not funny."

"Gallows humor, hon'. Watch yourself. Why don't you stay at the office today?"

I rolled my eyes and walked back into the kitchen. "Bye, Ian. Thanks for the news."

At the table, Remi pushed sausage gravy up the sides of her

bowl to disguise the amount she hadn't eaten. She looked at me. "Why didn't you get donuts?"

"Donuts every day isn't healthy."

"A lot of stuff isn't healthy." Remi sighed. "Everybody's worried about healthy all the time. You know, playing's good for me. Nobody worries about that."

"You might have a point," I drew out the words while I worked out the details of an idea. "An unintended point that has nothing to do with being healthy."

"Does it have to do with playing? I don't want to think about eating. Unless it's candy."

"It has everything to do with playing."

"Let's do it." She hopped from the bench. Four dogs popped out from under the table and danced around her feet. "What are we going to play?"

"You're playing with Aiden Jessup while I talk to his mother."

"What? No. I don't like Aiden." She stomped her boot and threw her hands in the air. The dogs slunk under the table. "Why is this boy always in my life? I can't get rid of him."

"I'll see if we can meet at a park."

Remi halted her histrionics. "We're going to a playground? Okay, then."

I wished my life with boys was that easy.

FORTY-THREE

#SilveradoPancakes #ParksAndWreck

---

*H*aving gotten permission from all parental units for the park playdate, I strapped a car seat onto Billy's bench and made Remi wear a bike helmet for good measure. Her body vibrated with excitement.

"This is so much fun," she exclaimed. "A ride and the playground."

"Maybe we can get donuts on the way home," I said. "If you're good."

"I'll be good," she promised. "I left my duck call and yo-yo at home."

I had no idea why that made her good, but I believed her.

We drove to the gate and discovered Nash's truck parked on the other side. I pushed the remote to open the gate, hopped out of Billy, and circled to unstrap Remi. No Remi. I turned toward the gate and spotted her climbing the fence.

"Mr. Nash," she screamed. "We're going to the park."

Nash had been slouched in his seat and jerked awake at Remi's shout. Before I reached the truck, she opened the door and clambered onto Nash. I entered the passenger's side and pulled her off Nash to sit between us.

He mopped his face and nodded, as Remi fired off the pros

and cons of the day, his truck, Billy, and donuts. "Okay, kid. Let me talk to your sister. You want to climb through the window into the back of the truck?"

"Can I?" I feared she might implode with excitement. Remi turned to me. "Maizie, oh Maizie. Please. Please."

At my nod, the back window descended. Remi slid through and bumped into the truck bed.

I watched her treat the truck bed like a bounce house before turning back to Nash. "I think I missed something in childhood. I had no idea parks and truck beds were so exciting."

"It's sweet of you to take Remi to the playground," said Nash. "I'll keep an eye on y'all. I took another vacation day."

"That's not necessary."

"We'll ride together. We can strap her booster seat on my jump seat. Stop and see Lamar on the way back."

Warmth over his proposal suffused me. The overpowering scent of Nash permeated the truck. Not an unwashed-man-who-sleeps-in-his-truck aroma. More of an intoxicating blend of pheromones and Acqua di Selva aftershave. His hand snaked along the back of the seat. I sidled closer to him.

Wait. We weren't just going to a park. Had Nash figured that out?

A playdate with Aiden's family seemed the perfect means for getting Aiden to trust me. According to Ian, the police couldn't get much out of Aiden, either. With his mom there, I hoped to suss out a better description of the people he'd seen at Lorena's. I also had a feeling he knew more about the night of the murder than he'd shared earlier. Remi had said Aiden had disappeared at the party during hide and seek. If I could get Aiden relaxed and off guard, maybe he'd remember more details.

I looked at Nash. He was studying me. "You don't—"

"I'm sorry about last night." Nash's voice deepened, "I missed finding you in my bed."

"I...well, the other night wasn't planned, you know. You see, I'm..." I couldn't concentrate when he looked at me like I was breakfast. The same way I looked at brown butter cinnamon apple pancakes. Topped with whipped cream. "Is that why you were sleeping in my father's driveway?"

"Come here." He pulled me into a long, hot kiss.

When he broke contact, I glanced out the back window. Remi had found his toolbox and was immersed in looking through it. I breathed a sigh of relief, then thought about what she could do with tools. Before I could warn Nash, he'd leaned into me again.

He stroked my face. "You mean a lot to me, Maizie."

"You mean a lot to me, too." I snuggled against him, then remembering Remi, inched away.

"When Gary almost stabbed you, I wanted to kill him."

That was kind of hot. I scooted closer, then reminded myself, as an independent private investigator, I couldn't support Neanderthal tactics. "About that—"

"I'll be a minute." Billy's keys dangled from Nash's fingers. His other hand gripped the door handle. "I'll move the Bronco, then grab Remi's car seat."

Hold up. How did he get my keys? What was going on?

I snatched the keys from his fingers. "Did you seduce me into allowing you to follow me on my investigation?"

"I seduce you because you're seducible."

I gave him a look. A look that (hopefully) spoke my disbelief.

"I thought you were headed to a park." He arched a brow and tried to control his smirk. "You never said anything about an investigation."

"You know exactly what I meant."

"You're not going to a park?"

"We're meeting at a public playground. Aiden's under police surveillance. I'm being careful."

Nash stared up at the stained fabric on his headliner. "You won't stop this investigation because you're afraid the press will say Ms. Cortez was an embezzler."

I bobbed my head.

"You insist on Rhonda and Aiden having police protection

because you're scared of what might happen to them. Even though Rhonda probably just needs counseling."

"Um. Yes to Aiden. Debatable for Rhonda?"

"You've made two men — Helmut and Gary — angry enough to attack you. Granted, one's a coward and the other is certifiable. And where I normally admire that kind of spirit, you left yourself open to attack."

"I mean—Well..."

"You're antagonistic toward the Clothing Kids' board members. All of whom you consider suspects."

"There are a lot of loose motives in that group. And they all had the means and opportunity for the crime. I think."

"Meanwhile the police have told you Kyler Blick, the man with a solid motive, is at large and considered dangerous."

I squished my lips together.

"You claim to not have seen this black vehicle that's reportedly following you. Now, I normally would discount a Crayola report, but it seems likely someone did listen in on your conversation with Johnny Sexton." Nash glared at me and his voice lowered, "Seeing how he was murdered."

I thought of the black car whipping out of Johnny Sexton's neighborhood. A car I'd tried to follow. I bit my lip. I'd kept that little factoid from Nash and Ian.

"And you've made your investigation completely public by taping it to the window of the PI shop. I mentioned that to you yesterday and it's still there," he growled. "You know who else can track your theories and movements? Lorena's killer. Why your boss would allow that kind of blatant..." His words were lost in muttered curses.

Craptastic. I hung my head. That was a dumb move.

"You need to carry your .38." Before I shook my head, he said, "But you're not going to carry it because you're afraid of using it."

I sighed.

"That leaves you with me as a human shield."

I propped myself on a bent leg to face him with a straightened spine. "Yes, I've made mistakes. I'm learning from them. That's what's important. And don't get mad at Annie. I haven't been entirely truthful to her as to the severity of the crime."

"You haven't told your boss there's been another murder?" Nash exploded.

"I haven't seen her?" I shook off my upspeak and regained my confidence. "It's my case and Annie has no problem letting me do my thing. She understands."

"She understands your mother owns the business." Nash pinched the bridge of his nose. "You weren't ready for this. I shouldn't have—"

"Shouldn't have what? You're not my boss anymore. Or my keeper. And for whatever reason Annie's looking the other way while I work on this *special project…*" I let those ill-fated words hang in the air for a long second. "She's allowing it. Maybe because she trusts me."

His jaw tightened. The broad shoulders were still rigid, but the icy blue eyes had melted. A little.

"You need to trust me, too." I cupped his cheek in my hand. "You know I need to do this and do it on my own. But I'm asking for help when I need it, right?"

"Debatable."

"I know you want me to be ready when we partner in our investigation firm. Nash and Albright Security Solutions, remember?"

He sighed. "Promise me you'll handle these situations with more care. I'm using my vacation day to take care of a few things. When you're done at the park, call me. We can meet up."

My eyes widened with excitement. "You want to get lunch?"

"I don't get the lunch thing. Ask your other boyfriend for that."

"Ian's not my other boyfriend." I punched him in the shoulder to disguise the awkwardness. "We're friends. We both like food and crime."

"From my perspective, it looks like he enjoys more than food and crime." Nash shot me a heated look. "But by all means, enjoy your lunches. Just remember, I'm dessert."

*B*lack Pine's All Children's Playground was situated at a park on the lakeshore. This suited me fine, except for the constant cold breeze that blew off the mountain and across the water. I didn't expect Lorena's killer to troll the lake in a black bass boat, so I chose a bench that put my back to the lake. The cop watching Aiden leaned against his patrol car in the parking lot across from the playground. Aiden's mom sat next to me when she wasn't hopping up to push a swing or coax a child down a slide. From her stroller, the baby watched the kids playing, content to be lulled by the back and forth glide driven by her mother's foot on the undercarriage.

Aiden and Remi had glowered at each other, then rushed to beat one another to the monkey bars.

"I'm sorry you have to deal with a police escort," I said to Aiden's mom. "It must be very scary for you."

"I can't believe this is happening." Mrs. Jessup's foot pushed and pulled, moving the stroller to a faster tempo. "Ms. Cortez was so nice. Aiden really loved her. We loved her. And now…" She shook her head.

"Have you seen anything? Or heard any news from the police?"

"They haven't alerted us. I'm too busy to notice anything outside my doors."

The stroller jerked, the baby fussed, and Mrs. Jessup slowed her foot. "I don't let Aiden outside anymore. That's why I agreed to come here. A public outing seemed safe enough. The policeman didn't mind. Thanks for offering. It's kind of you to think of my family and what we're going through."

My heart squeezed. My offer wasn't entirely motivated out of charity. I also had a job to do. "I hoped Aiden might open up to me. Tell me more about what he might have seen."

"You can try, but he won't say anything to me or to the police." Mrs. Jessup hugged herself. The tempo of the push-pull increased. "Our whole block is freaked out by the murder. Ms. Cortez was such a nice lady and we thought it such a cool opportunity for our kids to wear her costumes. She was famous. That's really something for their scrapbooks, isn't it? And for charity, too. We all thought it was such an amazing experience for the kids."

The stroller shot forward and the baby let out an excited shriek.

I retrieved the stroller. "I hope the police can quickly apprehend whoever did this. And when they do, you'll be able to make those scrapbooks and honor Lorena's memory. She really did love kids. She was a wonderful mentor when I was a teenager."

"I really hope so." Mrs. Jessup sniffled, then broke into a sob. "You know what I keep thinking? Because I wanted to see my kids wearing a famous designer's costume, I exposed them to evil. They have to live in danger, even with the police following us. Because I thought it was a cool idea."

I wrapped my arm around Mrs. Jessup while she cried. "It's not your fault at all. You can't think that. Who would know something this terrible would happen?"

The stroller stopped moving and the baby wailed. I grabbed the stroller handle and rocked it while rubbing Mrs. Jessup's back.

"You don't understand. When you're a mom, you blame yourself anytime your child's in danger. Just feeding them causes a lot of guilt and anxiety. But exposing them to murder?"

She ducked her head to find tissues in her baby bag. I rocked the baby. Aiden and Remi ran from the playground, stopped before the bench, and watched us for a long minute. Feeling flustered, I tried to think of excuses for making Aiden's mom cry.

"You got any snacks?" said Aiden.

"No," I said. "We just had breakfast."

Remi rolled her eyes and uttered a disgusted grunt.

His mom plunged her face deeper in the diaper bag and tossed out two bags of Goldfish crackers. "Aiden, stay with Remi and Miss Maizie. I'm taking the baby for a walk."

We watched her leave in awkward silence. "I'm sorry your mom was crying—"

"She cries all the time," said Aiden, popping a goldfish into his mouth. "Moms do that."

I didn't have a lot of experience with mothers other than Vicki and Carol Lynn, who were not criers. But they both seemed to be motherhood anomalies for different reasons. I ventured a segue, hoping to catch Aiden off guard. "Did your mom cry when you told her someone scared you?"

Aiden jerked his head up to deliver me a death glare.

I glanced at Remi who seemed on the verge of laughing, so I shot her one of my own. "It's okay to be scared. They might be dangerous. Did the police show you any pictures? To see if you recognized the person?"

He bobbed his head without looking at me.

"I know some…dangerous people. Maybe the ones you saw is someone I know. I brought pictures, too."

From my backpack, I pulled out photos I'd downloaded and printed from Facebook pages. I fanned out the pictures of Jennifer Frederick, Jan Martin, and Susie Newson on the ground in front of Aiden. He eyed them and quickly looked away. Then I laid down pictures of Kyler Blick, Gary, Spencer Newson, Dennis Martin, and Helmut.

"Are these like the pictures the police showed you?"

Aiden shrugged.

Remi picked up the copies and squinted at them. "I know some of these people. They were at the photoshoot. And at that costume party."

"Right," I said. "But maybe Aiden saw some of them at Lorena's house?"

He pushed the picture of Gary toward me. "He lives across the street."

"I know. I talked to him." And got him arrested. Twice.

I tapped on the photos of the Martins. "They're your neighbors, too."

Aiden turned around to face the playground, putting his back to me. Remi laid on her stomach to examine the images. "They were at the party, too. This lady yelled at me." She waved Jan Martin's picture.

"The party was at her house. Were you doing something you shouldn't?"

"Oh, probably." She gusted a sigh.

Aiden leaned forward then uttered a sharp yelp. Leaping up, he bounded to his feet and ran toward the playground.

"Hey, you're supposed to stay with me," I shouted and hopped off the bench. "Remi, follow us."

I darted after Aiden. He scaled the climbing wall, ran across the swinging bridge, and climbed the tubes to the top of the fortress tower. "Remi, get him."

She shoved a toddler out of the way and swarmed the climbing wall. While I apologized to the child's mom, Remi hurdled the top, grabbed a rope, and swung to the towers. I watched her pop out of the tube to confront Aiden. He shook his head and pointed toward the far side of the playground. I moved around the climbing wall to see what Aiden had spotted.

In a grassy area off the sidewalks by the parking lot, a group of women in hoodies and leggings stretched. Near them, a man stood under a tree. He also wore a sweatshirt but with the hood flipped up. He slowly swiveled, liked he searched for someone.

FORTY-FOUR

#StrangerDanger #WindowDressing

*I*n the enclosed plexiglass at the top of the fort, Aiden and Remi bounced and pointed at the far side of the park. I couldn't hear them, but I could tell they were shouting. I moved around the climbing wall, slipping under the slide to observe the hooded man. Behind him, the women prepared for their group walk. The man hadn't moved. He faced the park and seemed to be studying the playground.

Shiztastic. Did Aiden recognize him? Was he Kyler Blick?

At the other end of the parking lot, the policeman spoke to Aiden's mom. I didn't want to wave and attract attention to myself. I also couldn't leave the fort with Aiden and Remi still inside. Aiden's other siblings played on the smaller jungle gym for the younger kids.

I crouched beneath the slide, pretending to tie my shoe, and watched the man. After scouting the park, he began moving in a circuitous route toward the playground. Above me, children screamed and pounded over the bridge to the slide. I twisted to watch him as he skirted the swings and small children's area. He stuffed his hands in his pockets and walked slowly, his head turned slightly toward the playground.

My heart pounded, leaving my neck clammy and face hot.

The sharp, cutting wind off the lake blew tendrils of hair across my face. I pushed them back, then held my hair with one hand. Inching farther under the slide, I scooted beneath the bridge and angled myself behind the climbing wall. My stomach inched toward my throat, next to my heart.

The man walked at a rapid clip. His trajectory headed toward the climbing fort. I glanced at the parking lot. The policeman and Mrs. Jessup still spoke near his car. Her other children had joined her. I couldn't see Aiden and Remi from this position and hoped they'd stayed at the top of the fort.

Even if this wasn't Kyler Blick, the man seemed suspicious. What was he doing walking near the playground?

Unless, dummy, he's a dad. With a hood up due to the raw breeze off the lake.

Behind me, feet struck the ground. I swung around. Remi crouched on the ground. Aiden hung from the lip of a walkway.

"Get over here." The harshness of my voice surprised me. Remi and Aiden shot to my side, and I gathered them against me. "Who's that man? The one in the hoodie?"

The man had stopped walking, his attention fully on the children playing. The wind from the lake pushed against his back, forcing the hood forward and shrouding his face.

"I don't know," whispered Remi.

"We saw one of the women from your pictures," said Aiden. "She was near those other women."

I let the air whoosh from my lungs and pulled the children into a tighter hug. "It's okay. She's probably taking a walk with her friends. It's a big group and they're moving away from the playground, anyway. But let's get my pictures and you can show me which woman."

"Okay," said Aiden, casting his face toward the ground.

His small body trembled, and I knelt in front of him. "Was it the person who scared you?"

He shrugged.

I hugged him. "You did good, letting me know." Even if I had the wrong suspect. My heart still hammered and my stomach had soured, but the relief felt palpable, holding their little bodies against me.

Remi placed a hand on my arm. "You looked really mean and sounded scary. I didn't know you could do that."

J held their hands walking back to the bench. Below the bench, my backpack lay on top of the empty Goldfish bags and juice boxes. Aiden slunk next to me while Remi climbed on the bench, flipped over it, and ran around to do it again.

"Where are the pictures?" I muttered, looking inside my backpack. "Did they blow away? I thought they were inside my bag."

"Where's my mom?" said Aiden, clinging to me.

"She's in the parking lot with the police officer." I dumped out my backpack then tossed items inside. "Where are the pictures? And where's my notebook?"

"Did you get robbed?" said Remi.

I lightened my voice. "Nope, I've got my phone and ID in my pocket. The backpack is still here. And look, I had a granola bar in it. I brought snacks after all. But somehow I lost my suspect pictures and case log."

"A granola bar isn't a snack," said Remi.

"Yes, it is," said Aiden.

While they argued about the definition of snack and the worthiness of granola bars, I walked them to Aiden's mom. My chest had tightened again. Goosebumps had broken on my skin that had nothing to do with the raw wind. Anxious to get the kids safely locked in their homes, I moved us across the field at a jog.

"Thank you," said Mrs. Jessup. "Officer Hardy and I have been talking about a neighborhood watch program. Did you two have fun?"

I nudged Remi.

"Do you have any more goldfish crackers?" she replied.

"They had fun." I looked at Officer Hardy but decided against alerting him. I didn't know Hardy. Officers I didn't know liked official reports rather than an exchange of ideas. "Remi, we're stopping by my office before going home."

"Donuts. And Lamar," she chanted. "And Mr. Nash. I love your office."

"My other office. The new one."

She pouted on the walk to Billy. I strapped her into the booster seat. At Albright Security Solutions, she ran inside and flopped on a chair, still pouting.

I strode to the window and began ripping off the pictures. Annie walked out of her office to watch me. She left and returned with a bottle of Windex.

"Let me," cried Remi. "I love the blue stuff."

While Remi sprayed and wiped off my arrows and link lines, I dumped the sticky notes and pictures in a drawer and locked it.

Annie backed to my desk, keeping an eye on our window washer and her precious window. "What's going on?"

"I've been really stupid," I said. "Sticking all my notes on that window. People rarely come in here, but I didn't think about them seeing it from the street."

"Yeah, I wondered about that." Annie cracked her gum and leaned against my desk. "But it wouldn't mean anything to anyone. Especially the hand-drawn stuff. From the street, I thought it looked kind of artistic."

"We were at the park with the little boy who might have seen Lorena's killer. I had pictures of suspects for him to look at."

"Did he ID anyone?"

I shook my head. "Somebody has him freaked out. They must have threatened him. Now I'm freaked out. While we were at the park, someone stole my suspect pictures and my case log notebook."

Annie cut her head toward me. "Did you see anyone?"

"No. I was worried about a perfectly innocent man. Although

he could be a pedophile, I suppose." I sighed. "Annie, as hard as I try, I keep screwing up. I know you've been holding down the fort while I try to figure this thing out with Lorena. I appreciate it."

"You know, if someone did steal your case log and suspect photos, sounds like they're messing with you. Or trying to mess with your investigation."

"Or trying to learn who can implicate them." I sucked in a breath. "That means they think I know what I'm doing. When I don't."

"It also means you could be in danger. The local news said a celebrity reporter, Johnny Sexton, was found murdered." Annie eyeballed me. "Isn't that your guy?"

"Unfortunately, yes. And I reported the murder."

"Dude, why didn't you tell me?"

"Sorry. That's why I didn't come back to work." I grimaced. "I'm floundering, Annie."

"Investigations are tricky. You can only work with the evidence you have. It's not like you can pull all the suspects together and get one of them to spill, like in the movies. Nobody's going to confess like that. If you can't find physical evidence, you have to hope they slip up enough to clue you into a motive or something."

"Julia Pinkerton always had an 'aha' moment followed by a chase or fight scene. I guess I expected the same thing."

"If only it could be that simple." My phone rang and Annie strode to the window. "Hey, Remi. Try not to smear it so much."

"Ian?" I said, answering my phone. "Any news?"

"Where are you?"

"At the office with Remi."

"Stay there," he barked.

"I need to take her home. Before she destroys the office."

"I'll send a patrol officer over and they'll take her home."

"What happened? Did you find Kyler Blick?"

He let out an exasperated sigh. "I totally forgot to tell you this morning. Blick's moonlighting while he's doing that TV show. He was in New York meeting with retailers for some clothing line and didn't tell the producers or anyone else what he was doing. He had some underling report in for him."

"Oh, wow." I collapsed back in my chair. "I'll cross him off my suspect list. Back to square one, sort of."

"Maizie, enough already."

"Ian, I know things got a little crazy with Gary. But we didn't know he was—"

"Maizie," Ian interrupted. "Helmut's dead. Homicide. We found him in his hotel room. You're done."

FORTY-FIVE

#TheThinOrangeLine
#LikeAWreckingBall

*E*ither someone was killing off potential informants or someone really hated photographers.

My Julia Pinkerton 'aha' moment was more of an 'uh-uh' moment. Through my bumbling investigation, I'd gotten two men murdered while the killer covered their tracks. That kind of trajectory meant those I questioned were next in line. Possibly members of the board, including my parents. Aiden and his family. I'd exposed Rhonda to two of their homicides.

The evil had to stop. Now.

However, if the killer used my investigation to track anyone who could identify them, I was also a target. Again the irony rocked me. I was as clueless now as in the beginning.

Actually, not completely clueless. Our suspect with the best motive — Kyler Blick — had an alibi and our second-best suspect — Gary — was safely in a psych ward. It had to be someone local. Someone related to Clothing Kids and the missing money. Someone I had already questioned, which had clued them into my investigation.

Annie had given me an idea on how to pull off their mask. I had to make them slip up enough to indicate a motive. To lure them out, I had to present them with the opportunity to learn what I knew.

Or to kill me.

Not how I wanted to end my first independent case. But better me than someone else. I couldn't let them escape.

I had a great line to use on the suspects. A line that would sound innocuous to the innocent but had a lot of potential for getting the killer to react. If the killer exposed themselves, I'd get justice for Lorena with real evidence — a recording of an attempted murder. On me.

Okay, sounded better in my head.

My stomach flipped over. I took a long deep breath.

I had three big problems with my plan. Three besides the whole possibility of dying-thing. I had to get rid of Annie, Ian, and Nash.

I'd promised Ian I'd stay in the office. He was busy with a crime scene. If I worked on my plan quickly, Ian shouldn't get in the way. By bringing the suspects to me, I could stay where he asked and not risk him arresting me for interference.

The second of my problems, Annie, turned from the window, looking frustrated. A look one often got when dealing with Remi.

"Remi," I said. "You get a special treat today. A policeman is giving you a ride home in a real police car."

She dropped the Windex bottle and spun around. "Really?" Her excitement fizzled. "Why?"

"Yeah," said Annie, retrieving the cleaner and hustling it toward her office. "Why?"

"I told Detective Mowry I would stay here. I can't take you home." I glanced at Annie. "That means I can get a lot of this paperwork done. Why don't you take the rest of the day off? You've been working non-stop to cover me."

Annie glanced at the smeary window, the stack of folders on my desk, and at Remi. "Yeah, okay. Sounds kind of good. But I want to talk to you in my office."

I handed Remi a stack of sticky notes and a pen. "Do not move from this chair," I said with my mean voice.

She cocked her head. "Not as scary as at the park, but you're getting better."

In Annie's office, she left the door open and stood with an eye on Remi. "Something obviously happened," she murmured. "What did the cop say?"

"Helmut the photographer is dead. Murdered in his hotel room. I went after him when I learned he sold Johnny pictures from the party. His death is on my hands."

"How is that your fault?" Annie popped her gum, eyeing me. "Didn't the police question him, too?"

"I stuck his picture on the window, Annie." I paced the room. "I drew the green line from Helmut to Johnny. But I also drew an orange line between Helmut and Lorena. Orange lines meant they might have been at Lorena's house the night in question. Aiden also has an orange line. Thankfully, I didn't put Rhonda on the board."

Annie folded her arms and chewed her gum. "Yeah, I dunno about this theory. I've been looking at the window for the past few days and your color-coding wasn't that clear to me."

The front doorbell tinkled. I jumped and Annie said, "Easy, Tex." She stood to the side and I rushed out. Officer Hardy stood in the reception area looking around.

"Why aren't you with Aiden?" I said.

"Detective Mowry sent someone to relieve me. I'm getting off work and he asked me to take this one home." Hardy smiled at Remi. "D'you ever ride in a police car?"

Remi tossed me the stack of sticky notes and grabbed Hardy's hand. "Will you turn on the lights and the siren?"

"Sure." He chuckled.

"Good." Remi tugged him toward the door. "Wait and do it until we're in my driveway, though. That's gonna be real funny for my daddy."

Hardy cut his eyes to me and I shook my head. Hard.

They exited the door and a moment later, Nash entered. "What's going on?"

Annie popped her gum. "Photographer's dead and the detective said Maizie's got to stay in the office. He sent someone to take the kid home."

Nash looked at me. "Is Mowry sending a car over to sit in front of the shop? To arrest you if you leave?"

"No. I gave him my word."

He snorted, and I glared at Nash.

Annie glanced between us. "I'm heading out. So, the paperwork, yeah? Get on that."

While Annie grabbed her bag and sauntered through the door, Nash kept his eyes on me. The door shut behind her and he took a deep breath. "Helmut's been murdered, too?"

I took a step back. "How did you know a policeman was here?"

"You said you'd call when you were done with the park."

"I was busy with Remi, then Ian called. How'd you know I was done at the park? Have you been following me?"

He flashed a dark smile. "Why would I do that? I'm on vacation."

"You don't trust me." But of course, he didn't trust me. I came up with crazy plans like using myself as bait. Not a safe plan, but it was a classic trope for a reason. *Columbo* did it all the time. He loved trying to get the murderer to kill him.

Of course, Nash would point out I was no Columbo. But I would have to point out the killer was using my investigation and…

I just needed to get Nash out of the office.

"Mowry is coming here. He's bringing lunch."

"I could eat." Nash drew his shoulders back like a bowstring. "I'll call him and ask him to pick me up something, too."

Shizzles.

New approach. "If you weren't following me, were you following someone else? Like my father?"

Nash's eyes widened, then narrowed. "Why would you suggest that?"

"Because you've been obsessed with him and DeerNose."

"I'm dedicated to my job."

I stuck my hands on my hips. "I don't believe you."

He folded his arms. "And I don't trust you."

This wasn't good. I worried my lip. I had to get rid of him but this was Nash. He wasn't going to leave easily. And he'd never help me with my plan. Not when it might involve putting myself in jeopardy. There was only one way I could force him to leave.

Hurt him.

I internally winced. I loved Nash. At this very moment, every fiber in my being wanted to hash out this communication issue. Use all my years of therapy to work through the problems between us so we could build a healthier, happier platform for our relationship.

Plus, he was exceedingly hot when trying to protect me.

I'd have to resort to Neanderthal tactics.

My hesitation was lost to Nash who had his own Neanderthal tactics. He crossed the room in two long strides. Stopping before me, he jerked me into a tight hug, then pulled me back to look me in the eye. His cool blues assessed my sea glass greens for a long moment.

"I'm sorry, sugar," he drawled. "Of course, I trust you. How about I take you to lunch and then we'll come back here. I'm sure Mowry will let you leave the office if you're with me."

"I have a lot of work to do here." Panic bubbled and fizzed inside my chest. He wasn't playing fair. Almost like he knew what I was doing…

"Me, too. My laptop's in the truck. I'll grab it and we can work together. Like old times." Not only did his smile not reach his eyes, it snarled before it could reach his cheeks.

My brain pulsed inside my skull, searching for excuses. "Annie will be back any minute. We're going to do…spreadsheets together."

"Bull." He spat out the word. "I can tell when you're lying, Miss Albright. You're telling some big whoppers today. What gives?"

My stomach moonwalked and my throat constricted. I didn't want to do this. "I need my space."

He eyed me.

"I'm serious."

His ice chip eyes grew frostier. "Darlin', you may think you're handling this homicide all by your lonesome, but fun and games time has ended."

Tears pooled in my eyes. "It's too much. Taking vacation days instead of leaving work early like a normal person? Working crazy hours to impress my dad? You're jealous of Ian. Then there's the bed in the office and the tie."

"My tie?"

"That ridiculous camouflage tie. Stop wearing it."

"It's a uniform. I don't care what I wear to the office."

"At least, let me buy you a different tie—"

"Don't." He held up a finger. "Jolene tried to dress me. Don't start."

I sucked in a breath. He had never compared me to his ex-wife. I'd exposed his trigger. This was it. I had to go in for the kill or he'd never leave.

"You know what you're doing with that ugly tie?" I stepped to the side and folded my arms. "You're choosing Corporate Nash over my Nash. No, you're choosing your dumb job over me. Do you even want to go back to the way it used to be?"

"What do you mean?" The scar on his chin whitened with the tightening of his jaw. "As I recollect, the way it 'used to be' was *you* working for *me*. And that was it. There was no us. Us was on the back burner turned to a low simmer."

I shook my head. "That's not what I meant and you know it."

"Is it? There's been a lot of talk about the office not being an office. Or did you finally figure out I'm not good enough for you?" His scar pulsed. "You want the office to stay an office because you can't face the fact that I'm so broke, I'm living in it."

I swallowed, feeling sick. I couldn't do this.

But I thought about the Jessups. His mom's panic. Aiden's fear. Rhonda and Tiffany. The innocent members on the board, whoever they were.

Nash stared down at me, his eyes as hard as his jaw. Waiting for me to agree or give in. I'd done more than expose his trigger. I'd exposed his real fear.

Do it.

"Maybe you're right. I don't want to sleep in an office. Maybe I just want the job that's in the office."

"Honey, you've got the job," he snarled. "And an office with your name on it. What you don't have is me."

Oh my God. What have I done?

FORTY-SIX

#BarfBagged #MirrenMaiden

*W*hen Nash left, I threw up. Drank a Coke. Staged hidden cameras and microphones throughout the office. Thought about Nash. Threw up. Retrieved my pink .38 Special from the locked safe. Loaded it with real bullets. Threw up again. And borrowed a belt holster and a flannel shirt from Annie's office.

I hated the thought of having to use a gun, even in self-defense. But I wasn't stupid enough to put my life in jeopardy without some kind of protection. The very idea weighed on me more than the holstered revolver pulling down my jeans beneath the flannel. Hopefully, my suspects weren't used to spotting concealed-carry. Luckily, guns hadn't been the preferred weapon in this case.

The killer seemed to favor stabbing and battering their victims.

Now to keep my breakfast down. I didn't figure barfing all over my culprit would provide much defense.

I spent twenty minutes calling the Clothing Kids board with vague excuses about (fake) evidence I'd found. Wanting their help. Susie and Spencer. The Martins. Jennifer Frederick. My other suspects were either dead, in a mental hospital, or in New

York. If I didn't get a reveal from my original list, I would give up.

By spacing out their appointments, I'd hoped to eliminate them one by one. The Martins arrived first. Together. Even though I had called them separately. I worried my lip but reminded myself I had a loaded weapon on my hip. If necessary, I could pull it out while I called for backup.

That thought didn't make me feel better.

Jan and Dennis wore matching tracksuits, pink and red. I was surprised they didn't wear vintage to go with their historical home obsession, but then perhaps jogging suits were more fitting for murder.

Eyeing their striped, shiny pants, I ushered them into Annie's office. They took the chairs I'd placed before her desk while I circled around and poised myself on her desk chair. I'd left the office door open to keep a clear view of the reception area in case someone arrived early. I'd also jimmied a wedge beneath the door, so no one could casually close it. They had enough privacy to make a move if no one was in the bigger room. I'd left nothing to chance. Nothing in the open that could be used as a weapon. Hidden cameras focused on every inch of the space.

I also had the cover of the desk to slip my .38 Special into my lap for easy reach if they tried anything.

"What have you learned?" said Jan, leaning forward. "We can't get any information from the police."

"You're very interested in Lorena's case," I tried a *Columbo* tone. Then realized I was also using his New York accent. I switched to my mashup character. Straight to the point to throw them off guard. "Several times, I noticed you watching me."

"You were snooping." Jan shifted in her chair. "It's my neighborhood."

"I did a walk-through with a police detective," I said. "And surveillance with my boss. Private investigation is not snooping."

"You were across the street when my neighbor was arrested. He's such a nice man."

"Gary's got some issues. But he's in a better place."

"He died?" Jan's voice rose with panic. "I've been very anxious about what happened."

"Sorry." I grimaced. "By better place, I meant a hospital."

"He's done right by his gorgeous 1890's Greek Revival," continued Jan, still panicked. "What will happen to that beautiful house?"

At least Jan's priorities were consistent.

"What's going on with the case?" asked Dennis. "We have a right to know. Lorena was our neighbor and she died during our party."

"She was murdered during your party." I switched from my mashup to Hercule Poirot. Without the accent. "When I met you, you were both agitated and spoke of an emergency. I couldn't help but noticed you both wore gloves. Jan's gloves were damp. Like she'd just rinsed them out."

"We had on costumes," said Dennis, looking from me to Jan. "Jan's gloves weren't wet. Why would they be wet?"

"Just what are you implying?" Jan rose from her chair.

In my lap, I slipped my finger on the .38's safety, careful to aim it below the desk. "Jan, why were your gloves wet?"

"I have no idea what you're talking about." Jan stood and placed her hands on her hips. "This is ridiculous. If they were wet, it's because something spilled."

"When I met you, you'd just returned from leaving the party," I suggested, keeping my eyes on Jan. "Where did you go?"

"I didn't leave the party," said Dennis. "Jan, you didn't leave the party, did you?"

"The cookie closet is a convenient method for sneaking out of your house," I said. "A method you refrained from mentioning when we asked about exits."

"Cookie closet?" said Dennis. "What cookie closet?"

The man needed to pay more attention. To his house and his wife.

"She means the servants' entrance in the butler's pantry," hissed Jan.

"It must have been difficult having a famous neighbor," I continued. "The gala was a huge success, but you didn't get the credit. Lorena got all the credit."

"She did?" said Dennis. "We did get some nice thank you notes."

I ignored Dennis to focus on Jan, working my rival cheer-leader-motive on her. "Just like it must have been frustrating to know Clothing Kids, a new charity, diverted attention from the Historical Society. And then to have Lorena do something so unconscionable."

"I don't think getting murdered is unconscionable," said Dennis. "She really couldn't help it."

"I meant what she did to a piece of architectural history. Turning a bungalow into..." I switched back to a *Columbo* technique, pausing for dramatic effect. "An open floor plan."

"She tore out walls from a bedroom and dining room. Who does that?" Jan narrowed her eyes. "Wait, a minute. I know what you're doing."

"What am I doing?" I knew what I was doing. Using loaded questions and encouraging division between the couple. Leading Jan to admit to the crime, even if I hadn't accused her.

Thank you, Helen Mirren and the Reid Technique.

The office door tinkled. I looked past Jan and Dennis.

"Maizie Albright, get out here." Tiffany stood in the reception area, looking around.

Shizzles. This never happened to Columbo. Or maybe it did. I couldn't remember.

Tiffany spied me in the office. Her tiny, pointed face grew sharper. She stomped foward, the blunt ends of her blue-tipped bob swaying. "Girl, you have some explaining to do."

"I'm busy," I called. "I have clients in here."

"We're not clients," said Jan.

"That's right." I lobbed her a Julia Pinkerton sneer, still hoping for a quick confession. "Suspects."

"I'm not moving until you come out here," yelled Tiffany. "And I feel like breaking stuff while I'm waiting."

I hopped up. Then remembered the .38 in my hand. I shoved it into my belt holster.

"What was that?" said Jan. "Are you carrying a pistol?"

"Revolver." I moved around them into the reception area. They turned in their seats to watch me.

I couldn't catch a break. All I wanted to do was trap Lorena's killer. Why did Columbo make it look so easy?

"I've been trying to call you," I whispered, switching back to my normal Maizie Albright-self. Albeit a bit high-strung and nauseous. "How's Rhonda? Has she forgiven me?"

"We had a visitor this morning."

I felt my eyes round. "The stalker?" I breathed. "Are you okay? What happened? Did they make an attempt on Rhonda? Is she okay? Did you see who it was? Did you call the police? Oh my God, what did they do?"

Tiffany held her hand up. "No, to the first question, then I stopped listening. You talk too fast. The visitor was Wyatt Nash."

"Nash?" My heart melted. Then it stuttered. My stomach sank, then rose. I clapped a hand over my mouth. And rushed to the bathroom.

When I returned Tiffany sat on my desk. The pile of folders lay spilled beneath her swinging feet. Jan and Dennis waited at the office door, watching Tiffany.

I held up a finger to the Martins and rushed to face Tiffany. "Tiff, I'm sorry about everything. Really and truly. And I'm making it up to you. I promise. This is all ending today."

She rolled her eyes.

"I want to talk to you, but I really need to deal with them first." I jerked my head toward Jan and Dennis. "Can you like, come back? In around five hours?"

"Five hours?"

"Maybe four, if I work fast." I figured four or five hours would be enough time to get through my list of suspects and a possible attempt on my life. But I couldn't explain that to Tiffany. At least not in front of Jan and Dennis. I grimaced. If the culprit was Jan and/or Dennis — although Dennis really seemed unlikely unless he was an incredible actor — recreating that original tension would be extremely difficult. I'd have to step up my interrogation techniques into outright (fake) threats.

Before Tiffany could start a hissy fit, my phone rang. I held up a finger. I hoped it was Nash. Then prayed it wasn't Nash. Really hoped it wasn't Ian. Or Annie checking on my paperwork progress.

None of the above. Mrs. Jessup. "Oh, Maizie. Detective Mowry said you were at your office. That's not too far from here. I mean, he's never walked downtown. And he probably doesn't even know you have an office there. But I hoped, you know, he had such a good time at the park today."

"Um." I mentally peeled apart her words to gain the gist. "Are you asking if Aiden's here?"

"Yes," she breathed. "Is Aiden with you?"

My stomach repeated its ride on my emotional roller coaster. It dipped low, then rose steadily up my throat. "No, Mrs. Jessup. Aiden's missing? When did you last see him?"

Tiffany cut me a look. Behind me, I heard the Martins gasp.

"At home. We were in the backyard. I herded us all inside, but now I can't find Aiden." Her voice broke. "The police are here. I mean, more police are here."

"I'll be there in five minutes." I grabbed my keys and coat and ran out the door, abandoning Tiffany and the Martins.

Wishing someone had killed me, rather than face whatever happened to Aiden.

FORTY-SEVEN

#BananaArcana #WindowDressing

---

*a*t Aiden's home, police crawled throughout the neighborhood and alley. I parked in front of the Martins' home and walked to the Jessups. In her front yard, Mrs. Jessup and her other children crowded around Officer Hardy. The sun shone on the little group, and the air smelled fresh and green. But the breeze that occasionally rushed through still held the raw and frigid feel of winter. I approached cautiously, not wanting to interrupt, but Mrs. Jessup and Hardy waved me over.

"Remi's home. I spoke to her mother," said Hardy. "I came back on duty when I heard."

"What can I do?" I asked. "Can I help search for Aiden?"

"Detective Mowry would like you to stay at your office."

"Is Ian here? If I could talk to him, he might want help."

"He'll see you when he's free."

"But I'm an investigator..." I stopped at the curt shake of his head.

"Not now."

I hugged Mrs. Jessup, smiled at her kids, and hurried back to Billy, thinking about my earlier plan. Jennifer Frederick was supposed to arrive next. But I felt too distracted to focus on forcing confessions from anyone. I also feared the culprit had taken Aiden because they'd seen us at the park.

Or maybe because I'd made the move with the fake evidence. Which might mean I'd been on the right track in choosing suspects.

Except I wanted to be the intended victim. Not Aiden.

My stomach turned over. Again. I clutched my chest and forced my heart to slow. Heartburn caused by my screwups were the least of my problems, though. Aiden was the priority.

I glanced across the street. A policewoman walked through Gary's yard. They'd probably already searched Lorena's garden, too. But maybe not her house. Her house key would be in her evidence box and that might take some time to retrieve.

There was a chance the extra key might have returned to the flowerpot and the patrol cops didn't know about it.

Keeping my eye on the police, I moved up the Martins' empty drive and cut toward the side yard adjoining Lorena's. A walkway squeezed between a wall of azaleas, hiding the side of the house from the street. The grouping of bushes also hid the secret cookie door. And offered cover for anyone who wanted to sneak into Lorena's yard the night of the gala.

How convenient.

I cut through the tall azaleas toward the low fence separating the two properties. Checked for any police who might have misinterpreted my furtive movements. At the fence, I hesitated. Considering the proximity to Lorena's, Aiden's bear could have easily watched us from here. Jan Martin seemed particularly nosy.

Hopping the fence, I landed in a tight space behind a dense, overgrown row of camellias. The shrubs had once been planted and trimmed to form a long block, but Lorena had stopped pruning them. Their branches jutted naturally, making it difficult to maneuver behind them. I muscled my way along the fence, fighting the spreading branches, toward the back of the house.

A few yards before reaching the back fence and tool shed, I

found a break. Or rather, someone had created a break. The bush to my left had died back, and the neighboring camellia had taken advantage, pushing new branches into the dead space. The young branches had been bent to form a tunnel. The ground had a low depression cleared of leaves and other detritus. I exited near the back stoop and crossed to the herbs.

No key.

If Aiden's kidnapper had the key, they could still be in the house. My skin prickled and my throat constricted. Would a kidnapper really take a chance on hiding themselves next door?

I didn't know where else to look. Inaction would drive me crazy. I had to keep trying. Crisis-mode made me bananas.

I needed to calm myself. As much as it made me nauseous, I forced myself to think about Nash.

My mind automatically traveled to his parting shot. I winced, recalling his icy blue eyes. They'd been filled with pain, not venom. I'd really hurt him. My chest heaved and my shoulders convulsed.

"Stop it," I ordered myself. "Think like Nash, not about Nash."

I took a deep breath. Let it out. Centered my chi. Not that I was ever sure where my chi was.

Okay. Nash would stoically assess the situation. Go over facts he knew about Aiden. What we'd learned about the killer.

Think. Think. Think.

Aiden liked to hide. Maybe he wasn't kidnapped.

Hang on, Aiden had been agitated at the park. My logbook and pictures had been stolen.

Of course. Aiden had seen the killer at the park.

When he'd arrived home, he ran away the first chance he got. Ran or hidden.

I stared at the back door still warded by crime tape. Maybe Aiden did have the key. But would he know another way inside? I closed my eyes, recalling when I'd caught him in Lorena's back-yard. I'd ordered him home and he'd gone around the side of the house next to the Martins. Where he saw the so-called bear. He'd been deceiving me. Tricking me into letting him into the house.

I shook my head. Constantly thwarted by six-year-olds.

However, maybe he'd originally gone to the Martins' side because he'd planned on sneaking in another way. Then had heard the rustling in Lorena's camellias.

Worth a shot.

I crept past her back stoop and peered around the side of the home, checking for the police. I bent to kid-level to examine the house. Lorena's bungalow had a crawlspace, but other than venting fitted with a wire mesh, stonework hid the underside. Some of the mortar had chipped but was otherwise intact. The crawlspace entrance had to be on a different side of the house.

Anxiety fluttered inside me like a trapped bird. I chewed my lip, worried I wasted time. Missing something important. How else could a kid get inside the house? I looked up.

Bingo. A window.

The new windows were closed and locked. But I found a leaded, glazed window with a broken latch. I pushed and it swung out halfway. I noted the crumbling mortar beneath, creating toeholds for someone to climb up to the wooden sill. Perfect for a small boy.

Not so much for a normal-sized woman.

With great effort, I wedged my boot into a toe hold. Swung one leg up and hooked it through the narrow window. Teetered. Grabbed the frame. Hoisted myself until I could sit astride the sill. Looked inside. My leg dangled above a toilet. Thankfully, the bathroom door was shut. I sat in the window for a minute, listening. Not hearing any creaks or voices, I slid. Reached the awkward position of one foot not quite touching the floor and the other hooked through the window. And fell.

I lay next to the toilet for a long minute, panting and praying. With the window open, I could hear the shouts of people in the street and the squawks of radios. The room smelled like a cinnamon candle, but the breeze drifted in, rustled the toilet paper, and delivered the fresh scent of the winter thaw. A spring Lorena would never see.

My heart hurt. The silence in the house told me Aiden was likely not here. The police might have already searched the place. I'd wasted my time. But I didn't know what else to do.

I rose from the floor, shut the window, and crept to the door. Paused to listen, then opened the wooden door, gritting my teeth at the squeak.

Sweat broke out on my neck. I tiptoed down the hall, calling Aiden's name. After hunting in the master suite and guest room, I entered the office. The safe door still stood open. Careful not to touch anything, I circled the desk, checked underneath for hiding children, then studied the desk. Lorena's computer and other devices had been taken as evidence. An empty file drawer hung open. I closed my eyes, going over my walk-through with Ian, summoning up what he had pointed out. Then, I tried to recall what I knew of Lorena and her habits for dressing.

Her hair and makeup would be done first, of course. The night of the gala, she would have waited to dress until just before leaving. Lorena hadn't changed yet. The steamer had been on. She'd been busy with finishing touches. In the front room, when she'd been…

Okay, we'd deduced all that already. Why was the safe open and the papers everywhere? Who else would know the combination? She had no family nearby. Unless she'd told Spencer. But was Spencer the kind of lover to whom you'd give the combination to your safe?

According to the Black Pine mothers, earlier that day, Spencer Newson had argued with Lorena.

Spencer Newson had wanted Vicki to connect her personal banking to the Clothing Kids account and she'd dropped him like a bad habit.

However, Jennifer Frederick had said that system wasn't problematic.

Anyway, the money had been taken from the Clothing Kids'

account by Lorena and likely transferred to her account in Mexico. I still couldn't believe Lorena hadn't stolen that money. It didn't make any sense.

I opened my eyes. A soft scraping emanated from the front of the house. I rounded the desk and crept to the office door. A light metallic rattling broke the stillness. The air shifted. Wood scraped.

Someone was at the front door.

I held my breath, then realized I was trapped in the office. I shot through the doorway, tiptoe-ran down the hall, and entered the bathroom.

Shizzles. I hadn't checked the front room or the kitchen yet. Aiden could still be in the house. I pulled the bathroom door shut, leaving it cracked. Footsteps thudded on wood. The front door shut.

Who was in the house with me? And where was Aiden?

FORTY-EIGHT

#BathroomConfessions
#WhackaDoodleDoo

I shifted to lean against the bathroom wall with my ear toward the door. The clomping stopped.

"Don't touch anything. You sure he trusts you?" rumbled Ian's deep voice.

Ian had gotten the key from evidence to search for Aiden.

I hesitated at the bathroom door, then backed up. No way was I getting caught doing a crime scene B and E, even if my intentions were good. It would screw up the prosecution's case if anyone knew I was here. I tiptoed to the toilet.

"Give me a break, Mowry. It's not my first crime scene. I'm here to look for the kid, not compromise the integrity of a murder conviction."

Craptastic. Nash.

My toes snuck back to the door of their own accord. Stupid toes. I needed to get out before I was caught. But my body ignored my brain, plastered itself to the wall, and thrust my ear to the crack.

The men called out to Aiden. The clomping increased. I glanced back at my escape route. Luckily, climbing out would be easier than climbing in. The toilet increased my chance of success.

As long as I didn't break it.

"Check the kitchen. I'll look in the back rooms," said Ian. "But I don't think he's here. Unless he's in the attic."

"Is it a pull-down?" said Nash. "He wouldn't be able to reach."

"Dammit," said Ian. "What happened to that kid?"

I held my breath, hoping Nash would have a good idea.

"Where is she, Mowry?" Nash's voice growled. "The Bronco is down the street."

"Why're you asking me? I told her to stay in the office."

"Are you kidding? She's not staying in the office if a kid's missing."

My heart pounded. This was why my toes wouldn't listen.

The men called out for Aiden, treading toward the back of the house. I poised on my toes, ready to force my feet to hurry to the window. The clomping stopped.

Ian sighed. "I should've arrested her."

I gasped. Then quickly shut my mouth.

Nash snorted. "Right. What's that? Some kind of fantasy fulfillment?"

"Just what are you saying?" barked Ian.

"I think you know what I'm saying."

"You know me better than that."

"Been a long time, though, hasn't it, Mowry? I've not seen you take this kind of interest since the divorce."

Ian scoffed. "If we're going there, what's shaken your confidence? For a man who's got the world on a string, you sure as hell don't act like it."

"What the hell does that mean?"

"Is she getting tired of your BS? Women like to talk, Nash. You need to talk to her. Maizie's not like these local gals—"

"Don't tell me what's she like, Mowry," Nash's voice dropped to a low growl. I strained to hear him. "I know what's she's like. I probably know her better than anyone."

My heart swelled, then I remembered what I'd done. I

pinched my thumb hard but couldn't stop the tears. I had to get out of the house. My priorities should be finding Aiden then drawing out the killer. I had no business listening in on their conversation, no matter how juicy.

I edged backward from the door.

"Then what are you doing getting pissy with me?" said Ian. "I'm judging you by your behavior, man. If she's texting me about casework late at night, where are you?"

Good question. I tiptoed forward.

Somebody grunted, followed by a loud thud. The wall shook.

"You—"

A heavy thump shook the floor. Muttered curses were lost in scuffles and crashes.

I took their tussle as my cue to get out. Climbing over a toilet quietly was difficult enough.

Stifling my need to cry, I got on with my escape. If I didn't learn who was trying to kill me, it wouldn't have been worth what I'd done to Nash. Although, our relationship wouldn't have fallen apart so easily if everything had been right between us.

And if Nash didn't open up about where he went at night, I didn't know if we'd ever be right.

*T*he Martins' black Panamera sat in the drive, and from their porch, the couple watched the police. I stayed hidden among the azaleas, panicking over Aiden. I was trapped behind a wall of evergreens, waiting to be caught trespassing by the Martins, the police, or my crazy ex-boyfriends.

A black Mercedes pulled into the Martins' drive. Susie Newson. With Spencer.

Great.

The Martins moved off their porch and strolled into the driveway. The two couples stood behind the Mercedes. Dennis Martin pointed toward the Jessups' house.

Frigtastic. How long would I have to wait in these bushes?

A truck's engine started up somewhere in the alley. Nash's Silverado. Probably leaving to get away from Ian. Or me. He knew I was nearby.

I needed to get back to the office. Jennifer would arrive soon. I chewed my thumbnail. I didn't want to leave the neighborhood with Aiden missing. But I wasn't doing any good sitting in the Martins' bushes. I squat-walked onto the stone walkway, through the yard, and stopped behind the Panamera. I peeked out behind the car.

Next door, Ian stalked down Lorena's walkway to his truck. The two couples still stood behind the Mercedes. Fragments of their conversation carried on the wind. Dennis explained Aiden's disappearance. I caught my name. Connected to a five-letter word.

Totally awkward eavesdropping on a second conversation with myself as a topic. Especially while crouching behind a car. Much worse than hiding in a bathroom. Might as well continue my quest of knocking out suspects. Even if I humiliated myself in the process.

I popped up behind the car and casually walked forward.

Susie faced the house. At my pop up, she gasped, causing the other three to pivot.

"What the hell," said Spencer.

"What—" stuttered Dennis. "Where did you—"

"Were you in my house?" exclaimed Jan.

"Of course not. I was looking for Aiden," I said, fluttering my fingers in a vague direction behind me. "I'm sorry about earlier. Especially about the concealed carry. So you know, I have a license."

"I would hope so," retorted Jan. "I still don't understand what that was all about."

"What was what all about?" said Susie.

"Maizie accused Jan of having damp gloves at the party," said Dennis. "I'll be damned to understand a hubbub over wet gloves.

So Jan spilled a drink or something? It's not like she ruined the party. Lorena's murder did."

I gave myself a mental facepalm. Then gave Dennis one for good measure.

"Young lady," said Jan. "You might still have some status as a celebrity, but it doesn't give you the right to be rude."

"I—" I pressed my lips together before I continued with, "I was trying to figure out if you'd murdered three people." Not only had I lost Hercule Poirot, Columbo, and Helen Mirren, I'd also lost my mashup character. I was back to plain old Maizie, the screwup.

"You and your mother might have done 'Lifestyles of the Rich and Whatnot' in California, but it doesn't mean you can act so high and mighty here in Black Pine," said Jan. "I saw Vicki's topiaries on the Nextdoor app. And that headless statue. What did she mean by that? Did she cut off heads to make those obvious replicas seem real? How tacky. And completely unworthy of the Peanut Mansion's former glory."

"Someone put pictures of her statue on the Nextdoor app?" My cheeks flamed at the thought of Vicki's marbled partial-nudity displayed on the online grapevine for all of Black Pine to see...

Hang on.

"What do you mean by 'headless'? That statue and the topiaries had heads yesterday. And how could a marble statue lose its head?"

"Simple, it's not marble," said Jan. "A cheap imitation, like all her other renovations. That woman has some nerve passing off replicas like they're the real deal. I'm calling attention to it at the next Historical Society meeting."

"Vicki wouldn't knock off her sculpture's head," I replied. "Particularly if the statue looked like Vicki. She's too vain for that. If she wanted it headless, she would order it that way from the sculptor. Besides, she's not even home. When she left, the statue had a head. I was there."

"A stunt," said Dennis. "She had someone else do it."

"You're right. Someone else did it. Someone jealous of Vicki because of a history that has nothing to do with the Peanut Mansion." I narrowed my eyes at Susie. She and Spencer had been avidly following the conversation. While Spencer appeared bemused, Susie couldn't hide her smirk. "Someone who wanted to upset or threaten Vicki. They probably used the same weapon on the statue as the attack on my dirt bike."

"They used a weapon to cut off the statue's head?" said Spencer. "What, like a Whack-a-Mole?"

"Exactly like Whack-A-Mole. Their weapon of choice for murder is whacking. Stab, then whack."

"For murder?" Dennis looked at Jan. Jan looked at Spencer. But he stared at Susie. Her smirk had disappeared.

While we gawked at each other, Susie lunged toward the Mercedes, yanked open the door, and climbed inside. The car roared to life and reversed down the driveway. We scrambled, and the sedan nearly clipped Jan.

"Stop Susie," I screamed. "Where's Aiden?"

I had gotten my *Columbo* moment. At the wrong time.

FORTY-NINE

#ColumboMoment #NotSoSucky

Susie peeled out of the Martins' driveway and roared down the street. I darted toward Billy and pulled out my phone. In this particular case, it seemed Annie had been wrong.

My 'aha' moment would be followed by a car chase.

"What was that all about?" called Dennis. "Susie knows where Aiden is?"

"Yes, Dennis," I yelled while trying to text and run. Not so easy. "Go tell Officer Hardy that Susie knows where Aiden is."

"What history were you talking about?" said Jan. "I'm not jealous of the Peanut Mansion. I have the Tobacco King's house."

"Vicki's shared history with Spencer." I shot Spencer a venomous glance over my shoulder. "You snake. You turned Susie into the rival cheerleader."

"Susie's a cheerleader?" said Dennis.

I vaulted into Billy — and felt thankful for a doorless convertible — yanked on my helmet and cranked the ignition. Spencer hopped onto the seat next to me.

An issue with topless and doorless vehicles I had not foreseen.

I flipped the visor on my helmet. "What are you doing?"

"She's my wife. I'm coming with you." He buckled his belt. "You don't understand."

"I think I do." I shot him a hard look. "Susie might have lost it, but this is your fault, too."

"I know." Spencer's red-rimmed eyes appeared remote and despondent. "And I feel terrible. I can't protect her anymore. She probably drove home. I need to get to her before the police do."

"Whatever." I sighed, resigned. "The police will need to speak to you, too."

I pulled out from the curb, then waited for the Martins' neighbors to finish crossing the street. By the time I approached the corner, Susie's Mercedes had disappeared. I cut corners tightly, anxious to get out of the gridded blocks of the old downtown. Glancing at Spencer, I realized he was talking. Stopping at a four-way, I paused to pull off my helmet.

"...did the same thing to Jennifer, when Susie thought she'd figured out the truth."

The wind whipped my hair around my face. "I didn't catch that. Did what to Jennifer?"

"Like the statue and the topiaries. Except at Jennifer's house, Susie smashed all Jen's flowerpots and tore down her wind chimes. She also spray-painted a really nasty message on her sidewalk." Spencer's face reddened and he looked away. "She's young. And immature. I didn't know she wrecked your bike. I'm sorry."

I cut Billy's steering wheel to the right and pulled to the side of the road. "Say what now? It sounds like you're only talking about vandalism."

He mopped his face, then looked at me. "I fell hard for her. Things were really over with my wife when I met Susie. But I...I don't know. I ignored some red flags, like her possessiveness. To be honest, it was kind of a turn-on at first. But now, it's too much. I married a child."

In the distance, police sirens wailed. The police had gone

after Susie. Except Spencer thought the police were after a vandal, not a killer.

I stared at the clouds overhead. Counted to ten. Took three deep *ujjayi* breaths. Let them out. And turned to Spencer Newson. "What did Susie do to Lorena?"

"Lorena?" He reared back. "What do you mean?"

"Spencer, everyone knows you and Lorena were having an affair."

"Everyone— what? But I wasn't having an affair with Lorena."

I pinched the bridge of my nose, reminding myself of Nash. I yanked my fingers off my nose. "Susie lashed out at Vicki, me, and, as you say, Jennifer Frederick. None of us were having an affair with you. Yet she not only vandalized our property but also assaulted it. She battered my bike, decapitated a statue, and smashed flowerpots." I felt my patience give way to anger. "That's some aggressive violence. Why would she do that?"

He gusted a sigh. "I am having an affair. Just not with Lorena."

My stomach bottomed out. "With…"

"Jennifer."

I closed my eyes in relief. It wasn't Vicki. Opened my eyes and looked at Spencer, astonished. "Jennifer? Jennifer Frederick? The auditor?"

"For several years." He gave me a sheepish look. "I married the wrong woman. But I've been afraid of what Susie would do. I'm a coward. Whenever I bring up problems in our relationship, she gets hysterical. I'm afraid she'll hurt herself. Or someone else…"

"Like Lorena?" I twisted to face him. "Susie hurt Lorena, didn't she? Like everyone else, she thought you were having an affair with Lorena. Susie confronted Lorena while you were at the party. Things got out of hand…"

Spencer shook his head. "No, it wasn't Susie. It couldn't be Susie. The police questioned her. She had selfies on her phone from the party. The pictures were timestamped. She was at the party the whole time."

I gaped, then shut my mouth. I was so sure it was Susie. Columbo had failed me. Along with Helen Mirren and Hercule Poirot.

In fifteen minutes, Jennifer Frederick would meet me at my office. Maybe she was my homicidal cheerleader. She could have killed Lorena in a jealous rage. I couldn't imagine Jennifer the accountant getting worked up enough to murder anyone. But I also couldn't imagine her having an affair with Spencer. Might as well stick to my plan and give her another shot at homicide.

Three patrol cars shot past us.

"Can you take me home?" said Spencer. "Susie took our car. She's probably at our house. I should talk to her. Be there when the police arrive."

"A little boy is missing and a killer on the loose, Spencer. I've got places to be." I jerked a thumb at the sidewalk. "You're wasting my time. Get out."

"You sound like your mother."

Yikes. Not the person I hoped to emulate.

"Fine, I'll take you home. But I've got to hurry." I pulled away from the curb and sped toward the mountain. My hair flew, lashing my face and neck. I reached for my helmet, but it had rolled behind my seat.

Whatevs. Snarled hair was the least of my worries.

I thought about Jennifer and the slap, wondering if it was indicative of violence. What had she said just before smacking Spencer? She wanted to kill him, for "ruining everything."

Jennifer had played down the slap. Just like she'd dismissed Spencer wanting Vicki to connect her banking to the Clothing Kids' account. At the time, I hadn't known Jennifer was Spencer's paramour. Now I had a different perspective.

I looked at Spencer. He stared at the curving mountain road ahead, deep in thought. Somewhere up the mountain, the police sped to his home.

"You ruined everything for Jennifer." The wind carried my words, and I had to shout, "At the gala, she was really angry at you."

He gave me a sharp glance, then shrugged. "I have a bad habit of pissing off women, what can I say?"

I cut my eyes back to the road. "Is that what makes you sad? Regret?"

"I guess so."

"You must regret Lorena funneling that money into her Mexican bank account."

The line I'd planned for exposing the killer had been, "You must regret Johnny selling me the photos of Lorena's house."

Only the killer would be aware of Johnny taking photos at Lorena's the night of the murder. If the photos on the stolen camera had evidence of Lorena's killer, they would think I had copies. But my line also implied I'd bought other photos from Johnny.

I was proud of myself for coming up with that line. But I felt even better about changing it. Lorena had transferred the Clothing Kids' money into her Mexican bank account. There was no other way of looking at it. She'd also poured her heart and soul into creating Clothing Kids. She wouldn't abscond with the funds.

Lorena had been protecting her foundation by moving the money to a place no one could touch. She thought someone else planned to steal that money. And when she confronted them, they killed her. Then tore up her office, looking for a way to get into that Mexican bank account. They'd probably found the combination to her safe and looked in there, too. Leaving it open for crazy Gary to steal the crown.

Maybe I wasn't such a sucky investigator after all.

I refocused on Spencer. He still looked remorseful. But also astonished.

Holy Hellsbah. I wasn't in my office with cameras and microphones trained on him. I drove in an open vehicle on a winding mountain road.

Alone.

With the killer.

Dangit. I had to take all that back about not being a sucky investigator.

FIFTY

#ScratchThat #CarChaseKismet

*F*iguring out the motive for murder was one thing. Calling out a killer while driving on a twisty mountain road with your gun locked inside your glovebox is quite another.

Shiztastic.

I gripped the steering wheel. Hopefully, Spencer would allow me to drop him off at his house so he could talk to Susie about the evils of property destruction. The police would already be there. Perfect timing. His gated subdivision even had a guardhouse. When I stopped to give the guard the Newsons' home address, I'd take off my seatbelt and retrieve my gun.

Scratch that. The guard would get the wrong idea. Very wrong. Besides, Spencer might guess why I reached to unlock the glovebox. He could grab my .38.

New plan. Hop out of Billy and run.

Much better. And with a doorless vehicle, it couldn't be easier. Good ol' Billy.

The road curved sharply. I braked, slowing us down. My helmet rolled forward.

"Hurry up," said Spencer. "Susie's home by now."

"Safety first," I said with all the cheer I could muster. My hair slapped my mouth. I spit out the sticky tendrils and reached for my helmet. With one hand, I drew it into my lap. "I'm taking you home. Don't you worry."

"I'm really sorry," said Spencer.

"It's—" Was he apologizing for murder or theft? Should I offer a conciliatory "it's okay" for that?

No, my mashup would never go for that.

I glanced at Spencer. He'd unbuckled his seatbelt. "You really should wear a seatbelt. These roads are a little slick and as you see, Billy doesn't have—"

Spencer lunged and grabbed the steering wheel.

"What the—" I screamed. "Are you crazy? Get back in your seat this instant."

Billy skidded toward the shoulder. A steep drop-off fell into the woods below. I cut the wheel to the left. Spencer jerked it right. While we wrestled with the wheel, I pumped the brake. Spencer moved off his seat, yanking hard on the steering wheel. We veered into the left lane. A minivan popped into view in the opposite lane. I screamed. My hair lashed around my head. Spencer slapped at my flying hair. I jerked us back on the path.

The woman driving the minivan gave us an angry look and mouthed something. Hopefully, she'd report the crazy man almost in my lap, not my driving.

"Get off," I screamed.

His foot shot past the floor gear shift, bumping my leg. I kicked with my left foot. Awkwardly. He grabbed my seat with his left hand.

"You're going to kill us both, Spencer."

With a sinking feeling, I realized I'd revealed his brilliant plan. Deja vu prickled my nerves.

Fictional deja vu. Bad fictional deja vu.

Julia Pinkerton had a similar scene, in her first season. But Julia had been the passenger and the mountains were California hills. She'd been tailing the PTA president whose son headed a football doping ring. Julia suspected his supplier was his mom, a pharmaceutical rep. After cheer practice, Julia's car needed a jump. A football booster alumnus offered to take her home. It wasn't until they were driving on a canyon road that Julia figured out the booster had been the supplier. The winning season meant more to him than life. Literally. Julia had leaped from the car before he could crash it.

I was *so not* jumping out of a moving vehicle. My stunt double had worn a lot of padding. And had an ambulance on standby.

The road veered. I had the incline on my side, slowing us down. But it wouldn't matter with our swerving between lanes. I faced a mostly granite mountainside in the wrong lane and a steep fall into a forest on the right. Both options looked painful at any speed above walking.

Who was I kidding? Even at walking speed, either would hurt.

Spencer's foot shot out and hit the accelerator, flooring it. Billy's powerful V8 engine revved, gunning us up the mountain road. I stomped on the brake. Roaring and smoking, the Bronco slid.

Sideways.

I pulled my foot off the brake. We catapulted. My body jerked forward. My neck whipped back. My helmet dug into my stomach, wedged against the steering wheel.

Spencer clung to my seatback. The mountainside loomed before us. I jerked the wheel right. Spencer pushed left. We fish-tailed up the center line, heading toward another turn. Spencer shoved against me. His left foot slid off the gas and kicked my foot from the brake. His right jammed the accelerator.

He was going to kill us.

I fought against his imposing weight. Grappled the wheel with both hands. Used both feet to get around his legs to hit the brake. My mind spun faster than Billy's tires. I never apologized to Nash for that stupid ploy. Sadly, at the same time, I wasn't exactly lying. I'd been frustrated. I'd felt guilty for him losing his business, but he'd given up so quickly. Applied his work habits to corporate life. Maybe PI work wasn't his dream, just mine. Maybe I didn't know him like I thought.

Maybe the Nash in my head wasn't the real Nash.

And I'd tried to become the old Nash.

Look where it got me. Dying in a car accident that would be deemed my fault. They'd add manslaughter and reckless driving charges to my eulogy.

Friggin' Spencer Newson. The cheater. I hadn't trusted him from the beginning. I should've gone with my gut.

My arms and shoulders hurt. My shins and ankles stung from his kicking. And my hair felt like nettles slapping against my skin. I longed to put on my helmet, but I couldn't let go of the wheel.

My heart ached. As much as I wanted Nash to be the man I imagined, I still loved him. Stupid camo tie and all.

A truck passed us, blaring its horn.

Spencer pulled hard to the right again. Billy tilted. We skidded toward the graveled shoulder. I counter-steered.

The tires dropped.

He wasn't just going to kill us. He was also killing my convertible. The steering wheel felt close to breaking. My tires were probably shredded. The brakes felt spongy. Spongier.

"Spencer, what did you do with Aiden?" I yanked the wheel again and fought his feet, digging my heel into the top of his foot. "Does Jennifer have him?"

"She's got nothing to do with this," he shouted. "Leave Jennifer out of this."

"She took my pictures and case log at the park, didn't she?"

"I don't know what you're talking about."

"She was covering for you, you troll. Jennifer knew Lorena had hidden that money and she knew why."

"I needed that money. My ex-wife took everything."

"You probably deserved it," I shouted and rammed my shoulder into the hand that clung to my seat.

He grunted. I focused on steering us around the next curve. We were nearing the turn off to Vicki's. Around the bend, I knew the road dipped sharply before resuming the incline. We'd pick up speed. My arms were tiring.

My seat bounced. I didn't dare take my eyes off the road. Spencer's left hand reached over my head toward the steering wheel.

Oh, God. I wasn't strong enough to grapple the wheel against two of his hands.

I knew what I had to do and it would hurt.

Badly.

FIFTY-ONE

#DeathGrip #ShameOnMe

I grabbed my helmet with one hand. With my right, I held the steering wheel in a death grip.

Literally.

Spencer seized the wheel with his left hand and jerked the wheel. Billy careened toward the drop-off. Bracing myself against the seat, I pulled on my helmet. Released the seatbelt.

And jumped.

Muscle memory from years of stage combat and martial arts classes took over. I tucked, crossing my arms over my chest. Shoved my hands in my armpits. Rolled. Felt my clothing tear. My skin rip. My shoulders might have caught on fire. But I was on the pavement.

Still moving.

I looked up. An oncoming car rushed around the bend. My body tightened like a coiled spring. But I forced myself to roll into the right lane.

The car whipped by, honking.

I lay in the road for what felt like minutes but was probably seconds. The crash broke my stupor. Dragging myself to my feet, I hobbled to the soft shoulder and eased onto the steep embankment. Sank to the ground. Then collapsed. I lay looking up at the sky through my tinted visor. My right hip ached. My back throbbed. My arms stung liked they'd been scourged with a fiery lasso. Pretty sure I had whiplash. I didn't have the energy to take off my helmet anyway.

I drew my phone out of my back pocket. The cracked screen lit up. I pressed 9-1-1, opened my visor, and balanced my phone against my helmet's opening. Then let my arms collapse on the ground.

*W*hen Nash arrived, he found me sitting in the back of the ambulance. A victim blanket wrapped around my shoulders. I had another deja vu flash, but it wasn't to a *Julia Pinkerton* scene. I'd flashed to my recent ambulance sit at Lorena's house. This time it wasn't my mind in shock. It was my body. I had terrible road rash and bruising. Possibly, cracked ribs. My coat and clothes were shredded. My hair resembled a bird's nest. Again.

But there was a crack in the back of my helmet that could have been my head. Billy was a mangled mess. Spencer Newson was barely alive. I knew when to count my blessings.

Despite their attempts to stop him, Nash pushed past the police and ambulance crew. He stopped in front of me, breathing hard. A muscle in his jaw jumped and his eyes narrowed into slits.

"Did they find Aiden?" I said. "No one will tell me anything."

He placed his hands on his hips. "You need to go to the hospital."

"Did they find him?"

He blew a long breath out of his nose, then cut his head sharply to the right.

I tried to shrug the blanket off my shoulders and winced. "I've been thinking…"

"Have you?" The steely edge in his voice cut through the ringing in my head.

I winced again. But I was too tired to protest. "I know who can find Aiden."

"Tell Mowry."

"He's not here." I pulled in a breath at his murderous look. "The police will scare Aiden. I need to go. Will you take me?"

Nash didn't reply.

"Please?" I blinked back tears and shook off the blanket. The cold bit through the rips in my clothing. I shivered.

He crossed his arms and lowered his chin. "What are your injuries? Anything broken?"

"Just my convertible. It's dead."

"Better Billy than you." Nash held out a hand. I took it and slid forward. He caught me before I hit the ground. His left hand spanned my waist. At my grimace, he yanked his hand off. "I was looking forward to fixing that Bronco. Shame."

"Yes, I'm going to miss Billy." I blinked up at him.

"That's not what I meant," he said curtly and dropped my hand.

I felt worse than when Spencer tried to kill me.

The road going up the mountain was closed off for all but first responders. Nash waited while I changed into borrowed scrubs from an EMT. He helped me into his truck, and we headed back toward town. Instead of attempting an awkward apology and near-death confession, I called the cabin and asked to speak to Remi.

"Do you remember playing hide and seek at the party?" I asked her. "You said nobody could find Aiden. Did he go next door to Lorena's?"

"That's cheating," said Remi.

"I know. But you said Aiden's a cheater."

"We already looked at Lorena's," muttered Nash.

I turned to him. "I know. But Remi said he's really good at hide and seek."

"I didn't say he was *really* good," squawked Remi.

"How did you know I looked at Lorena's?" said Nash.

"I might have been hiding in the bathroom. And left through the window."

He pressed his lips together and the veins in his neck bulged.

"I, um, kind of overheard your argument with Ian, too."

"Was that before or after you rigged your office with cameras and invited your suspects over to play true confessions?"

"How did you—"

"Because I know you," he spat. "If I hadn't been at the office, trying to wring a confession out of Jennifer Frederick, I could have stopped Spencer Newson from getting into your Bronco."

"That was an issue with a doorless vehicle I hadn't foreseen."

He cut his head to the right and glared at me. "You think?"

"Maybe he's not a cheater," whispered Remi.

"He's a cheater all right," I said. "Cheating on his first wife, then cheating on Susie with Jennifer. Did she confess to that?"

"Frederick confessed to not reporting the missing money because she knew why Lorena had hidden it," said Nash. "She confessed to checking your investigation board and taking your case logbook to help Spencer. And she confessed to being an idiot in love with a weak man which made her do stupid things. Sound familiar?"

I wanted to ask which part, but I could guess. "You're not a weak man. Far from it. And I'm stupid on my own."

"Wasn't talking about me."

"I'm sorry," cried Remi. "Please don't fight."

I turned my attention to the phone. "No, I'm sorry. You shouldn't have heard that."

"Aiden's not a cheater. He didn't go to Lorena's. He is really good at hide and seek." She moaned. "I don't like him being better than me. Please don't tell Momma. She'll get on me for lying."

"Where did he hide?"

"They have a little room with a hidden door."

"The cookie closet door? But that exits outside."

"Aiden hid under the sink. But before hiding, he opened the cookie door, so we'd go outside to look for him."

"Ingenious," I gasped.

"Isn't that kind of cheating?" whined Remi.

I put my hand on Nash's arm. "The Martins. Aiden's at the Martins' house. He must have snuck in through the hidden door. He's in the butler's pantry."

FIFTY-TWO

#AllsWell #ThatDoesn'tEndWell

---

*A*fter the Martins let us in and I'd coaxed Aiden out of their cabinet, we walked him to the Jessups. The parents and siblings bawled and hugged him — except for the baby who reached for me and bawled when I left. Nash and I walked back to his truck. However, instead of feeling the Jessups' joy, I only felt the cold seeping through the thin fabric of my borrowed scrubs. I huddled inside my victim's blanket, serving as a shawl.

"How angry are you?" I stared at my feet so I wouldn't have to see his face and confirm what I already knew.

"I have never been so angry in all my life."

"Okay." I swallowed. "Annie can probably pick me up. I'll figure it out."

"Stop trying to figure everything out."

"I know I screwed up—"

"Yes, you did." He jerked his thumb back at his truck. "I should take you to a hospital, but I'm sure you'll have your own idea of where to go."

. . .

*I*n his truck, the tension was unbearable. I asked Nash to drop me off at the office. The new office. I'd probably never get to return to the old office. I already missed the scent of donuts. The visits with Lamar. The dirt and dust and worn furniture. The stupid bed.

But what I really missed sat beside me in stone-cold silence.

I pinched my thumb to the point of bruising but still couldn't keep the tears from rolling down my cheeks.

The Silverado stopped in front of Albright Security Solutions. I slid out of the truck. He sped off while I stood on the sidewalk, holding the remnants of my belongings in a plastic grocery bag. The name on the storefront window mocked me.

Wasn't this what I really wanted? I'd flushed out Lorena's killer and found Aiden on my own.

I'd lost Nash in the process.

Stiff and sore. Beaten and bruised. Heart, body, and mind hurting, I shuffled through the door. I prepared to humble myself into asking Annie for a ride home. And hoped she wouldn't make me stay and finish all my paperwork first.

"About time you got here." Tiffany sat behind my desk, tapping on the computer. The folders she'd knocked down had been re-stacked, and Annie stood behind her.

"Wrong column." Annie snapped her gum and pointed at something on the screen.

"Maizie." A body gripped me in a painful hug. A hug that smelled of Maybelline, Matrix, and mango. Rhonda loved fruit-scented body lotion. "I'm glad you're okay. We heard about the car crash."

Wincing, I pulled back to study her. "You look great. You did your hair and makeup." I hugged her again. "Have you forgiven me?"

"Forgiven what? Get over yourself." Rhonda gave me a grin and patted her extensions. "Tiffany did my hair. It was time for a change. But girl, you look like you've been to hell and back."

"Kind of feels that way, too." I touched the squirrel's nest that used to be my hair. "Are your brothers still mad at me?"

"They're just glad it's over." She eyed me. "It's over, right?"

I nodded. "Susie didn't threaten you. That note was for me. It accompanied her trashing of Lucky. She must've thought I was making the moves on Spencer." I stuck out my tongue. "As if. He went to school with my parents."

"Ew," said Rhonda. "That girl is seriously disturbed."

"Not as much as her husband," I said glumly.

"You're gonna need new wheels," said Tiffany. "Rhubarb's doesn't do refunds. But if we sneak out tonight and salvage parts, we might get a trade-in."

"I like the way you think." Annie cracked her gum. "Maizie should get a Jeep."

"I no longer want a convertible, that's for sure." I looked at Annie. "Am I out of a job? It looks like you're training Tiffany."

"Is it really your job, if you haven't been doing it?" Annie smirked.

"You're right. I'm sorry." My shoulders slumped. "I suck. I wanted to be like you and Nash. Stay cool under pressure. Make good decisions."

"Well, you didn't die," pointed out Rhonda. "That's pretty good, considering."

"Are you kidding me?" said Tiffany. "You solved Lorena's murder in a week. I thought I'd have to stay on you for months. Good thing, too. Now I can call that bartender. I didn't want him smelling Rhonda in my house."

"Hey," said Rhonda. "I was in shock."

"It's not like you saw the *Psycho* crime scene," snarked Tiffany. "A shower's not gonna trigger PTSD. Seriously, Rhon."

"Girl—"

"And you got your mom out of town," said Annie, saving us from a pointless argument. "I owe you big time, Maizie. No meetings with Her Highness for a few weeks."

"I didn't have anything to do with that."

"Don't care." Annie grinned. "Vicki's happy, so she's off my back. I doubled our profits, but we need help in keeping up. I'm hiring some part-timers for the paperwork. You're good at the fieldwork. You should stick to that."

"I'm good at fieldwork?" I blinked. "Wait. You're hiring Tiffany for real?"

"And me." Rhonda sashayed forward. "I'm your new receptionist. I think we need to knock down walls and increase the office space. Talk to Vicki about that. Tell her it's an investment in quadrupling the profits."

"Truth be told," said Tiffany. "LA HAIR fired Rhonda for missing so much work."

"Then they fired Tiffany for threatening Faye for firing me," said Rhonda. "But don't worry, we're still your personal stylists. I've got to keep up my blog and InstaFace. How do you feel about shaving your head and starting over? Documenting your hair regrowth could give me weekly content."

I opened my mouth, then shut it.

"Maizie," said Annie. "You don't look so good. Considering you were in an accident, I'm giving you the rest of the day off."

"Okay." Feeling overwhelmed with all the good news, I walked out of the new office — the new office on the cusp of becoming the new-new office. Then I remembered didn't have a vehicle. Not even a dirt bike. My feet continued to move. Numbly, I let them take me down the block, around the corner, and up the street. They stopped in front of the Dixie Kreme Donut shop.

I'd had help, but I'd successfully closed my first independent case. Despite all my mistakes. I'd been rewarded with a dream promotion. My new mentor was cool. Not only would I see my besties every day, but they'd also do the stuff I found boring. Who could ask for more?

Me. Because I was still selfish. Maybe my brattishness was a vestige from a previous celebrity lifestyle. Or maybe humans always wanted to have their cake and to eat it, too. On a silver platter. With a silver spoon.

Enough with the metaphors.

I sucked in a breath of donut air for comfort, then opened the side door. I shuffled up the stairs, skipping the one that sounded like a gunshot. I knocked on the old Nash Security Solutions office door, then tried the knob. Locked. I fished out my key from the shopping bag, unlocked the door, and went inside.

The bed was gone.

His desk was still shoved against the wall, covered in boxes from his bygone private-eye days. But the bed was gone. So were his clothes. The file cabinets had been emptied.

I closed the inner office door so I wouldn't see the emptiness. I climbed into Lamar's recliner but didn't pop the lever. I pulled my knees up, hugged them into my chest, and rested my forehead on them. Nash had been right. A murder investigation did change me. And not for the better.

The hall door opened. I looked up, my face wet with shame-filled tears.

"What do I always tell you?" said Nash. "There's no crying in PI work."

"I'm not crying over the investigation."

He sighed. "I guess we need to talk."

I didn't want to have *that* talk. I was sticking to investigation-talk. "All I wanted was to be like you. Calm, competent. The person to call in an emergency. I thought I was doing that, but I made a mess of everything. You didn't think I was ready for this and you were right."

"Maybe I wasn't completely correct."

"No, you were. I couldn't stick to a role. I spent more time developing backstory than understanding my victim. And I was too focused on proving myself."

"You figured out Susie and Spencer."

"Almost too late."

"And you found the kid. Because you're you. You kept your

head when Spencer tried to kill you," said Nash. "I was too angry to say this before, but I'm proud of you. Don't beat yourself up so much. You made mistakes, but we all do."

I sniffed, feeling better. "Thank you. I guess I did keep my head in an emergency. Particularly because I remembered my helmet."

"I'm buying you a new helmet. A thicker one. Mowry's mad as hell, though."

"His suspect is in a coma. And I sent him to arrest the suspect's wife for vandalism, not murder."

"It was his job, too." Nash folded his arms. "But that's not why he's angry. He's ticked because he wasn't there to save you."

"I wasn't relying on him to save me. I don't need him to save me. I wanted to save myself."

"Maybe he's worried you don't really need him anymore."

I cocked my head, wondering if we were really talking about Mowry.

"Here's the thing." Nash paced to the window and turned his back on me. "A man may think a woman is perfectly competent at doing a job. Even if she's new at the job and the job is danger-ous. He'll encourage her and support her. Want her to do well. He believes she'll do well."

I lowered my knees and stood up, readying myself to leave. I wasn't sure what Nash was trying to say, but I couldn't take any more rejection.

He turned from the window to face me. "But when that woman is put in harm's way, the man will fight like hell to get her back to safety. He can't help it. It's instinct. Primeval."

"Neanderthal?"

Nash shrugged. "Maybe. But he especially feels this way when he loves her."

"Are you saying—"

"I'm not talking about Mowry." Nash rubbed his neck. "Hell, maybe he's in love with you. I don't know. But I'm not talking about Mowry."

I moved toward him. "Are you saying you love me?"

"Of course, I love you." He glared at me. "How can you think I don't love you?"

I stopped in front of him. "I thought we broke up."

"Maizie, you pushed the wrong buttons today." He softened his look. "But that happens in relationships. We're going to get angry with each other. Get annoyed. Fight. We'll have to work hard to get back on track. It won't be easy. Especially with our histories."

"*Our* histories?"

"Jolene wanted me to be something I wasn't. I tried. And when I couldn't do it, she rejected me." He sighed. "And I was an idiot about it."

I bit my lip. As much as I wanted to trash talk Jolene, I was smart enough to leave that subject alone. "Any time things got rough with my boyfriends, we broke up."

"They're idiots, too."

I touched his hand. "I didn't mean all those things I said today. I was trying to get rid of you."

"I knew what you were doing. But I let it get to me anyway." His fingers threaded mine. He squeezed our palms together. I winced — road rash — and he relaxed his hand. "I have the best intentions when it comes to you. But the worst delivery."

I inched closer to him. "I needed you before. I still need you now. But not in the way I thought I needed you. As much as I want us to be partners again, I realized our relationship is more important. When I believed I might die, I wasn't thinking about my name on the window. I only thought about you."

He drew me into a tight hug then loosened his grip when I flinched. "You did fine without me, Miss Albright. You learn from your mistakes. Not many people do."

"The lone PI role is not for me, Nash."

"From the look of your office tonight, you're not alone. The way Rhonda talks, sounds like a *Charlie's Angels* remake is coming your way." I buried my head in his shoulder and he kissed the squirrel's nest. "I circled the block after dropping you off. I'd cooled off and went inside the shop. They told me."

"I still want to be partners with you," I whispered.

"We will," he whispered back. "Maybe sooner than you think."

"I knew it." I drew back. "You weren't at DeerNose all these nights. You've been working on a case."

"DeerNose is my case." He moved me against his chest again. "That's why I didn't want to involve you."

"I don't understand." I pulled back to look up at him. "What are you saying?"

"DeerNose stinks and not of deer pee." Nash's jaw tightened. "But I'm doing what I can for your father."

"My father knows?"

"Not exactly."

"Then I'm helping you."

He shook his head then gazed at me. "Miss Albright, I love you."

I gazed back. "Mr. Nash, what happened to your bed?"

The End
But Not Really.
Maizie & Nash will continue with their next case(s) in 19 CRIMINALS, coming soon!

Movies and TV Shows Mentioned in 18 1/2 DISGUISES

A League of Their Own
Billions
Charade
Charlie's Angels
Cold Case Files
Columbo
CSI
Dazzled
Empire
Friday the 13th
Halloween
Hercule Poirot
Homecoming Court
Julia Pinkerton, Teen Detective
Kung Fu Kate
Lady in Cement
Mad Men
Man on Fire
Prime Suspect
Psycho
Raiders of the Lost Ark

Scooby Doo, Where Are You?
Scream
Snapped
To Catch a Thief
Toy Story 2
The Bodyguard
The Dukes of Hazzard
The Lion King
Tony Rome
"Who's On First" (Abbott and Costello)

Larissa's Gift For You!

"It's sassy, sexy, and southern suspense at its best."

DEVILISHLY DELICIOUS BOOK REVIEWS

THE PIG'N A POKE

A FINLEY GOODHART CRIME CAPER SHORT

LARISSA REINHART
Wall Street Journal Bestselling Author

THE PIG'N A POKE

A Finley Goodhart Crime Caper prequel

When a winter storm traps ex-con Finley at the Pig'N a Poke road-house, she finds her criminal past useful in solving a murder.

Free For My VIP Readers!
Type this link in your browser to join Larissa's email group where she shares exclusive content, news, and giveaways — www.larissareinhart.com/larissasreaders — and receive *The Pig'N A Poke* as a gift.

Note: Larissa will not share your email address and you can unsubscribe at any time.

Larissa's Series

The Maizie Albright Star Detective series

15 MINUTES

16 MILLIMETERS

NC-17

A VIEW TO A CHILL

17.5 CARTRIDGES IN A PEAR TREE (novella)

18 CALIBER

18 1/2 DISGUISES

19 CRIMINALS

"Child star and hilarious hot mess Maizie Albright trades Hollywood for the backwoods of Georgia and pure delight ensues. Maizie's my new favorite escape from reality."

Gretchen Archer, *USA Today* bestselling author

Ex-teen TV and reality star, Maizie Albright, returns home to Black Pine, Georgia, determined to start a new career as a private investigator, modeled after her childhood starring role as a "Julie Pinkerton, Teen Detective." Unfortunately, Maizie's chosen mentor, Wyatt Nash of Nash Security Solutions, is not a willing teacher and her learning curve includes becoming her own person after spending a life under the thumb of managers, directors, and producers, particularly her stage-monster mother.

A Cherry Tucker Mystery series

"Readers who like a little small-town charm with their mysteries will enjoy Reinhart's series." ~Denise Swanson, *New York Times* Bestselling Author

A CHRISTMAS QUICK SKETCH (prequel)

PORTRAIT OF A DEAD GUY (#1) (and audio)

STILL LIFE IN BRUNSWICK STEW (#2) (and audio)

HIJACK IN ABSTRACT (#3)

THE VIGILANTE VIGNETTE (#3.5)

DEATH IN PERSPECTIVE (#4)

THE BODY IN THE LANDSCAPE (#5)

A VIEW TO A CHILL (#6)

A COMPOSITION IN MURDER (#7)

A MOTHERLODE OF TROUBLE #8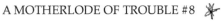

Meet Cherry Tucker, big in mouth, small in stature, and able to sketch a portrait faster than kudzu climbs telephone poles! The Cherry Tucker Mystery series (Henery Press) begins with Portrait of a Dead Guy, a 2012 Daphne du Maurier finalist, a 2012 The Emily finalist, a 2011 Dixie Kane Memorial winner, and a Woman's World Magazine book club pick for 2018!

"Reinhart manages to braid a complicated plot into a tight and funny tale. The reader grows to love Cherry and her quirky worldview, her

sometimes misguided judgment, and the eccentric characters that populate the country of Halo, Georgia. Cozy fans will love Cherry Tucker mysteries." ~Mary Marks, *New York Journal of Books*

Finley Goodhart Crime Capers

"As fun as it is moving and at times heart-breaking, never the more so when the final page comes and readers are only left wanting more."

Cynthia Chow, *King's River Life Magazine*

THE PIG'N A POKE (prequel, short story)

THE CUPID CAPER

THE PONY PREDICAMENT

THE HEIR AFFAIR

Ex-con Finley Goodhart finds her criminal past--and criminal ex-boyfriend--useful in catching crooks. Can she make up for her past by helping victims double-cross their swindler? More importantly, can she convince Lex that going straight is the best (and most challenging) hustle of all?

"Faced paced, bold, heartbreaking, this book has it all. It takes us deep into the world of hustlers, cons and dirty business. Yet it gives us glimpse of just how pure-hearted some of the worst con artist can be. Highly recommended for lovers of mystery and thrillers."

About the Author

Wall Street Journal bestselling and award-winning author, Larissa Reinhart writes humorous mysteries and romantic comedies including the critically acclaimed Maizie Albright Star Detective, Cherry Tucker Mystery, and Finley Goodhart Crime Caper series. Her works have been chosen as book club picks by *Woman's World Magazine* and *Hot Mystery Reviews*.

Larissa's family and dog, Biscuit, had been living in Japan, but once again call Georgia home. See them on HGTV's *House Hunters International* "Living for the Weekend in Nagoya" episode. Visit her website, LarissaReinhart.com, join her VIP Readers' Group, and get a free short Finley Goodhart story.

facebook.com/larissareinhartwriter

instagram.com/larissareinhart

bookbub.com/authors/larissa-reinhart

pinterest.com/LarissaReinhart

CPSIA information can be obtained
at www.ICGtesting.com
Printed in the USA
LVHW112207070921
697290LV00005B/270